THE KINGDOM
SHALL FALL

THE KINGDOM SHALL FALL

Until Philosophers Become Kings Book Two

A Novel

Chris Thomas

ISBN: 0996560726
ISBN 13: 9780996560726
Library of Congress Control Number: 2017911370
Chris Thomas, Denver, Colorado

To my dad. Thank you for being a storyteller.

Acknowledgments

My heartfelt thanks go to the following people for taking the time to read various drafts of the manuscripts for both Book One and Book Two as I took this quixotic journey and for providing me their valued opinions and support: Mic and Mindy Gumb, Neal and Nora Quitno, Ted Baird, Art Cudworth, Scott Guetz, Karen Gumina, Sue McIlvennan, Harvey Brandt, Phil Schwartz, Pete Graham, and Donna Wilkens. A special thank you to my proofreader and ardent supporter Madison. Also, to my brother Dan and my sisters, Kathy, and Tere, for not only reading the manuscripts but also for having the honesty to tell me what they really thought. Lastly to my wife, Nan, and our three kids, Sarah, Wil, and Sam, for their belief in me and the dream.

The society we have described can never grow into a reality or see the light of day, and there will be no end to the troubles of states, or of humanity itself, till philosophers become kings *in this world, or till those we now call kings and rulers really and truly become philosophers, and political power and philosophy thus come into the same hands...for it is not easy to see that there is no other road to happiness, either for society or the individual.*

—**Plato**, 428 BC–328 BC, *The Republic*

Battle not with monsters, lest ye become a monster, and if you gaze into the abyss, the abyss gazes also into you.

—**Friedrich Nietzsche,** 1844–1900
Beyond Good and Evil: Prelude to a Philosophy of the Future

Prologue

Colegio Militar Road
Near General Ignacio Pesqueira Garcia International Airport
Hermosillo, Mexico

The black luxury SUV with darkly tinted windows was just one of a dozen vehicles parked along the gravel shoulder of Colegio Militar Road adjacent to the tall security fencing that defined the perimeter of Hermosillo's international airport. This part of the road was a favorite with many of the younger local residents because it passed so near the northeast end of runway 23, and landing aircraft passed very closely overhead as they descended onto the airport's principal runway. The noise and jet blast from the powerful engines of the larger commercial aircraft as they touched down within several hundred feet of where they parked or stood watching provided a rush for some who frequented this spot. Today was special, as the country's president was flying in. A presidential visit to Hermosillo was big news anytime, and most of those parked along the road were there to observe up close the landing of Mexico One, the new US-manufactured Boeing 787 jet carrying President Raphael Fernandez and his entourage. The occupants of the SUV were parked there, however, for more sinister and deadly reasons.

Of the three men in the luxury SUV, it was the youngest of the occupants sitting in the front passenger seat who dearly wished he were anywhere but here—unlike the brutish and dangerous-looking driver with the black Belgium FN five-seven semiautomatic pistol in his lap or the well-dressed but menacing older passenger in the rear seat, who were parked there for a specific purpose. The older man in the rear seat—Eduardo Vargas, to those in the criminal drug underworld of the northern Mexican States who knew him—glanced at his expensive Swiss watch. If the presidential flight was on time, he and his driver/bodyguard were only minutes away from carrying out the plans of their leader, a mysterious and powerful criminal force known to but a few called El Condor de Muerte, the Condor of Death. The Condor was the unchallenged leader of the drug cartel of which Eduardo and his driver were members. To Eduardo, the Condor was Pablo Vargas, his cousin, whom he'd known since they were young children raised a few houses down from each other in the poor and dangerous Hoyo del Infierno (Hell's Hole) neighborhood in Chihuahua. As one of his cousin's oldest friends, he operated as his close confidant and chief lieutenant within the cartel. Eduardo alone knew the details of their purpose this day and what it would lead to in the days that followed.

As the scheduled time for the president's arrival drew near, all other air traffic into the airport was temporarily diverted, and an eerie silence fell over the international airport as all takeoffs and landings ceased. Eduardo was watching out to the north and, although it was late morning, could easily see the bright landing lights of what had to be the president's new jet against the backdrop of the dark rain clouds that thirty minutes earlier had dumped rain on the airport.

"Roll down his window," Eduardo said casually to his driver, who immediately complied. The scared young passenger was looking straight down the runway from his seat, his view unobstructed except for the thin metal fabric of the chain-link security fencing. In his right hand, he held a cell phone, preprogrammed to execute certain specific functions with the touch of a key, once the proper arming code had been entered. The young passenger turned in his seat enough to face the unidentified older man in the rear seat, evidence of the fear and dread he was feeling obvious in his appearance and in his shaking hands. "I...I...can't do this," he said feebly. "I won't. I know you're going to kill me anyway; you might as well do it now."

Eduardo looked coolly at the younger man and then said, "You misunderstand, Senor Nieves. It is not you we shall kill. If you cherish the lives of your wife and your three young daughters, you will do as instructed, or you will watch them die. You? You will be allowed to live, if you can, with the knowledge your cowardice ended their short lives."

Nieves swallowed hard, choking back the tears the mere thought of seeing his beautiful girls shot to death brought on. "I will do as you say," he finally said weakly.

Eduardo simply nodded and said, "Of course you will. Now, enter in the first code. You have perhaps two minutes until the landing, and your timing must be perfect."

The two small but sophisticated explosive devices that Nieves had been forced to place within the right landing gear well of the president's new jet the day before in Mexico City would in all likelihood perform as expected; they were of a very reliable design and expertly constructed. Because of his job as one of the lead aircraft mechanics for the president's new jet, the man in the back seat had taken his family and given him no choice but to help destroy the president's aircraft. He knew precisely where the devices should go to ensure Eduardo's objectives. What was more important, however, to Eduardo was that the small explosions be precisely timed with the jet's landing, for if they were, to all observers, the resulting catastrophe would appear as nothing more than a tragic accident.

If Nieves performed this final forced deed as instructed, the first of the two small explosions would shatter the telescoping strut of the down-lock mechanism of the sophisticated landing gear where it fastened to the heavy-duty four-wheel carriage assembly. The severe landing forces from so much aircraft weight and velocity being applied so abruptly to the damaged strut could not help but have the devastating result of a complete collapse of the gear. As the landing gear collapsed, the powerful Rolls-Royce-manufactured Trent 1000 high-bypass turbofan engine suspended beneath the right wing would strike the concrete runway with more catastrophic results. The meticulously planned, inevitable destructive actions would then be supplemented a millisecond later by the second small explosive device that was attached to the main fuselage fuel tank of the aircraft, also accessed from within the landing gear well. The resulting explosion of so much Jet A-1 fuel ignited by the shaped plastic explosive would be horrific, and Mexico would suddenly be in need of a new president—precisely the result Eduardo's cousin and leader desired.

The glistening new jet, painted in the white, green, and red of the national colors, roared closely overhead a minute later. Nieves forced the thoughts of his wife and daughters from his mind and focused on the landing, closely watching for the telltale blue smoke that would be released as the motionless tires of the extended landing gear made contact with the concrete runway and were instantly accelerated to near 140 miles per hour. The sophisticated cell phone in his hand had acknowledged with a tone the preprogrammed contact with the devices on board after he had entered the first required code. All that was necessary now was that he press zero and then the pound key, and his grisly tasks in a presidential assassination would be complete. Nieves's view was perfect down the runway. As the nose of the graceful jet rose slightly, indicating that the senior air force colonel flying the president was beginning to flare the aircraft expertly for landing, Nieves knew the moment was at hand. He saw the brief whiff of blue-gray smoke and did what he had to do to save his family. Despite the devastating reality he thought he knew was coming, the sudden collapsing of the landing gear and the subsequent impact of the right engine with the runway, coupled an instant later with the massive explosion from the tens of thousands of gallons of ignited jet fuel, still shocked him. He involuntarily recoiled away from his locked door in horror, images of the flight crew he knew well and the now-dead president flashing through his mind.

The older man in the back seat leaned forward, patted him on the shoulder, and said, "Well done, well done. Now, let's return you to your family. And remember, say nothing to no one, not even your wife."

Eduardo reached into the inside pocket of the expensive sport coat he was wearing and took something out.

"Take this," he said, handing what turned out to be a formal bank document and a bank card. "Five million pesos has been placed into an account in your name at the National Bank. This and other evidence of your actions here today have been carefully laid back to your doorstep. If at any time the authorities believe this was not the tragic accident it appears to be and choose to look elsewhere for a cause, what they will find if they look hard enough is you. So stay silent and enjoy this financial windfall wisely, and in time, you will put all this behind you as you and your wife watch your beautiful daughters grow up."

1

W hen does good end and evil begin?

For Ray Cruz, that simple thought was always there in the back of his mind, his own personal sword of Damocles hanging over him. It dominated his thinking, no matter the situation, and was there again this morning as he stood in the architecturally magnificent rotunda of the Mexican presidential palace and watched the newly sworn-in president of Mexico enter his official office. Raul Ortega, the president's closest friend and head of his personal protection group, a privileged group called the inner circle that remarkably Ray was also now a part of, followed the president. The country needed a new president because the preceding one, Raphael Fernandez, and most of his closest aides had died the day before in the horrific air crash of Mexico One. To the world it appeared to be a tragic accident. To a very few within the cartel of El Condor de Muerte, it was a masterfully executed assassination. The very few that did know this also knew former Secretary of Public Security Jacques Alvarez, now elevated to the presidency, was the Condor. And he now led not only a country but the most powerful cartel in the Western Hemisphere. The Condor's father, long since dead, killed by business rivals, had founded the family's illicit business almost forty years earlier. Like his son, who had only become involved with the trafficking to protect a father, the father had only become involved to protect a wayward younger brother. In the end Alvarez's father hadn't been able to save his brother—or himself—from their rivals.

1

Alvarez's father had selected three of the four members of his son's protective inner circle many years before. With the exception of his two cousins in the north that ran the day-to-day business of the cartel, they were the Condor's closet friends, in addition to his bodyguards. Ray had been undercover on this op for six months now and had only known Raul for the last three terrible long months he had been inside the cartel. However, despite the short time frame and the difficult realities associated with being inside a cartel, he could not help but to think of Raul as a friend. How that could be was still confusing and deeply troubling to Ray, as the man had orchestrated the assassination of the former president. Despite his intellect, training, and experience as an undercover operative within the DEA, Ray nevertheless had been drawn into the assassination plot and failed to prevent it, a failure that still tormented him in his every waking hour. He had managed to maintain his covert identity and stay alive during the plot—no easy task, as it turned out—but others had perished with the former president in the carefully planned crash of his official jet. In certain confidential circles within the government, there were many unanswered questions about the dead president and whether he himself had been a cartel criminal. Some were even speculating that the crash may in fact have been deliberate somehow, the result of cartel infighting. But the other passengers lost in the crash of the presidential aircraft were innocents, and those deaths weighed heavily on Ray's conscience.

Six months undercover could change a man. It had changed him, and that was something Ray would have never believed possible when he had taken this assignment. The shrink that conducted his psych evaluation during the preparation for his operation had mentioned how such changes were possible and had warned him of the signs. Nevertheless, Ray had written off the kind doctor's concerns and his science as psychobabble bullshit and had never given it another thought. God, how could he have been so arrogant and so wrong? he wondered. Not only had the circumstances and the constant pressures and life-threatening risks of being deeply undercover changed him, but he'd also killed two men—one of them a longtime member of the inner circle he was now a part of. He had never killed before this mission;

he was certain he couldn't do it again. Ray had stabbed to death his fellow bodyguard to keep him from raping the daughter of one of Raul's pawns in the presidential assassination. The possibility that he might have to kill had been a part of his mission brief, but in his gut, he really hadn't believed he would ever have to. The miserable shits he'd killed deserved it, but he'd been brought up Catholic, and while he hadn't been to Mass or confession in years, his conscience still struggled with what he had been forced to do.

A uniformed presidential guard closed the doors to the presidential suite of offices and took up his post, more or less at attention, as the many other government staffers that had witnessed the new president's morning arrival sat back down at their desks and returned to their respective duties. The echo of the closing door in the harsh acoustics of the marble-clad rotunda brought Ray out of his deep, depressing thoughts and into the here and now. He slowly shook his head and walked off toward the polished marble stairway that curved gracefully downward into the lower floors of Los Pinos, as the official presidential home and offices were known.

The security offices were located a level below the rotunda behind an overly dramatic steel door, Ray thought, as he entered and prepared to assume his official security duties. Another uniformed guard smiled warmly at him as he walked in.

"Good morning, Senor Ortega," the older man said as he smiled his toothy, disingenuous smile and bobbed his head, acknowledging the vast difference in their ranks within the presidential guard. Ray just nodded back, the man's innocent greeting painfully reminding him once more that his days as Ray Cruz, his true identity, were tragically behind him now, a result of his own weaknesses and failures during his operation. He sat down at his assigned desk but did nothing more than just lean back in his chair, looking past the array of computer monitors and displays in front of him, staring at the blank far wall of the security center, once more trying to understand how things had gone so terribly wrong.

Ray had once been a highly decorated young undercover cop in the Narcotics Division of the Sacramento Police Department. His dad was the captain in command, but never had there been even a whisper within the department about nepotism at the position he had attained so quickly. The many successful drug busts Ray had organized for the department from within the gangs and other criminal organizations he successfully infiltrated at great personal risk silenced even the most cynical of observers.

His undercover work brought him to the attention of Bennie Santiago, the special agent in charge of the US DEA's Special Operations Unit, after a successful joint task-force raid conducted by his unit and the DEA in Sacramento. Bennie had been impressed with his professionalism and cool under stress. There were also Ray's looks and language skills. He was completely fluent in Spanish, and though he was twenty six, he looked younger and therefore less dangerous. Bennie had taken a run at recruiting him and Ray had been ready for change and for an opportunity to get after the root sources of the illicit drugs that were flooding into his hometown.

Bennie had serious problems within the DEA and was looking for a team of new agents to help him solve it. Several DEA regional field offices along the border with Mexico were no doubt compromised by the cartels. Agency operations were failing more often than succeeding in their interdiction efforts and producing less intelligence, all at the expense of the lives of good agents. Theodore Mills, the new director of the DEA, and his number two within the agency, Charley Willis, the new intelligence director, had tasked Bennie to take charge of the agency's counterintelligence and tactical units and identify the traitors within their agency. Both DEA executives were old, reliable friends of Bennie's, and he took the job after first turning down the operations director slot, the number three position in the agency. He would have been tied to a desk in DC had he accepted the job, pushing high-level paper around. Bennie knew he was a street guy, not a desk jockey, and had taken the SAC position instead.

After Ray agreed to join Bennie's unit in the agency, he spent his first month studying the drug-trafficking epidemic from the DEA's long perspective. Bennie then started preparing him for his first mission. Bennie had carefully constructed a Mexican identity for him with a true legacy and family history and then prepared a criminal record for him as a smalltime trafficker and suspected murderer out of Albuquerque named Ray Espinoza. Once established and Bennie was satisfied that Ray was ready, Bennie had him placed in a Texas state detention facility in El Paso. The DEA was holding several high-profile suspected traffickers there, and Bennie's plan required Ray to be incarcerated for months in the facility if necessary, as the cellmate of the most interesting one.

The target's name was Carlo, last name unknown, and that made him more interesting than others being held. The near-total lack of information on Carlo in any of the DEA or other law enforcement data banks, including the Policía Federal Mexicana, also made the man a target for Bennie. Carlo had been captured in a local El Paso police counter-narcotics operation and identified by others looking to cut deals to mitigate their sentences as an important cartel leader from Mexico, but a leader no one knew much about. Bennie's plan was simple. In lieu of trying to deal their way into the cartels, a tactic that never really worked against the more sophisticated and experienced organizations, Bennie's idea was to have a known cartel leader personally take an agent with him back to whatever cartel he operated out of, wherever it operated, after their freedom was arranged. All his agent had to do was survive months in jail as another trafficker and somehow manipulate the target into befriending him, all without raising any suspicions. Operation Trojan Horse, Bennie's designation for Ray's operation, was dangerous and risky for Ray. However, Ray had seen the subtle genius of Bennie's plan and signed on.

Ray was lucky, and if asked, he would have told anyone that had always been the case during his short career. As Carlo's cellmate, he did not have to do much at all to approach the older prisoner. Ray was by nature a quiet, reserved, intelligent young man, where Carlo was the opposite in every way and had sought out Ray's company instead. Carlo was at least fifty and was outgoing, noisy, and openly hostile to the Anglo population on their cellblock. The inmates were only allowed a couple of hours a day in the yard, and soon after Ray had become Carlo's cellmate, some angry white trailer-park trash had attempted to knife Carlo in the yard. If Ray had not intervened when he had and disarmed the attacker, the man would have succeeded in seriously wounding Carlo or even killing him. For all his ignorance and ruthlessness, Carlo, in his own way, valued honor and was grateful to his young cellmate for saving his life. As a result, Ray's relationship with the mysterious older man was sealed.

Initially, everything worked out pretty much as Bennie had planned. Bennie's special unit had skillfully carried out Ray and Carlo's "escape" from incarceration during a routine prisoner transfer, and Carlo had indeed taken Ray south into Mexico with him. However, from the moment he stepped foot into the large guarded estate in the foothills west of Chihuahua, one of three estates that Carlo's family operated their cartel from in northern Mexico, Ray's life had not been the same. The challenges and difficulties began the very first day after Ray learned just what cartel he was now a part of. Carlo was the younger of the two Vargas brothers, thought by the local state police to be nothing more than hired enforcers to any nefarious group willing to pay. They were in fact the chief lieutenants to their mysterious cousin and leader the Condor. Ray had prepared diligently for his mission and had pored over all the classified briefing intelligence the agency had on the six largest and most notorious of the Mexican cartels, and a couple dozen lesser ones, and in all that material, there was no mention of the organization he was now a part of. He also discovered that several of what were believed by his agency to be among the largest and worst of the cartels were in fact just fronts for the one he was now a part of. This huge hole in the agency's intelligence summary had flabbergasted Ray. Then his life got worse—much worse.

Ray's job for the first several months inside the cartel was as a personal bodyguard and friend to Carlo Vargas. This had turned out to be a safe position for Ray, as neither Carlo nor the others he surrounded himself with were all that bright. Ray had passively gathered intelligence and, on several rare occasions, safely passed the valuable information on to Bennie with single-use cell phones purchased for the occasion. He was lucky again, as he was trusted, not only for saving Carlo in prison but also for his actions during their escape. To be so new to an organization and so unknown, yet trusted, was indeed rare in an environment where no one really trusted anyone at all outside his immediate group. As part of Carlo's security and given Carlo's importance within the cartel, they—along with Eduardo Vargas and his security people—traveled as part of the tightly controlled entourage that accompanied the Condor all over northern Mexico as the Condor and his cousins conducted their illicit business.

Two months into his undercover assignment, Ray's life was irrevocably changed for the worse when, during a business meeting between the Condor and several other traffickers aligned with his organization, one of the other leaders had attempted to assassinate the Condor. That was when he had been forced to kill for the first time. Ray had been tasked by Carlo to be the personal bodyguard to Eduardo Vargas, the Condor's assigned second at the meeting, because of Ray's skill with knives. Ray had messed around with knives for fun while growing up and, after becoming an undercover cop, always carried a concealed Heckler Koch four-inch auto-opening switch knife literally up his sleeve in a scabbard strapped to his right forearm. None of the attendees at the meeting or their bodyguards were supposed to be armed, but Carlo wanted his cousin protected at the meeting, so he had selected Ray, believing he would be able to get his knife past the security checks. Carlo's plan had worked, and it had saved the Condor's and Eduardo's lives. The two other leaders, Gerardo Barega and Ramon Vasso, had been conspiring together to kill their powerful rival, and one of Vasso's guards had been allowed to pass through security with a small-caliber handgun. The assassin, a bodyguard and killer for Vasso for many years, had been standing to Ray's left, just beyond the Condor's longtime protector and head of the inner circle, Francisco Ortega. As the meeting went on and Vasso's assassin had waited for the right opportunity and worked up the courage to attack, his actions had not gone unobserved. Ray was very observant by nature as well as training, and something about the man standing not six feet away from him had bothered him enough that he kept a careful eye on him. Sure enough, when the assassin had finally gone for his concealed weapon to attack, Ray had been ready and surprised the attacker, his H-K in hand. When it was over, Ray had unintentionally killed the first assassin, and Francisco had killed a second but also lost his life, a victim of the single shot the assassins could get off. Later that night, after the entourage had returned to the estate near Monterey where they were currently operating out of, Ray had been flabbergasted once again when, in the Condor's private study, with just he and the Condor present, the Condor had elevated Ray to the inner circle.

Saving the Condor's life and being elevated to the position as one of his personal guards brought with it more unintended consequences and radical changes to Ray's life. For starters, because of how he had killed the assassin, Carlo had given him the name El Cuchillo, the Knife, and the name had stuck within the cartel. Ray hated it, as it was a constant reminder of what he had done and the life he had taken. Secondly, it had brought him into close contact with Raul Ortega, the now-dead Francisco's younger brother, whom the Condor had named to replace Francisco as the head of the inner circle. Unlike Carlo, whom Ray had spent so much of his time with in the cartel before being elevated to his current job, Raul was not only friendly but also surprisingly intelligent. Much to his surprise considering where he was and whom he thought he was involved with, Ray soon discovered that like the Condor, Raul was formally educated.

The Condor had been an enigma to Ray at first. In his day-to-day interactions with other business associates and even with the lower-echelon members of the entourage, he presented himself as the ruthless, coldblooded cartel leader he was, but in private, when alone with Ray or the other members of the inner circle, the Condor was a quiet, well-spoken, and one could even say a kind man.

From the beginning of Ray's time within the cartel, every couple of weeks as the entourage shuttled between the three large private estates the Condor maintained in the northern states that bordered the United States, the Condor and his personal guards would take a sophisticated luxury private plane and leave for destinations unknown to Ray and the others. Two or three weeks later, typically, they would return, always careful to arrive at a location different from where they had departed weeks before. Ray suspected that no one within the cartel, except for Carlo and his brother, Eduardo, knew where or why the Condor disappeared as he did.

After becoming a member of the inner circle, Ray learned to his amazement that the Condor was not only the ruthless leader of what was looking to Ray like the most powerful cartel in Mexico, but also that the entire Condor persona was a ruse. The Condor was really Jacques Alvarez, the secretary for public security in the Mexican president's cabinet and the second most powerful politician in the country. The Condor's regular travels took them from the northern states through Baja Sur, where the Condor first changed his identity and his physical appearance to that of a reclusive wealthy entrepreneur by the name of Nicolas Pena—also a ruse—and then he was transformed once again to his actual identity. This was accomplished more easily than Ray could have ever imagined due to the Condor's talents for altering his appearance and the adjacency of the Pena estate and the Alvarez family estate on the coast of Baja, overlooking the beautiful and tranquil Pacific Ocean. From Baja, after having passed from the Pena estate to the Alvarez estate unseen via a sophisticated tunnel, the well-known Alvarez, now in his true identity and accompanied by his official security detail that Ray was now a part of, could leave the private and secured compound that was the longtime Alvarez family estate and return to the Mexican capital. Ray had learned on his first trip as one of the Condor's personal bodyguards that he had been operating successfully with his multiple identities for years. In the several weeks that had passed since Ray had learned of the Condor's deceptions, he still had trouble believing that in the three months he had served as one of Carlo's bodyguards and had seen the Condor almost every day he was at the estates, he'd nevertheless been totally fooled by the Condor's appearance, his long, flowing white hair, and the matching beard. It had never occurred to him that the man had been in disguise. He'd been totally sucked in; such were the Condor's talents.

To his further amazement, Ray learned that the Condor's father was the one who had started the family's illicit trafficking business years before, but he had sheltered his young son from the trafficking business for his entire life. Alvarez's father had also carefully and brilliantly invested the vast amounts of laundered drug profits into many well-known legal family businesses, making the family not only one of the wealthiest in the country, but also one of the most generous through their many philanthropic trusts. Twelve years ago, the young Alvarez had been a very successful prosecutor in the federal judiciary and had been promoted at age thirty-eight to the position of deputy attorney general of Mexico for organized crime. Alvarez's father, fearing that his son would discover the family's terrible dark secret, confessed to his son, wishing to turn himself in order to protect the young Alvarez's increasingly bright political future. Alvarez was presented with a Hobson's choice no son should have to face: arrest and prosecute the father he worshiped, or join the illicit family business and somehow save his father, himself, and the family name. From his philosophy studies years earlier at the National University, young Alvarez wanted to believe if he controlled both the politics of his country and could become the most powerful cartel, he could then slowly end the trafficking menace, becoming not unlike the philosopher kings described in Plato's *Republic*, one of his favorite works. By rising within the government until such time he could seize the reins of political power in his country—all the while as a leader of his father's organization, secretly destroying his country's enemies, the other criminal cartels marauding throughout the country killing innocents by the thousands—he believed deeply he could save his country.

Learning of Alvarez's history and plans had greatly surprised and confused Ray, as a big part of him found the Condor's goals truly noble. Infiltrating a serious cartel, getting intelligence back to Bennie in the north so the DEA and his government could better fight the scourge that illegal trafficking was, had always been Ray's mission. To discover Alvarez's truth and then discover that helping Alvarez could do more good than fighting him was a moral dilemma that Ray could never have contemplated, and he was still trying to see his way through that reality.

When does good end and evil succeed? As Ray sat at his desk in the well-guarded security room of the presidential palace, he didn't have an answer. His conscience was overwhelmed with guilt at the innocent lives that had been lost in the assassination of the corrupt president that elevated Alvarez to the presidency and closer to his dreams. And Ray's mission, as originally envisioned, was now in question. Ray believed himself a good man, a decent man, but people could believe about themselves what they wished, but it was the actions they took in life that revealed them for what they were. That was an increasingly hard truth to face.

2

Jacques Pablo Alvarez walked slowly around the ornate, historic antique desk that was the centerpiece of the expansive office of the president of Mexico. He paused and stared out the large windows behind his desk, taking in the beautiful view of the park and majestic pine trees that surrounded the presidential office and official home of the president. His thoughts returning to just how he had achieved his new position, he turned and placed his hands on the high-backed executive chair, slowly caressing the old green leather. He looked up, his face not reflecting the satisfaction, pride, or happiness that achieving the presidency of a major country in the Western Hemisphere might bring to another, but rather had a pensive look, perhaps even sad.

His oldest and closest friend, Raul Ortega, stood opposite the desk, quietly watching the new president, and then asked, "What is it, Pablo? You are troubled; I can tell. We are almost there. Come Saturday with our planned raid on the Gang of Four, your dreams and plans will have been almost completely fulfilled. You will have eliminated the worst of the cartels. You've succeeded."

Alvarez stared at his friend for a very long time before responding, "Perhaps, but at what cost, Raul? Emilio? Your brother? The many innocents lost when our actions could not avoid it?"

11

Raul was shaking his head. "Pablo, let it rest. We have saved thousands of lives with what we have done and with what we will be doing in the immediate future. Collateral losses, however regrettable, were always unavoidable. If you have taught me anything over the last twelve years, it is to keep our focus on our end goals, the greater good. Do I have to remind you again? You are a good man; that has not changed. You—we—are doing good. I will always believe that. Our enemies are the worst of mankind. Our country, our citizens, were in terrible danger, still are, until we finish what you started. You are righting many wrongs. Do not forget that, please."

Alvarez's look didn't change as he listened to his old friend, and then he turned away once again, facing the magnificent vista of the Bosque de Chapultepec, before responding, his voice soft, subdued. "We are trying to do good. I do believe that, Raul, but Emilio's death for one was not unavoidable. How am I to live with that? Manuel, may he rest in peace, was not only a good brother to you, but he was a good friend to me. I knew he would try to protect me as Emilio got closer and closer to the truth. I should have stopped him. I could have, but I did not. Now my sister is without her husband and her children without their father, and I lost a dear friend in Emilio. Ultimately, you lost your brother because of my plans and actions."

Raul, whose look became very sad at the mention of his brother, responded, "You had nothing to do with Manuel's death. How are you responsible for our enemy's assassins? Manuel was where he wished to be: at your side, helping." Raul paused and then went on, his tone becoming even more melancholy: "What's done is done, Pablo. I, of all people, understand what he did and why. I say again, what we do, the burdens we bear: they are for the greater good."

Alvarez had no idea that Raul, like his brother before him, also had been placed in the difficult position of having to save Pablo Alvarez from himself. Emilio Rodriquez had been a great attorney general for the country, a relentless investigator and prosecutor of the cartels and their trafficking operations. His older brother, Alberto, was now the most senior member of Alvarez's cabinet, as secretary of public security. Before that, Alberto had been the longtime courageous leader of the Federal Police. Raul liked

Alberto very much, but Alberto, like his brother, was brilliant and an expert investigator. The odds of him discovering Alvarez's several concealed identities, their cartel, and some if not all of their many illegal actions taken over the last twelve years was likely a sure thing in time. Raul had long realized such a possibility, and as Pablo Alvarez's friend and chief protector, he had carefully planned for Alberto Rodriguez's elimination. But when the time had come to do as his older brother Manuel had and end the threat, he hadn't done so.

Despite the fact that for the last twelve years, he had been the chief protector and confidant to Mexico's most powerful yet carefully concealed and unknown cartel leader, Raul had never personally killed. He had organized and ordered the deaths of a great many of the worst criminals in Mexico, but others within their cartel, hired for such purposes, had done his bidding. Alberto was neither a criminal nor an enemy, really—just a threat. And as he was one of Pablo Alvarez's last living close friends, the plans for his elimination had to be kept secret. Raul knew that if Pablo ever found out, he would have stopped it, for no matter the risks, the guilt he felt over Emilio Rodriguez's death at Manuel's hand was simply too great.

Raul's plans were known only to himself and his young protégé within the president's inner security circle, Ray Espinoza—now Ray Ortega, after some manipulations of several government data bases. With Ray's elevation to the inner circle following the recently failed assassination attempt on Alvarez, Raul had a new life history created for Ray and had the cartel's IT genius, Geraldo Baca, insert it into all the relevant government databases, in case anyone bothered to look. Ray's new identity made him Raul's nephew and a decorated local police officer from the Hermosillo police in the north. Hermosillo's police records had been chosen because that department, more than any of the several they controlled, was the most deeply penetrated at all levels. With their move to the capital, Ray was seen for what he now was: a personal assistant and guard to the new president, and as a result of Raul's planning, he had the official bona fides that supported the fiction.

Over the last several weeks, as they had carried out their plans and eliminated the corrupt previous president, elevating Pablo to the presidency, eliminating the most serious threat to his friend had become imperative. Raul discovered he couldn't do it; he could not kill Alberto Rodriguez. He was sadly certain he had doomed them all.

Alvarez was looking carefully at his oldest friend. Something in his manner suggested secrets, but he would not ask. He trusted Raul with his life and had done so since he was twelve years old and Raul eighteen, and his father had selected Raul and his older brother to be his personal bodyguards before sending him to the capital city to begin his formal education. Raul would tell him in time what was bothering him. Alvarez simply nodded at his friend's statements and then said, "As we entered this office and all that it represents, all I could think about is how today my father would be seventy-two, had he not been killed by our enemies."

Raul's eyes widened a bit, and then he wistfully shook his head. "My apologies, Pablo. With all that has happened, I had forgotten today was his birthday. Forgive me. He was a great man."

Alvarez, his lips pursed, responded, "Was he, Raul? Really? I loved Father, but the path we have struggled down these past twelve years, he created. That reality continues to haunt me."

One did not normally sit down in the presence of the president without being invited to, but the president before him was the only family he had left. Raul sat down in one of the two large chairs fronting the president's desk and then spoke. "Yes, my friend, he was a great man, as are you. He only went down the path he did to try to save his brother all those years ago. And once involved with the trafficking, remember all he has done with the profits, all the good that has come from our legitimate businesses, and from his philanthropy—and now yours. He gave you no choice, admitting his complicity in the trafficking, with you the new deputy attorney general of the country. Is a son really expected to send his father to jail for life? You chose the more difficult road, in my view. Yes, neither one of us will ever be the same. But, my friend, we have rid the country of so many of the worst criminals, and we have saved thousands of innocent citizens from their despicable actions. With our coming plans against the Gang of Four, if successful, we will control most of the trafficking into America, and now, with your ascendancy to this office, we have the political power to slowly start reducing that flow. Worthy dreams and accomplishments, Pablo."

Alvarez's expression hadn't changed the entire time Raul spoke, and while he appreciated what his friend said and his continued loyalty and friendship, he knew he had had a choice twelve years ago, and he had picked his father over the rule of law. He also knew from the Jesuits who had educated him through secondary school and from his study of philosophy and the law at the National University that he owned his choices.

For the last twelve years, he had done what he could to save his family name and save his country by eliminating by whatever means possible as many of the criminals producing and trafficking the huge quantities of illicit drugs within the country. His goal had always been to gain control of the trafficking by being smarter and more ruthless than his enemies. He had built a highly sophisticated and powerful criminal empire and taken on the persona of El Condor de Muerte, leader of his largely unknown cartel. A ghost leader, for most of the law enforcement in his country and in America had little accurate intelligence on him or the cartel. One by one, over the years, he had convinced loyal lieutenants to infiltrate the other powerful cartels, and those who had survived had risen in those organizations and would now do his bidding. His cousins had been his father's chief lieutenants, before they had become his own. Carlo was the loyal and obedient enforcer, the one who did whatever was necessary if asked, no matter how evil the task. Eduardo was smart and responsible for all intelligence gathering the cartel relied on to achieve its ends. With his cousins', Raul, and his brother Manuel's help before him in the role as chief protector, Alvarez had finally made his organization the most powerful cartel in all of Mexico. Now with his ascendancy to the presidency, he could finally achieve is goals and undo, to a great degree, the wrongs his father had created for himself and his family when he had started the family trafficking business, decades ago.

He had made the terrible choice years before to assist his father. Once he committed to that path, now a criminal in his own right, and after learning just how powerful and cleverly concealed his father had made their organization, thoughts and philosophies from his studies of Plato years before began to form him and drive him. He grasped onto the possibility that if, as in Plato's *Republic*, he could fashion himself in the mold of a benevolent and wise philosopher king, doing what was right for the country and his fellow citizens, his choices and actions, however criminal, could in the end be justi-fied. Good could be accomplished, perhaps even his country finally saved. There was a nobility to that dream that kept him going, even as the deaths piled up because of his actions and assaulted his deeply held religious beliefs. He could only hope a benevolent God would indeed understand his motives and forgive him his transgressions when he ultimately faced his Maker.

3

Captain Danny Irwin loved his job as the "hoot owl" shift commander for the US Army Border Corps Recon Squadron. From midnight to 0800 of each duty night, he was responsible for the planning and execution of all the search patterns in the area his team of Predator pilots and sensor controllers patrolled. The recon squadron was responsible for the overflight of some nineteen hundred miles of the Border Security Structure, as the new walls and fencing on the border with Mexico were referred to. Danny was responsible for the five hundred miles that meandered through mostly deserted dry desert landscapes from Nogales, Arizona, in the west to Presidio, Texas, in the east. As part of the US Army's expanding role for border security under the new immigration law, Congress had authorized the formation of an aerial reconnaissance company, complete with three of the newly enhanced MQ-9 Predator systems and the personnel to man them. A Predator system consisted of four new advanced MQ-9 drones, the pilots and sensor operators that maneuvered the craft and operated the array of sensors and cameras on board, and the necessary support staff to maintain and service the aircraft themselves. All told, each team was made up of fifty-five men. The other two shifts were commanded by majors. The senior-most one also acted as the recon company commander, so this assignment, on paper, was a plum assignment for a young captain looking to move up and out. Captain Irwin, however, was not the least bit interested in moving up or out. He not only liked his job; he needed it.

As shift commander, he took great pains to pour over the maps and satellite images available to him through the office of the G-2, the tight-assed colonel who served as General Rodriguez's deputy chief of staff for intelligence, and plot the flight patterns his drones would use that night. Danny could see no logical reason why an American army base located in the middle of bum-fucking nowhere in west Texas needed an intelligence section anyway. His team plus the other two Predator teams were the only ones on the base doing anything remotely connected to intelligence gathering, and then that was really more for the local cops, the DEA, and the ATF, and not for the army anyway. While few people on the sprawling base were even aware of the existence of the recon company, it was not a secret; most people just weren't interested, and the recon group's real mission was known to very few. Those who thought they knew were certain that the drones were assisting in stopping the flow of human traffic in either direction across the border. Those who knew the mission orders knew they were there to help in the multiagency attempt to stop the flow of cartel drugs north and cartel guns south.

Each night before he took command of the shift, Danny had already laid out which sectors of the wall his troops would watch that night. Their mission was to pilot the unmanned flying camera platforms at an altitude of five thousand feet and focus the many night vision and infrared cameras on the rugged terrain below, searching for anyone who might have thoughts about entering US territory illegally. Since the passage of the new immigration law, the Predators also looked for those wishing to return to their native country without being properly outprocessed, a mission that always bothered Danny. He could see no reason why the army, or anyone else for that matter, should be bothering with illegals trying to leave the country. The more the better, thought Danny. Documentation in both directions, north and south, had become very important to a lot of people in Washington. As a political science graduate, Danny thought the outprocessing was a colossal waste of time and money. That stopping the flow of guns south was a primary mission of the border corps had escaped Danny's intellectual grasp, so focused as he was on the sad people returning home. On those occasions that the Predators did spot illegals attempting to breach the wall, Danny had had to keep his personal feelings to himself and call it in so soldiers of the border corps could be vectored out from the nearest barracks either by chopper or, if close enough, by Humvee down the road that ran between the two lines of new, tall fencing and pinch the poor bastards. As much as this bothered Danny, it didn't bother him enough to not do his job well. He wanted to keep his job, which meant excelling; his habit demanded it.

Danny thought the Predators were amazing platforms. The new -9 series were a major jump in performance and technology over earlier systems. Their range had been upped from the 550 miles of the -3 series to over 1,000. If they weren't required to carry the deadly laser-guided AGM Hellfire-2 missiles that each drone could carry, auxiliary fuel tanks could be added instead, and an additional 150 pounds of fuel could be taken aboard, increasing the drone's range to 1,400 miles. Though capable of a top speed of 300 miles per hour, at an average flight speed of 150 miles per hour, the predators could fly out to an area and hover over it for hours before returning to base.

Their cameras bays had been upgraded to the latest improvements in optics, and the image-intensified real-time TV could see from five thousand feet with the digital clarity as if from twenty. Danny was certain he could read the watch of an illegal from five thousand feet if the sucker would stand still long enough. The night vision and thermal imaging equipment were also upgraded, making observation at night even easier and more accurate than the daylight flights. The software improvements in their operating systems allowed them to program out small radiating sources like rabbits and coyotes that could distract an operator's attention and focus on their true targets: men and machines.

Danny turned over command to the major commanding the first daylight shift, had a quick meeting with his four lieutenants who were responsible for all the follow-up paperwork, and headed out of the building. It had been a quiet night for a change. Building R-24 looked no different than a great many others that were lined up and down on both sides of Pershing Road, the central boulevard of the base. He hopped into his Honda Accord and headed east on Pershing and made his way down to Robert E. Lee Drive and out the Lee gate to grab breakfast at his favorite dive and to meet his friend Alex Guerro. To call Alex his friend was a misnomer, he thought. When he got right down to it, they never hung around together, shot pool, or grabbed beers. Once a week they meet at Harry's Diner on east Montana Avenue on the northeastern edge of El Paso. The breakfasts at Harry's had the necessary requisite grease to classify Harry's as a dive, the coffee was decidedly not Starbucks but closer to bitter brown water, and the plastic tablecloths where usually sticky from someone else's day-old syrup. But Harry's was cheap, and hardly anyone from the base ever went there. Danny did, regularly, to meet Alex, who supplied him his weekly fix of cocaine in exchange for information on where the army's drones would be flying on a given night.

Danny was the clean-cut ROTC type to look at him whom no one paid much attention to in high school in Kansas City and then again at the University of Kansas at Lawrence. He looked like the last person you would suspect of having a drug problem, but a problem it was. He had been more than a casual user after he had first been introduced to cocaine in high school by the older brother of a girlfriend in Kansas City. He initially funded his purchases from money his wealthy parents gave him and income from his various after-school jobs. In college on an ROTC scholarship, his taste for it had grown, and he had moved into dealing, which posed far greater risks but also ensured a steady affordable supply. After his graduation from Kansas, he owed the US Army five years for his education and was attracted by the technology of the aerial reconnaissance assets the army used. With his extremely high aptitude with computers, he did well in the testing and was given his chosen field.

After additional training and education, he spent a lot of time out of the country his first two years as part of the First Recon Squadron assigned to duties in Afghanistan. That was a rough two years for Danny. In spite of the worldwide reputation Afghanistan enjoyed as one of the heroin-producing capitals of the world, he had used very little on that tour. He had drawn the line at heroin usage and only used coke occasionally, and that had mostly been on leaves. Coke was hard to come by at Bagram Air Base in Afghanistan, where the members of the army recon squadron worked with the air force boys. It was available but was really bad shit, cut so often as to be hardly recognizable as coke and then at a terrible cost. But the cocaine gods had smiled on him after he was promoted to captain. He had been rotated out of Afghanistan and assigned to Fort Bliss and the recon company there, where he stumbled into a great source in Alex.

Alex originally was just a dealer he had found through other users on the base he had come to know. But early in their relationship, during some typical small talk as they transacted business, Alex had asked Danny what exactly he did for the army. After the pleasantly high Danny explained his duty in some detail, a reflective and thoughtful Alex had scratched his chin and suggested that he might just know some people who would be very interested in exactly where Danny's drones were looking each night—or more specifically, where they would *not* be looking at any given moment. Alex went on to say that having such information might well earn the gratitude of his friends to the point that Danny would have a generous and no-cost supply of his favorite candy.

Danny had realized a long time ago that he had certain character flaws that made him susceptible to poor decision making. The possibility of having a steady, completely free source of coke was way beyond his capacity to say no to. Alex had contacted his business associates and had become the go-between that passed Danny's information to the people who were bringing the coke out of Mexico. Knowing where the army's drones would not be looking was indeed a very valuable piece of information, and Alex's friends were generous in their gratitude. Danny's capacity for rationalization was as great as his need for the coke. He reasoned that his cooperation with drug traffickers was in no way a violation of his officer's oath to protect the country against all enemies foreign and domestic, because his contact was really not an enemy. Alex and his business associates were not hurting anyone in Danny's view but rather providing a harmless recreational service.

Alex had the smooth, classy appearance of a successful Mexican businessman without being garish in any way, and therefore he did not draw attention to himself. He looked prosperous but normal. If one watched him more closely, however, one would see that his eyes never stayed focused on one place for any length of time. He could be having a detailed conversation with you, yet his eyes would be taking in his surroundings, always darting here and there, noticing who was coming and going, always looking for anyone or anything that might tip him to a possible tail or surveillance.

Alex was waiting for Danny in one of their usual booths in the front dining area of the rundown restaurant from which both the parking lot and the front door could be watched. He smiled and greeted Danny as if they really were friends. Danny had been introduced to a senior DEA guy the day before and informed that his mission assignments would be changing. In what way, Danny wasn't sure, as the DEA honcho had mysteriously left the base in a hurry for Washington. He was nervous about any changes in his routine because the information he regularly provided Alex was his currency for the great coke he received in return. He decided that Alex needn't know about potential disruptions just yet, because he really didn't have any details, so why rock the boat?

After breakfast and the simple but discreet exchange of coke for the flight schedule for the upcoming week, the "friends" parted company: Danny to his billet to blow a little coke, hook up with his new girlfriend, and enjoy his day off, Alex to the American location of his legitimate Mexican-based import-export business.

After taking care of a few items at his warehouse, Alex got back in his car and made the drive south into Mexico through the manned and patrolled Bridge of the Americas entry-exit point between El Paso and Ciudad Juarez, Mexico. Once in Juarez, Alex went to a safe house his employer maintained and passed his reconnaissance information up the line, his principal task as a member of the cartel complete.

4

The large Boeing 767 was hurtling smoothly through the air at its assigned altitude of forty thousand feet, halfway through the five-hour flight from Dulles International outside Washington, DC, to Mexico City. The two seasoned flight attendants who catered to the well-heeled first class passengers were having coffee in the galley, as their passengers had already been served their breakfast. Aside from strolling through the cabin occasionally to take care of minor requests, their principal service tasks on this flight were complete.

Most of the passengers were napping, reading, or engaged with the multichannel entertainment systems available to them at their large, comfortable leather seats, but not the serious, well-dressed older passenger in seat 4B. To the observant senior flight attendant, this was a troubled man in some way, as the look on his face seemed to oscillate between grim to sadness and back, the wrinkles on his brow and the circles under his eyes marring what was otherwise a pleasing countenance. She took a quick glance at the manifest and determined he was one of the several passengers aboard flying on a diplomatic passport. This wasn't unusual for this route, nor did it convey any particular status, as many differing levels of diplomats or embassy personnel flew with such credentials. The manifest identified him as Mr. Benjamin Santiago, US citizen, but to anyone who knew him well inside or outside the Drug Enforcement Agency he had worked for going on forty years, he was simply Bennie. But none of that information was present to the senior flight attendant in the manifest. Despite the fact he had his headphones plugged into his personal iPhone and appeared to be concentrating, she nevertheless approached him and touched him on the shoulder. He had to have been in deep concentration, as her simple gesture startled him a bit. He jumped slightly and then quickly removed his headphones, looking at her with a question in his eyes but saying nothing.

"Excuse me, Mr. Santiago, for the intrusion, but is there anything at all I may bring you? I know you passed on breakfast—a cup of coffee, perhaps?"

Bennie's look softened under the flight attendant's very nice smile, and he responded, "No intrusion. Coffee would be nice. Cream and sugar, please."

She nodded and walked gracefully back to the galley as Bennie watched. He shook his head, glad, to be honest, for the brief contact with the lovely woman and the momentary diversion from having to think about the serious work that was confronting him down in Mexico. The flight attendant returned with his coffee, smiled her dazzling smile once more, and then moved on down the cabin.

Bennie sighed; he was nearing sixty and had been a widower for a great many years. He had met the occasional interesting and attractive woman, but the requirements of his chosen occupation made it difficult to form any new lasting romantic relationships. More often than not, what few private and personal pleasures that had come to him over the years were from encounters with ladies not unlike this flight attendant who were involved with or supported some aspect of the travel or hospitality industries that catered to his very frequent business travels. Home had once been in Los Angeles but now was a small, cluttered apartment in the DC suburbs near the DEA headquarters. Bennie could have been sitting in a plush office on the executive floor of the DEA headquarters at 700 Army Navy Drive in Arlington as director of operations, third in command of the entire agency, instead of flying into what was certainly a dangerous scenario that could well turn out to be a deadly one in Mexico. But he had turned the promotion down months earlier when offered the post by his friend and the new director of the DEA, Ted Mills.

As pleasant as the brief exchange with the flight attendant had been, the furrows on his brow returned as he sipped at his coffee and returned to the grave problems facing him, the likes of which the observant and professional flight attendant could never have imagined. According to the official DEA manning chart, Bennie worked out of the director's office as a "special assistant" to the director. Exactly what he did was not specified, but most in the agency knew Bennie was the agency's go-to guy for field operations against the major cartels out of Mexico and South America. As such, he regularly took a leadership role, usually as senior advisor or tactician, for all the major operations the various field divisions were conducting under the auspices of the new operations director selected by Ted after Bennie had turned down the posting. The current ops director and Bennie had known each other for years but weren't close, and the new director had expressed his annoyance on more than one occasion to Ted regarding the movements and actions of "that loose cannon Bennie Santiago," but to no avail. Whatever Bennie was doing and reporting to the director of the DEA was privileged information, and the annoyed ops director simply had to live with it.

Bennie's duties, as observed by others in the agency, were nothing more than a smoke screen obscuring what he really did. His role as the tactical planner and leader of the agency's raids on cartel assets and sites in the United States, while important and valuable, obfuscated his principal responsibilities to the director and the number two man in the agency, Charley Willis, the director of intelligence. It was clear to the two most senior leaders of the DEA that a serious number of field offices in the southwest part of the country that bordered Mexico had to varying degrees been compromised by the wealthy and dangerous cartels. Ted and Charley had tasked Bennie with quietly ferreting out the traitors in their midst, in addition to increasing the agency's intelligence take on the cartels in northern Mexico. To this end, Bennie had come up with a clandestine program to infiltrate deep undercover agents into the cartels in rather unorthodox ways that would protect their true identities and hopefully ensure their survival. His first such operation had been designated "Trojan Horse," as it involved placing one of his very best young agents into a state prison in El Paso, Texas, for an extended and dangerous period to allow him the time to try to befriend a suspected serious but virtually unknown cartel leader being held there. Agency efforts at infiltrating cartels as potential buyers or sellers had mostly ended in failure, as the bigger and smartest of the cartels trusted no one outside their tightly controlled leadership structures. For Bennie, failure had usually meant the death of a colleague, and he was tired of it. It was a long shot to believe that whatever cartel Ray ended up inside would be responsible for corrupting any one of the southern field offices, but even if it wasn't, Ray surely would be able to provide actionable intelligence that could help the agency in its efforts.

Surprising Bennie greatly in spite of his careful and detailed planning, Ray's infiltration had been more successful than Bennie could ever have imagined. The older cartel leader and Ray had become friends during the three months they had shared a cell. The planned prisoner transfer escape Bennie had orchestrated had come off without incident, and Ray had indeed been taken south to Mexico. The suspected cartel leader turned out to be named Carlo Vargas, a senior lieutenant and cousin to a previously undiscovered yet powerful cartel operated by a leader referred to as the Condor. From the two brief reports Ray had been able to transmit back to him during his first month in deep undercover, a very real intelligence coup, Bennie and the agency had learned a great deal about this powerful, previously unknown cartel. Ray's messages not only confirmed the existence of this cartel but also gave Bennie the locations of a cartel safe house near Las Cruces and another near the border, which they were now watching. Ray was also able to detail his route from the safe house down into Mexico. Most importantly, Ray had given them detailed information on the three principal estates the Condor and his entourage operated out of in the northern states. However, just when Bennie was beginning to believe that Ray's infiltration was going to be a great intelligence success, things had turned to shit.

Nothing bothered Bennie more than to not be able to maintain constant contact with, and in fact control, any agent he had undercover. After

Ray's second report several weeks into the Mexico part of his mission, there had not been another word from him in over two months. Contact had simply ceased, and Bennie had no idea if his man was even alive. Bennie had become so desperate to find a way to reestablish contact with Ray that he had gone to Fort Bliss, the sprawling army base outside of El Paso, Texas, and the headquarters for the newly established US Border Corps, to seek the help of the commanding general Manny Rodriguez. Bennie had done so for two very important reasons. First, the general had drone assets under his command that Bennie wanted to use to try to get eyes on Ray by watching the three large estates Ray had given them. If the general cooperated, they could keep an eye on the comings and goings at these estates, and there was at least a chance they could spot Ray, if he was still alive.

Secondly, the general was a close first cousin to one Alberto Rodriguez, who was the head of the Mexican Federal Police and one of the few men Bennie knew he could trust in the Mexican political hierarchy. The general had turned out to be very cooperative, for his close cousin, Alberto's younger brother, Emilio, had been ruthlessly assassinated leaving his estate in Mexico City in the last couple of weeks. Emilio had been the director of Mexico's version of the FBI, and his death had sent shock waves throughout the Mexican and American agencies charged with fighting the cartels. For Lieutenant General Manny Rodriguez, anything he could do to help the DEA, he would do if it meant catching or killing those responsible for the murder of his cousin.

Bennie's plan to use General Rodriguez's drone assets was just getting organized nicely when what appeared to the world as a tragic accident occurred, and the Mexican president and many in his entourage were killed in an air crash in Hermosillo. But appearances could be deceiving, and Bennie and General Rodriguez were part of a small group who knew that what appeared to the world as a tragic accident had indeed been a very well-orchestrated assassination of the Mexican president. Furthermore, the source of the privileged and vitally important information that had come to them through Alberto Rodriguez had as its source the no-longer-silent Ray Cruz.

Alberto unknowingly had been passed a note during a social gathering in memory of his slain brother, hosted at the palatial home of his old friend and superior in the government, Secretary of Public Security Jacques Alvarez. With the death of President Fernandez in the air crash, it had been a certainty that Alvarez, as the most senior member of the cabinet and long-time rising star in the dominant political party, would be selected by the presidential commission in charge of such duties to fill the remaining four years of the dead president's single six-year term. Ray's note and a subsequent call from Ray to Bennie at the message-drop number Ray had been provided before his infiltration revealed to Bennie just why Ray had gone silent for several months.

In a twisted, unlucky string of events, the powerful cartel that Carlo had taken Ray into was in fact run by the new president of Mexico, Jacques Pablo Alvarez, for he was also the Condor. Somehow—and Bennie had no idea how—Ray had gone from simple young friend and bodyguard to Carlo Vargas to one of the three personal bodyguards and confidants to Mexico's new president. From Ray's call, Bennie knew his young agent was on the brink of totally losing it, if he wasn't in fact already lost. As a member of Alvarez's close personal circle, Ray had been sucked into the conspiracy to assassinate President Fernandez, and despite his courage, training, and experience, Ray had not been able to stop it. The deaths of Fernandez and the others killed alongside him in the air disaster were clearly weighing heavily on young Ray. More distressing to Bennie was Ray's belief that he had failed Bennie and the agency, and as a result, he believed his life as he knew it was over. The last thoughts Ray shared with Bennie in the message drop were to say the only way forward he could see was either to kill the new Mexican president to end his control, an act Ray would likely not survive, or to join him. It was clear from Ray's call that in some weird way Bennie could not even begin to comprehend, Ray admired Alvarez for what he was doing. But joining truly did mean leaving a decent law-abiding life behind him. Either thought sent chills down Bennie's spine, and he was damned if he was going to lose his man.

As the flight neared Mexico City, Bennie sadly sat fiddling with his special encrypted iPhone, trying to figure out just what he could do for Ray. He plugged his headphones back in and listened to for what had to be the twentieth or thirtieth time the last few agonized seconds of Ray's message: "I'm sorry, Bennie, for failing you like I have. I did try, but one thing led to another, and I couldn't stop it or control it. Listen, whatever happens, could you get word to my dad? Tell him I tried to see right from wrong…but the gray…the gray just got too hard to see through. Tell him, Bennie. He'll understand what I'm trying to say…and tell him I…love him."

Bennie stopped the recording and accessed the copy of Ray's note to Alberto Rodriguez, rereading it again. He'd read it so often over the last several days that he knew it word for word without looking, but he read it nevertheless, slowly shaking his head in what was still disbelief.

ALVAREZ IS CONDOR DE MUERTE
OF CHIHUAHUA, ALSO NICOLAS PEñA
OF BAJA SUR. PRESIDENT FERNANDEZ TO
BE KILLED MONDAY IN HERMOSILLO
"ACCIDENT." YOU TO BE ASSASSINATED
MONDAY BY A BOMB IN YOUR CAR.
ALVAREZ WANTS THE PRESIDENCY.
CONTACT BENNIE SANTIAGO, US DEA ONLY.
REPEAT: ONLY. CONDOR SPIES ARE
EVERYWHERE. TRUST NO ONE.
SIGNED, TROJAN HORSE

The pilot's voice over the intercom system broke through Bennie's concentration, announcing they were beginning their descent into the capital city of Mexico. Bennie slowly and sadly shook his head, knowing that his mission was simple yet perhaps impossible. Somehow, with Alberto Rodriguez's help, he had to try to rescue his agent, his friend, out from under the nose of the most powerful and dangerous cartel leader in the country, who was also now the country's president. Alberto had pledged whatever support Bennie required, for there could be no doubt that with the high-risk passing of the note, Ray had saved Alberto's life, for the car bomb that had in fact been placed on his car had been safely removed.

Taking on cartels was always a dangerous and deadly business, but Bennie had been doing that for years. What he'd never even contemplated was that there would come a time he would be taking on the president of the country. Bennie's close friend and the intelligence director of the agency had asked him before putting him on the flight to Mexico, "How do you plan on saving Ray and not getting you both killed in the process?" Bennie had told Charlie he didn't know, but he was honor bound to try. As the sleek Boeing 767 continued its descent into Mexico City, Bennie knew he was no closer to knowing how he was to save Ray and live.

5

F orty-six-year-old Lieutenant General Manny Rodriguez was an imposing figure, even when dressed in the nylon-and-cotton camo army combat uniform he usually wore around the huge grounds of his command of Fort Bliss, Texas. Still an athletic and trim six feet two and 210 pounds, he was viewed by almost everyone who knew him personally or professionally as a true modern-day warrior. Manny's father, Henri, was the brother of Alberto and Emilio Rodriguez's father, Ernesto. Henri had come to the United States upon his graduation from the National University in Mexico City to pursue graduate studies in international business at the University of Texas and had decided to stay. He had met Manny's mother on the first day of classes, and that had been that, as they said.

Manny had many interests while growing up, but early on he dreamed of nothing else but a career in the army and eventually easily earned one of the two appointments granted by the senior US senator from Texas at the time. From the day he entered the parade ground at West Point, he knew he had found a home, and he excelled at every level.

Advancement in the US Army was available to all and largely dependent upon the intelligence, education, experiences, and skills of individual officers. The very best young officers followed a proven similar path up the command ladder, from small unit commands to senior staff positions and eventually to the command of battalions, regiments, and divisions. During the slippery climb up the ranks, more education was required for the few who had earned the right to be selected to attend the army's advanced officer schools. In addition to the army postgraduate schools, officers with their sights on general rank also earned postgraduate degrees at other universities in a variety of subjects intended to round out their personal and professional experiences. This rigorous path up the ladder for the most part identified the truly best and brightest of the officer corps and resulted in senior officers of enviable educational and command-experience backgrounds.

From Manny's first command as a platoon leader assigned to Bravo Company, First Battalion of the Seventy-Fifth Ranger Regiment at Fort Benning, his career had followed an aggressive path up through the ranks. He had assumed command of an infantry company in Operation Desert Storm in what history now called the First Persian Gulf War when his captain had been injured in training and couldn't carry out his duties. Manny had been seriously wounded and decorated twice for leadership and courage as a result of several night actions he had conducted as the acting company commander against elements of the crack Iraqi Republican Guard. For Manny, however, the best thing to come out of his first unit-command experience wasn't the Distinguished Service Cross or Silver Star medals he had earned—and the recognition and respect that went with such high honors—but rather his close friendship with his Command Sergeant Major Jefferson Green. Nevertheless, because of his cool, courageous leadership during the deadly actions in the harsh desert, his career had been brilliant and noticed.

As a highly decorated junior officer, Manny had quickly received promotions and choice assignments. During a two-year staff assignment in Washington, DC, while recovering from his wounds from Desert Storm, he had the opportunity to further his education and did so by earning a master's degree in international relations from Georgetown University. For the next twelve years, he continued to receive early promotions and assume commands in increasingly higher and more important positions in the army. The years also saw him involved in nearly every overseas deployment made by the US military. Manny's actions as a combat commander in Somalia, two more tours in Iraq, and one tour in Afghanistan saw him decorated time and again for his leadership and courage under fire. Between overseas deployments, he continued to further his education with appointments to the US Army Command and General Staff College in Fort Leavenworth, Kansas, where he earned a second master's degree in military arts and science, and then the US Army War College at Carlisle Barracks, Pennsylvania, where he received his third postgraduate degree, a master's in strategic studies.

On the twentieth anniversary of his graduation from West Point, Manny achieved a significant accomplishment in the life of a career military officer when the president of the United States nominated him to the rank of brigadier general. His appointment hadn't gone go unnoticed within the military establishment, for it was a remarkable achievement to have reached flag rank in just twenty years, and he was the first of his academy class to do so. Since his appointment as brigade commander at the Point, he had been on a fast track to the star he received. His courage and leadership in battle had earned him even more respect and admirers in the upper ranks, and at the time of his appointment to brigadier general, there didn't exist in the US Army a more highly decorated, battle-tested colonel, and there were few better-educated ones.

Despite Manny's training and experience, as well as the awesome military power he now commanded, he felt completely powerless as he sat in the simple kitchen of his quarters with his old friend the sergeant major. One thing his new command quickly taught him was that the enemies he was charged with containing, the brutal and elusive cartels of northern Mexico, were as dangerous as any he had ever fought. The miserable part of the assignment was that all he was empowered to do was contain or intercept and keep the bastards south of the border. Of the fifty thousand troops under his command, only the six thousand troops of the recently organized US Border Corps were doing any effective soldiering. And then there was little they actually did except make their general presence known with the endless patrolling up and down the nearly two thousand miles of wire. This dirty, thankless task was augmented by the intelligence take from his squadrons of

Predator drones that patrolled the skies each day and watched for the elusive enemy from overhead. *Glorified camp guards*, he had thought more than once—only the camp was Camp USA.

South of Manny's picket wire, real fighting was going on against the cartels of Mexico, and his cousins were at the front lines of that battle. These heavily armed and wealthy criminal organizations were rampaging and killing all over northern Mexico, protecting their profitable business interests, and it was his cousins with their police forces and law books who had been doing the real fighting—only now, one of them was dead. It didn't take three silver stars on your shoulders to understand that the good guys were losing—and losing big—down there. They were outgunned, out financed, and as far as Manny could see, outfoxed when it came to intelligence information, the absolute bedrock of requirements for an effective combat leader. The Mexican authorities, his cousins in particular, were constantly looking to expose and prosecute traitors in their own camps, bought off with small pieces of the billions the cartel leaders reaped in profits every year, if the report given to him recently by the DEA was to be believed.

Command Sergeant Major Jefferson Green, all six-foot-four, 250 pounds of him, was chewing on an unlit cigar just staring at his troubled general. They were waiting on the general's G-2, the deputy chief of staff for intelligence Colonel Scott Cudworth to join them at the general's quarters for lunch.

To Manny, his senior noncommissioned officer looked exactly the way a command sergeant major with thirty years of service should look—erect in bearing, with a totally squared-away personal appearance, always crisply dressed, even in his dungarees—and nothing on the base, much less in the ranks, missed his sharp, experienced eye.

Manny had given a great deal of thought about how he was going to deal with his staff regarding his cousin Alberto and how he was going to help him. In the two weeks since his very close cousin Emilio had been assassinated leaving his home in Mexico City, Manny had thought of little else. He took his officer's oath seriously, and the idea of lying in any circumstances was repugnant to him. He therefore decided he would tell his staff the truth to a point, however out of context the truth may be. That his staff would think that the general had received sensitive orders from FORSCOM or above would be their natural assumption. He simply would not disabuse them of any conclusions they might logically jump to.

The G-2 arrived as scheduled, and over lunch, Manny explained to him there was great concern in Washington regarding not only the growing refugee camps of the recently deported Mexican citizens to south of the border under the new immigration law and the troubles brewing there but also the increases in cartel trafficking and violence as the Mexican army was shifted from cartel interdiction in the northern states to aiding in the Mexican government's relief efforts at the camps. As a result, Manny said, the US Army Border Corps had been requested to assist the DEA and the Mexican government with a highly sensitive reconnaissance and intelligence-gathering joint operation, and all information regarding the operation was to be strictly on a need-to-know basis.

"Scott," Manny said, "all I can tell you is that we have been tasked to cooperate with the DEA on a plan devised by their agent in charge, Bennie Santiago, and that the less people who know about this, the better. They need our help trying to get eyes on an agent of theirs who apparently is in the deep shit, and they need some of our drone assets to accomplish this. I'm told there have been serious security breaches on other joint operations, so this thing is going to be held close. Nothing to do with Mr. Santiago or his mission is to be discussed with anyone outside this group, understood?"

"Yes sir, of course. Anything I can do," the G-2 said.

"What I need you to do first is get on the horn and call Captain...Jeff, who's got the hoot owl shift?"

"Captain Irwin, sir. Danny Irwin," Sergeant Major Green replied after removing his well-chewed cigar.

"That's right—Captain Irwin. Have him meet us at his office. I understand he worked the hoot owl last night, and it's his day off, but this is important." Manny returned his attention to his intelligence chief and went on. "You, me, and the sergeant major will brief the captain on what must be done and impress upon him the importance of this operation and who he will be taking his orders from. Jeff here will coordinate for us and report to Colonel Romero."

The G-2 nodded and began pulling out his cell phone, but the general stopped him, smiled, and said, "Finish your lunch, Scott. The DEA and your young captain can wait another half hour before we get this shit show on the road."

The Palms Apartments
El Paso, Texas
Tuesday Afternoon

Danny Irwin was sound asleep in his off-base apartment, having partied very hard all morning since leaving the base after his all-night shift. His new girlfriend was as sexy and good-looking a woman as he had ever had. That she was attracted to him almost exclusively for his ability to provide her with great cocaine when together, as opposed to actually being interested in him for his personality or even his average looks, was something Danny was willing to overlook. The sex, especially coked-out morning sex, was just way too good to get all hung up on honest motives. When it came to getting laid, Danny had zero ego. His cell phone ringing and ringing brought him out of his slumber.

"What." He snarled into his cell phone, once he located it on the floor.

"Captain Irwin, this is Colonel Cudworth. Something's come up, and I need to see you in your office in thirty minutes."

At the recognition of the G-2's voice, Danny was jolted by an adrenaline rush into a greater sense of awareness quicker than he would otherwise have been given his condition. Danny was terrified of the colonel.

"Yes sir, thirty minutes. On my way in, sir."

Danny stumbled out of the sack and into the shower. He felt like complete shit. The one problem he was becoming increasingly aware of with having basically a free supply of unlimited high-quality coke was that he had a tendency to overindulge, knowing that there would always be more. And off duty, when he partied hard, the resulting hangovers could be brutal.

Besides the typical bloodshot eyes and sore nose and throat, his head was pounding, and his hands shook so much he nicked himself several times shaving.

In the days prior to his relationship with his new supplier, Alex, money had always been the determining factor as to just how much fun he could have. Good coke in the open market was expensive, and he was in the US fucking Army and not on some college campus, so dealing, as he once had, was a very dangerous proposition to supplement both his income and his supply. As a result, his stash had been rationed: only a certain level of partying and then sharing with only a select few. His complex relationship with Alex had changed all that.

He knew whatever the colonel wanted to see him about would require his attention and focus, and the pounding in his skull and the raw burn in his nose and throat would make this difficult at best, if not impossible. His new girlfriend worked a late shift at one of the more popular bars that serviced the base. She'd met Danny at his apartment after his breakfast with Alex and was still in a deep sleep after coming off the earlier high, and she had not stirred at the call or his rushing around the room getting dressed. He scrawled a hasty note saying he had to go into work and that he'd call her later about getting together that evening.

He only lived a couple of miles from the base and made the short drive quickly. He passed through the main gate and made his way to the restricted parking area of Building R-24. He could not help noticing that the base commander's three-starred vehicle was there, parked beside the colonel's car.

What in the hell is the general doing here on a Tuesday afternoon? Danny thought. *Jesus, please let him be here for something that does not involve me.*

As fearful as Danny was of the colonel, the idea of meeting with the general was far worse. Generals were so far above Danny, not only in rank but in perception, that just being in the same room with one was uncomfortable, and this general was a powerful force. The general's confidence and all-knowing intelligence and power, all traits that Danny severely lacked, just radiated from him. Danny had been introduced to the general just after he had taken over command and had been touring the base and all his various subcommands, but other than a quick salute and handshake as part of the entire recon unit, that had been it.

He passed through the tight security screens required to enter Building R-24 and headed toward his first-floor office, a terrible feeling in the pit of his stomach making him momentarily forget the pounding between his ears. As he walked down the hallway, he had to pass the main conference room for the building. Standing there at the door was the hulking presence of the general's command sergeant major. The sar major tossed Danny a casual salute and said, "Afternoon, Captain. In here, if you would, please, sir."

Danny returned the salute and felt an ice ball growing in the pit of his stomach as he walked into the large conference room. He saw the commanding general and immediately popped to attention and said, "Sir, Captain Irwin reporting as ordered."

"At ease, Captain. Grab a cup of coffee, if you want, and take a seat. Jeff, close the door, please."

Danny immediately recognized everyone in the room. In addition to the general and the sergeant major, there was his immediate superior, Major Gumina; the recon company commander; the major's boss, Colonel Cudworth; the G-2; and the general's chief of staff, Colonel Romero. All in all, there was enough gold braid in the room to make Danny's pulse rate jump a few beats higher than it already was. Danny suspected this meeting was the follow-up to his introduction a few days earlier to some DEA bigwig out of Washington. Danny took the general up on his offer and poured some hot coffee, splashing it all over as he did so, as his hands were shaking so badly, and took the first open seat next to the G-2.

"Gentlemen," Manny started, "for the record, everything that is discussed in this room is to be considered restricted and strictly on a need-to-know basis. No one outside of this group is to be told anything about the mission to be discussed without my or Colonel Romero's permission. Is that understood?"

The general was greeted with a chorus of "Yes, sir."

"Captain Irwin, we're here to put into operation the general plans explained to you several days ago by DEA Special Agent Bennie Santiago. He has been called away to Washington, and I assured him before he left that we would carry out the mission tasked to us in his absence. As the sergeant major explained to you when he brought Agent Santiago here the first time, you and your team have been assigned to help him. From today, until otherwise ordered, you will be taking your mission orders from the chief of staff, through the sergeant major. He will tell you what he needs and when he needs it. If you have any questions of a purely military nature regarding your orders, you will make them known to the sergeant major, who will then get Colonel Romero or me involved. Is that clear?"

"Yes, sir." Danny croaked.

"Major Gumina," Manny said, shifting his focus to the company commander, "sorry to fuck up what's left of your command, but it's necessary. You are to make the necessary adjustments to your command to maintain our basic intelligence-gathering mission as best you can, given the reduction in your resources and manpower. The G-2 understands the importance of this special mission and will be amenable to any suggestions you may have, as well as your concerns about the diminution of the intelligence take as a result. In other words, Major, do the best you can with what you got. No one will be breathing down your neck on this one. Most importantly, I don't want your other troops wondering where Captain Irwin's team has gone, and I definitely do not want them kibitzing with Captain Irwin's people over beers in the club or the NCO slop chute. The sergeant major will help you make this point with the men, understood?"

"Yes, sir, and thank you. We'll be able to accomplish most of our responsibilities, General."

"Fine. You're dismissed, Major. Get working on your plan, and get with Colonel Cudworth later today. Scott," Manny said, turning to his G-2, "you can go also. Let's plan on meeting tomorrow morning, say at ten hundred hours, and take a look at how things are working, and thanks for understanding."

"Of course, General. Ten hundred tomorrow."

After the colonel and major closed the door behind them, Manny turned to Danny Irwin. "Captain, we have already begun calling in those members of your team who were on base, and they will be arriving shortly. You are directed to set up in Auxiliary Control, transferring all Predator control for your group to that room. Only your team and Agent Santiago, should he return, are to have access to that area. The sar major will give you the mission details. Any questions?"

"Sir, what about our hoot owl shift scheduled to begin tomorrow night at midnight?"

"Not your worry, Captain. From now until relieved, you and your team work when the sar major says you do—clear?"

"Yes, sir, General. Sir, what about records, logs, and reports?"

"The sar major will tell you what reports and in what manner they will be recorded, but this mission is classified, as will be any reports. We're keeping this tight, Captain," Manny responded.

"The sergeant major has been briefed on all aspects of this mission and has his orders. He knows everything I do, and when he speaks, he is speaking for me, understood?"

"Of course, sir!" Danny said, tossing a quick glance at the intimidating force that was the sergeant major. Rank or no rank, captains at Fort Bliss treated the sergeant major with almost the same respect and awe as they did the general. To cross the sergeant major was the same as crossing the general, maybe worse.

Manny stood up. "Captain, I leave you in the hands of the sar major here. If there's anything you need, Colonel Romero's and my office doors are open."

The others stood as Manny did, casual salutes were exchanged, and Manny turned and walked out, followed closely by Colonel Romero, who had said nothing in the meeting. They walked out of the building and climbed into the general's staff car. Sergeant Morehead, the general's driver, saw the general coming and already had the rear door open and then closed it behind Colonel Romero and quickly took the driver's seat. The general said, "The office, Harry," but other than that seemed deep in thought, and not another word was spoken by either soldier on the short drive. When they got to the headquarters building, Manny turned to Colonel Romero and asked him to come to his office for a second. Colonel Romero followed Manny and closed the general's office door behind them and assumed an at-ease position before his desk.

"Sit down for a second, Romey."

The colonel did as he was ordered.

Manny had a serious, contemplative look on his face and then said to his chief of staff, "I'm afraid you have drawn the shit end of the stick again, Romey."

Colonel Romero, a puzzled look coming to his face, asked, "How so, sir?"

"For all the reasons you can come up with yourself, the security on this operation has to be airtight. I'm way out of bounds for setting this up as I have, and I'm willing to resign my commission if this gets to FORSCOM or the Pentagon. But for selfish and personal reasons, I want us to succeed in helping my cousin, his country, and ours. But mostly, I want to keep Al alive, and in my mind that means getting that Condor bastard before he gets Alberto. If this desire is coloring my judgment, then so be it. I can't have word getting up the chain on our side and blowing this. That means we need to watch our people working with Bennie. In this day and age of cell phones, texting, e-mails, and instant messaging, I don't have a clue how we keep a lid on this, which is why I'm lateraling it to you. We can't have those men talking about this mission outside of Auxiliary Control."

"I already had some thoughts about this, General, and shared them with Jeff. By now he has impressed Captain Irwin and his troops about the need to keep their mouths shut. Also, by tomorrow, I will be meeting with the group and will review the added penalties for violating National Security Directive such-and-such. As to just what directive they would be violating, I will know myself just as soon as I write it up. Let me do some additional thinking, and I will come up with a plan and put it into works. At a minimum, sir, it will probably mean getting Billy Ames involved. I will likely need some manpower, and his CID agents would be the best people, all things considered. I don't see using his people without letting him know why."

"No, you can't," Manny said slowly, his look to the colonel clearly indicating he was considering the ramifications of expanding their group. "But let's keep what we are doing tight, Romey. Colonel Ames needs to know only that we are involved with something clandestine using Captain Irwin's drone team. He doesn't need to know the mission. On my authority, go ahead and get him and his CID involved. As soon as there is a security plan, I'd be interested in seeing it."

"Yes, sir." The colonel stood up. "By your leave, sir?"

"Thanks, Romey. This is a shitty business, spying on our own troops—but necessary."

6

Back in the conference room of Building R-24, after the general and his chief of staff had departed, Captain Irwin, trying to project more authority than he was feeling, looked at the sergeant major and asked, "Well, Sar Major, seems I'm working for you. What do you suggest we do next?"

It was all Jefferson Green could do to mask his contempt for this particular young captain, but he did and answered politely. "First things first, Captain. Let's get your troops and get things set up in auxiliary. We need to get a secure area up and operating first."

The rest of the day was spent setting up the captain's Predator unit in Auxiliary Control and instructing the rest of Danny's team about their mission. The team consisted of the four lieutenant team leaders, the four drone pilots, and twelve sensor operators that operated the array of sensors and cameras on board the four advanced MQ-9 drones.

All told, in addition to the sergeant major and Captain Irwin, twenty of the team's men would know of the mission. The thirty maintenance personnel and mission-intelligence specialists that also made up Danny's group did not need to know where or what the drones were looking at once they left the base.

Once they were assembled, Sergeant Major Green spent five minutes reviewing the military penalties that junior officers and the troops would face if it ever came to the sergeant major's attention that someone had shot off his or her mouth to anyone outside the group about any aspect of the classified operation they were now all involved in. As Jeff stood before the assembled team and read them the riot act on security, a scared Danny Irwin couldn't help thinking that if he were not in the position he was, he'd have been pissing his pants. The sar major was one intimidating son of a bitch when he wanted to be, and he seemed to want to be twenty-four seven.

The access-card reader for the door into auxiliary was reprogrammed, and new security cards were issued that would grant entry to the limited group. The sar major told the captain he could dismiss the men until 0600 the next morning. Once the men left and it was just the two of them again, he got into the mission. Jefferson Green had been dealing with sensitive and or covert missions for most of his adult life and had given a lot of thought on exactly how to explain to the captain and his people just who they were helping the DEA look for. Remembering his own orders from the general on security, in the end he defaulted to the most fundamental, tried-and-true approach: he mostly lied.

"Captain, our mission is to locate several important individuals that escaped jail here in the United States who the DEA believes are deeply involved with a particularly effective drug cartel in Mexico. The 'why' the DEA wants these mutts and the 'what' they intend to do if we find the bastards for them are not important to you. What is important is using your birds to locate these individuals."

Sergeant Major Green broke out a map of northern Mexico that Colonel Romero had given him the night before and sat it on the desk.

"We have information on three probable cartel compounds that we need to bring under surveillance for the DEA. If we find them in the course of just watching the compounds, we also need to try to identify anyone else of interest we may stumble upon."

The sar major produced the booking mugshots of a "Carlo," no known last name, and a Ray Espinoza. "This is the guy we're after."

He handed Danny the mugshot of Carlo.

"He is sometimes accompanied by the younger dude who we think is nothing more than a bodyguard but seems to go wherever this Carlo asshole goes, so we will keep an eye out for him too. I've circled the general areas we know from DEA-provided intel where these cartel bases are located. Here is a detailed description of all three and also a description of the drive from each city to the estates. Using this information, your first task is to simply locate and verify the exact estates. Once you have done that, we need to keep an eye on them and see if we can locate these people."

"Sounds like a pretty simple mission, Sar Major, and frankly, more fun than just flying up and down the fences," Danny said as he started looking at the written information and maps the intimidating senior sergeant had with him. Danny told the sar major that he'd have the team's search plans all ready by 0600 the next morning. And unless these cartel boys were good at camouflaging their estates, he felt certain they would locate them sooner rather than later. The sar major simply nodded and, without another word, left Auxiliary Control.

Danny was all smiles and nothing but the accommodating team leader until Sergeant Major Green left the room. Alone, he quickly reverted to the truth of the moment. He still felt like shit and now would have to spend the rest of his day off here in Auxiliary Control plotting flight plans based upon the DEA intelligence he had and arranging work schedules for the team. This was a bummer, for it meant that the lazy afternoon and evening he'd planned of sleeping some and then getting high and laid again was now blown completely out of the water. Worse, however, was the realization that with the change in assignment, there was probably no way he could make his next regularly scheduled Tuesday-morning breakfast at Harry's.

Fuck, Danny thought. *I'll need more coke. I wonder if this search will fuck up my arrangement. Maybe his people will stop the supply if I can't tell them what's happening on the border. Goddamn it! This is a disaster.*

Danny and his lieutenants finished up the necessary planning work for the next day's shift and left aux control by late afternoon. When he got back to his apartment, he was alone, as he thought he would likely be. As he was changing out of his uniform, he glanced into the bathroom and noticed a small empty plastic bag and the hand mirror lying on the counter. His so-called girlfriend had clearly helped herself to his coke while he was out and then had likely taken with her what she hadn't blown. He'd enticed her into his bed the first time with his bragging on how much of the nose candy he had and could get with a snap of his fingers.

Well, that's just great, Danny thought. *That was supposed to last me till next week, the greedy bitch.* Danny knew she could be a problem—very needy of the highs he could provide her and very superficial in her affections toward him—but hey, she was gorgeous and did things to him that other girls had never considered. He had his weaknesses too.

As ironic as it seemed, Danny was well aware of his weaknesses; he simply lacked the will or judgment to do anything about them. It was like that part of his brain that contained the centers for reasoned thought or judgment had been lobotomized right out of him. The intellectual side of Danny, which was significant, sometimes viewed this deficiency as if from afar and wondered, *What the hell are you doing?* But in the end, he could not help himself.

Danny cleaned up the incriminating mess and went to the kitchen table, sat down, and thought reflectively for a few minutes. Then he scrolled through his cell phone until he found the name he wanted—Alex. He punched in the cell number, listened, and then hung up disappointed as he was sent to voice mail. He next looked up Alex's business number. Alex had only reluctantly given Danny this backup number, and it was only to be used for emergencies—for example, if any of the confidential plans Danny provided every Tuesday morning were somehow changed. Well, as problematic as that situation would be, in Danny's mind there was no greater emergency than being out of coke and likely not being able to meet next week. That was a real emergency, so he dialed the backup number. After several rings, he got nothing but voice mail. Alex was always warning him about security and not writing anything down or leaving messages, but he reluctantly stayed on the line. At the beep, he kept it short and sweet: "Alex, call me. My situation on the base has changed. It's important we get together. I need to talk with you." With that he hung up. *Good,* he thought; only Alex would understand the message and know who it was from.

It was far too soon for the kind of security measures Colonel Romero might have liked to have in place on the small group of soldiers working in Auxiliary Control, and even then, there was not much he could have done to intercept a cell phone call from off base. But luck was with the colonel in ways he did not even know, for DEA colleagues of Bennie's, not privy to anything Bennie was doing out at Fort Bliss, had been interested in Alejandro Guerro for a very long time. The illegal tap on Alex's US business phone automatically recorded all calls, and the DEA technician with the duty not only noted the day and time, but with his sophisticated equipment, he also had the incoming phone number. It was a cell phone, as was almost always the case. US citizens might be protected by the Constitution from such an invasion of privacy, but the previous leadership of the DEA, desperate to make more arrests under great pressure from Congress, had taken the gloves off when it came to Mexican nationals in this country. Once the new intelligence director Charley Willis found out about this operation, it would be made lawful or terminated, but until then, the current SAC (special agent in charge) wanted leads, so this team kept eavesdropping. The SAC would use the niceties of the Constitution and its protections, if and when the illegal leads led him to US citizens.

As Danny assumed, the call would have sounded benign to any layman who might have overheard the short message. But the DEA tech listening was a seasoned professional. He knew he had a nugget of information and flagged it for the agent in charge of the surveillance. Come morning when the tapes were reviewed, the SAC responsible for this particular surveillance would add another contact and potential distribution suspect to their growing list. This contact would be worth tracking down, for as innocuous as the message was, it did mention two words worth following up on: *the base.* Interdiction of narcotics was important anytime, but interdiction of anything illegal to the sprawling Fort Bliss was a top priority. The team would run this lead down fast, and the first step was to identify who owned the cell phone that had placed the call. With a quick couple of keystrokes on his computer, the tech had the database he required and entered the number.

In several seconds he had his name—Captain Daniel Irwin, US Army—and his off-post address. This information was also flagged for the SAC, who would likely call the provost marshal at the base and give him a heads-up as a professional courtesy.

7

When the pilot announced that they were beginning their descent into Benito Juarez International Airport and would be landing in twenty-five minutes, Bennie pocketed his special iPhone, closed up his briefcase, and looked out the window, anxious to get his first look at the capital.

He need not have bothered. The seasonal monsoons, with their dense cloud cover, obscured the land below with only the tops of various mountains poking up through. All visibility was lost once they dropped down into the puffy-looking gray clouds. Bennie traveled so much he was very comfortable with flying and never gave heavier-than-air flight much thought, except when he could not see out and the turbulence got bad, as it now did. After fifteen uncomfortable minutes of bouncing around the sky in the big Boeing 767, they finally popped out of the soup into a real rainstorm, but Bennie could at least somewhat see the ground. At first all he saw was lush green mountains as they made their steep approach to the city below. Unbeknownst to Bennie, because their approach was from the southwest due to the winds, their flight path first took them over the neighboring western city of Toluca, which Bennie had at first mistaken for Mexico City, having never flown in here before. Had he known, he would have recalled that it had been from Toluca that Ray had made his fateful call to Bennie of a few days ago, declaring that his life as he knew it was over—the result of what

49

Ray believed to be his failure to stop the assassination and prevent the loss of innocent lives he now carried on his conscience. They quickly passed over the much smaller city and then over another low range of mountains or hills. Before Bennie knew it, he was now seeing the sprawling capital of twelve million people. Viewed through the mist and rain, the city looked like a textured sepia-colored quilt from the wet, muted colors of millions of clay roof tiles on mile after mile of ramshackle housing all jammed together. The stitches in the quilt were the ribbons of narrow crisscrossing streets, most at ridiculous angles to one another, that cut here and there in nonsensical patterns.

Christ on a crutch, Bennie thought. *They never hear of the grid system?*

His first impression of the capital city was not flattering. He had the same feeling he usually got whenever he flew into Los Angeles in the daylight: a crush of humanity and all of the associated dysfunctional systems of a large urban area jammed into a small area that had probably once been beautiful.

After a nice landing under the conditions and after quickly deplaning Bennie followed a stream of his fellow passengers and made his way out of the concourse and into the large modern space that was the customs area for arriving international passengers. He was approached by a tall well-dressed young man of perhaps thirty with penetrating eyes and a not-too-well-concealed shoulder holster and pistol who asked him in Spanish, "Senor Santiago?"

"Yes," Bennie responded in his impeccable Spanish, instinctively recognizing a fellow cop, "I'm Bennie Santiago."

"The secretary offers his apologies for not being able to meet you personally and has asked me to be of service and take you to his home. He will meet you there within a few hours."

"Sure," Bennie said. "Thank you."

Before leaving Dulles, Bennie called Manny and told him Charley was up to speed. He also told the general he would keep him informed of his progress, or lack of it, once he hooked up with Alberto. Manny took down his flight information and told Bennie he'd give his cousin a heads-up on his arrival, which obviously had led to this greeting committee.

The aide asked for his baggage-claim ticket and handed it to another man, who, to Bennie's well-trained eye, was also a cop and had appeared out of nowhere after a subtle nod of the head from Alberto's aide. Bennie was quickly cleared through customs, merely having to show his diplomatic passport. The second cop had his baggage stub stamped Diplomático Ninguna Inspección (Diplomat No Inspection), and after a quick, almost embarrassing description of the suitcase from Bennie, set off to retrieve the well-worn bag.

The tall young aide led the two of them out of customs and through the main terminal. They walked out the automatic doors of the terminal at street level to a waiting limousine sandwiched between two oversized black GMC SUVs. All were parked in an obvious No Parking zone right in front. There was an armed driver for the limo waiting patiently beside the open rear door, and each SUV was manned with two more security types. As soon as they entered the limousine, the door was closed, the caravan pulled out, and they made their way into the heavy traffic that seemed to envelop the crowded airport area.

Bennie was impressed with the security that Alberto afforded him but could not help thinking that it was in a motorcade not unlike this one that Emilio Rodriguez had been ruthlessly ambushed and killed. Though the limousine was likely armored in some way, it was little protection indeed from rocket-propelled grenades. He wasn't concerned about assassination; he was a very small unknown fish. If anything, all the fuss surrounding his arrival and the ostentatious show of protection probably put him in more danger than a simple cab ride would have. He forced those thoughts from his mind and tried to take in the views as they left the airport grounds. Bennie was innately curious and loved exploring new places and surroundings. Visiting a new city always was something he enjoyed, and he often found time from his duties to just explore.

It was still raining hard as they left the airport grounds, their route meandering through a mix of run-down housing and retail areas in the northern outskirts of the central business district of the capital city. They were heading toward what Bennie thought was mostly west and passed some very interesting ruins, likely of an Aztecan or Mayan nature, that Bennie made a point to remember to ask Alberto about. They finally intersected a major avenue that seemed to knife its way diagonally across the lesser streets, which Bennie was told by the aide was the Paseo de la Reforma. In contrast to the short drive through the lower-class neighborhoods surrounding the airport, which had taken a full thirty minutes to navigate due to the circuitous route and terrible traffic congestion, now on the grand avenue, they passed more quickly, even with the traffic. As if on cue, because of the much nicer neighborhoods they were beginning to transit, the rain stopped, as if nature was saying that only certain areas of the city required the occasional washing. The first slanting rays of afternoon sunshine began peeking through the overcast sky.

The broad avenue, with its upscale retail stores and high-rise office and apartment buildings lining each side, led them into a very large parklike area. The aide saw Bennie's interest in the landscapes passing by their windows and told him they were now in the Chapultepec area, which had at its heart the grand and beautiful Chapultepec Park, a large, natural open space of over sixteen hundred acres. Bennie could see that the large park area was surrounded on all sides by an eclectic assortment of old and new residential areas, glitzy-looking retail establishments, upscale and modern new office buildings, and many of the capital city's finer examples of historic architecture. It was not unlike the city views from the heart of Central Park in New York, thought Bennie. After a ten-minute drive on the grand avenue, they turned off Reforma into an older, quiet, very handsome residential and commercial area.

In all his years at the DEA working almost exclusively on the interdiction of drugs into the United States from Mexico, Bennie had never been to the Mexican capital. His visual sense was at first overwhelmed by the great diversity in new and modern versus old and decaying, the obvious wealth of the Chapultepec area, and the poverty evidenced in some of the neighborhoods they had passed through in the drive from the airport.

Bennie was very impressed with the home of Alberto Rodriguez as they made the turn off the cobblestone-paved residential street and passed through the heavily guarded main gate of the estate. Beyond the tall stone and plaster walls that surrounded the large estate were lush lawn areas, blooming floral gardens, and a canopy of mature trees. They followed the long curving drive until stopping in front of the older, very elegant Italian Renaissance mansion.

Bennie was hopelessly middle class, he had come to realize over the years, and glad of it, very comfortable with the modest lifestyle of his parents and now his own. There were the public schools, community colleges at first until he was recognized for his gifts and given a scholarship to UCLA. After his graduation from college and joining the DEA, there had been a number of warm and comfortable homes, Chevys in the driveway, neighborhood bars, cold beer from a bottle, and the occasional round of golf on the burned-out, patchy fairways and greens of the nearest public links. Simple, to be sure, but there were also the friendships found and maintained by the simplicity of such lives—associations based on the content of a man's character and actions as a neighbor, not the breadth of his portfolio or the size and shine of his personal toys.

His long career in the DEA and the successes he had achieved because of his talents had exposed him from time to time to the wealth and power in those he came into professional contact with. He was as comfortable sitting on the patio of a US senator drinking fine old scotch whiskey—as he had done just a few nights earlier in Arizona—as he was with sitting in an El Paso dive swilling cold Coors with other cops, as he often did. He was very comfortable in his skin and had never been envious of the lifestyles that came with great wealth that he saw in others. He was satisfied that he had contributed far more to the safety and well-being of his country than most. He wasn't without his weaknesses, such as they were, and had developed tastes for really good single-malt scotch whiskeys and deep, complex red wines, and he was the first to admit that a thick steak was a helluva lot better than a burger, but there was no harm in that, no betrayal of his root character.

The meeting two days earlier near Prescott, Arizona, with the junior US senator from Arizona, Pete Martinez, and three-starred General

Rodriguez, had been arranged by Bennie's boss, Charley Willis. As director of the Intelligence Division of the DEA, Charley had his fingers in all sorts of pies as he tried to develop and keep current the agency's ongoing picture of the trafficking business. It had been Charley's idea to approach the general about using some of his drones to surveil the three estates in northern Mexico that Ray had passed information about in one of his two early communications. It was a desperate move, both Charley and Bennie realized, to think that watching the estates might actually get eyes on Ray, but as Charley had noted, it was better than sitting around DC with their thumbs up their butts and not doing anything. The senator had been General Rodriguez's West Point roommate, was on the Senate Intelligence Committee, and was the principal author of the recently passed new immigration bill that was rounding up millions of illegals in the country and staging them in efficient deportation camps near the border and then processing them back to Mexico in an orderly manner. Ostensibly, this sort of documentation and processing would then allow for the legal reentry of some of the Mexican and other South and Central American citizens back into the United States. The government of the late president Fernandez had totally botched their end of the processing by not properly constructing or staffing what amounted to refugee camps on the Mexican side of the border. Chaos, disease, and violence had spread as a consequence.

Back in the moment, as he stared out the window of the limo and took in the private estate and home of Alberto Rodriguez, he was more aware than ever that there were people out there who operated in very different worlds from his own. He might as well have been on Mars the differences were so great. A formally dressed butler was standing on the front steps with an unopened umbrella waiting to greet the limo. *Man, oh man*, Bennie thought, *cop or not, this guy lives in another universe.*

Before he could open the door, the butler approached the car and opened it for him.

"Senor Santiago, welcome to Senor Rodriguez's home. I am Alejandro, sir, and I am at your service."

"Thank you, Alejandro," Bennie said as he straightened up after passing out the rear door of the limo and extended his hand in greeting. "Nice to meet you."

Alejandro seemed puzzled for a second, and then slowly, after moving the umbrella to his other hand, shook hands with the stranger from America, quietly amused but not showing it and a little taken with being recognized as a person and not a servant.

"If you will follow me, Senor, I will show you to your room, where you may freshen up after your long journey."

The Rodriguez aide that had brought him to the estate also got out of the limo and said, "Senor Santiago, I must leave you now. The secretary should be here between five and six."

"Thanks," Bennie said, also shaking his hand. "I appreciate you meeting me and the ride. Uh, any idea where my suitcase is?"

"It will arrive shortly, Senor. I hope you enjoy your visit to our country."

The aide, who was still nameless to Bennie, turned and got back in the limo. Bennie started to follow Alejandro but first stopped and admired the two large carved stone lions that sat on their haunches as sentries on the ends of the low, curving stone walls that flanked the wide, shallow entry steps. Alejandro showed him through the impressively tall double front doors of the mansion into the grand foyer.

That's what my front porch has been missing—a couple of big-ass stone lions. Really punches the place up, Bennie thought as he entered the foyer.

The high-ceilinged foyer space was almost entirely made of polished stone, most of which Bennie did not recognize. Bennie had done a European vacation with his late wife on an anniversary once, before the cancer had finally claimed her. The foyer of Alberto's house reminded him of the lobbies of some of the boutique hotels they had stayed in. The polished, patterned floor and stone-wainscoted walls and trim gave way to two identical curving stone stairways on the left and right sides of the beautiful space, leading to a second-floor balcony. Above and below the balcony, framed by the staircases, Bennie could see through a wall of tall windows divided by a hundred small lines of delicate metal mullions at what appeared to be formal gardens and fountains. He was amazed that he could see through so large a mansion from front door to rear, and his curious mind decided he would explore this peculiarity of the mansion's layout given the chance. Alejandro stopped in the middle of the foyer, and Bennie almost ran into him, as he was looking up at the magnificent chandelier that hung high above the center of the large entry space. After he made his apologies to Alejandro for nearly running over him, Alejandro pointed out the formal living area and the dining room to Bennie, all open and accessible and, from his quick glances at the rooms, very beautiful Old World elegance in their decoration and detail.

They climbed the left marble stair, Alejandro walking with professional purpose, back ramrod straight, eyes fixed straight ahead, his left hand formally on the small of his back, while the habitually slump-shouldered Bennie trailed behind, admiring the carved, polished balustrades and the fine art that adorned the walls. At the second-floor balcony, from which the rear formal gardens and pool areas were now fully visible, Alejandro took them down a long, wide corridor that was fancier than any hotel corridor Bennie had seen. Alejandro stopped in front of a formal door, turned the elegant gold lever handle, and led Bennie into the room.

Bennie's so-called room was actually a very nice three-room suite. He and Alejandro entered into what was a decent-sized living room, complete with a wet bar, flat-screen TV, and a nice fireplace, which was fronted by a comfortable-looking couch and several overstuffed chairs. Through the living room were the bedroom and a large bathroom, most of which, like everything else Bennie had seen, was polished stonework, mirrors, and gold trim. When he came out of the ornate bathroom, another manservant of some kind was delivering Bennie's battered three-suiter suitcase, setting it on the appropriate piece of furniture in his bedroom. It looked totally out of place in this setting, making him wish for a second that he had bought a new one by this time. Just about every time he pulled out the larger, older suitcase for a trip, he thought to himself, *Jesus, replace this piece of shit*, but there never seemed to be enough time, so he still carted it around, scars and all from all the endless traveling he did in his job.

Alejandro looked at Bennie. "I trust these accommodations are satisfactory? Is there anything we may do for you while you wait for the secretary?"

"Thank you, Alejandro. The rooms are just fine—more than fine. I thought I'd take a quick shower first and change. Afterward, would it be OK to explore the house and the estate while I wait for Senor Rodriguez?"

"Certainly, sir. Any of the public rooms with open doors is available to you. Ask any of the security people on the grounds should you go outside, and they will escort you around the estate. May we fix you something to eat or drink?"

"Do you know what the secretary has planned for us this evening?"

"Dinner here, Senor, at eight."

"Well, then maybe something light, Alejandro, after my shower. I'll be quick, about ten minutes."

"Very good, Senor."

Bennie's mind had been a rat's nest of never-ending thoughts, it seemed, since the teleconference with Alberto the day before from General Rodriguez's office at Fort Bliss. It was during that call that he and Alberto had been introduced to each other, and Alberto had given them Ray's message, resulting in Bennie being down here. As he emerged from the refreshing shower and looked at himself in the mirror, he realized that he had not thought of Ray from the time he had pulled up in front of the Rodriguez mansion until this very moment, perhaps something on the order of thirty minutes.

Shit, I must be bushed if I let a little thing like unbelievable luxury and a real butler dazzle and distract me like that, he thought as he stared at his tired reflection.

As he got dressed, his thoughts returned to contacting Ray. He had been thinking of little else in the twenty-four hours since Ray's voice mail telling him he had been sucked into the assassination conspiracy and then had failed to stop it. Because of that—and the two men Ray said he had killed during the mission—Ray was convinced he was lost to Bennie, beyond reach, and could no longer return home. A broken Ray believed the only way forward was to either kill the new president, hoping to survive that and expose Alvarez's twisted history, or to join him. Ray had also said he believed Alvarez was a good man and his plans noble. Bennie was very disturbed at this line of thought from Ray, for no matter how many bad guys Alvarez was eliminating for them, he was still a trafficker, still a murderer. To hear Ray's voice, his despair and remorse, had affected Bennie deeply, for in his mind, Ray had done nothing wrong. In fact, Bennie believed his young operative to be heroic. Somehow getting close to Ray without exposing him and then telling him he was still his man was something Bennie knew he was morally obligated to try. While he had some ideas, he needed to hear from Alberto on what was possible.

His first hope was to be able to accompany Alberto to a meeting with Alvarez, perhaps on the pretext of reviewing the upcoming action against the Gang of Four. If that could take place and Ray was in the presence of Alvarez, at the very least, Ray would know that Bennie was around and that he and Alberto had received his desperate message. Perhaps between Alberto and himself, they could figure a way to actually talk with Ray and maybe even slip him some of the electronic gadgets Charley had thought to provide for him for this trip. Taking one last glance at his reflection in the full-size mirror in his bedroom, he decided he looked decent enough in his best dark-gray suit to take dinner with Mexico's new secretary of public security.

He left his room and descended the first curving stairway he came upon. Alejandro appeared seemingly out of nowhere and greeted him as he reached the bottom. *I wonder how he knew I was coming down just now. Just a good professional, probably, but be careful. Alvarez's spies are everywhere is what the note said. You can only trust Alberto, so watch what you say and who you say it to*, Bennie thought.

"Excuse me, Senor, but you expressed some interest in a light lunch and also appeared interested in Senor Rodriguez's gardens. The afternoon is quite nice, so I have taken the liberty of setting up an informal luncheon on the patio for you, if you would like to accompany me?"

"Sure, Alejandro, and thank you."

Bennie was shown through the wood-and-glass rear doors of the foyer out to an intimate patio on the edge of the formal gardens adjacent to one of many fountains scattered about the rear grounds. At a small glass-and-wrought-iron table for four was a place setting for one person. Like everything else he had seen so far at the estate, everything associated with the simple luncheon reeked of Old World affluence and style. The china was old and gold trimmed and the silverware a bit oversized, and each handle was embossed with a family crest of some kind. Bennie sat down, and Alejandro asked, "Would you care to start with a soup or perhaps a *sopa seca*?"

"It's a nice day and a little too warm for a soup. How about just the *sopa seca*."

Alejandro turned to the serving cart and removed one of several silver domes covering various dishes on the adjacent rolling cart, picked up the dish, and placed it in front of Bennie.

"Your *sopa seca*, Senor." Bennie was served a very nice linguine with roasted garlic and chipotle chilies with wild mushrooms and tomatillos. It looked and smelled delicious.

"Thanks, Alejandro. This is perfect."

"We have a very nice burgundy blanco, Senor, if you would care for some wine?"

"Sounds nice. Thanks," Bennie said.

"For your main course, we have several selections available—perhaps the pork loin?"

Bennie looked up and smiled at Alejandro. "I thank you very much, but this pasta will be more than enough. With dinner in less than four hours, I better pass."

"As you wish, Senor. After you have finished your luncheon, if you would like to explore the estate, simply set out, and one of the security officers will join you and answer any questions you may have."

"Thanks, Alejandro, for all your kindness."

With a formal nod of his head, Alejandro turned and left Bennie alone. He gazed around the opulent estate as he ate his lunch, using his cop's eye to pick out the various security arrangements he saw, and there were plenty. He reminded himself again that Alberto Rodriguez's brother had been attacked with RPGs and blown all to hell and gone not far from here just a week or so ago and that Alberto was a high-profile target even before his promotion today to the top secretary in the new cabinet.

Looking around at all the luxury, Bennie recognized there was an incongruity between the man he had spoken with over the general's hookup the day before and what he was now surrounded by. Everything Bennie ever had read about Alberto Rodriguez and what had been confirmed by their face-to-face video conference yesterday was that Alberto was a courageous, tough, no-nonsense, experienced cop—a high-ranking one to be sure, but a real cop, and Bennie had been almost immediately comfortable with him. For all the differences from organization to organization or state to state—even country to country—there did exist an unspoken brotherhood between law enforcement officers, at least the very good ones. He and Alberto had felt that connection in their short conversation of the day before. One of the things that was really different between their two countries was the stark class divisions down here. Alberto had been right about that in their conversation. The poor were really poor, and the rich, well, looking around the grand estate and the fabulous mansion behind him, he saw they were really rich. Alberto was descended from a very old wealthy family, yet he and his brother had made the decision early on to serve their country, and not only to serve but to do so in a way that put them directly in harm's way every day with the worst the Mexican underworld had to offer. He respected and admired the brothers more than ever as he thought about that, and he had never actually met either of them.

Bennie recognized that as focused as he had been on getting Ray back safely, he also now had to consider Alberto's position. To go up against a nation's president under any circumstance was a formidable and dangerous, if not impossible, task. This would not be a long, drawn-out culmination of events, like the *Washington Post*'s Bob Woodward and Carl Bernstein taking on the Nixon White House in the 70s. There would be no opportunity to chip away at the presidential corruption with painstaking investigation to build a grassroots swell of public discontent as the fabric of that fetid administration slowly unraveled, revealing the lies and corruption. This was an extremely popular new president rising out of the sorrow of a national tragedy that he had ironically caused, who, come Saturday, if everything went well, would be fresh off a major victory over the very criminal elements he was associated with. There would be dancing in the streets in celebration of the attack on the Gang of Four if successful, once the details of the action were made public. Then in the middle of this, somehow Alberto Rodriguez and two foreigners, Bennie Santiago and Ray Cruz, would have to point out to everyone that despite what appeared obvious to the masses, their president was not a new national hero but rather a criminal, no different than the cartel leaders he'd just killed or captured. And unlike the Nixon White House, who fought back against the *Post*'s attacks with lies, cover-ups, and misinformation to maintain their powerful positions, this president may well fire back with armed mercenaries toting automatic weapons and RPGs.

Jesus H. Christ, Bennie thought as he finished off the fine white wine, *how in the living hell are we supposed to pull something like this off? Ray's word against Alvarez alone will not fly. We will need to convince people to actually look into the connections that we know and those that Ray hopefully can provide us. Alberto controls a lot of the government apparatus around here, but he is trumped by the president. Who else in the government is part of Alvarez's organization? What about their trumped-up political party? Is that also dirty? How deep do Alvarez's contacts and control go? This cannot be a long, protracted exposure. We have to hit Alvarez hard and quick and in a way that the evidence is irrefutable to others in the leadership around here and the people. But for the life of me, I don't see how we do this. I sure hope Alberto can see a way.*

Finished with his lunch, Bennie glanced at his watch—almost four thirty. *Jesus, I need another nap*, he thought, feeling the lethargy that often came to him with a late lunch. He stood up and walked out past the pool into the gardens; walking always gave him energy. From what Bennie could see, the entire estate was surrounded by very tall walls, ten or twelve feet anyway, made of stone and plaster. There was a continuous line of tall, mature trees of a type Bennie did not recognize just inside the walls and many others scattered about the grounds. There appeared to be small houses or casitas along the perimeter wall in and toward the corners. He supposed that this was where the servants and guards lived. Without him having done anything but get up and start walking, a uniformed security guard appeared and approached him. Bennie needed time to think, and he did his best thinking while walking, so he simply nodded at the guard and started strolling slowly around the grounds. He noticed CCTV cameras and exterior lighting discreetly mounted everywhere in the trees and along the walls. The emphasis was clearly on a perimeter defense, which made Bennie think again about the warning in the note, *Alvarez spies everywhere.* No amount of closed-circuit coverage or other electronic systems could detect that sort of treachery.

Bennie's walking took him around the mansion to a large car-park area at one end. He passed through the area, which was thick with security types, all of whom looked suspiciously at him, even followed as he was by one of their own. He passed through a tall hedge following a walkway and found himself on the long, curving front entry drive. To his left was the main entry gate that he had come through earlier, to his right, the mansion front entry; he turned right. As he started up the drive, the guard suddenly touched his arm and said, "Senor," and pointed back to the main gate, which was in the process of opening. "Senor Rodriguez is arriving."

Bennie stood off to one side and watched as a four-vehicle caravan came through the gate. After it passed, Bennie followed the cars and walked toward the front entry. Both front doors of the trailing SUV opened simultaneously, and two well-dressed men got out and immediately turned toward Bennie with firm, purposeful looks on their faces.

They see a stranger where none is supposed to be, thought Bennie. The guard walking with Bennie waved in recognition, and this appeared to do the trick, as the bodyguards clearly relaxed their appearance, and Bennie and his escort continued walking up the drive. Alberto stepped out of his car and turned to Bennie and waved. Bennie waved back, and as he approached the tired-looking but smiling Alberto Rodriguez, he was thinking that despite their collective years of experience in law enforcement, it may not be enough; the problems before them seemed unimaginable, the new president of Mexico just too powerful. Everything depended on safely contacting a twenty-six-year-old undercover cop who had been in the DEA for less than six months and hope against hope that he had the key, the information they'd need to bring down a sitting president. Bennie had been involved with many dangerous operations in his thirty-plus-year career, but none compared to what he and the tired man he was now approaching faced. It was a lead-pipe cinch that people were going to die before all was said and done. He only hoped it was the bad guys.

8

Like his cousin the general, Alberto was over six feet tall and very fit. He walked up to Bennie, his hand extended, a genuine and warm smile on his tired face, and in impeccable English, said, "Hello, Mr. Santiago, and welcome."

"Thank you, Mr. Secretary, for seeing me and for the hospitality—and it's Bennie."

"Has Alejandro taken care of you?"

"More than I am sure I deserve, I'm afraid."

"Come, join me for a drink. It has been a very long and interesting day." They walked into the mansion where the ever-present Alejandro was waiting.

"Hola, Alejandro. We shall be in my study and will serve ourselves."

"As you wish, Senor."

They walked through the foyer past the entry into the formal living room and stopped at another typically ornate door. Alberto placed his left thumb on a wall-mounted pad in the jamb of the doorframe that Bennie had not noticed at first glance, and there was the sound of an electric lock clicking open. Alberto opened the door, allowing Bennie to walk in, and then closed the door behind them. They entered a magnificent two-story library that was Alberto's private study. The first thing Bennie noticed was how most every surface that wasn't a book or a piece of furniture was dark, beautifully lacquered wood. Bennie was no expert, but the first thought he had was mahogany. The second thing he noticed was the sheer volume of books that lined the shelves on the sides of the room. The built-in shelves were so tall there was a narrow decorative metal balcony eight feet off the floor to access the higher shelves. The balcony was accessed by a metal spiral stairway adjacent to the entry they had just passed through. A stone-trimmed fireplace was centered in one wall with a comfortable-looking group of furniture around it. A handsome antique wood desk sat at the far end of the beautiful room with a wall of heavily mullioned glass windows behind it that looked out into the rear gardens. Bennie thought the glass had that funny different green look to it, as if it was thicker somehow—say, enough to stop bullets, similar to the drive-up teller window of his bank back home.

Alberto walked to the desk and set the briefcase he was carrying down. Bennie noticed the closed shape of Alberto's see-tee on the credenza. Obviously no one was allowed into this room except Alberto and whomever he wished to bring in. Alberto walked over to a section of wall not covered with books and opened a panel, revealing a full bar.

"Now that we are alone, I will call you Bennie, as you requested."

"Thank you, Mr. Secretary."

"Please, Bennie; it's Alberto. I suppose in public or in front of others, we should observe the appearance of a more formal relationship, but not in here. What may I fix you?"

"I like old scotch whiskey whenever I can get it, the older the better," said the smiling Bennie. Alberto smiled back, nodded, and opened the leaded glass door of a cupboard above the bar and pulled two crystal decanters from the shelf. He poured a healthy amount of a golden liquid from the first decanter into a heavy crystal tumbler and handed it to Bennie. He grabbed a second decanter and poured himself a glass of something different.

"Old single-barrel American bourbon for me, Bennie, a gift from my cousin Manny. I acquired a taste for it on a visit to your Kentucky when Manny first became a general. I fear I like it too much. Cheers."

They touched glasses and drank some down. Bennie was impressed; Alberto clearly knew his fine whiskey. The decanters were obviously cooled in some manner, as the exceptionally fine whiskey was slightly chilled without being cold. Because of this Alberto had not considered offering Bennie any ice, and Bennie knew better than to chill his whiskey further, so he had not asked.

"Please, Bennie, let's sit over here. We are free to speak openly within this room. I have the mansion swept regularly by trusted staff." Bennie nodded his understanding at the security reference and then followed Alberto to the sitting area in front of the fireplace, where they made themselves comfortable. "You had a nice flight, I trust?"

"I always used to say anytime I walk away from a plane ride, it's been a good flight. Considering the events of the last couple of days, maybe that's more true than ever."

Alberto smiled again and nodded his agreement.

"You said it was an interesting day, Alberto—can you tell me about it?"

The small, friendly smile on Alberto's face changed to a rather tight, grim look, and there was no missing the great sadness in his eyes.

"Yes, Bennie, it was. I am not sure 'interesting' is an appropriate description, however; perhaps 'tragic' or 'surreal' is more accurate, but those words are also so much more melodramatic. But I must say, to be required to stand next to Alvarez and be witness to his swearing in as president of my country was the most difficult thing I think I have ever been asked to endure, especially knowing he most likely was the one who ordered Emilio be killed. It took all my strength to not wear my old Colt .38 Police Special and just shoot the bastard and end this all right then and there on national television—and take my chances on explaining everything. If it comes to it, I am prepared to do just that—kill him, that is—but I would prefer exposing and convicting him. I have had many such dark thoughts on this situation in the last thirty-six hours, both emotional and professional. The only conclusion I have reluctantly come to so far is that Emilio must have discovered some aspect of the Baja connection through our counterintelligence efforts, perhaps a link to the identity of this Senor Pena alias, and instead of keeping that information just between us brothers as we swore to do, he must have told Alvarez. That is why he was killed."

"As careful as I hear you and your brother have been, why would Emilio have done such a thing, Alberto?"

"Emilio and Alvarez were very close friends for many years. Second only to me, Alvarez was Emilio's closest friend. They were roommates at Saint Matthews, a preparatory school associated with the Latin American University here in the city we all attended as teenagers, and then also at the National University following that. They then went on to law school together. Emilio's widow is Alvarez's younger sister."

Bennie was surprised.

"By the look on your face, Bennie, it seems you did not know this."

"No, I did not. The general filled me in on the circumstances that resulted in putting your family and Emilio's family up at his base, but he never mentioned that connection."

"Then perhaps you can understand more fully the depths of my despair when you realize that we are dealing with a man who, in the course of achieving his apparent goals, likely did not hesitate to order the murder of not only his best friend in life but the husband of his sister and the father to his sister's children. I can think of nothing more cold blooded. Not exactly the act of the Jesuit-educated friend and classmate of my youth. To know Pablo Alvarez as I have for these many years and to now know of his deceptions and the great cruelty he is capable of...well, there is not much I am certain of anymore other than he must be brought forward to face the consequences of what he is and has done."

Bennie also now had a grim look on his face and was just slowly shaking his head as Alberto opened up to him. Then he said, "Alberto, I just don't know what to say. Whatever my troubles have been in the last few months, I know they're nothing in comparison to yours and your loss. I'm sorrier about that than you can know. And I will not sit here and tell you I know how you feel, because that would be a damn lie. But the one thing I will say—I have to say—is that you cannot take Alvarez out by yourself. Even if you could somehow convince your country that you were not just another wide-eyed assassin, your country needs you. We will find a way to get through this in a way that the decent, responsible, law-abiding people in your government believe you, and Alvarez is dealt with. Don't go sacrificing yourself in this mess."

"I appreciate that, Bennie; thank you. As much as I would personally like to handle this, I will not. I do not wish to become a martyr. If it comes to it, I have concluded that using Los Pueblos Fantasmas, I could probably make it appear as if the cartels have struck back for this Saturday's attack on them, another senseless tragedy for the people to absorb."

"Excuse me, Alberto, but what is Los Pueblos Fantasmas?"

Alberto sat back in his seat, his eyes a little wider and a smile beginning to cross his tired face as he shook his head slowly.

"Jesus, Bennie, I must be more weary than I thought. I see my tight-lipped cousin has again lived up to his reputation for honor. Well, no time like the present. I felt you would have to be told of some of my secrets if we were to be working together on my problem. To put it simply, Los Pueblos Fantasmas, the people's ghosts, is a private clandestine army that Emilio and I built over the last several years, funded initially by us and then eventually with the captured cartels funds we have managed to lay our hands on. It is a small, very close group, totally self-sufficient in a military or police organizational sense. We have our own military strike teams, reconnaissance assets, intelligence and counterintelligence, communications, medical, transportation, logistics, you name it—all unknown to all facets of the government, including our new president, and run by Emilio and me from a concealed location away from the capital."

Alberto gave Bennie a thirty-minute synopsis of his organization from birth until today, telling him in some detail of the very successful strikes they had conducted in the last year and the intelligence and resources they had acquired—not to mention the huge cache of contraband they had recovered. Alberto paused after his summary, sipped his drink, and then looked at Bennie and went on.

"So you see, Bennie, perhaps second only to Alvarez, I may be the greatest criminal currently at large in my country. On my orders, I say

known—but the correct legal term would be 'suspected'—drug traffickers and murderers have not only been killed and captured without warrants or due process, but in addition, those whom we have incarcerated
have, on my orders, been subjected to the most aggressive of interrogation methods possible in order to squeeze every bit of information we can
out of them. I have denied them the most basic of civil rights. And what
is worse, perhaps, those we have incarcerated and treated so badly cannot,
will not, ever see the light of day again, much less a courtroom. At least
not until the last vestiges of the evil that now attacks my country is gone.
I suppose the only thing that separates me from my enemies is that I do
not profit from my illegal acts. If anything, morally and ethically at least,
I am the poorer for it."

Bennie was amazed and could not keep from showing it. "Well, that
was quite a confession of sorts. I don't have to guess what your cousin said
when he heard this. No doubt his reaction was the same as mine. Please
pardon my vulgarity, Alberto, but I say way to fucking go. You're no criminal. You're in an almost no-win war, for Christ's sake." Bennie paused for a
moment, looking at a clearly sad and reflective Alberto. "I want to tell you
a short story from my country's history. Our greatest president was a fellow named Abraham Lincoln. He assumed the leadership of our country at
a time we were irreversibly headed into civil war. He took unprecedented
actions as the chief executive, and many of his actions were deemed illegal,
but it did not stop him. He was fighting for a greater good, the Union.
Because of the great crisis exploding all around him, he suspended one of
our Constitution's most protected rights, that of habeas corpus. He sent
men to prisons with little hope of the right to a speedy trial because it was
necessary to save the country. Even his friends in the legislature said that he
was committing an impeachable offense, and you know what he told them?
'Let's save the Union first; then do what you must,' or words to that effect.
He did what was necessary, Alberto, to save his country. He wasn't a criminal, and neither are you. He was a hero, and that's exactly what I think you
are. It's a privilege to be at your side. He saved us and got himself killed in
the process, struck down soon after the war was over by an assassin's bullet.

As far as I'm concerned, you get this war won, and then you fold the tent on this Los Pueblos Fantasmas as if they really were ghosts."

Alberto smiled at Bennie. He really liked this man, and not because he agreed with Manny or looked favorably on his illegal actions—this was a good and smart man. They would be friends for a very long time, he thought, if they managed to survive the next couple of weeks or months.

"Thank you, Bennie. Manny did indeed say much of what you have. I do not want to end up as your President Lincoln. I know of him, of course; I have a book of his speeches somewhere in here. There is a passage from one of them that I have thought of often as I have struggled in this fight; it goes something like, 'I do the very best I know how—the very best I can; and I mean to keep on doing so until the end.'

"There is little in life I want more than for all of this to end; my problem is I do not see how it does. I want very much to publicly try and convict Alvarez, but I may or may not be given that choice. Assassination is an idea of last resort, of course, but, Bennie, absent any other solution, I am prepared to follow through on this. I admit to you I have had many dark thoughts about my old friend Pablo since Emilio was killed, and one that keeps coming back to me, haunting me, is from Voltaire: 'Clever tyrants are never punished.' Pablo Alvarez, it seems, has been very clever, and he appears to have become the worst of tyrants, but he must not be allowed to go unpunished. I may have no choice but to punish him myself. However, before events get that far, the professional in me wants to know how he has accomplished what he has and also, from a very personal perspective, why? To know these things means we must have the opportunity to interrogate Pablo Alvarez, not kill him."

Alberto paused and shifted his gaze to the beautiful gardens beyond the thick windows. He sipped his bourbon again and returned his focus to Bennie, and Bennie could see on his face the doubts and questions the man had been keeping bottled up.

"It is so difficult to get my head around all this. The man I have known since we were very young men and the man who now controls my country are two different people. I see him, and he treats me like a brother as he always has, but to know who he really is? Well, there is a great disconnect in me. I have given that reality much thought over the last two days. I have so many questions. Is it possible he is truly ill—a multiple personality, for example—or has he just gone mad? And if so, what has driven him to this course? Who could do the things he has done and not be criminally insane? If not insane, he has demonstrated that he is a self-absorbed psychopath, and that is not the man I grew up with or the man I thought I knew."

Alberto sighed and took a drink of his bourbon and was lost in thought again for a second before going on. Bennie recognized that Alberto was getting some deep personal feelings off his chest and simply drank as well, not wishing to interrupt the obviously deeply troubled man. But truth be known, at that moment, he didn't know what to say.

"You would need to know Pablo Alvarez as I do, Bennie, to fully appreciate the disconnect I am feeling. There were times as we were growing up together Emilio felt certain that Pablo would become a priest. He was very spiritual when we were younger. I used to think he had that deep goodness in him, like one believes about a priest. That young man changed as we grew older, his thinking more serious and reflective, especially in his study of philosophy, but that innate goodness never left him. I could always sense it, this great desire to do good for others.

"He is, or was, an amazing man, Pablo Alvarez. In our last year of preparatory school—we couldn't have been more than thirteen or fourteen—he decided he wanted to be a stage actor. Never acted a day in his life, as I recall, and then he auditions for and wins the lead in our school's one big drama production of the year, an adaption of *Don Quixote*. I'll never forget. He persuaded Emilio to try out as well, and he of course ended up his Sancho Panza. Ironic, it seems to me now, looking back on the years, how so often Emilio really was Sancho to Pablo's Don Quixote. Emilio was always the smarter of the two, or of us three, really, but somehow, it was Pablo Alvarez who ended up leading. Funny I had not thought of that in those terms until now. When I am at my lowest, as I was after learning of Emilio's death, I have thought that the fight we take to the cartels is not so different from Quixote's quest, the chasing of proverbial windmills."

Bennie leaned in toward Alberto. "Well, I think you're being too hard on yourself, Alberto. You're fighting the good fight—against terrible odds, I might add—and if I may quote Lincoln myself, 'A friend is one who has the same enemies as you have.'"

Bennie smiled at Alberto and tipped his glass in a salute that a smiling Alberto returned, and then Bennie went on. "So you see, my friend, you are not in this alone. I am, however, a little fuzzy on my literature—been a few years, and it was never my bailiwick—but as I recall, Don Quixote was quite mad. Seems like your old friend is also…only thing that makes sense."

"Perhaps," said Alberto. "But he did have a thing for the theater and did some amateur theatrics well into college, always escaping into other characters. We used to tease him about that, as if he was not comfortable with who he was. Yet that is the one small part of his history as I know it that makes some sense now. He obviously has at least three personas and must be acting out in two of them. I'm just not sure which of his personas the true one is. After knowing Pablo for almost forty years, I realize I do not know him at all. This fact and one other scare me the most. It is clear he believes he has, or will, get away with this. Where does that sort of confidence come from? What can it be based upon? How can you keep a secret as big as his so quiet? Emilio and I had a brotherhood of two, and only two, and yet even at that, it was not possible to keep our secrets safe, it seems."

Bennie just shrugged his shoulders slightly. "Emilio did that, Alberto. If your guess is right, he broke the first rule. He trusted someone other than just you or your cousin. He made a mistake. But given the difficulties we both are having with the truth lately, I think we can cut Emilio some slack here. It was a mistake I could have seen myself making in his shoes. Hell, what did he do that we ourselves are not doing at this exact moment, Alberto? Confiding in one another like we are? Emilio had no idea of the depth of the treachery he was faced with. Hell, we do know it, and even then, it's hard to accept."

"I suppose you're right, Bennie. But Alvarez has kept the biggest of secrets secure for at least twelve years; I know because I checked the Internet last night on just the basic facts of the life of one Nicolas Pena, one of Pablo's apparent aliases. The first substantive news article dates from then, twelve years ago. I find that unbelievable."

"I will grant you that point, Alberto—that is something, especially when you consider the business he has been in and the kind of money that's thrown around, especially for betrayal. The character of the types of people who are involved in their little enterprise is not exactly honorable. Hard to believe he has not been betrayed—speaks well, in a sick kind of way, to his group of friends and family. Must be a small group, and they must be true believers for whatever reason. Like I say, hard to imagine. Also goes a long ways to explaining why Ray has been so careful to communicate, or *not* to communicate, to be more accurate. I can't imagine the enormous pressure he must be under. I have no clue how he is passing himself off as a true believer. The kid must be better than I thought he was, and I thought he was the best I ever saw. I prepared him for this assignment, but no way did I prepare him for what he is evidently doing."

"I am sure you must be right, Bennie. But if I am not to be reduced to an assassin, it would seem we are greatly dependent on your young man. Tell me of him; he indeed must be something special."

"Like I said, Alberto: the best young undercover cop I've come in contact with."

Bennie told Alberto the entire story in great detail, everything from the leaks and betrayals in the southwest offices that led to setting up his special operations unit through the recruitment of Ray from the Sacramento police. He detailed Ray's infiltration and how he had sweated out the first couple of weeks Ray had been undercover and missing, waiting to hear from him and worrying the entire time that Ray had been summarily killed after reaching a cartel. He told him of the euphoria he had felt after receiving Ray's first report, then the second, and being able to act on the intelligence Ray had provided before the past eight weeks of nothing. Bennie told Alberto what he had never shared with Charley: the sense of foreboding that somehow Ray had been discovered, executed, and dumped in some arroyo in the desert. He had never let on with Charley that he felt that way deep down, always telling Charley that Ray was alive and just hemmed in by security somehow.

"Alberto, I was happy yesterday morning for the first time in months. I don't know what all your cousin has shared with you, but at some personal career risk, the general has generously turned over one of his squadrons of Predator drones to us, and based on the intelligence Ray provided us in his second report, we think we can locate the three estates in the north the Condor operates out of. Our thinking before your call telling us about the assassination and you receiving a message from Ray was that if he were alive and just out of communication, we would find out once and for all if we simply covertly watched for the entourage that travels with the Condor. The idea then was for me to come down here and try to make contact with Ray, if only visually, so he would know he was not alone. I was preparing a snatch and grab of my own to get him out of harm's way if I had to. Then came the call from you, and everything's been blasted to hell and gone. On the one hand, I was unbelievably relieved to find out Ray was alive, but between the circumstances and the truth about Alvarez and Ray's new position in this whole mess...well, frankly, I'm back to feeling like shit. I'll be dammed if I have a clue what we do from here, Alberto, except get me in the same room as Alvarez, and hope as an aide or bodyguard, whatever the hell Ray is, that he at least sees me and knows that his gamble passing you the note paid off."

"I also have given this much thought, but before I go on, you say you feel certain you will be able to locate Alvarez's estates in the north? Manny had not mentioned this covert reconnaissance to me."

"No doubts at all, Alberto. Ray's reports contained very solid descriptions, both of the estates themselves and their general location with respect to the cities they're located near. The estates will not be hard to spot. They will be large, isolated, walled, and fenced, and have armed guards patrolling the grounds and at the main gates—hard to see from the road as you pass by maybe, but easy to see from overhead with the powerful cameras on the drones. And as I said, we have mugshots of this Carlo guy, and we had a description of his older brother, Eduardo Vargas, from Ray's second report. We now know that these brothers are Alvarez's chief lieutenants in his whole operation. Once we locate the estates we will see these guys, I'm sure of it. Snatching them would be very helpful. In his second message Ray said that the total traveling entourage is about twenty men, so we will watch for motorcades capable of moving that many men. Has to be five to six large SUV's at least."

"I agree this surveillance no doubt will prove helpful in the future, Bennie, when we can act on the intelligence you develop and get these brothers. It begs the question: Do we go after Alvarez directly first, or do we go after his organization and perhaps flush him out that way?"

"The only way to get Alvarez, in my opinion, is through Ray. That's as far as I can get with my thinking. Ray will certainly have further intelligence on this guy, and with that, perhaps we can formulate a strategy. I will tell you one thing, however: until you mentioned your Los Pueblos Fantasmas, I had no idea how we could even go after the cousins once we find the bastards, let alone Alvarez, not knowing who all you can trust down here. I'm beginning to like the idea of snatching his cousins with your private army. What the hell would Alvarez do if his two top lieutenants just up and went missing without a word? Would drive the son of a bitch crazy—maybe make him make a stupid move."

"I agree. A most interesting idea, especially since you say you can provide accurate, actionable intelligence with your surveillance. With Alvarez here in the capitol and his cousins always remaining in the north at one of their estates, they would likely have their guard down and travel in smaller groups. Catching the cousins on a day trip in a lightly guarded motorcade could easily be done with my strike teams. They are very good, especially in snatch and grab. We need to talk more of this. For now, contacting your man without exposing him is the key. Let me think more on this, but first, how about I fix us another drink?"

9

Cuidad Juarez Mexico
The Estates of El Condor de Muerte
Near Monterey Mexico
Late Tuesday Afternoon

A lex Guerro was in a dangerous business, even on the periphery of actual trafficking as he was. He also was the kind of person doing the types of legal business that would attract the police and the federals even if there were no crimes being committed. He was a Mexican national living lawfully in the United States whose business required he pass back and forth through the border on a daily basis. He knew anyone matching those few criteria drew the attention of the border patrol and others even more dangerous. He had been pulled over "randomly" on many occasions and asked to stand idly by as his personal car was inspected in detail for contraband. Alex expected to be stopped, and he expected to be under surveillance occasionally. Those were just the facts of his life, and as a consequence, he was very careful and had never transported a gram of narcotics over the border.

Alex was not a mule, at least not in the common understanding of the term. He was a mule for information. He had been set up by his employer in a good small business with a steady income and a comfortable lifestyle with strict orders to commit no crimes, other than the little distributing he did to a select few sources. The dealing that he did was really a front for his actual job. He was a generator and a conduit for information, a front-line operator in a larger, very complex intelligence network run by his employer. He was directed to drops on the American side—bars and restaurants usually but also other public places where people would meet him and give him information. Sometimes the information was written, most times just spoken, and he then made his reports from his business on the Mexican side, always using one of the prepaid cell phones that FedEx delivered to him at his warehouse from a variety of addresses in various Mexican cities on a regular basis.

He was clean, as numerous background checks had attested. No record, no arrests, not even a traffic ticket: he was an educated, successful young Mexican businessman conducting lawful business on both sides of the border. The fact that his record was clean was testimony enough, Alex had thought on more than one occasion, to the power and connections his employers had, for Alex was all too aware of his real history. The fact that the American authorities thought him a clean, law-abiding Mexican citizen and had granted him a visa based upon his record was a mystery to him and a blessing, and it went beyond just the name change.

Danny thought of Alex strictly as a dealer, which he was not, but Alex wasn't offended by the label. He had done enough of that in other days in another life in his native Chihuahua, but those days were in his past. He did worry that his new responsibilities would raise his profile to a point where he could be picked up on the border patrol or DEA's radar as a dealer. This was now certainly possible if Danny or any of the other few soldiers from the huge, sprawling base he was servicing and working for information ever got caught and talked, and that talk led to him. He made it clear just what would happen to anyone that did. The army better kill them, he had warned, because Alex's people certainly would. The threat was a real one, and he drove that point home. So far none of his special projects had been discovered using.

After the passing of the new immigration law and the delegation of the border's security to the US Army, his employer had expanded Alex's role to a developer of intelligence and did so with the intent of getting to people on the ever-expanding US base. It was necessary, he was told, to try to develop information out of this border army, and he was of an age and a level of intelligence to get it done. He had even been shown how to do it, although considering his past experiences, he would have known how. He would have known to frequent the local bars and clubs the young soldiers went to when off base and cutting loose without being told. He knew how to spot the weak ones who were into drugs. He was also given several dealers in the area who worked for his bosses and whom he could direct to the soldiers he had flagged for possible compromise and make the initial dangerous contact without exposing himself. His dealers were the ones running the risk of exposure, and they maintained their relationships until, from time to time, a soldier with a potentially interesting job was discovered. Then Alex took over and worked the soldier for information. He had three "Dannys" he was working, but the real Danny was the only one that had come through so far, and in such a big way. To know what areas the border corps would or would not be watching at any given time had pleased his employer greatly. Within a week of his first report, Alex had received a package out of nowhere with $50,000 cash in it. A brief note had also been included, stating simply this was a small reward for his efforts. A small reward, he thought— Jesus Christo! He would work Danny to death if he could.

There was a downside, and Alex was very aware of it. Danny was a flake of the highest order, careless in his personal life and almost certainly a stone-solid addict. Addicts were horribly flawed humans and always eventually got caught. Alex knew he would have to mentor and counsel his addict or risk losing him earlier than he would want. That meant watching him when he could and keeping him from self-destruction. Alex drilled Danny and the others many times on just who they should reveal as their suppliers if they ever did get caught. Alex's bosses had been thorough enough to provide the names and numbers of suspected dealers from rival gangs or cartels. But Alex was not naïve; once Danny was caught, the army interrogators would require about ten minutes to get Alex's name and numbers out of Danny— he was that weak. Such a happenstance would mean the end to Alex's way of life, and he was not about to lose it. He had been down that road before only to have miraculously landed in his current situation. Such a break was not likely to happen twice in his life.

Alex had been a policeman once in another life—a smart, tough young detective on the fast track to a better and quite legal life, but he had gotten arrogant and greedy and had gone into business with a local drug lord in his hometown whom he had considered stupid and manageable. Just as he thought he had control of the situation, forcing the dealer to pay him large cash payoffs not to arrest him and expose his organization, he had found himself arrested and up on charges for his corruption. His trial had followed quickly, and he had been convicted by the jury in a few hours. Within days of his conviction, he had been loaded into an uncomfortable, beat-up police van and shipped west from Chihuahua to the federal prison in Hermosillo. He never made it. One moment he had been weeping in the back of an overheated van on a dusty highway headed to prison for ten years, and the next he had been at a small, comfortable house in the country outside Chihuahua. He had been brought before a man he had never seen before, an older, well-dressed, obviously educated man who had told him he had a choice: Continue on to prison, where it would become known he was a convicted policeman and therefore would be unlikely he would live ten days, forget ten years. Or he could go to work for the older gentlemen with a new name and identity, with the opportunity to prove his worth and loyalty. The choice was easy, and he had been released into the custody of others at the small, neat house; retrained in his new business; given time to learn and accept his new identity; and then placed into service as a conduit of information for the sources the older man had inside America.

He now understood that his role as a conduit had merely been a first step, a proving ground of sorts of his loyalty and abilities to handle his position. With the recent expansion of his role, he now understood that for whatever reason—his background, his education, his age, his language skills, something—he had been ruthlessly recruited into a highly efficient intelligence-gathering organization for one of the major cartels. It was the only thing that made sense. Which one, he was not sure; it could be one of three or four. All he knew was he was not about to fail now; the consequences were far too grave.

In the meantime, back at the safe house, the information Alex had carried over was reviewed, and then he made a call from one of his prepaid cell phones to an unlisted number. The person who answered did not identify himself—merely said, "Yes?" listened to what Alex had to say, and then thanked him for the information and hung up. Alex was not sure, but he suspected the voice was that of the older man who had given him his life's choice. It was not.

The head of this particular intelligence operation was a very careful man. There were always intermediaries. The unknown man who had taken Alex's call lived in Juarez and resided only a few miles from Alex's office, but Alex had no idea. That man then made a call to a cell phone number that changed on a regular basis and passed Alex's information along, his part in the pipeline completed. He had no other responsibilities in the operation.

After passing on the information, Alex left the safe house and touched base with his business in Juarez, before once again making his way through the border point and entering the US legally with the valid visa he had with his passport. Another twenty minutes and he was once again in his comfortable upscale apartment not far from the UTEP campus and its collection of lovely and available coeds—that is, available to a man with means. And Alex was indeed a man with means.

In Monterey or, if the day was different, Hermosillo or Chihuahua, Eduardo Vargas turned his cell phone off and returned to the other papers he was reading before being interrupted with the updates on the flights at the border. Eduardo had good people working this particular transshipment route. Smuggling drugs through tunnels at the border had been one of the very first crude and, early on, most efficient ways to move large quantities of drugs north. Increases in US border patrols and then recently the new border fences and walls with the added troops of the US Army had shut down routes like this and had put most of the smaller operations out of business—or at least forced them to find new methods. Most of the alternative methods available to these small operators meant more risk with greater exposure to the authorities and less efficiency. Even the Gang of Four saw a major curtailing of this crude form of smuggling, and several of its members had been doing little else for a very long time. In part, the disruption of these crude transshipment routes was one of the driving motivations forcing their enemies to get together and talk about it, thought Eduardo. And in so doing, it handed his cousin and him the golden opportunity to finally eliminate those vicious bastards, once and for all. Meetings such as the one coming up were very rare.

The other cartels had been loosely aligned only a few years and still did not fully trust each other. But the recent actions by both the US and Mexican governments had not only eliminated some of their transshipment routes but had also resulted in the loss of some very valuable men and forced the meeting. What the Gang of Four did not know was that it was Eduardo's people doing the most damage to the Gang of Four, not the federals. Based upon the informants his cousin had placed in the enemy camps over the years with painstaking patience, Eduardo and his cousin not only knew about the summit but also the location and time. They also knew the general composition of forces each of the leaders would be bringing. This information was passed on to the government through yet additional resources at the Condor's disposal. And between the federals and Eduardo, few if any at the summit would survive. There would be those in the government who would likely want prisoners for interrogation purposes, but even that possibility had been planned for by Pablo. Any cartel leaders who might be captured would never make it to an actual interrogation. Accidents happened randomly in life, and retribution happened all the time in this business. Following the attack on the others, there would be plenty of both. There was nothing random about retribution; it was as predictable and as certain as the sunrise, and Pablo wanted retribution for his father. If it were not for the one nagging unanswered question that was bothering both him and his cousin, Eduardo would truly be content with the way things stood with his planning.

The facts were that not only had a number of key people in the Gang of Four gone missing recently, but several of Eduardo's own people were also missing or dead. Eduardo knew he was not responsible for this, and the Condor said the government also was not. And when it came to getting information out of the government, the Condor had no equal. It was the one attribute that made him so very different and special from any others in their business. So where had these men gone, and who had gotten to them?

The only logical answer to Eduardo was some quiet infighting or retribution between members of the Gang of Four or individual personal vendettas by some of their people. But his people in the other cartels were just as much in the dark as he was. No one knew what had happened or where the missing men might be. They had just up and vanished like farts in the wind. It was a mystery, and to a man like Eduardo Vargas who thought he had all the relevant information regarding trafficking and crimes against persons available in his country at his fingertips, this was unsettling.

While the new border security was disrupting some of the operations of the Gang of Four, it was having little to no impact on Eduardo's operations. Eduardo had not used tunnels at the border for years, even before the new fence had gone up, Pablo's creative methods of transshipment being so far superior. But he had also not abandoned their few as-of-yet-undetected tunnels, using them mostly to get people back and forth across the border as the need arose—like getting poor, stupid Carlo back after he had escaped incarceration in Texas. But when one of his US operatives passed on to Eduardo's people that he might be able to provide information giving Eduardo and his associates the schedule of the US Army's reconnaissance craft and the position of their troops at any given time, well, that had opened up all sorts of possibilities for Eduardo. Several of the small gangs that had been taken over by El Condor de Muerte had no other transshipment methods other than crude smuggling. So instead of retraining them or simply eliminating them, Eduardo had put them to work with the methods they understood, but with a far greater chance of success given the intelligence being provided. If the Condor had said it once, he'd said it a thousand times: "We live or die based upon what we know and how we use it, not how many soldiers we have and how many men we can kill." From the very first day that his cousin had become involved in the family business, Eduardo had witnessed the value of Pablo's wisdom and approach, and he had learned.

Based on the information from his source in the US Army, Eduardo was able to move product north in several different ways. On the prearranged nights that his man's source said there would be no aerial observations or patrols by the army or the US Border Patrol people in the areas near where he had existing tunnels, Eduardo's men would run vehicles up to the previously deserted and undiscovered tunnels and pass the product through with human mules.

His best method of transshipment in these areas, however, was his helicopters. The family owned two Bell 407s. Each chopper was painted a midnight blue, had no markings, and was configured for two pilots with the rest of the cabin space clear for cargo. In addition to the two pilots, each chopper could carry two thousand pounds of product, fly at 150 miles per hour, and handle a round-trip range of 380 miles. Eduardo had storage facilities up and down the border that were unknown to all except the family. Typically they were concealed in the open as a warehouse facility for a perfectly respectable business in the industrial area of one of a dozen towns or cities near the border. Delivery trucks would move the product to prearranged locations, where the product would be loaded onto the helicopters and then flown nap of the earth across the border in the areas his sources said the US Army would not be looking, there to be met by his people in America. His principal distribution lieutenant from San Antonio, Texas, would have made the long drive down timed to arrive at night at the spot on the border that Eduardo had been informed would not be observed. The distributor would bring with him enough men to quickly unload the helicopters, and by the time the sun rose the next morning, the distributor would be well on his way down I-10 toward San Antonio. Pablo had at first looked skeptically at the idea of tunnels or the use of helicopters, when compared to their other more elegant and large-scale methods of shipping, but Eduardo also reminded him that with the elimination of the Gang of Four, there would be a lot more product for them to ship. Until their other sophisticated methods could be expanded, these older approaches, with the assistance of the US Army, would mean a reasonably safe way to get several tons of product a month into America. The Condor nodded his acceptance of the reasoning and left the details to his very capable cousin; as long as Eduardo had the army's schedules, why not?

10

On the flight down to Mexico, Bennie had imagined a lot of possible scenarios he might find himself faced with once he got to Mexico City, but the pleasant surroundings he now found himself in had never occurred to him, nor had the intelligent conversation and new possibilities.

Alberto walked from the built-in bar back to the comfortable seating area fronting the large fireplace and handed Bennie a fresh drink and then sat down before going on with their conversation.

"Let me tell you the schedule of events and what I have arranged thus far. Tomorrow will be a busy day, what with Fernandez lying in state for the people's viewing and the world's dignitaries arriving for the funeral on Thursday. I am dealing with the advanced security teams of forty countries at last count. If that is not enough, we have the mundane but important work to continue of just getting the government reconstituted. You may stay here or accompany me to my offices tomorrow; your choice. Thursday of course is the state funeral; I will be occupied all day. I can get you cleared for the requiem Mass as a representative of your government, should you desire to attend, without you having to go through your embassy or be a part of their delegation. Free of that bureaucratic burden, you would be more free to see if Ray is present and perhaps at least make eye contact. The interment will be at Panteon Dolores, our most important of cemeteries, and is intended to be a simple family ceremony. The president will be going, and I'm expected to attend, but few others will. My guess is that Ray will not be there. Alvarez's closest aides tend to stay in the background out of the public eye. They are always close by in private—at his home or in the office—but they are never a part of his public entourage here in the city. I now understand why, I think."

"You lost me there, Alberto. No one sees these guys? How is that, just out of curiosity?"

"It is speculation on my part, but my guess is that when he is playing his role as the Condor in the north, your Ray and the others of his personal guard in fact do act more as his bodyguards, replacing the capital police and my Federal Police. In that role we can assume they no doubt come in contact with many nefarious types who would likely recognize them if seen on television here in the capital. Clearly, Alvarez in his aliases must also change his appearance somehow so as not to be recognized by those he does business with; that's all still a mystery to me, of course, how he goes unrecognized. We have seen with Emilio's death the ramifications of sharing a secret. The only way for this charade of his to have worked all these years is that very few people must be aware of the truth, and the few that are aware are, as you say, most loyal."

"Well, speculation or not, it makes sense to me, Alberto. And anything we can logically put together on how and where Alvarez operates helps us nail him. We know where his organization lives and works now; we know his principal associates, and we now have them under surveillance; and my people are recording everything. Someday soon you will be able to mount an operation against his operations based upon this intelligence, and that will hurt him and his organization. From what Ray was able to pass along, it sounds if all control is vested in Alvarez and his two cousins, supported by a few others. That reminds me—does the name Baca mean anything to you? According to Ray's second message, he apparently is the key communication and computer guy that goes everywhere with him."

"Damn," Alberto said quietly as a very troubled look came over him. He shook his head, sighed, and said to Bennie, "Geraldo Baca is who you are likely referring to. This is bad, very bad. I have been worried all along about who all in the federal government may be working for Alvarez. I suspect several that are close to me, principal deputies of mine, but I did not suspect Baca. Damn silly of me for not doing so."

"Jesus, who is he?"

"He unfortunately is the director of our national crime information center within my new office and concurrently holds the position of director of information technology for all my secretariat's departments. He was the sole person responsible for bringing all our criminal databases and information-management systems into the twenty-first century. Our record-keeping and criminal databases were positively Byzantine. Then along comes Geraldo Baca. For lack of a better description, he is a wizard when it comes to IT technologies and programming. He is a graduate of our National University here but also of your Massachusetts Institute of Technology. He is simply brilliant at what he does, and what he does and did was singlehandedly design or procure all our information technology systems, program them, and organize the databases and then got all our systems to talk to one another in an efficient and organized way. I should add that he was also the architect of all our security and encryption systems that are in place to safeguard the very sensitive information now within our systems. If he is indeed in with the Condor, then our job just got exponentially more difficult."

"That doesn't sound good, but I'm a dummy when it comes to this kind of stuff. It's clear that having this Baca guy on his side gives Alvarez access to the same information we may access, but he and Baca have always had that access, so how are things worse?"

"They are worse, Bennie, because his single greatest responsibility as head of both our NCIC and IT divisions is as the gatekeeper. He designed all the access programming. Anytime I or any of my reliable people accesses a database to conduct a search of anything, a name, an association, anything, Baca will most certainly know of this as soon as I have done it. I am no doubt being watched very carefully. In all modesty, Bennie, I am Alvarez's greatest enemy; I pose the greatest threat. This explains a lot, don't you see? Baca and his unlimited access to all our systems has allowed him to keep Alvarez informed on any investigation or inquiry any of our law enforcement and justice division task forces have been doing. With the sort of information Baca could provide, coupled with everything Alvarez was already privy to, no wonder we could not get a fix on his organization. Baca could manipulate our databases to add wrong information or omit information that might have helped us. To further illustrate what this means, I may or may not have told you, but I have met your operative just last week in Alvarez's office."

"You did mention yesterday seeing him—or knowing who Ray was—but not that you actually met him," an excited Bennie responded.

"Yes. Last Thursday, Alvarez returned to the city after being with his mother for a week and asked me to his office to discuss some important business he did not want to do over the phone. It was at that meeting he advised me incidentally that he intended to leave the government and was recommending that I be appointed the secretary. A complete farce, as we now see, tied to his assassination plot, but a convincing one at the time. In any event, as is usually the case, two of his security people were in the office as well. One was Raul Ortega, who has been with Alvarez for as long as I can remember. But your Ray was there, and he was a new face. He was introduced as taking the place of Manuel Ortega, Raul's older brother, who I was told had suddenly died when Alvarez was visiting his mother in Baja. After I got back to my office, I had my administrative assistant give me a typical background synopsis on Ray—where he was from, education, past experience, that sort of thing, just routine for my edification—and that's what I received and reviewed. A complete file, all very ordinary and what I expected to see on one so young placed in such a sensitive position: good background, good education, and a nice record as an officer in the Hermosillo police, I think it was. His entire life story right there for all to see, if ever anyone wanted to look. That is what Baca can do. How long has your man been involved in this, three months? Yet he lives in our databases as if he has been here since birth, a complete history. The possibilities are endless and also quite frightening."

"I take your point," Bennie said with a grim smile on his face and a shake of his head. "I'm sorry if I appear amused, but it just occurred to me that we are after a guy with three identities we know of, and our greatest weapon, ironically, is an undercover operative who now also has at least three identities I know of. I hope Ray remembers who the hell he really is and who he's working for."

Bennie paused, took a long drink of his whiskey, and looked hard at Alberto. "I'm worried about him, Alberto. He called our message drop yesterday after the assassination. First time I'd heard from him in months. He was despondent, so low, at not being able to stop it. He feels responsible for all those who died in the crash. You and I know that's foolishness, but he doesn't. And even though Alvarez orchestrated the crash and is by all accounts one of, if not the most, powerful cartel in the country, Ray, in some strange way, finds Alvarez's actions noble. Jesus Christ, I still can't believe that. I'm hoping I haven't lost him for good, Alberto."

Alberto was sadly shaking his head. "I understand your concern, my friend. And from my own experiences with Pablo Alvarez, I understand Ray, I think. There is no doubt that my old friend Alvarez is the one who has provided us with the most actionable intelligence on so many of the cartels and gangs. He is responsible for a great deal of good—I see that—but it is his base motives we must act on. His family is made up of criminal traffickers and murderers, and he chose them over the rule of law. In the end, he is no better. As for Ray, once we can get to him and get him away from Alvarez, I'm certain he will remember who he is. Take heart, my friend."

Bennie smiled. "Thanks for that, Alberto; sorry if I appeared to be crying into my booze. I think you're right about Ray. As for Baca, I see the problem, and it then begs the question: How many more backgrounds like Ray's exist in your system? It also explains why we had nothing on Carlo Vargas in our systems. This explains a lot; how can we know what or whom to believe and trust now with what you just told me?"

"You are unfortunately quite right, Bennie. I would suggest to you that if getting Alvarez is our first priority, capturing and interrogating Baca just became our second. We must have him alive and then get from him all he knows, or I will be living and dying with his organization, with or without Alvarez."

"With respect, Alberto, I would say our first priority is getting Ray out alive. Besides my selfish interest in making that happen, I would suggest what he knows is our best alternative for figuring out how to get to Alvarez."

"Yes, of course, Bennie. I agree and did not mean to imply otherwise. My train of thought was to our actions after we have contact with Ray. With Baca in with them, they will be able to track both the progress and the direction of any investigation we may undertake using the information in my systems, so we cannot use them."

"I just had another chilling thought," Bennie said. "Now that you know about Baca, what does Baca know about you and your operations—your Los Pueblos Fantasmas, I mean?"

Alberto smiled, a small one to be sure but genuine nonetheless.

"Absolutely nothing, Bennie, but damn near everything. I almost recruited Baca to help us. As ironic as it is given recent events, it was Emilio who talked me out of it. He said we needed a clean break from our agencies if we were to build a truly untraceable organization. We instead retained some smart US contractors and developed our own independent systems and databases. Neither Emilio nor I ever conducted any Los Pueblos Fantasmas business on our government systems. Baca, I am relieved to say, knows nothing."

"You said you suspected several of your deputies—can you tell me who?"

"Sadly, the new head of the Federal Police, Alejandro Quito-Perez—my former deputy, whom Alvarez suggested for the post—and Hector Garcia Ramirez, who was the senior deputy to Emilio at justice but who was today appointed the temporary head of my AFI, also at the suggestion of Alvarez. I have no real evidence on either of them of a connection to the Condor, but they are not the intellectual equal of either Emilio or Alvarez, so why the coat strings to higher office? I have my doubts that it is simply based on old friendships."

"Goddamn, Alberto, if you will pardon my blasphemy. The deck, as they say, is really stacked against us. But don't knock your intuition. I'd be dead several times over without mine."

"In time I can get rid of Garcia Ramirez and Quito-Perez."

"One last question, Alberto. Let's say we get to Ray, and he gets us some evidence beyond what he could offer in testimony, and maybe we have whatever it is you can dig up on this Pena alias, and we then somehow can make the connection to Alvarez—who in the hell do you go to? Where can you make a case against a sitting president, a national hero, assuming this raid on the Gang of Four comes off? Who in the living hell is going to believe us?"

Alberto looked at Bennie and then shook his head slowly. "Right now, I just don't know. We will have to figure that out when we know more. And to know more almost means snatching Baca first—after contacting Ray, of course—and opening him up like an empanada."

Alberto paused, turned slightly, and stared out at the gardens beyond the green-tinted windows, the same serious look on his face he had had earlier when in thought, and then turned back toward his guest.

"I am beginning to like the thought of getting Alvarez's cousins more and more, but we must get Baca also. He's the key to really understanding all that Alvarez has done."

"I require no convincing, Alberto. Anything we can do to distract Alvarez and those around him probably helps my man out. We just need to gather a little more intelligence and then come up with a plan. In the meantime, what happens next?"

"As to our immediate schedule, following the funeral on Thursday, there is to be a reception at Los Pinos, our White House, for senior people in the government and the diplomatic corps and dignitaries that have come for the funeral. I must be there, and I will take you as my guest and introduce you to Alvarez. I suggest our cover story is that you are in the city for the funeral and to discuss subjects of mutual interest. Should he want to know more about these mutual interests in private, it is our coordination efforts against the Gang of Four. I have no way of knowing if Ray will be there, but it is worth a try. Our next opportunity to be with Alvarez, and therefore his retinue, will be Friday late afternoon or evening. He mentioned he wanted to hear my final plans for the raid and asked me to come by his home for cocktails to discuss them. I of course said yes. I will also take you with me to that meet. Let us both hope that you get an opportunity to see your Ray."

"It's a start, Alberto, and we gotta start somewhere. For tomorrow, I think I'd like to go in with you—to your office, I mean—and then maybe just check out some of the sights. Maybe look over the cathedral where the service will be or just cruise by this Los Pinos, to get a feel for the lay of the land."

"A reconnoiter, eh, Bennie?"

"Let's call it sightseeing. Can you hook me up with a car and a reliable driver? Hopefully someone you know that's on our side?"

"I have just the man, Bennie; he met you at the airport today."

"He looked very competent, very professional. We can trust him?"

"I do, Bennie, with my life. He is my nephew, my sister Angela's oldest son, Roberto. A captain in my Federal Police and a fine young investigative officer with a bright future, should we all live through this mess. He is also a member of Los Pueblos Fantasmas."

"We will live through this mess, Alberto, we got a couple of young hotshots on our side to help us old men," Bennie said, smiling, and then asked, "Any chance I can get some more of your whiskey? You serve really nice stuff."

Alberto smiled back, liking Bennie Santiago more and more with each passing minute. "Certainly, my friend, and then let's go see what Alejandro has planned for dinner. Do you like fine red wines, by any chance?"

"Almost as much as I do old Scottish malt," Bennie said, smiling again.

"Well, then, let me freshen up our drinks, and let's go dig around in the cellar and see what we can find. Did I mention that there is a nicely stocked old wine cellar in the basement?"

Bennie chuckled. "No, you did not, and you may well end up regretting you shared that little piece of intelligence."

11

Sergeant Major Green was sitting at a high-tech-looking console next to Captain Danny Irwin, studying the images being sent back by one of the Predators. The drones had been on station over the Hermosillo and Chihuahua areas since dawn. Because of the relatively short distances from Fort Bliss to the targets, the nearly invisible birds could loiter over the area for hours. Monterrey had posed greater challenges given the four-hour flight each way.

When the sergeant major had arrived at Auxiliary Control a little after six, Captain Irwin and his troops had been all ready for him. Over coffee, Danny had showed the sar major what he had come up with for a schedule and for the search patterns. He had even taken the written descriptions of the estates and sketched up some site plans of what they generally must look like. He had then reviewed this with the troops so they had a visual image of what to look for. The team had four birds, three of which had been readied for departure. After the briefing, the orders had been issued to launch the drones.

Now, some three hours later, the Hermosillo and Chihuahua Predators, birds 1 and 2, respectively, were still doing careful searches of the general areas the DEA intel had indicated the Condor's estates were located. From Ray's detailed descriptions of the routes from the cities to the estates, the search areas were able to be narrowed to a few square miles. Each estate within the geographic box defined—and there were many—was being over flown and carefully looked over for the detailed criteria Ray had passed to Bennie and then eliminated if it failed to meet the description.

The predators had started at an altitude of ten thousand feet and had slowly been dropped down to roughly six thousand feet, allowing for very detailed views of the various haciendas. The GPS coordinates of those estates eliminated were noted in the computer, and the birds never flew the same territory twice. Bird 3 was still en route to Monterrey and would not be on station for another hour. Bird 4 was kept in reserve and was still on the base.

The operator controlling bird 2 called out, "Captain, I think I'm on a target."

The sar major and Captain Irwin walked quickly over to his station. His bird was orbiting at seven thousand feet vertically and a mile horizontally over a very large estate that was walled and had the necessary outlying casitas, the collection of SUVs, and the most revealing aspect—a secure-looking front gate with armed guards cooling their heels just inside the gate. The sar major went slowly thorough the DEA description of the Chihuahua estate, line by line. Everything seemed to fit, right down to the cobblestone curving driveway, the porte-cochere, and several large fireplace chimneys.

In the next two hours, the operators for birds 1 and 3 had located the Hermosillo and Monterrey estates as well. Once they knew what to look for after pinpointing the Chihuahua estate, the others had been easier. Ray's intel he'd passed on to Mr. Santiago had been right; the estates were almost identical looking from the air, as if built from the same design. Bird 3 had begun its return almost immediately after the GPS coordinates of the Monterey estate had been recorded. The other birds were still in medium-altitude orbits, focusing their cameras on every individual they could see coming and going. The sar major's first impression was the Chihuahua estate was the most active: more people visible, more vehicles, more comings and goings. From what Bennie had told him, the Condor and his entourage of twenty men moved between the three estates, leaving only the permanent house staff and guards at the locations they were not occupying. It looked clear to Sergeant Major Green that the Hermosillo and Monterrey estates were pretty quiet. But things were happening in Chihuahua.

From an altitude of five thousand feet, the Predators would not be heard, nor would they be seen, unless you really were looking hard and had the help of radar, which, given the Predator's small size and stealthy profile, would really not be much help. From this altitude, the incredible lenses of the real-time and still cameras could focus in tightly on individuals to the point that facial characteristics could be easily identified. The sar major had Captain Irwin's operators focusing on finding the Carlo guy. Carlo had more unique identifying features, making him easier to spot. His size and shape; big, rounded shoulders; and a toothy smile were easy to see, and where Carlo was, perhaps Bennie's agent was also.

There was a buzzing of the main-door solenoid, as someone with the correct clearance was obviously coming in. The general came through the door, followed by Colonel Romero. Manny barked, "As you were," as those not actually involved with flying the Predators started to pop to attention. The sergeant major walked over to Manny and greeted him.

"We've got all three haciendas pinpointed, General."

"Good job, and so quick."

"It was the intelligence we had on the locations, General. That got us within a few square miles, and the estates just jump out at you once you know what you're looking for. Not a lot of neighbors, as you can imagine, and lots of armed guards in strategic places. They are not shy about showing muscle, which makes them easy to see."

"Well, I'm glad you're off to a good start," Manny said. Colonel Romero got everyone's attention, and the general gave the collected recon group a quick pep talk on the importance of the mission and the required secrecy. When done, he turned to the sar major and asked to see him in private. They went into the one private office off the Auxiliary Control room and closed the door.

"Jeff, anyone question your orders when you ordered the birds south into Mexico?"

"Not one bit, General. Captain Irwin and his lieutenants simply nodded and started poring over the maps and the intelligence I gave them and started plotting courses. I don't think anyone gives a shit about where they're flying. Truth be told, I overheard a couple of the troops saying how glad they were to finally be doing something worthwhile. Not that the routine stuff isn't, of course."

Manny responded with a smile. "After doing the work these guys were doing in Afghanistan and Pakistan, they've got to be bored silly flying up and down the wire. You aren't telling me anything I don't already know. Well, good luck with the search; I've got a mountain of paperwork on my desk to get at this morning. Call me with anything interesting."

"Yes sir, General."

The general left, and the sar major returned to his monitor. One of the very good features of searching this way, other than it was mostly risk-free, was that the controllers could fly the Predators where ordered, at whatever altitude, and then zoom in on anything of interest. The operator of bird 2 over Chihuahua called over to Jeff, "Sergeant Major, I've got a two vehicle convoy approaching the estate, both big black SUVs."

Jeff went over and stood behind the technical sergeant and watched the feed. It seemed to him all the cartels ever rode around in were black Escalades. They might as well have had the name of the cartel painted on the side, they were so obvious. The two SUVs were stopped at the gate only momentarily and then waved through; clearly, the occupants were known to the guards. The vehicles made their way up the private drive and pulled into and through the porte-cochere. Only the second SUV was obscured by the projecting roof, but given the position of the drone and the angle of view, the cameras could see halfway under the overhangs, so they were not fully blocked out. The occupants of the first SUV were obviously guards, for they jumped out of their vehicle and walked quickly to be in place to open the rear doors of the second. Two men got out of the second SUV and seemed to gather a few guards around them and were gesturing, as if giving instructions. Jeff said, "Zoom in on the two guys giving the orders. I want pictures, good pictures, for possible identification." The video controller at the station next to the flight controller did as he was told.

"Can you fly this thing in a little closer without tipping them off that we're watching?" Jeff asked the flight controller.

"Yes, Sar Major, I can. We are at five thousand feet vertically and almost that same range horizontally. That's almost a mile. Our tests have shown that at a half mile, we cannot be heard except under the most ideal of wind and audio conditions. And we're so small that we are virtually invisible at half a mile."

"Get us close and quick, Sergeant. I'd like to identify the two guys giving the orders."

The video controller kept his cameras on the group in the driveway as the flight controller guided the Predator in closer. He dropped to three thousand feet and brought the bird in to about the same horizontal distance. Flight data from the bird told them they were downwind from the estate, which made the possibility of being heard very remote. They also had the morning sun at their backs, so visually they were in a perfect spot to see and not be seen. The tech flying the drone was doing lazy figure eights to keep the bird over this relative position. All the while the cameras continued to adjust to the drone's flight to keep its cameras on the target. The image data from the cameras were digitally being filed away, their shots clear and crisp, as if the cameras lens were only thirty or forty feet away from the subject. There was no doubt in the sergeant major's mind that the shorter, heavier of the two was the Carlo guy that Mr. Santiago wanted, confirming they indeed were watching the right place. It was just a guess, but Jeff's first thought was that the older, taller of the two might well be the older brother, Eduardo Vargas, that Bennie had mentioned and described. From what the DEA intel had said, the Vargas brothers were a part of the traveling entourage of the Condor. If they were here in Chihuahua, there was a very good chance that the Condor, and therefore Bennie's agent, would be there as well.

"Captain Irwin?"

Danny Irwin had been looking over the shoulder of bird 1's controller, "Yes, Sar Major."

"Captain, bird two is over Chihuahua, and it's hot. We have a positive ID on one of the characters we're looking for. I want twenty-four hour surveillance on this estate, and if caravans, say a minimum of two of those big bastard SUVs go somewhere, I want them tracked. Can you make that happen?"

"Yes, Sar Major. We have bird 4 in reserve. We can get it on station timed to arrive with the departure of bird 2. If we abandon one of the other searches, I can get you continuous coverage over Chihuahua."

"OK, Captain, on my authority, for the time being, drop the Monterrey surveillance, save all that flying, and get multiple birds on Chihuahua. My gut tells me this is where the action will be, and if not, maybe these characters will lead us to wherever it is."

"Yes, Sar Major, I'm all over it."

12

Departamento de Seguridad Pública y Justicia
(Department of Public Security and Justice)
Mexico City
Wednesday Morning

A fter a delightful dinner with Alberto and his first good night of rest in months, aided by all the wine they had drunk, Bennie had forced himself to get up early and accompany Alberto to his office. On the way into the city, Alberto reminded Bennie to not mention anything sensitive when they got there. He was not yet certain of how secure it was from electronic eavesdropping. Over the two bottles of Bordeaux at dinner the night before, Alberto had told Bennie the uncomfortable truth: that with very few exceptions, he trusted no one in his new office.

They were each having a cup of strong coffee on the couch in Alvarez's old office and Alberto's new one, as Alberto was giving Bennie an overview of Saturday's raid on the Gang of Four, when his secretary knocked on the door and showed in Roberto Rodriguez and two other security types. After his secretary had closed the door behind herself, Alberto said to Roberto, "You and your team will be accompanying Mr. Santiago today; he will let you know his agenda. If you would just give us another minute or two, he will be right with you."

With a silent nod, Roberto went to Alberto's desk and opened the brief-case he was carrying. The other two security men joined him and each took a handheld electronic device from the case and began making quiet passes over all the surfaces and furnishings in the room. Roberto sat at Alberto's desk and began assembling a small device that, for lack of a better description, looked like a telephone answering machine, only smaller. Alberto kept up his dialogue as Bennie watched the three men with interest. Roberto finished up whatever it was he was doing and brought the device over and placed it on the bookshelves nearest the couch. Roberto glanced at his two associates, who simply nodded back. For the first time in the ten minutes he had been in the room, Roberto spoke, but very softly.

"As best as we can determine, the room is clean, Uncle, but I would still use caution here. The device on the shelf emits electronic noise at a very high frequency. In other words, you cannot hear it, but it will mask any conversation in this area if there are electronic listening devices here of a type we cannot detect. All that will be picked up on such devices is static. Your conversation will go undetected."

"Thank you, Roberto. Bennie, I have a briefing in ten minutes, so I must excuse myself. Let's plan on meeting back at my home after five. You can fill me in on your tour of our city then. If my schedule should change in any way where I think an opportunity arises for you to meet the president today, I will contact you through Roberto here."

"Sounds fine. Thanks for the coffee and for the use of Roberto."

"Seeing the president" was their agreed-upon code phrase in front of all others for seeing Ray. Another thing they had agreed to the night before was that the nature of Bennie's true reasons for being in the capital would remain just between the two of them. Emilio's likely breaking of this kind of security discipline was front and center in their minds. They shook hands, and Bennie followed the security team to the elevator and down to the garage, where a limousine was waiting. Roberto held the rear door open for Bennie and then joined him in the back seat while the two security men got in the front.

One to drive, the other to ride shotgun, no doubt, Bennie thought. *Only down here riding shotgun really means just that. I wonder what weapons they carry.*

Roberto asked Bennie where he'd like to go first. "I probably should have mentioned this before we came down here, but I thought since we were here at the Zocalo, I could check out the cathedral where tomorrow's service will be held."

Roberto smiled for the first time in Bennie's presence. "For that, Senor, we need not necessarily take the car. It is of course right across the Zocalo at Catedral Metropolitana de la Asuncion de Maria. Henrico," Roberto said to the driver, "take us to the National Palace, the diplomatic drop-off. We will leave the car there and walk across the plaza to the cathedral."

With a nod the driver headed for the parking-garage exit. Alberto had pointed out the National Palace to Bennie as they had taken in the view from Alberto's office overlooking the Zocalo. The palace made up almost the entire east side of the great plaza, and the cathedral dominated the north end. The diplomatic drop-off was just off the Zocalo on the north side of the dominating western facade of the centuries-old palace. Alberto told Bennie that Alvarez would be splitting his time between his new office in the Executive Department located there and the more modern and more easily accessible office at Los Pinos, the official residence of the Mexican president. As they merged into the traffic that snaked slowly around the perimeter of the grand plaza and made their way up the east side, the six-hundred-foot-long, four-story-tall stone-covered facade filled Bennie's passenger-side window.

"That reddish stone, Roberto—what is it? I don't think I have ever seen anything like it before," Bennie asked.

"It is called *tezontle*, Mr. Santiago, a volcanic stone indigenous to Mexico. It is said that much of the stone of the palace dates from the time of Montezuma II."

"Really old, in other words, Roberto."

"Yes, Senor. From about the time Columbus of Italy was discovering the West Indies and your country for the Spanish, if I am recalling my world history correctly."

"You're talking the 1492 Christopher Columbus, Roberto? This palace dates from way back then?"

"Yes and no, Senor. A palace has existed on this site since then. The building itself has been rebuilt on many occasions through the centuries, but as the seat of power in our country, it has always been here. It was on this site that the Aztec kings, including Montezuma, ruled, then the Spanish after their conquest, and eventually the modern Mexican government."

"We are so young as a country," was all Bennie could think to say softly, as if to himself. Roberto only looked at him and then fell silent, not understanding the older man's comment. As they continued the short ride in silence, in Bennie's mind, the metaphor of a country as a human being was on his mind, but Roberto was the wrong guy to talk to about it. The cartels were a cancer on the body of the old and vulnerable Mexico. And like cancer in the elderly, it was consuming it, as the older body's defenses were overpowered by the disease.

We are vulnerable, thought Bennie, *to insidious cancers like the cartel organizations. The increases in the violent-crime rates in our Southwest are the first symptom of this. Maybe for the first time I really understand why Charley drives the agency like he does. Now I'm here, assisting a man who for all intents and purposes has formed the nucleus of an organization whose goal is to depose the current leader of a democratic country, by assassination if necessary. A leader who just happens to be the worst of bad guys, and only five or six of us good guys know this. Jesus, what a mess.*

The driver turned onto the Calle de la Moneda to the north side of the Palace and slowly drove through an arched opening in the facade into the covered diplomatic reception area. The security man riding shotgun was first out of the car, which had drawn the attention of the uniformed presidential guard detachment in the area, and showed them his credentials. Bennie and Roberto got out of the back, and Roberto went to the guard in charge and had a few words, at which point the guard snapped to attention and nodded. Roberto returned to Bennie and said, "Our car will be fine here. Please, if you will follow me, we shall visit the cathedral."

They made the short walk to the Zocalo along the festive Calle de la Moneda, entered the plaza, and strolled toward the front of the imposing old cathedral where Fernandez was lying in state. There was already a long line of citizens snaking out the huge, ancient front doors. Bennie couldn't help himself; like any other tourist, he simply stopped and, in awe, took in the highly decorated facade of the National Cathedral. There did not seem to be a surface that was not adorned with a statue or some other decoration or relief in the stone.

"Jesus Christ," Bennie said without thinking, "it's magnificent. Evidently real old as well and also the same red stone, huh, Roberto."

"Yes, Senor. Construction began in the late fifteen hundreds and took several hundred years to complete. The president is lying in the entry portion of the nave, the narthex before the Altar of Forgiveness. He will be moved this evening deeper into the cathedral to the central nave at the crossing before the Altar of the Kings for the actual service. All told, about five hundred dignitaries will actually be seated for the service, yourself included."

"Anyway we can get inside without waiting in line?"

"Certainly, Mr. Santiago, if you would follow me."

The people wishing to pay their last respects to their slain president began gathering hours before the front doors had been opened, and with the assistance of both the capital police and the presidential guard, who brought order to the chaos, were formed into a queue that came out of the front doors, ran to the east, and then continued north up the east side of the imposing old church. This kept the thousands that wanted to see their president and pay their respects out of the always-crowded traffic lanes surrounding the Zocalo.

The line never stopped moving. People shuffled along at a very slow pace, but they were moving. Once people gained access to the sanctuary and were actually in the presence of the large draped coffin, they only had a moment to say a quick prayer or cross themselves or both and then were ushered out the west entrance of the narthex. It was to this exit that Roberto led Bennie. He showed the guards there his credentials, and with a nod of the guard's head, he, Bennie, and the two others slipped by the mourners who were exiting and stepped into the dimly lit great cathedral. They kept to the wide side aisle that ran parallel to the central nave and observed the procession going reverently by the coffin from the opposite side. Bennie was taking it all in, trying to see if any one spot would give him a better view of tomorrow's crowd and, if Ray was there, perhaps see him. But he quickly concluded that spotting or being seen by Ray here at the service would be a fool's errand. The place was going to be packed, and unless he was miraculously seated close to Ray by pure chance, there would be no seeing him. Alberto told him he thought it unlikely that Ray would even accompany Alvarez to the funeral or the interment—too many cameras, too great a chance of being seen by people in the north if Alberto's speculation was correct. Bennie's great reconnoiter idea was going right out the window. As he concluded that espying Ray here or at the cemetery was unlikely, he had another thought.

"Roberto," he said softly, both out of respect for place and also so as not to be overheard incase the acoustics of the nave would betray him, "did I understand correctly that the president's official residence is a museum of sorts?"

"That is correct, Senor. Los Pinos is not only the president's office and residence, but it can also be toured by the public."

"What say we head to this Los Pinos? Will we have time to see it and be back at the secretary's place by, say, five?"

"Certainly, Senor; my uncle lives less than two miles from Los Pinos. They are both in or near the Bosque de Chapultepec."

"Well, how convenient. Let's get the hell out of here and go there."

Bennie knew his best chances for bumping into Ray would be tomorrow at the diplomatic reception or Friday at the informal briefing at the Alvarez mansion. His next best chance was if Alvarez had his closest aides with him at his office, and that meant Los Pinos, if he could get a private tour. It was a long shot, but that was all his team had going for it at the moment. At least this way, he might actually be in the same building at the same time as Ray. It was worth a shot.

They made their way out of the cathedral and back to where they had left the car and headed for the Chapultepec area. After a short drive, they turned off a major avenue onto a smaller street that was framed on either side by sweeping white decorative walls that led into the park. There was no gate, but brass signage on each wall said "Los Pinos," so Bennie recognized this as a special street of some sort. They had not gone far before the street ended as a cul-de-sac before an ornately decorated security gate set in a white cut-stone wall. Sitting on an island in the center of the cul-de-sac was a small, attractive stone guardhouse with several uniformed guards sitting inside. Bennie had come to recognize the uniform of the Estado Mayor Presidencial, or EMP, the Mexican Presidential Guard. Unlike the US Secret

Service, which had few uniformed members and more members dressed in business attire, the Mexican guard was the opposite. The few members of the guard around the president wore suits; the majority wore military uniforms because the EMP was a division within the army.

Either they were going to be allowed through the manned gate, or if not, they would circle around the guardhouse and head back the way they had come. Bennie realized now that what he thought had been a street leading into the park was really the main entry drive to the presidential mansion, only the gate was set well into the park.

Bennie's driver pulled up to the guardhouse, rolled down his window, and showed his credentials to the curious guard who came up to the car. As the guard was looking over the driver's credentials, Roberto opened the rear door and stepped out to have a word with the guards. This attracted the attention of the second man in the guardhouse and clearly made the first guard a little nervous. Whatever Roberto had to say to the guards made them relax a bit, and they talked together another minute before Roberto returned to the car.

"Senor Santiago, I apologize for this. This is the public entry to Los Pinos, but due to recent events, public access has been closed. These men are part of the presidential guard. I have let them know that you are here as the personal guest of the secretary, and they are calling the office to confirm this, and they have also called their commander for instructions. I am told that the president is here, and I have told them that you do not seek to be anywhere near the presidential offices, simply that you wished to tour the public areas as if they were open to the citizens. I think we will get in if we show some patience."

"Sounds fine, Roberto. I'd like to get in if we can, but not to the point of ruffling anyone's feathers."

They sat in the limousine, and ten minutes later, a marked car arrived from the direction of the mansion. Two uniformed gentlemen got out of the back seat and passed through a man door in the wall and approached the guardhouse. Roberto got back out and went to join them. After a brief discussion, Roberto signaled Bennie to join him. Bennie could see that the older of the two men had much shiny gold decoration on the brim of his slightly oversized cap and gold-braid trim to his uniform. He also had a silver star and gold eagle on his epaulets signifying his rank as brigadier general.

"Mr. Santiago, may I introduce you to General Ramos, commander of the presidential guard. General Ramos, may I introduce Mr. Benjamin Santiago, a special envoy of the US government and the personal friend and guest of Secretary Rodriguez."

"A pleasure, Senor Santiago, and my apologies for the precautions that have required you to wait so long."

"Thank you, General. Sorry if I'm upsetting anyone with my visit. I have no duties to attend to today, and wishing to stay out of the secretary's way, given all he does have to do, I was just playing tourist. If this is in any way inconvenient, just say so, and I'll understand and be on my way."

"Not at all, Senor; we merely had to check with the secretary's office. As the secretary is a very important cabinet member and also a personal friend of the president, we will of course allow the visit. If you will return to your car and follow me, we will take you to Los Pinos."

With a handshake and a smiling nod, the general returned to his car with his aide, and the other guards opened the large gates electronically. Roberto looked at Bennie with raised eyebrows and a quizzical look once they returned to their car but said nothing. His gesture seemed to say to Bennie, *I don't know what all is going on, but here goes nothing.*

They followed the general's sedan along the winding paved drive, and Bennie was immediately taken by the incredible beauty of the place as they slowly meandered into the park. The drive was lined with neatly trimmed hedges and shrubs, and for most of the drive, they were almost completely covered by a canopy of lush trees. Bennie now understood why the president's home was called the Pines, as unlike any of the trees he had seen in the neighborhoods he'd been in so far in the capital, there were huge pine trees everywhere. There were also beautiful fountains sitting among a type of palm tree Bennie had not seen before. *Almost like passing through an arboretum*, he thought. *Incredibly beautiful.* At regular intervals along the drive were cast bronze busts sitting on polished stone bases. Roberto explained these were the past presidents of Mexico since the revolution of 1910. He went on to say that this had been the home for the president since 1934.

They emerged from the garden-like setting and continued past a nearly deserted parking area hidden by hedges and followed the general's car right to the front of the impressive structure that was the president's home. Not unlike the home of the American president, the mansion was mostly of white and warm-gray stone but was of an architecture he was unfamiliar with. He recalled from somewhere that the White House was Colonial Georgian, and Los Pinos obviously was something entirely different, but there was something strangely beautiful about the large mansion, set as it was in the lush garden setting. On the flight down, Bennie had glanced at the inflight magazine at a travel article on Mexico. There had been several pictures of the more popular Aztec or Mayan ruins, and looking at the front of the mansion, he was reminded of some aspects of these temples.

The general got out of his car, and Bennie and Roberto did likewise. As the general approached them with his toothy grin, Bennie thought, *This guy's a first-class phony. I wouldn't trust him any further than I could throw him.*

"Senor Santiago, duties call, so I will leave you in the care of my aide. He will escort you into our official residence, and there will be an usher to show you around. I hope this meets with your approval?"

"You have been too kind, General—my thanks. This is more than I expected."

"Good, then I will take my leave; enjoy your tour." With that the general smiled again, nodded, and returned to his car. The young aide—a major, if Bennie had the Mexican insignias figured out—was as unsmiling as his general was toothy. Bennie judged that he felt he had more important things to do than play tour guide or nursemaid to some low-level diplomat with friends in high places.

"If you will follow me, Senor, I will take you to the one who will serve as your guide."

Bennie thought that he would be led to some secondary entry of the sort more suitable for a low-level visitor like him, but instead he followed the major up the wide front entry steps that led right to the front doors of the presidential residence. The tourist in Bennie was looking forward to the tour, but the senior DEA agent was hoping to somehow bump into his operative. One of the tall, decorative metal entry doors had already been opened by a member of the presidential guard, and they walked right into the entry lobby. The serious, unsmiling major turned Bennie over to the assistant head presidential usher, a nattily uniformed man named Delgado, who turned out to be very pleasant and seemed genuinely happy to be conducting a private tour of the mansion for the American diplomat.

Senor Delgado explained to Bennie and Roberto that the presidential office suites were in the north wing, and as the president and his staff were in, that area could not be approached; however, all the principal ground-floor public rooms were available. In addition, as the new president and his family were not going to reside at Los Pinos, a tour of the family quarters could also be accommodated. Bennie told Senor Delgado that he had plenty of time and would like to see whatever was permissible in whatever time he had available. Bennie's motives were to spend as much time at Los Pinos as possible in the hopes of running into Ray. With that, they took a very pleasant ninety-minute tour as the excited Delgado told story after story of the history of this room and that. Bennie smiled and nodded the entire time and heard virtually nothing as he stole glances here and there, hoping to see Ray by chance as they came upon the occasional staffer. If Ray was here, he had not been anywhere near the public spaces Bennie toured. His tour concluded, Bennie enthusiastically shook the usher's hand and thanked him, disappointed inside that he had not made contact. A presidential guard showed him and Roberto to their car, and they drove off. Bennie knew his two best chances of running into Ray were ahead of him, so he wasn't completely disappointed. This impromptu visit had been a long shot, and long shots rarely paid off.

13

Los Pinos Presidential Residence and Office
The Bosque de Chapultepec, Mexico City
Late Wednesday Afternoon

Life in the real world was a capricious thing. What Bennie did not know, not being clairvoyant, was that his long shot had paid off; he just wasn't aware of it. As had been arranged prior to Bennie's arrival at Los Pinos, the assignments of the Alvarez inner circle had Ray paired with Raul this day so that Raul could show him the ins and outs of not only Los Pinos but what their duties would entail. The EMP had primary responsibility for the president's safety, but anything and everything of interest or concern that came to the attention of the EMP commanders in the course of their guard duties was relayed to Raul on their communication net. Attached to Raul's belt was a second small receiver transmitter, and tucked behind his left ear was a discreet two-way com link. Raul didn't monitor all traffic on the net; rather, he was just on the command circuit and therefore only contacted when the captains in charge of various command groups decided that contacting their superior commanders was necessary. Raul then would begin to overhear the discussions or requests made of the majors or colonels and determine for himself if it was necessary to follow events. It was at times a nuisance for Raul to be conducting business with someone and at the same time to be listening in on a conversation—like trying to concentrate on work and listening to the broadcast of a baseball game at the same time. More often than not, the communications on the command net were of a trivial and unimportant nature, and Raul was learning to tune these out.

Because Los Pinos was closed to the public, and only those who normally staffed the presidential mansion or worked for the executive were actually on the grounds, there was very little from a security standpoint requiring anyone's attention—that is, until Roberto and his security people showed up outside the closed gates, flashing very serious credentials and escorting an American diplomat of some kind requesting a tour. The guards at the gate called the officer of the guard, a lieutenant, who then called his captain in charge of this particular company of guards, who bumped it up the chain of command to the colonel manning the office of the presidential guard this particular day with the president in residence. Normally, General Ramos would be found in his office at the National Palace at the Zocalo, but this day he was with the president's staff reviewing security arrangements for the funeral and interment the next day. As the general was in the building, the colonel interrupted the general in his meeting by sending in an aide with a note requesting his immediate attention on an unusual item that had come up. General Ramos excused himself from the other staffers with a comment or two that indicated he was annoyed by both the interruption and the inability of the lower ranks to solve problems, and he headed for the colonel's office. In truth, he was glad to be out of the meeting and also glad to have the chance perhaps to solve some issue that would get noticed by the new president.

There was an intrinsic problem with elevating men like Ramos to positions of importance, for they more often than not revealed the character flaws that had led them to be compromised and used by others in the first place—unlike Alvarez himself, who had been diverted from an accomplished and honorable life by the unexpected and surprising revelations of a criminal past by his father; it could hardly be called a "grievous character flaw" to love and honor one's own father. In most circumstances, the love and loyalty shown by Alvarez would have been thought to add depth and humanity to his character, not be a subtraction from it. However, the flaws of those he sought to compromise through the years ran the gamut of the worst in people from simple greed and envy to more serious flaws such as addiction, arrogance, cowardice, or hubris and the worst, an obsession for power or adulation. Where Alvarez had controlled the direction of his life with determination and intelligence after his flaws had made it impossible for him to do what was right, the flaws in those he had subordinated through the years simply led to their eventual ruination, discarded after they ceased to be useful, like the recently murdered Fernandez and the soon to be murdered Barega.

In the case of General Ramos, it had been a combination of factors that had turned him into a traitor and lapdog for a distant and powerful criminal leader: his insecurities and vanity for his personal appearance, for starters, but also his basic cowardice and his desire to be respected and admired, even feared. These were attributes that had to be supplemented through false achievements and advancements. Now that he had a star on his shoulders and was known throughout the country as the head of the presidential guard at a reasonably young age, his future was set in his eyes—and at such a small price in his opinion: information.

Ramos entered the colonel's office as an aide held the door open for his superior.

"What is so important, Colonel, that I am interrupted in a very important meeting regarding the security plans of a dozen world leaders?" Ramos said, feigning anger.

The colonel was a few years older than the general and, unlike his commander, had earned his way to his rank through hard work, intelligence, and at times great courage. He had been being groomed by the former head of the presidential guard, General Lopez, to one day take his place—and would have had not the events of this past Monday not shattered all his plans and dreams when the general had perished in the air crash. It hurt his pride that the man he had outranked for so long, and who he knew without doubt was a bad officer, had received the promotion to replace Lopez. He was the senior colonel and he should have ascended to the post, but the new president had passed him over. It had been a cruel stroke, yet he would do his job and do it well, for as little character as the general had, Colonel Mariano Cordova had character in abundance.

"With apologies, my general, there is an American diplomat, a personal friend of Secretary Rodriguez, who is at gate one and is requesting a tour of Los Pinos. As he is a personal friend of Senor Rodriguez, and knowing in what esteem the president holds the secretary, I felt we should not just say no, not today. Because you yourself issued the orders closing the public access to the grounds, I felt it necessary to seek your approval. I have already checked with the secretary's chief aide, and the gentleman is indeed a personal friend and a houseguest of the secretary."

"Yes, yes, I see the problems. No, Colonel, you acted correctly. Where is this diplomat?"

"He is still at gate one in his car, waiting for word on a tour."

"Thank you, Colonel. Please contact my aide and have him meet me with my car at the front entrance. Also, please inform Senor Ortega, the president's personal aide, of the situation and let him know that on my authority, I am allowing the informal visit. Then contact the head usher's office and arrange for a tour guide for this person, someone with enough knowledge and skill to escort and entertain this man. I will go to the gate and escort him to the front entry personally. Might as well impress him a little, eh, Colonel?"

"Yes, General."

It was obvious to the colonel that Ramos was trying to curry favor with the president. The man was pathetic, but he was a general and the colonel was but a colonel, so he started making his calls as the general turned and walked out.

Raul was showing Ray the central security room in the basement and the very private secondary security room, where the ever-present Geraldo Baca and his select team worked their particular magic. It was necessary that the EMP members of central security knew and understood who Ray was, and it was important for Ray to know where to track down Geraldo whenever Jefe needed his particular skills. Raul was in midsentence explaining to Ray how and where to access the security facilities when he received the call over the net from the colonel in the north wing. He just paused in midspeech; raised his hand as if to say to Ray, "Hold it a second"; and listened.

Ray had seen Raul do this before, so he knew he was being updated over his earpiece. As Ray could hear nothing over his, this meant that it was the EMP net. "Come with me for a second, Ray; a minor item has come up, but it will be of interest to our group."

What made the colonel's message interesting to Raul was the report that the American diplomat, whoever he was, was a personal friend of Alberto Rodriguez and a guest at his home. In short, any friend of Rodriguez's was a likely enemy of the Condor, so best to identify and keep track of such a man. They moved from central control into Geraldo's office.

"Geraldo, can you bring up the cameras at gate one for me?"

"Of course; go to the empty desk, and use that monitor. I will have the gate camera shots for you in a second. Is something wrong?"

"Nothing wrong—just a person of interest, an American diplomat by the name of Santiago staying at the home of Secretary Rodriguez whom we will want to create a file on if we have no file already."

Santiago? Ray thought. *Is there a chance?*

Geraldo's fingers were flying over his keyboard as he quickly completed several tasks. The first was getting the cameras online, and the next was creating a new file for this particular video to be saved. Lastly, he began to access the database that would give him the names and identities of all the American officials that would be attending the funeral. Raul sat at the desk, and Ray stood to the side and slightly behind so he also could watch. It was a very good thing that he was slightly behind Raul and that Geraldo and his men were all busy doing what they did and not paying Ray any attention, for when the images of the first camera popped up on the monitor, there was a conversation going on between the peacock of a general that Alvarez had appointed as head of the EMP and a tall young-looking official Ray had never seen. The screen split, and now Geraldo had the images from two different cameras on the split screen. The second camera was focused on the diplomat's limousine. The man speaking with the general turned and gestured toward the car, and the security person standing nearby opened the rear door, and the diplomat got out and walked over to the others.

Had Raul or any of the others been watching Ray closely, they would have seen an obvious momentary reaction from him, for even as professional as Ray was, he had shown just a fraction of wide-eyed astonishment at the image of his DEA control agent ambling over and smiling kindly and shaking the general's hand. Ray quickly gathered himself, but just as some of the poorer poker players back on the force in Sacramento had blushed slightly at the sight of a winning draw, therefore telegraphing their hand, Ray felt a little flushed and knew he'd better get control fast. Thinking about being executed was a good way to get himself focused.

Ray couldn't believe it. *Bennie's here! And he's with Rodriguez, thank God. That can only mean that Rodriguez got the message; that has to be it! What's he doing down here, if not to try to get to me? Maybe all is not lost—is there a chance? I need to try to see Bennie to confirm this, but I'm not prepared. Shit. You should have had a second message prepared. I will correct that tonight. Maybe Bennie will be part of the reception tomorrow or, better yet, be at the final planning session for the big raid. I have to get word to someone on Alvarez's trip north.*

They continued to watch the monitors as everyone returned to their cars, and they proceeded through the gates. Geraldo asked Raul, "Did you say the American's name was Santiago, Raul?"

"Yes, that is what I was told."

"There is no Senor Santiago on the American diplomatic roster, Raul; I just checked."

"Check again, will you, Geraldo, and also check lower-level embassy people, especially their military and security rosters."

"I have already done this. There is no one attached to the embassy with the surname Santiago, nor is there a Santiago on the roster of those traveling with the American vice president. We just updated all those files as well."

"Any ideas or guesses, Geraldo?"

"I'm thinking perhaps this man is nothing more than a personal friend, perhaps through Rodriguez's family in America—something like that."

Raul thought about it for a second. "Perhaps, Geraldo. Start a file on this man, and let's do nothing further for now. Maybe after the funeral, he will just leave, and that is the end of it. If he stays on, then we will explore other possibilities. If nothing else, we can send an inquiry from the Office of the president to the ambassador asking for a dossier on the man."

They watched the monitors for a few more minutes, right up to Bennie reaching the lobby, and then Raul had seen enough.

"Geraldo, learn what you can without going outside the circle."

Geraldo nodded his acceptance of the order, and Raul and Ray continued on their way. Raul took Ray all over the backroom areas of the mansion, explaining various procedures or precautions at each new stop, but never did they venture into any of the public spaces Bennie might be in.

For Ray, the rest of the day was uneventful and even boring, but inside, his emotions were running high and needed to be masked. Late in the afternoon, he and Raul took their car and returned to the Alvarez mansion. The president would not be at Los Pinos until later, so they would not be dining with him. Ray simply wanted the night to come so he could work out his next message drop. He'd have two chances and two chances only, and he meant to be ready.

14

Harry's Diner
El Paso, Texas
Thursday Morning

A lex had called back on Tuesday night and left a message at Danny's apartment scheduling their breakfast for early Thursday morning, the soonest possible time Danny said he could meet. This was better than nothing, but Danny had spent an uncomfortable Wednesday at Aux Control and later in his apartment, both physically and mentally—physically because he had not been high since Monday and really craved it and mentally with the growing awareness that he might be losing control of his recreation. He would get his delivery, but so too would he be more prudent in his use. No more binges with bitches, as he had come to calling his excessive partying with the beautiful and shallow women he called girlfriends. He had also spent Tuesday night worrying about what Alex's reaction would be to the fact that he could not tell him anything about patrol patterns at the fence. He did not want to fuck up this relationship, and not providing his dealer with the information he wanted seemed to be the surest way to do just that.

During the routine surveillance of the two estates on Wednesday, since the DEA bigshot was off to Washington, he had grabbed a cup of coffee and wandered into the main recon control room to shoot the shit with the major in command and pick up what he could on flight patterns, to be in a position to throw Alex something. That attempt was short lived, as no sooner had he gone over and begun talking with the major than the general's hulking sergeant major showed up. After making his manners to the major, he had asked to speak with Danny personally on a matter. They had gone into the hallway, and the sergeant major had stood in front of him akimbo and suggested the captain's time might well be better spent focusing on his own fucking job.

Danny knew he did not have a very commanding presence with the troops who worked for him—or any others, for that matter—but he was an officer, and as long as he wore the bars and was fair and respectful in his dealings with the men, he maintained a certain level of respect from them. The sergeant major, on the other hand, made him look and feel like the hollow man he really was and could barely disguise the contempt he seemed to hold Danny in. Any fleeting thoughts he may have had on bringing the sergeant major up on a complaint of insubordination were just that: fleeting. He was an extension of the general himself, and Danny had seen full-bull colonels not be able to hold his gaze. An irrelevant captain, who most people on the base didn't even know existed, had no chance. He had scurried like a rat back to Auxiliary Control and tried to look busy.

Later at his apartment, after a long twelve-hour day of overflying the Mexican estates they were tasked to keep an eye on, he had felt humiliated at the memory of how cowed he had been before the sergeant major and had spent a bad night thinking about it. Normally he would have blown a few lines and forgotten all about it. But alone in his apartment and unavoidably sober, it worked on him, bringing back dark thoughts of the adolescent hazing he endured through high school that had ultimately driven him to drugs. He hated those memories. He hadn't slept well as a result and had gotten up earlier than he had wanted, showered and dressed, and headed for the diner. He and Alex were to meet at six thirty. This would give them an hour to have breakfast and talk and allow him to get to the base by eight. He had left word the night before with one of his lieutenants that he had some personal business in the morning and would not be in at six, as was the new routine. If the big black bastard had a problem with that, Danny had decided he'd tell the sergeant it was none of his fucking business when he, as commander of the unit, came in and to butt out. Or maybe, as reality returned to his troubled mind, discretion being the better part of valor and not wanting to rock the boat and make himself any more conspicuous than he was, he'd have a little toot and just forget about the big bastard. Rarely did Danny show up at work high; it was just too dangerous. This morning would be one of the rare exceptions to his rules. He needed it badly.

It was just after six when he pulled into the gravel parking lot of Harry's Diner. The lot was half-full and would fill up fast as the regulars all arrived. Harry's had a faithful breakfast following for a dive, fueled mostly by its homemade biscuits and pork gravy. The coffee, though, was the shits, and as was his custom, he picked up a double espresso at the drive-through Starbucks on his way. The two older regular waitresses had no problem with his drinking Starbucks inside as long as they could add the extra buck and a half to the bill that Harry's charged for their bottomless cup of joe. He grabbed a paper and sat in the only open booth. He knew Alex would prefer the last booth in the front dining area where they usually met for the privacy and for the ability to see who came and went, but the fat-assed trucker who was already there seemed to be settling in for the duration, so he had no choice but to take what was available. This meant a booth in the rear dining room. It had the privacy, but you couldn't see shit from there. No way could he and Alex conduct their business at the counter or one of the tables in the middle of the front dining room. Alex would not be happy he could not watch things, as seemed to be his habit.

Danny was really worried about how Alex was going to take not getting this week's flight plans and had come up with an alternative idea. He had no choice but to tell him the truth that he had been temporarily reassigned, but he could also tell him about the surveillance he was now working on. He really did not know as much as he would have liked in order to dangle it in front of Alex, but it was enough to know that he was working on trying to find a trafficker who had escaped from the El Paso jail and who was thought to be well connected to a cartel. This, and apparently the DEA wanted him back real bad. So bad, in fact, that for the first time ever, against all previous orders, they were flying deep into Mexican airspace. The odds of Alex knowing the guy were no doubt slim, but surely Danny reasoned that if the guy was not an acquaintance of Alex's people, then that made him a competitor or maybe even an enemy. That might be information a rival gang or cartel might want to have. Information was the gold standard for people like Alex, and Danny had information. Danny liked that train of thought, and if Alex bit, he would pass out information slowly to keep him coming back until he could get back to his normal routine. For now, he would only say he was looking for some escaped asshole named Carlo and that the search was happening deep in Mexico and not at the border. That would be enough for now. Next week he would reveal one of the estates, maybe Monterey, and the week after, one of the others. He would drip the information out just like a faulty faucet. The more he thought about it, the more he liked his plan.

He was staring at the sports page going over in his head what he now considered his brilliant alternative when Alex found him and slid into the booth, predictably unhappy at the choice of seating. He was also a bit early.

"Hola, amigo," Danny opened.

"Cut the shit, Danny. I don't like you calling me," Alex said quietly and without friendliness under his breath, as his eyes quickly scanned the room.

"Why couldn't this wait until next week? This had better be important."

Alex hoped he had put the right amount of pissed-off attitude in his greeting. He wanted Danny subservient and a little uncomfortable. The anger was not totally feigned, however; he had been real clear about calls to him: don't do it unless it was real important. Not showing for a prearranged meeting was an issue of concern, but Alex would have contacted Danny in that event later on, at his apartment. And he could have used one of his prepaid cell phones in case Danny was compromised. There was no real reason for Danny to call him unless it really was an emergency. Given Danny's attitude this morning, that did not appear to be the case, which meant that his call hadn't been necessary. He had no reason to think Danny had gotten himself caught, so he had showed up this morning. His other two sources on the base who knew Danny socially had heard nothing alarming. But Alex's bosses had been clear about operational security and the need for caution at all times; Alex had no intention of getting caught now.

"I'm sorry, I'm sorry," Danny said equally quietly as he leaned in toward Alex. "I've been temporarily reassigned to a very hush-hush surveillance project and it's changed my schedule."

Betty, one of their regular waitresses, came strolling by the booth, and Danny sat back in his bench and smiled at her.

"Hiya, fellas, the usual?" she asked as she removed her pencil from somewhere in her hairdo.

"Sure, Betty. Sounds fine," they said in unison. Their once-a-week breakfasts together were enough to get them recognized as regulars. Danny actually was, as he had breakfast at the diner several times a week. As Betty hustled off to get Danny his smothered omelet and Alex's huevos rancheros, they both leaned in a bit to continue their conversation.

"What's this about a reassignment? What does this mean? Do you not have my information?"

"No, Alex, I don't, but it's not my fault. I have to follow orders, you know. But I may be into something even better. Give me a chance to explain."

Alex simply nodded as if to say, "Go on." As pissed off as he tried to look, Alex was actually very curious and even a little hopeful that Danny was right and his new information was better. New lines of intelligence often meant big cash bonuses. Danny gave Alex a general overview of the new assignment, the setting up of a small group under very tight security and the general's personal interest in the project. He told Alex that he was now taking his orders directly from a DEA guy in charge named Mr. Smith but that he thought the name was a phony. He promised Alex he would work on that. Mr. Santiago's real name would be a nugget he'd give Alex in a future meeting. *Drip, drip, drip*, thought Danny.

"So far you are not impressing me," Alex said. "My bosses will not be happy to learn that you cannot tell us where the army will be."

Betty came back with breakfast, and as she served, Danny thought about it and knew he had to give Alex more than just the setup. So after Betty served their breakfasts and left, he leaned in once again. "What I've got so far is the name of the guy the DEA is all hot and bothered to locate. He's an escaped prisoner named Carlo. I don't have a last name, but I will also work on this. He was in the El Paso jail and somehow escaped. He is apparently someone important because we are looking for him in Mexico, not at the border. The DEA has some idea where he lives or works, and that's what we are looking for now. I'm telling you, Alex, I think this is hot information—this guy is important somehow."

Danny was getting desperate, and it showed in his voice and his mannerisms. Alex almost felt sorry for the weak little shit. He softened his look; he knew he had subtly pushed Danny as close to the edge as he dared. He had to be careful not to push him over.

"Are you out of coke?"

"Yeah, bitch girlfriend took all I had left Tuesday morning while I was at the base getting into this new assignment. I'm not well, Alex. Please tell me you have something for me."

"Give me your paper, and eat your breakfast. Betty might think there's something wrong with that shit and ask questions. I've got some for you, so relax. My bosses might just be interested to know what the DEA has going down. Eat, compadre."

An obviously relieved Danny tried to force some breakfast down his tight throat.

Outwardly, Alex changed his countenance from "pissed off" to "all might be OK." Inside, he was excited. Anything to do with DEA operations at the border was highly desirable intelligence. An operation into Mexico would really be well received; he had never heard of such a thing. Danny had mentioned nothing of a joint operation; this was all DEA, no Federal Police involvement. That was unusual, and that made it special. The name Carlo meant absolutely nothing to Alex, although he did seem to recall hearing something about the escape some months back on the news. Even if his bosses did not know this Carlo, someone would pay for the information, and his bosses seemed to know everything going on at the border. It was impressive what all his bosses knew.

Alex read the paper and, as he did, slipped the small plastic bag from his pocket into the fold of the paper. Danny was watching him the entire time, and the relief in his eyes as he recognized what Alex had done was pitiful. *This is a weak man, and don't you forget it,* Alex thought again. If ever a source would betray him, Danny would be the one. He was just so weak. After Danny finished his breakfast, Alex slid the paper back, drank a last sip of the truly awful coffee, stood up, shook hands with the still-sitting Danny, and left. For all appearances, they were just two friends parting after a nice breakfast together, to the average person who might have noticed.

The middle-aged woman in Levi's and work shirt at the table across the dining room, sitting with what looked like her middle-aged husband, was anything but average. The exchange she had witnessed and had been quietly describing to her partner and the others on her network picking up her soft transmissions was anything but casual friends meeting, eating, and parting; this was a drop. The twitchy captain had looked panicked when he came in and terrified talking with his so-called friend. And there was no doubt in Chief Warrant Officer Pam Greer's mind she had seen a transfer. This sniveling little captain was spilling his guts about something and doing it for drugs, if the tip from the DEA on this Alex Guerro was correct.

In all there were six troops, including her, in Pam's Criminal Investigation Division (CID) squad working this tip from the DEA. The base provost marshal, Colonel Donny Schaplowsky, had been contacted by the DEA yesterday morning and advised of a possible problem with one of their soldiers. Colonel Schaplowsky had listened to what the DEA had and then immediately contacted Pam's boss at CID, Lieutenant Colonel Billy Ames, and delegated the investigation to him, who in turn had given the investigation to her. Colonel Schaplowsky took no special notice of the named suspect the DEA had turned over. There were about a thousand such captains on the base; CID would either make a case or not depending on where the evidence led them.

Pam, a twenty-year veteran with a criminal justice and police sciences degree from the University of Iowa, was also a distinguished graduate of the Army Military Police School at Fort Leonard Wood, Missouri, and the FBI National Academy. Every criminal in every case she had ever worked had either underestimated her or, as in most cases, were never even aware she was around until it was too late. She was short at five feet four, her soft brown hair cut on the short side but still attractive, and she was a touch voluptuous—full figured, she liked to say. With her charming but plain midwestern looks, she came off as everyone's harmless aunt Pam from Des Moines, not the keen-minded bulldog of an investigator she was. Once Pam got a hold of you, either you went to Leavenworth, or it was determined you really were one of the rare birds that was innocent. While she always got her man, Pam especially despised traitors. She watched as Danny got up, left cash on the table, and, after carefully picking up his newspaper, quickly left the booth.

"Leroy," Pam said into her carefully hidden Bluetooth mic and earpiece unit, "I want pictures of this captain to confirm the ID, and tell me you got pictures of the Mexican perp."

Team B had been sitting at the end of the counter in the front dining area when Danny had come in, and after Danny had settled in the back, he had paid for their coffee and gone back to their pickup truck in the parking lot. Leroy Johnson, one of Pam's best and her team B leader, acknowledged her net call.

"Got the Mex, and Tiny is getting some nice Polaroids of the dipshit captain as we speak. Tiny said the name 'Irwin' is stenciled across his uniform. That confirms what's in the DEA report."

Elmore "Tiny" Washington was Leroy's partner and, at six feet five and almost 280 pounds, was not only the muscle end of their squad but also their principal photographer. While Leroy watched, Tiny was taking an entire series of digital pictures with his motorized Nikon D90 SLR with 180mm lens. "He's got a nice shot, Chief—face and name badge. C team is on the perp and headed down the road."

Team C had staked out Danny's apartment and trailed him to this diner, which had also been mentioned in the report from DEA. They were parked across the highway and had never left their old, beat-up Ford Bronco, leaving the inside surveillance to their squad leader and team B. Pam and her partner, Jimmy Burton, had taken a table in the back dining area for the same reason Danny had a short while later: no available booths in the front. She had picked a spot that gave her full view of all the other available booths, which she was sure the suspects would want. Fifteen minutes before Danny had shown up, Pam had placed herself at a rear corner table so she could watch the room and not be overheard talking with her team. Team C was now carefully tailing Alex but would keep it loose. He was probably headed to his El Paso warehouse, and a colleague of hers had his team covering that and Alex's apartment already. If Alex twigged to a tail, team C would drive on by and disappear. Alex instead went directly to his regular border crossing and then to one of the safe houses in Juarez to make his report. Team C had no choice but to let him go and reported to Pam as such, for they could not yet detain him. They'd be patient, knowing that later in the day, he'd return to the United States, and then his ass was theirs.

Team B would be on Danny, but they knew where he was headed also. They would see where exactly on the base he ended up, which would further confirm his identity.

"Acknowledged, Leroy. Dipshit is a Captain Irwin."

"That's a confirm, Chief."

Danny got back in his car, and after a last look around to confirm no one was watching, he quickly unwrapped his package and, using the small stainless steel coke spoon he kept in the ash tray, quickly bent over and took a couple of snorts. In his agitated state, Pam could have been standing right next to the car, and Danny wouldn't have seen her, his focus was so intense on getting a hit. The rush was what he expected and just what he needed. He laid his head back and closed his eyes, just letting the euphoric first feeling wash over him, spreading out in him from his tongue and throat like a warm shower over his body. Unlike the shit that a few guys tried to pedal in Afghanistan, Alex's coke was uncut and pure. The highs were the best he'd ever had. He desperately wanted more, but using what little discipline he had, he didn't. No doubt the big black bastard sergeant would be waiting for him when he got in, and he'd need his wits if confronted.

He started up the Honda and headed back to the base, pleased with what he had accomplished with Alex. He almost hoped that this recon gig would last awhile, for he knew now he could indeed string Alex along. He'd told him almost nothing and had him clearly wanting more. Drip, drip, drip.

Pam's teams followed their targets, and each went to the predicted destinations: Alex to his office and Danny to the base. Leroy stayed back far enough and kept a vehicle or two between him and the suspect; Leroy was good at tails. Once on the base, they followed Danny until he slowed, turned, and parked in a reserved spot in the lot adjacent to Building R-24. Leroy called it in to Pam, who was almost on base and heading to the office of the provost marshal to meet the colonel and her boss. The colonel wanted an update on the suspect as soon as Pam had it, so her orders where clear, report in first, and then head to Personnel and Records and start doing some homework on this Captain Irwin. One of her other teams was detailed to check out his quarters, on post or off. Pam never made it to P and R.

15

Pam was expected and walked briskly into the office of the provost marshal to brief the colonel, and her boss in CID, who were already there waiting for her. She was addressing the provost, but as soon as she mentioned Captain Irwin's name in her verbal report, her boss, Lieutenant Colonel Ames, did a quick double take and interrupted, asking her to repeat the name.

"Captain Daniel Irwin, sir, works in Building R-24—or at least that was the first place he stopped. He's there now."

"Jesus Christ," the agitated lieutenant colonel mumbled under his breath. "Colonel, may I use your phone, sir?"

"Sure, what's the problem, Billy?"

As the lieutenant colonel picked up the phone and began dialing, he said, "With all the respect I can muster, sir, I'm working on another case, a counter-intel one for the general, and am under orders not to divulge anything to anyone. This captain whom Pam is working in her case may be involved in both…get me Colonel Romero in the general's office, and do it double quick," he barked in the phone as soon as it was answered on the other end. A few seconds later, he said, "Romey, Bill Ames. Got some shitty news, I'm afraid. Based on a DEA tip we got yesterday, we were following up on a potential drug contact between one of our captains and a Mexican national off post. I just got an ID on the captain, and he's on your special-projects list, a Captain Danny Irwin. He just left an apparent drop at an off-post breakfast spot and headed right to your special projects building. Problem is it doesn't look like a regular buy. The CID warrant officer in charge says no doubt the guy scored some drugs this morning, but he did a lot of groveling and bullshitting before his contact delivered the goods. If I had to guess, I'd say this guy shot his mouth off—about what, I leave to you to consider."

The provost, Colonel Schaplowsky, and Pam had no idea what the other operation being discussed was—nor, given the tense tone of the exchange, did they think they'd be finding out anytime soon.

"Goddamn it," Colonel Romero said softly on the other end of the line. "Thanks, Bill. Do me a favor, would you? Don't say anything just yet, but bring the warrant officer, and the two of you come to headquarters. I think you just ruined the general's day."

"Yes sir, Colonel; we're on our way. What do I tell Colonel Schaplowsky?"

"Give him the phone; I'll square things with Donny."

Colonel Romero hung up the phone after explaining to the provost marshal that he could not tell him anything more given the classification of the project. He then picked it right back up and dialed Auxiliary Control from memory. Whoever picked up the phone answered it as he had been instructed, simply repeating the extension. "4105."

"This is Colonel Romero for the sergeant major."

"Yes, sir. He's right here."

There was a brief silence, and then the familiar gruff voice of the sar major was on the line. "Yes, sir."

"Jeff, Romey. Need you here on the double."

"Be there in five, sir," was all Jeff said and hung up the phone. Jeff didn't make small talk or ask stupid questions ever, but especially not over the phone. He'd been about to have a word with Captain Irwin on his showing up two hours later than his team, but that little personal enjoyment would now have to wait. Eating stupid young captains' new assholes in a respectful but clear way was always fun, and this one struck him as dumber than most. He looked forward to it, but other duties called.

As the CSM of the post, Jeff had his own personal Humvee. As such, it was the cleanest, best-maintained vehicle on the base, second only to the general's official vehicle. The boys at the motor pool weren't stupid; they knew who could fix a problem if ever the need arose. Jeff climbed in, and after the short drive over to the headquarters building, he parked in his reserved spot and headed for the commanding general's suite of offices. He passed through the outer office area and noticing the general's door was open and, knowing that he was expected, walked right in. Jeff knew immediately by the occupants of the general's office and the looks on their faces that the shit had hit the fan somewhere. As command sergeant major of the base, he was usually aware of any potential shit flying long before it ever worked its way up the ranks. Being able to keep the general from being surprised by unexpected events from the ranks was one of his top jobs and one he took seriously, both personally and professionally. There was no man on earth Jeff admired more than his general, and protecting him was a privilege.

Jeff knew he was up for command sergeant major of the army, the top NCO slot there was, and, following that three-year posting in DC, retirement. He hadn't told anyone yet, and the general would fight him tooth and toenail, but when it came time to take the CSM of the army promotion, he was going to pass. If he only had three more years in this man's army, it would goddamned well be doing what he enjoyed, what he lived for, and not pushing paper around a desk for whatever brass-hatted four star that might be occupying the army's top command as the chief of staff. Knowing his luck, it would be that four-star asshole at FORSCOM, and his black ass was having none of that. The general would be getting a four-star posting of his own in two or three years, and Jeff would go with him. He could serve out more than three more years if the general wanted him. And while the general would press him to take the top NCO spot, his friend Manny would want him with him. That's the way he'd finish his time in the green machine.

Seeing the head of CID and one of his warrant officers standing at ease to one side of the general's desk along with Colonel Romero was an ominous sign to Jeff. If CID was involved, this was not good. Jeff had his meaty hands into everything on the base except CID. They were an autonomous group and came and went as they damn well pleased. Except for "liaising" with some of their noncoms at the NCO Club over the occasional beer in an effort to stay up on whatever it was they were looking into, he really never had a clue what they were doing, and not knowing everything on a base was a pain in the ass for a good CSM—and he was the best.

"Close the door, Sar Major," the general said as Jeff entered. "You of course know Lieutenant Colonel Ames; this is one of his agents, Chief Warrant Officer Pam Greer."

Jeff simply nodded as he took up a position of parade rest in front of the general's desk.

"Jeff, it seems our Captain Irwin has a drug problem. The provost got a tip from the DEA yesterday regarding a dealer they've been watching and a contact he had here on the base. The provost rightly lateraled it to the colonel here, and the chief and her team were conducting the…what, the stakeout, right, Billy?"

"Discreet surveillance, General."

"Right, a discreet surveillance. Seems Captain Irwin met this DEA person of interest this morning at breakfast and in the process had quite the chat and then apparently received some drugs in return."

"Anyone get what they were talking about sir?" Jeff asked.

Chief Warrant Officer Greer responded after glancing at her boss. "No, Sergeant Major. My partner and I were close enough to witness a probable drop and to observe the agitated conduct of this captain, but not to hear what was discussed."

"Did I hear right, ma'am—a probable drop?" Jeff asked sternly. Despite his size, years in the service, and position, a warrant officer still outranked a CSM, and Pam was a feisty one at that. Without hesitating, she shot back just as sternly, "It was a drop, Sar Major, no doubt in my mind. These people just don't hand this shit over; it was all done under the table or, more precisely, on top of the table—in this case, in a newspaper exchange, one to the other. This captain took possession, all right. We just didn't see the package. It goes from probable to actual when I get my hands on the goods."

Jeff nodded, a sign of acceptance and respect to the lady.

"Jeff, the colonel and Chief Greer are not need to know on our mission and Captain Irwin's role. Given the sensitivity of the mission, what Romey asked the colonel to do was come up with a plan for generally keeping an eye on Irwin's team. All Billy really has to this point is the list of people to keep an eye on; there has not been time to set up anything else. Catching the captain in this indiscretion was simply a coincidence, a case of two investigations randomly crossing. He received the chief's report this morning on the progress of the drug case, and he recognized Irwin's name and called us. Question is, what do we do next? I wanted your input."

"Question for the chief, sir."

"Go ahead, Sar Major," Manny replied.

"This breakfast this morning—the captain go anywhere afterward, or did he just report to work?"

"Drove straight here, Sar Major," Pam said. "FYI, one of my guys watching the diner parking lot swore he thought this dipshit sampled a little of his take right there in the lot."

Jeff nodded his thanks, returning his firm look back at his general, and said, "Simple, sir. I go back to R-24 and drag the captain's raggedy ass to the brig. We shake the captain down right the hell now for the drugs, and we own him. He's either carrying it on him, or it's in his car, one way or the other. We give him a pee test at the brig to confirm that he is really the dipshit he appears to be, and then we ask him none too nice what he spilled."

"General, I don't know what you got this captain doing, and I don't want to know, but does he even know anything that this Mexican national might be interested in? Is he really some kind of security threat?" Colonel Ames asked.

"Yeah, afraid so, Billy. He's into some sensitive areas. He and his team were required to sign an NSA declaration, so we have more than just a dumb captain caught using recreational drugs, if that's what it turns out to be," Manny responded glumly.

"OK, Billy, so how do we do this?" Manny asked.

"Well, unfortunately, unless you got someone else watching this guy on the inside, because we don't, we've given him the chance to stash his delivery somewhere in the building while the sar major has been here, if he suspects anything. Pam's got her team still watching the guy's car outside, so we'll know if he's gone out there, but what I suggest is we have Pam and the sar major go back, the CSM gets this Captain Irwin out of wherever he is, and then Pam arrests him, and as the sar major said, she drags his ass to the brig. You or whoever you want can interrogate him there."

"OK," Manny said. "Let's do it that way. I want those drugs as leverage as well as evidence. Romey, you and the sar major will do the interrogation. Alert the JAG, and make sure there is a lawyer there for the confinement booking. We need to know what he said this morning, and we need to know the extent of his relationship with the Mexican. Get him to waive the right against self-incrimination so you can talk with him in private. I want his lawyer out of the room if possible. You both know what's riding on this."

"Yes, sir," Jeff and Romey said in unison.

They all left the general's office, and Chief Greer followed the sergeant major and hopped into his spotless Humvee. She immediately alerted her team watching building R-24 via her net that she was en route and for them to report. No one had gone in or out of the building in the twenty minutes since the sar major had left, they reported. As Jeff accelerated his vehicle out of the headquarters parking area, he said to the chief without looking at her, "No disrespect meant with my questions back there, Chief; just trying to understand the situation."

"None taken, Sar Major. Sorry we had to spring all this on you."

"Some days it just don't pay to get out of bed, ma'am."

Pam turned and smiled at the CSM. "That's an affirm, Sar Major."

They made the remaining four-minute drive in silence. Pam of course respected the sergeant major greatly, based upon observation and reputation, and he was now certain she was a good hand. He liked tough women who could do the job. Jeff had come to accept and respect women in the ranks. All that was ever important to him, even in the rocky early times, was whether they could do the job, and Chief Warrant Officer Greer sure as shit had the reputation for doing hers. Based on her reputation, which he was well aware of as CSM, she'd have been the one whom he would have had the occasional beer with to keep up on things at CID, but as a warrant officer, she drank at the O Club and he at the NCO Club, so he drank with their top sergeant instead.

They pulled into the parking area, and Pam told her team to meet her in front. After telling them the plan, she and the sar major went in.

"You wait here, ma'am. I'll be back in a second with the dipshit."

Funny thing, thought Pam, how great minds tended to run in the same vein. That was how she thought of the soon-to-be-busted captain.

The hulking presence that was the sergeant major nodded to the curious desk sergeant at reception and keyed in his passcode to access the rest of the building. A second code was necessary to gain entry at Auxiliary Control. He keyed in his second passcode and entered the restricted area. Captain Irwin glanced up from the desk he was occupying, and Jeff could see something in the captain's eyes, but not the typical fear or intimidation of the last several days. There was something else there—more confidence, something. The chief's man was probably right: he'd sampled what he'd picked up. That could explain it, thought Jeff. God, he hoped so. They'd get him to pee in a cup first thing. Not much you could do in this man's army with a confirmed drug test, Jeff thought.

It didn't look to Jeff like the captain had moved an inch in the twenty minutes Jeff had been gone, so the contraband had to be on him or in the car. He stopped and looked around the room, as was his typical custom. Don't spook the target. Satisfied that all looked routine, he went to the captain, who, despite his usual intimidated body language, did not rise but did look up.

"Morning, Captain."

"Sergeant Major," Danny said with little confidence.

"Sir, the general had some information come in this morning and asked me to pass it along to you. Could you join me in the front conference room, sir?"

"What kind of information, Sergeant Major?"

"From Mr. Santiago in Washington, sir, best discussed out of earshot of the troops. Please, sir, if you have a moment."

Danny relaxed a bit because of the sergeant major's civil and respectful tone.

Jeff turned and walked over to the senior lieutenant. "LT, something's come up, and the captain and I will be gone a bit. You've got command."

"No problem, Sar Major—everything's under control," the solid young lieutenant replied. Jeff nodded; this was a good kid, a good officer. He could handle the job he had no idea he was inheriting. He'd be a captain within the month as a result. Jeff walked to the door, where Captain Irwin joined him. They headed for the conference room off the lobby instead of the secure one. If Danny thought this unusual, he did not seem to show it. Jeff opened the security door to the lobby and stood aside to let the captain pass through first, as was customary. Danny didn't pay any attention to the small woman in civvies talking to the desk sergeant until she turned and walked directly to him, blocking his path. Danny stopped, annoyed that the small civilian had suddenly impeded his way. By this time, the sergeant major was standing uncomfortably close behind Danny.

Chief Greer said, "Captain Danny Irwin, by order of the commanding general, you are under arrest, sir." Before the stricken Danny could say a word, she grabbed him by the arm and spun him around, snapping on her cuffs as she did so.

"What's this about—why am I being arrested? I haven't done anything!" Danny managed to croak out of his tightening throat.

The sergeant major grabbed Danny under one arm and practically lifted him off the floor as he headed out the front doors, with Pam holding on to the other arm. Neither said a word until they shoved Danny up against the sar major's Humvee.

One of Pam's team came walking over and said, "We've got some evidence from the vehicle, Chief, and pictures of the interior, but not the drop itself." Pam turned the grief-stricken Danny around and forced him face forward up against the vehicle, kicked his legs further apart, and started going through the pockets of his green woodland-colored ACUs. In addition to the two front blouse pockets, which were empty, she went through the two shoulder pockets, also empty. The pants had standard Velcro-secured thigh pockets, which had his wallet and keys, and a bellowed calf pocket. It was in the calf pocket that Pam found what she was looking for. She removed the sealed clear plastic bag and the white powder it contained and showed it to Jeff.

"More than a gram, I'd say, Sar Major. More like three or four; looks like we have enough for intent to distribute, street value of about a thousand. Only I didn't see any grand going the other way across the table this morning. Don't believe the Mexican national would leave the diner emptyhanded, Sar Major. What do you suppose the captain here used to pay for this shit?"

"I sure as hell intend to find out, Chief," Jeff said.

They none-too-gently got Danny into the back seat, where Pam settled in beside him. Jeff got in the front, and they drove to the brig with Pam's team following, bringing what evidence they had found in Danny's car and the car itself. The day was warm already, probably going to be a hot one, and the windows of the sar major's pristine Humvee were down. Even then, there was the distinct smell of urine.

"Jesus Christ, Sar Major, I'm sorry to have to tell you this, but the dipshit just pissed himself all over your rear seat," Pam said, smiling at Jeff's reflection in the rearview mirror.

He was shaking his head in disgust. "Goddamn, Chief. Like I told you earlier, some days it just don't pay to get out of bed."

It was five minutes to the office of the provost marshal and the brig. They hauled the now stunned and frightened Danny out of the back seat and took him in a side door and down a hall to a booking room. Danny was uncuffed, forced to strip, and then re-dressed in a one-piece jailhouse-orange jumpsuit and a pair of slippers. Pam re-cuffed him, and she and the sar major took him to an interrogation room, while members of her team took his clothes to the lab for testing. The interrogation room, like most such spaces, was a small windowless room with a mirror on one of the pale-blue walls. The harsh fluorescent lighting of the room reflected off the light-colored vinyl flooring and made everyone look pale and unhealthy.

Pam shoved the captain into one of the three metal chairs surrounding the small gray metal table that was bolted to the floor. He looked pathetic, on the verge of crying. She stopped by the break room, grabbed a couple of bottles of water, cracked one open, handed it to Danny, and said, "Drink."

She looked at the sar major and said, "We can probably get the drug results off this asshole's pants or your rear seat, but we want him hydrated and want a sample as soon as he can produce it."

Pam left the room to go file her investigative report and the arrest record, while Jeff stayed in the booking room. They were alone for fifteen minutes. Danny was breathing rapidly, short, quick gasps of air, clearly scared out of his mind, while the large, confident CSM starred at Danny with total contempt. Neither man said a word before Colonel Romero walked in with another captain, a tall, good-looking blonde with intelligent eyes and an attractive curvature to her summer uniform. Both pulled up chairs and sat down opposite Danny, who looked up from his jailhouse slippers with wide, frightened eyes.

"Captain Irwin, I'm Captain Elena Amado; I have been assigned by JAG Corp as your attorney. You're going to be charged by the provost marshal with multiple offenses. These include simple possession of a controlled substance, but because you had more than one gram in your possession, you are also being charged with possession with intent to distribute.

"In addition, Captain, you are also being charged with a far more serious offense: that of violation of the Espionage Act. I have been advised by the office of the commanding general that you recently took command of an operation that falls under the act. You may recall having to sign an acknowledgment of your participation in this command, which also spelled out certain requirements and procedures. Chief among these is to report any contact with foreign nationals. You not only failed to do this, but in your act of meeting a foreign national, the arresting agent says that you appeared to trade information for drugs. Now, Captain, as your lawyer, I am telling you that under Article 831 of the Uniform Code of Military Justice, you are protected against self-incrimination. The colonel here has asked to talk with you with the understanding that your cooperation will mean some room for leniency. I must advise you that given the photos I have seen and the evidence collected in so short a time, plus the likelihood of a positive drug test, the army's case against you on just the drug charges is strong. Help yourself if you can, Captain. Do you wish to voluntarily speak with the colonel?"

Danny looked up. "What do you mean by 'lenient,' sir?"

An obviously angry Colonel Romero stared at Danny for a few seconds. "Captain, how lenient will depend entirely on how much assistance you give us on the EA violation. And by assistance, I mean tell me everything about your contact and what you divulged. Convince us you are not a traitor to your uniform and your country. Do this, and your sentence will be reduced; don't cooperate, and we throw the book at you. You would be looking at forty years. Now, what's it going to be?"

Danny looked at his lawyer. He remembered having seen her at the O Club and not having the nerve to walk up to her and introduce himself. She was so much more naturally beautiful and classy than the string of girl-friends he had collected who had no real interest in him but a great interest in the diversions he could offer. "Captain, I'll talk with the colonel."

"Captain Irwin, do you understand that anything you tell the colonel can and will be used against you at a court martial?"

A clearly frightened Danny hesitated just a second and then, in a barely audible voice, said, "Yes, ma'am."

"Colonel, I will note for the record that this officer has volunteered to speak with you and that he has been apprised of his rights of self-incrimination. Go ahead and ask your questions."

"Thank you, Captain. In so much as the prisoner has agreed to speak with me, we will be discussing classified information. I'm going to have to ask you to leave the room."

Captain Amado nodded, as this possibility had been discussed with her prior to her and the colonel entering the interrogation room. After discussing the colonel's request with the JAG commander, she had agreed to it, as long as Captain Irwin agreed to waive his right under Article 831. She got up and left the room, closing the door behind her.

"Captain Irwin, I want you to know that it is likely at this very moment, the DEA has your dealer, one Alex Guerro, downtown under lock and key, and before this day is out, he will have spilled his guts on everything you two have been up to in order to reduce his time in an American jail. It was the DEA that gave us you. They have been watching your guy for months. In other words, you lie to me, you little shit, and I will know about it. Now, how long have you been seeing this Guerro, and what have you told him?"

Exactly like Alex had feared, Danny told the colonel everything, including who else on the base was likely talking with Alex. Danny's circle of friends and acquaintances that liked to party together was small for the obvious reasons. One of them had steered Danny to Alex. It only took a few minutes to tell his story, as there really wasn't a whole lot to tell. He had committed the same crime over and over: that of divulging the flight plans in exchange for cocaine. He had no knowledge of just what Alex did with the information, just that he wanted it on a weekly basis. Danny was adamant with the colonel that this morning's exchange had been his one and only regarding the Predator surveillance program into Mexico and that he had only told Alex they were trying to find a guy named Carlo that had escaped jail up here. He swore that was all he had told him. Colonel Romero believed him. This was a weak, broken man, and he was too scared to lie.

"I find out you have lied to me, Captain, and all bets are off. You will go to Leavenworth and be one fucking old man by the time you get out. Is that understood?"

Danny was looking down at his clenched hands on the table. It sounded as if he were trying to hold back a sob. He looked up. "Colonel, I swear to you I've told the truth, but I'm scared. Alex said if I ever told anybody about this, his people would have me killed. He said there was nowhere I could hide, including the base. He said his people knew everything, had spies everywhere. You've got to protect me, sir."

Given the possible connections to the cartels and especially this Condor, Romey was pretty sure what the stupid kid had just said was likely true.

Colonel Romero got up and looked at the sergeant major, who had been present the entire time.

"Sar Major, go get one of the CID agents, and have them put the captain here into custody. And Jeff, I want him watched."

Jeff nodded and left and returned a minute later with two of Pam's team, who escorted the now totally broken Captain Danny Irwin to a cell where he would be tested and placed under a suicide watch. The sar major looked at the colonel and asked, "Does the DEA have the Mexican, sir?"

"If you will recall, Sergeant Major, I said that it was *likely* the DEA picked up the dealer. To be honest, I have no fucking idea what the DEA has done."

Jeff smiled at the colonel. Jeff didn't smile all that often when on duty, so this was an occasion. "Colonel, you are one devious and mean son of a bitch, sir, and I say that with respect and admiration."

"Thank you, Sar Major. Coming from you, I accept that as a compliment of the highest order. Let's go talk to Colonel Ames and then brief the general. We need to know where the others who Irwin mentioned were when you and the warrant officer took down the captain. We can't have word getting back to this Alex guy that his source has been arrested. And we need those people watched as of now. We also have to get word to Mr. Santiago down south—see what he has to say and what, if anything, he may want done. Who's running the recon operation while the captain is in lockdown?"

"That's under control, Colonel. There's a top LT down there who can run the show."

"OK, Jeff. Fine. Stay on top of things over there. In the meantime, we need to get back to the DEA up here as a follow-up and thank them about the tip without spilling any information. I've got some ideas on how we might turn this fiasco to our benefit."

"Figured out a way for that worthless captain to help us, have you, Colonel? Maybe feed a few bullshit stories to the bad guys and see where it leads to?"

"Something like that, Sar Major."

Colonel Romero and Sergeant Major Green met briefly with Colonel Ames, who said he would contact their DEA liaison and thank them for the tip and let them know they had their end under control, but nothing more.

Regrettably, it mattered little what level of caution the colonel took in thanking the DEA unit that had contacted them, for the unit was dirty. All it ever took was just one person to turn traitor, and all the good work that this electronic eavesdropping team had accomplished would be all but forgotten. The agents who had been working and flagged the taped communication for action had no idea that they had a traitor in their midst. All the good work they had been doing, even if some of the raw information they were collecting was with illegal wiretaps, would not be remembered if ever the traitor was exposed…all because of one mediocre middle-aged agent with a bruised ego at having been passed over for a promotion several years before.

As soon as the entire team met with the SAC on Monday morning and discussed this new lead, later in the day, the information would start making its way south in the conduits established by the traitor's unknown sponsor. If the Condor had a special gift in the intelligence-gathering business, it was that he had educated his lieutenants in the art of finding those people who were vulnerable, with a grievance or weakness, and being able to exploit those vulnerabilities. Many a flawed but decent person had been turned because of a sympathetic ear and total understanding of just how unfair life had been to him or her. That and the money—there was always the money, and it was significant. The Condor's intelligence-gathering network that Eduardo ran was expansive, with multiple layers of control and reporting. The sheer size of his organization assured a steady stream of information and operational security for the leaders but also proved cumbersome at times, as important information could be treated by those working for the leaders with the same level of interest as the unimportant or trivial. It all depended on the knowledge level of the lieutenant handling a particular information stream or tip. Eventually the information would get to the people with the knowledge to know what was or was not important. As with most anything of importance, it seemed, some would benefit from the delays, and others still would be harmed.

16

As excited as Ray was with the events of the day before, for Bennie, yesterday had been a complete bust. He could not know that Ray had seen him, but he also knew that his best two opportunities for seeing and contacting him would be in the next two days. As he had nothing else to do after the tour, Roberto took him back to the Rodriguez mansion. It was just after noon, so he had little to do but have another fine lunch by himself and explore the house some more. He ended up in his suite just killing time until Alberto returned home. Bennie went down to the first floor at five thirty and sat in the foyer and then the living room and back to the foyer. He finally decided to join the stone lions and sat out front to await Alberto. At least it was a nice day, and he wasn't cooped up anymore in the lap of luxury.

With the new encrypted iPhone that Charley had provided him, he could speak with his old friend about less sensitive subjects and feel comfortable that their discussions would remain secure. He called and gave Charley an update, and Charley let him know that he had just returned from Fort Bliss. Bennie's team leader on the Las Cruces surveillance he'd set up based on Ray's intel was now on their net with the same secure communications. Bennie was a little embarrassed to admit that since leaving Arizona to initiate the Predator overflights, he had not thought about his Las Cruces team, so totally consumed as he was with locating Ray. He called his team leader, who was glad to finally hear from his boss, and received a thorough and complete update on that particular surveillance and investigation.

They had all the principal players and facilities of this particular distribution network identified and located. More important to Bennie, however, was the positive identity of the few players who were actively engaged in contacts with DEA agents. Cops were cops all over the world, and after a shift they tended to congregate at comfortable watering holes that catered to them to have a few belts and blow off steam. Several of the Condor's people were regulars at two such El Paso bars. Bennie's team leader had already managed to get people into both bars as either bartenders or servers. A short list of DEA people who appeared to communicate with the Condor's people was being compiled. Bennie was sure he would have the worst of his leaks plugged soon, all a result of Ray's undercover work.

Alberto had mentioned earlier they would check in with Manny and the others on the see-tee at six, so there would be at least something to do then. True to his word, despite what must have been a crushing agenda of items to be concerned with, Alberto's motorcade arrived a few minutes before six. After a brief warm greeting, Alberto led Bennie back to his secure study. Once in contact, the general gave them an update on the overflights, which seemed to be going well, but other than that, there was nothing further to discuss, so they signed off, agreeing to keep in touch. Bennie and Alberto enjoyed a fine dinner together and drank and talked into the night, enjoying each other's company and getting to know each other better. After a pleasant evening, they called it a night and headed off to their respective suites.

Bennie was moving a bit slowly the next morning, a result of all the traveling he'd been doing but also because of the several bottles of wine he and Alberto had consumed during and after dinner. He was sitting on the edge of his bed when Alberto called to say his cousin had called him and urgently needed to speak with them. Bennie told Alberto he'd take a quick shower and join him downstairs. Alberto was already in his study when Bennie joined him twenty minutes later. There was a coffee service sitting on his desk, and after greeting Bennie warmly, Alberto told him to help himself. Bennie poured a cup of coffee and watched as Alberto logged on to the see-tee. No sooner did he hit send than the image of Manny came up with Colonel Romero and the sergeant major in the background.

"Hola, Manny. Bennie is here with me. How are you?"

"Not good, I'm afraid, Al; get Bennie on the horn, would you."

Bennie, who was sitting in one of the chairs opposite Alberto's desk, which put him in the background of the transmission, got up and walked around the desk. "I'm here, General—what's gone wrong? We lose a bird or something?"

"Bennie, I'm sorry to report it's potentially worse than that—we had to arrest Captain Irwin this morning."

Alberto rose out of his chair and motioned to Bennie to sit down.

"Jesus Christ, General," he said softly. "On what charge?"

"Drug possession but also the Espionage Act; it seems the young captain has been sharing classified information on our border surveillance with one of the cartels or gangs in exchange for a steady supply of cocaine. Essentially, he tells his Mexican national contact and dealer where our birds will be looking at any given time. In the wrong hands—or right hands, depending on your point of view, of course—this would mean that smugglers could move drugs north at specific places with little worry about my people catching them. He's been doing it for months. Some of your DEA people apparently have been watching this dealer and his phones and intercepted a call from Irwin to this Mexican national arranging for a drop at a local diner. DEA told us because the call came from the base. Our CID people began sitting on Irwin as part of a simple drug investigation. Only my head of CID has knowledge of our special project, and then all he had were the team names. At my request, he was arranging for some discreet surveillance just to keep an eye on our troops. After getting an update on the drug case this morning and discovering the name of the individual involved, Colonel Ames realized he had a common name to both cases. We busted the captain when he got on base and have him in lockdown in the brig under a suicide watch. Romey interrogated him after he waived his rights, and he is cooperating. Bennie, he told this dealer that we were looking south for a guy named Carlo who had escaped jail up here. Someone has got this information. Now, given what all you have told me on these cartels, it could be anyone of six groups—maybe even one of the gangs you mentioned. But we can't eliminate the possibility that Alvarez's group got the intel."

Bennie was shaking his head slowly. He was unaware of any electronic surveillance of Mexican nationals out of El Paso, so the operation that nailed Captain Irwin was a holdover from the past administration, another headache for Bennie to solve sometime soon.

"General, given what all we know about the cartels and the way they operate, I'd say the odds are pretty good we're talking about Alvarez's group. He seems to value intelligence and establishing networks to a much greater degree than the others. Did the shithead mention Ray?"

"Apparently no, just this Carlo guy."

"Well, that's something anyway. Maybe keeps the focus off my guy."

"Any progress, Bennie, with contacting your agent?" Manny asked.

"None yet, General, but our first real opportunity comes today at a diplomatic reception. If we don't see him there, then Friday at the president's home, if Alberto can get me in."

"He will be with me, Manny," Alberto interjected. "We are meeting to specifically finalize Saturday's raid. To have a DEA representative as a courtesy is logical. There will be no problem having Bennie accompany me. The real challenge is discreetly contacting the agent, if he is indeed at either event. We need some luck, frankly."

"What's the old saying, Al?" Manny asked. "If I didn't have bad luck, I'd have none at all, or something like that. We need a break, guys."

"Manny, I think you should know that if we cannot make some luck here, I'll be forced to resort to an alternate course of action. Under no circumstances can I allow Alvarez to continue as president for long."

"You're talking Los Pueblos Fantasmas, aren't you, Al?"

"If there is no other alternative, yes, Manny."

"Jesus, Al, should that come to pass, wouldn't that likely make you president? Who'd believe your motives if something like that came out?"

"If it comes to that, Manny, we all had better hope we can keep a secret as least as well as Alvarez has these past years."

The Condor Estate
The Foothills West of Chihuahua, Mexico
Thursday Afternoon

Eduardo Vargas had just finished a late lunch when his cell phone for this week rang. Not only did Eduardo regularly change his phone and number, but the list of associates who would be told the number was very limited. His cousin had taught him that—the need for vigilance always in all matters of security. *Always assume that your enemies are at least as smart as you are*, Pablo said. *Never underestimate them.* Better to put up with all the seemingly silly nuisances like trading out cell phones regularly or never meeting a person in the same location twice or never taking the same route twice than to discover that you had made but one mistake. *In our business, Eduardo, we are not allowed one. It will mean our death or incarceration. Don't forget that.* If there ever need be a reminder of this philosophy, it had been his and Pablo's miraculous escape of the recent Vasso-Barega assassination attempt. Both of the miserable shits had been controlled without realizing they were controlled for a very long time. Eduardo had known them for many years and did not consider them a threat. Yet they had collaborated on the attempt and mustered the courage to try, and if not for the uncanny instincts of the young Ray Espinoza, or Ortega, as he now had to think about him, all their plans would have died along with him and his cousin. *Remarkable series of events when considered in the abstract*, thought Eduardo.

In all his years, it was the one and only time Eduardo had ever seen his cousin underestimate an enemy. It was Eduardo's second time, and the first had resulted in the death of Pablo's father. Eduardo still grieved over that mistake. *Keep your friends close and your enemies closer.* How many times had Eduardo heard Pablo say that? *Remember your Sun-Tzu*, Pablo would always say. *Remember it—shit, I never knew it*, thought Eduardo, smiling and shaking his head at the memory. He glanced at the number coming in and answered his phone; it was one of his men in Juarez. "Yes," he answered.

"My apologies, Jefe, for not calling until now—a problem, it seems, in getting your new number. I have some information from our source at the US Army base in El Paso."

Eduardo became more interested than usual. He had scored a major coup he felt by compromising several soldiers in sensitive positions on the large, important base. The intelligence coming in on this network had proved to be very valuable. "Continue," Eduardo said casually.

"Our man in charge of providing the positions of the soldiers and their observation craft has been diverted to a more sensitive matter, it seems. He has been ordered to look deep into our country for an escaped Mexican citizen from the jails in El Paso. Someone named Carlo."

A now-startled Eduardo set up in his chair and, raising his voice, which was rare for him, asked sternly, "When did you receive this information?"

"Just this morning, Jefe."

"And you are only now passing it along?"

"A technical difficulty, Jefe, with my phone. It had to be replaced, and I only just received your number."

Eduardo regained his composure. It was important to not let it appear that this information was any more important than any other. This link in the chain had been set up by still another intermediary. This caller had no idea who he was talking to or that Eduardo had a brother named Carlo.

"We will let it pass; no harm has been done. Instruct your people to ask when we might start getting our regular reports. And as always, share this information with no one. Be assured that if you do, I will find out about it."

"Of course, Jefe," the clearly terrified operative responded. Eduardo ended the call and then sat back and considered the possibilities.

Have any other Mexicans by the name of Carlo escaped incarceration from a US jail anytime in the last three months? If not, is the Carlo mentioned my brother? How to confirm this? Why the interest suddenly in finding Carlo, if it is indeed my brother? Has one of Carlo's people in the north gone missing and maybe given the authorities information that makes Carlo appear more valuable than he really is? Have the Americans discovered a link from Carlo to Pablo? Is there any connection with this information and our men in the other cartels who have gone missing? Who gave the Americans the permission to fly their aircraft down here? Pablo certainly did not, or I would know about it. Are the Americans suddenly taking a more unilateral active role down here, one we are unaware of? Just too many variables. I need Baca's help, and I need to make Pablo aware of this. Send Corro north first, I think, and get me more information before I bother Pablo. He has enough on his mind.

Eduardo picked up his phone and speed-dialed a number.

A voice answered on the other end. "Yes, Jefe."

"I have a matter of the utmost secrecy that I wish run down. I want you to personally handle this. Contact all of our people in the north who had any contact with my brother when he was detained. I especially want to find out where those we had to burn to get Carlo out of the El Paso jail have been taken and who they have been talking to. I want them questioned if possible. The Americans are looking for Carlo, and they are looking down here. I want to know why. I want to know who of our people may be talking with them, and if found, I want them silenced, but only after we have a chance to interrogate them. There is no logical reason for the Americans to be seeking out Carlo unless they now believe he is more than he appeared to be when in jail. Go north to the safe house in Las Cruces. Make sure you have the proper papers. Do not get arrested for as much as a traffic violation. And, my friend, move quickly on this, and get me answers. I expect to hear from you daily."

"Yes, Jefe." Valentine Corro put his phone down. He had been running informants in the north for Eduardo Vargas for twelve years. Eduardo had always taken care of him and his family, ever since he had refused to bow down to the now-dead Mendoza brothers and use his legal access to the north to run drugs for them. Eduardo could not return his kidnapped child to him—the young boy was just gone—but Eduardo had gotten him out from under a death sentence when he had attempted to kill the oldest Mendoza brother, whom he knew was responsible for his missing son. It had taken years, but Eduardo had let Valentine participate in their recent killing, although his weapon had been information and deception to lure them into Eduardo's trap south of Chihuahua.

Valentine was not a violent man, but he was very aware that he was involved with those who were. He and Eduardo were of a similar age, even appearance, as both were far grayer than they may have wished, and both had intelligent eyes. It had been Valentine who had recruited Alex Guerro and many others for Jefe, and it was Valentine who set up the intermediaries that moved information up the intelligence pipeline Eduardo had created. Jefe was insulated from all but him and had nothing to fear, for he owed him his life. All Valentine did was seek out information and then get it delivered. He knew who Jefe worked for; he'd figured that much out, and it had not been difficult, not with what all he knew. But as long as he was not required to hurt anyone or to actually traffic in narcotics, he was happy to do his job. He owed Eduardo Vargas that much. It required he use his head and not a gun, and he had a good head on his shoulders. He went into the bedroom of the small but well-kept house he shared with his wife of many years and started to pack.

"Where are you going, Val?" his wife quietly asked as she followed him in.

"I must go north on business for a while; I do not know how long. Do not worry, my little dove. I will be fine," he said with a reassuring smile as he gently touched her cheek.

He knew she worried whenever he did these trips. She was unsure of what exactly his work was, but she knew enough to know it was probably illegal and therefore dangerous. Their friends in their middle-class Cuidad Juarez neighborhood, as well as the border patrol and immigration officials who occasionally checked his papers, believed Val to be a salesman for a Mexican auto-parts manufacturer that sold to American companies. He did not get up and go to work like the other husbands in their neighborhood, as it could be credibly said he could work his territory from his home office. They had no financial worries, and it had been that way for a very long time now. Val's wife had no idea how much there really was. Their children's children were set for life. The trusts Val had set up would see to that.

He picked up his leather duffel and walked to the garage, kissing his wife before he left. It was a short drive to the border and then only an hour or so to the small farm south of Las Cruces. He didn't visit the farm often, preferring to stay in hotels in El Paso, but Jefe had said to work out of the farm, and so he would. When he thought about it, it was probably safer than a hotel, as there was no registration involved, so no paper trail for the authorities to follow—and the food would be so much better. No one would be looking for him anyway, but certainly not at the farm; he could conduct his inquiries in safety.

Life, however, was full of twists of fate and disappointments. Of all the places the decent but terribly compromised Valentine Corro could go in America, the least safe within the world he operated in was the small farm south of Las Cruces. Bennie's surveillance team on that project had thoroughly wired the Alonzo Martinez farm for sight and sound. Once made aware of the safe house by Ray's first intelligence report, Bennie's team, recruited almost exclusively from DEA offices in the northeast and the northwest and headed up by an old friend named Johnny Walker from Long Island, New York, had waited until the older couple who owned the farm went into town for their weekly shopping and then had descended on the small house and barn like locusts. With the detailed intelligence provided by Bennie, it had only taken a few minutes to discover the hidden basement in the barn, and this area had both listening devices and miniature CCTV cameras. It would be in this space that those of interest to Bennie's team would be located, so the cameras were necessary. Bennie had no desire to eavesdrop visually on the old couple. They would listen with their sound-actuated devices, but they would also respect their privacy—an oxymoron, to be sure. The team had both doors to the neat and tidy little house covered with all-weather cameras from nearby utility poles, so it was enough to know the faces of those allowed in and then have just their voices digitally recorded. Bennie's team could sort out who was who when necessary.

For ten weeks, the team had been watching the safe house, and the surveillance had blossomed as more and more new faces were identified and their roles and responsibilities were sorted out. The surveillance had revealed several warehouses in the El Paso industrial suburbs that, despite the names and businesses advertised on their front doors or the sides of their delivery vans and trucks, were in fact key distribution points for the Condor's product. With the surveillance of the warehouses came the transportation methods being used to bring the illicit product north in bulk. The trucking and rail interests were carefully logged and the key people in charge added to the growing list of those involved. The Mexican-based auto-parts company that shipped inexpensive and much-needed quality parts to the Toyota truck-assembly plant outside San Antonio had seen their trucks identified as the principal transportation method for the product. Bennie's people had not yet identified just how this was being done, only that it was. Bennie's team was uncertain if the auto-parts company itself was involved or just people within the company who handled transportation. That was often the case: good company, bad workers on the dock. They would discover the answer in time.

Others who passed through the farm were clearly involved in information gathering or dissemination. The locations where they met with the few bad apples in the DEA, local police, and immigration control were now under surveillance. Once Bennie's people developed the list of all DEA agents frequenting the same watering holes on a regular basis as the messengers from the Martinez farm, it had only taken the simplest of investigative skills and approaches to take the access granted by the warrants issued by the federal judge in the Fifth District out of San Antonio and identify the traitors.

A prosecutor friend of Bennie's had once told him that criminals by and large were the dumbest group of human beings he had ever seen, yet believed themselves to be brilliant. They would think a crime through using their limited capacities and break the law, thinking they had outwitted law enforcement, only to leave obvious footprints in their path that made capture and conviction easy. For the three DEA agents whom they had identified as the likely traitors in the El Paso office, all had failed at advancement, had limited potential beyond the day-in, day-out jobs they were currently in, and lastly, seemed to have financial difficulties. The only way they could not be caught was if no one ever questioned them or investigated them, and that was unlikely given the careers they were in and the people they could come in contact with. Footprints—always there were footprints.

Meanwhile, the decent human being that was Valentine Corro, who, in a weak moment twelve years before had made one poor moral and ethical judgment out of grief for a missing child, was destined to disappoint his wife and family because of his relationship with El Condor de Muerte. Not all involved with the trafficking of illegal drugs were evil, but all were guilty of poor judgment, and in the end, their lives would be ruined.

17

Before Bennie had gone to bed the night before, he had told Alberto he was going to attend the funeral service. He just could not sit around the Rodriguez home another second with so much in the balance. He had rationalized to Alberto that while his chances of seeing Ray were pretty much zero at the public events, he sure as hell wasn't going to find Ray if he sat on his ass in his room. Alejandro had followed Bennie to his suite when he and Alberto had finished the last of the wine and offered to touch up his suit for the next day's events.

"Just leave it on the rack here in your sitting room, and we shall take care of it, if you wish, Senor," Alejandro had said. Bennie had a change of clothes, of course, but his dark-gray pinstripe was his most formal, and even after successive days of use, Bennie thought it was probably fine. Obviously the ever-professional Alejandro thought differently. Bennie had not been offended by the offer but instead accepted it. Bennie had not noticed before, but the door to his suite from the hallway had no lock, but his bedroom door did. Apparently those who were accustomed to servants would have known this, but Bennie was on new and different turf here. Before turning in, he laid the suit on the rack as instructed and, true to Alejandro's word, when Bennie got up this morning, his suit had been cleaned and pressed and was hanging on a hook near his bedroom door. He also noticed that his shoes had been shined, and that had been unintentional on his part. After Alejandro had left the suite, Bennie, as was his custom, had kicked off his shoes and sat with his stocking feet on an ottoman and watched CNN before heading off to bed. He had simply forgotten to take his shoes with him. Now here they were, looking better than they had the day he bought them.

Who am I kidding, Bennie thought. *I could get real used to this treatment.* He noticed that Alejandro and the rest of the staff were treating him very well. This might be expected as the houseguest of Alberto, but Bennie couldn't help but feel he was getting extraspecial attention. He liked it.

Alberto had the press of his duties and left early for his office at the Zocalo. Roberto came by for Bennie at eight thirty to take him to the great cathedral for the service at ten. The crowds were expected to be enormous, and they were. The five-lane boulevard that snaked around the perimeter of the Zocalo had been closed to all but screened traffic, so the great plaza had even more room for all the citizen well-wishers. Bennie and Roberto were allowed into the cathedral by virtue of the passes they had been issued by Alberto's office. There was a long line of limousines queued up to drop all the important or seemingly important leaders from around the world, directly in front of the five-hundred-year-old religious edifice. Roberto and Bennie repeated their walk from the diplomatic entry drop area of the National Palace across the street so as to stay out of the limelight. The world's press was in attendance, and Bennie wanted to be no more noticed than any other face in the huge crowd.

They were allowed to enter from the side entrance into the narthex. Their reserved seating section was two-thirds of the way down the great columned and high-arching space just behind the really important guests. Bennie chose to stand in the rear and watch for the Mexican president's entry before taking his seat. Alvarez was one of the first to arrive just after 9:30 a.m., and he looked both solemn and serious, as might be expected, as he exited his car and, with his beautiful young wife on his arm, entered the church. From Bennie's vantage point, it appeared that Ray was nowhere to be seen, as the security people all were EMP, according to Roberto.

Bennie had been raised Catholic, and the long, formal service in Latin brought all the memories back from his youth. His parents had given him and his brother the option when they reached ten and twelve years of age of attending church further. Both had gradually attended less and less, more so because such attendance conflicted with the Sunday-morning broadcasts of NFL football. But by the time Bennie had gone off to college, he was officially in his mind a fallen-away Catholic. He still believed in Christ and still enjoyed occasionally reading the stories, but the institution of religion had made him cynical and unsupportive of their domain. He had been pressed by his elderly parents a time or two at family gatherings to explain why he no longer went, and he generally wussed out under the firm stare of his mother and simply gave work as the reason. Point of fact, while Bennie believed in Jesus Christ, he had long since stopped believing in a supreme deity. He had seen so much death and misery in his work over the years that what little faith he may have ever had had long since been flushed out of him by the realities of the street. His mother didn't need to know all that; she was on her knees praying for his safety on a daily basis as it was. The last thing he wanted her doing was praying for his salvation as well.

The service mercifully drew to a finish. A very small delegation was going to the interment, but for a majority of those in attendance, their duty was done. All told about eighty of the higher-level diplomats and representatives of the many countries in attendance would reconvene at Los Pinos beginning at four for an official reception. Not unlike an Irish wake but far more stuffy, the occasion allowed old acquaintances from around the world in the rarefied air of government or diplomacy an opportunity to drink and socialize. Bennie had a few hours to kill, so he had Roberto take him back to Alberto's home. He contacted Charley and gave him a heads-up on the electronic eavesdropping operation that had snared Captain Irwin. Charley was as surprised as Bennie was and said he would be on the next flight to El Paso to get to the bottom of it and would report back later.

Bennie grabbed his briefcase and began extracting some of the devices Charley had thoughtfully provided him and started organizing them into two piles. He had given this a lot of thought in the last twenty-four hours, and in order to be prepared for a chance encounter with Ray, he wanted him and Alberto to each have a small package that could be discreetly passed to Ray if the chance presented itself. The packages would be identical, each consisting of one of the slim encrypted cell phones, a small burst transmitter, and a simple note on their use and confirmation they had received his message.

The burst transmitter was disguised as a jewelry-quality cigarette lighter that, when activated, would send a GPS signal to one of several communications satellites in synchronous orbit above the equator. There it would be bounced back to earth and routed to Bennie's iPhone, giving Ray's exact coordinates. In this way, if he was unable to use his cell phone, which also was GPS capable, at least Bennie would know his location if he moved and they again lost contact.

The kinds of monitoring systems that Alvarez's people likely employed were set up to intercept the normal radio frequencies that cell phones used. The special encrypted phone Bennie hoped to get into Ray's hands was a frequency-hopping device and encrypted, which sounded like static on detection devices to the untrained ear. The frequency hopping alone made it nearly impossible to get a fix on this type of device. Ray could also use simple text messaging, which was even more difficult to detect given the short duration of transmission.

Bennie took pencil and paper and wrote out two brief notes on the operation of the devices that he intended to use. He wrapped the note around the two ultraslim devices and taped them together. All told his package was no more than two inches by four inches and about a half inch thick. He and Alberto had talked at length about the packages and being prepared if the opportunity presented itself. They had agreed that unless they were certain a transfer could be made safely, they wouldn't try. They may have to settle for Ray just seeing Bennie. Bennie would try to give him a look confirming that his message had been received, but compromising Ray at this stage was out of the question.

Alberto returned home at two thirty just as Bennie was finishing up his packages. There was a knock at his suite door, and Bennie went to the door quickly to make sure it was not one of the servants.

"Hello, Alberto. Come on in. I'm about finished. How was the interment—I don't suppose Ray was actually there?"

"No, it was a very small service, mostly family and a few friends and of course the president and his wife. Panteon Delores is one of our oldest and most important cemeteries and is actually very crowed already with the dead. In fact, if you must know, I spent the entire time wondering who the devil the president had ordered moved in order to find a place for Fernandez. His family is from the north, Hermosillo, so they would not have had an existing family crypt. Yet there was one there for the late president. I seem to recall reading that this site has been full since the late eighties. But it is our most prestigious of burial grounds, so a place had to be made for a fallen president. How do your packages look?"

"I think they'll do the trick. They're small enough to be palmed and passed with a handshake or palmed and slipped into a coat pocket, like Ray evidently did to you. Here's yours. For God's sake, don't try passing it unless you're sure it's safe."

"I won't, Bennie. We both need to be very careful. I will be required to be part of the diplomatic receiving line. I have no idea how long that will take. You will be free to circulate around the room. I will introduce you to Alvarez as soon as we are finished with the receiving nonsense. The diplomatic reception room is on the first level of Los Pinos and is rather like a very nice lobby with many seating areas and several nice fireplaces, that sort of thing. It will be very full. I would think that if your Ray is there, like most security people, he will be positioned to make himself unnoticed. If we circulate separately, you will have the greatest opportunity as an unknown diplomat to do what is necessary. Shall we go? There are several people downstairs I would like you to meet, including Roberto's mother, my sister Angela. She oversees much of our family's businesses while I attend to government matters. She is an exceptionally bright woman."

Roberto and his mother, along with several security-looking types, were waiting for them in the downstairs great room. After the brief introductions between Bennie and Angela, Alberto turned to his sister and said, "Angela, dear, would you excuse us for a minute? I need to speak to these gentlemen in private."

"Of course, Alberto—where would you like me to go?"

"No, no, you stay here; we will use my study. Just ring for Alejandro should you desire anything. Gentlemen, if you would accompany me?"

Bennie had no idea what was going on, but Roberto and what looked like his two bodyguards turned and followed Alberto toward his study, so Bennie did as well. Alberto closed the door behind Bennie, and then they joined the others in the middle of the room. Alberto turned to Bennie. "Bennie, please allow me to introduce you to Colonel Vicente Portillo, my chief of operations of Los Pueblos Fantasmas, and Major Antonio Justo Garcia, my strike team leader. They masquerade as some of my sister's bodyguards so we can meet on occasions when necessary. Because they look and act like security people, given our societal structures, they are largely ignored—call it class anonymity. Gentlemen, Senor Bennie Santiago, a special agent of the American DEA." Handshakes were exchanged.

"We don't have much time, so let me tell you all why I have brought us together. Bennie, I want my people to begin planning for an assault on the estate you have discovered in the north near Chihuahua. At some point in the very near future, I feel it will be necessary to our special classified mission to disrupt the Condor's operations. We may need to provoke a response or an action from him on our timetable, and in my mind that means getting his top deputies. If we do and he has no idea who or what has done this to him, and he does not know where his cousins have disappeared to, we may be able to force a mistake. Your thoughts?"

Bennie had picked up on both of Alberto's signals: the reference to a classified mission and the referencing of Alvarez as the Condor. It seemed

Alberto took compartmentalization seriously even with his most trusted of subordinates.

"Sounds like a good idea, Alberto; we would want those characters at some point anyway. If we can rattle the Condor's cage, I say do it. Frankly, I'm a little tired of reacting to him all the time. How do you want to proceed?"

"First things first, Bennie: we need your intelligence on the compound where you have located these men. For today a general review of the area, but as soon as you can arrange it through your contact in El Paso, a copy of some of your real-time surveillance, the GPS coordinates, that sort of thing. With that Vicente and Antonio can begin making plans."

"Can we have the room alone for a minute, Alberto?"

"Certainly, my friend; gentlemen, if you would rejoin my sister, I'm sure Alejandro has refreshments for you."

The three others left the study, and Bennie looked at Alberto.

"Good-looking men, Alberto—tough, intelligent eyes."

"Yes, they are. That young major is truly a ghost, he and his team. There are only thirty men in the strike team, but they attack like three or four times that. Very skilled, very disciplined, and quite lethal, I might add. They have run a dozen operations in the last year without so much as a scratch to any of our men. The major has his own sargento mayor like Manny's Sergeant Green. In fact, I'm sure that the two know each other; they just do not know they are involved in the same action. He is one of Manny's old sergeants, Sammy Montoya, a very skilled soldier."

Bennie had been surprised to learn that there were American ex-military involved when Alberto had first told him about his private army.

"I know time is short today, Alberto, and we have to leave for the reception. What I was thinking is that we fire up that super laptop of yours and see if we can raise the general right now. I'll explain what we need, and between him and his team, they can get it put together."

"Yes, let's do that."

They were lucky. They caught Manny in his office and, after updating him on their plans and schedule, got his promise to get a video and data package put together. They agreed to contact each other later that night, at which time that information could be transmitted from see-tee to see-tee and then down loaded onto a disc. It was more than Alberto could have hoped for. He would have his sister for dinner, and that would keep his Los Pueblos Fantasmas team here until late, at which time they could review the data together and talk about plans.

Alberto and Bennie and their security entourage, led by Roberto, made the short drive south on Calzada Chivatito to Calz del Rey, the entry street into Chapultepec Parque Nacional (Chapultepec National Park) that led to the entry to the forested grounds of Los Pinos. Several hundred yards into the park at the actual entry gates of Los Pinos proper, the presidential guard and the capital police had Calz del Rey blocked off to all traffic but for the stream of flagged embassy limousines and SUVs going to the reception. A careful check was made of every vehicle wishing to proceed past the little stone gatehouse and down the lane leading to the presidential mansion.

The dignitaries who were allowed the privilege of sharing the hospitality of the Mexican people as extended by their new president were dropped off at the front entry, where colorfully uniformed members of the presidential guard opened the rear doors and escorted the guests up the stairs, through the main lobby, and into a large receiving room off the diplomatic reception hall. Alberto and Bennie did not join the other dignitaries in the receiving room but rather were greeted warmly by Senor Delgado, the senior usher who had given Bennie his tour the day before, and escorted to a side entrance into the large and beautifully decorated diplomatic reception hall. The guests who would be entering from the prefunction space would be passing through the ritual metal detectors now standard at such events. Alberto told Bennie that they would be circumventing the screening by going into the guarded side entry, passed through on Alberto's authority. This would allow them to carry their special packages into the reception without being subjected to any questions regarding the devices or the odd notes. Except for the Los Pinos staff members who were busily putting the final touches on the various tables of finger foods and liquid refreshments placed along one side of the grand room, they were alone.

Senor Delgado said, "Mr. Secretary, the president will be here short-ly, and the receiving line will be formed. You will be to Senora Alvarez's right, then the other senior cabinet ministers, the leaders of the Chamber of Deputies and Senate, and then the chief justice."

"Fine, thank you, Senor Delgado. Will you assist my good friend here while we go through these formalities?"

"Of course, Mr. Secretary; Senor Santiago, if I may suggest you stay in this area and, as more guests arrive, circulate as you wish."

"Thank you, Senor Delgado. Anywhere you suggest, as long as I am out of the way," Bennie said. "I have no official duties to perform or specific people I must see. I simply want to pay my respects and enjoy the reception."

"Very good, sir; I will be overseeing the staff. Anything I can do for you, simply get my attention, and it will be my pleasure."

As they were having their conversation, more of the senior members of the government were arriving. These included all the senior secretaries and deputies, the leaders of the military, and the members of the Supreme Court. Several came over and exchanged warm greetings with Alberto. From the far end of the room opposite the entry that would be used by the visit-ing guests and well-wishers, a door opened, and the new president and his wife came strolling through, followed by Raul Ortega and the two other members of Alvarez's inner circle. Bennie was standing outside the circle of government officials that Alberto was a part of, very nearly with his back to the wall. He saw the president and his entourage coming in almost immedi-ately and was filled with many emotions as he saw that Ray was a part of it. The kid was alive and looked good to him. He hadn't changed really in the last three months except for his attire and maybe longer hair, but he did look older, more serious—but that was to be expected he thought, given where he had been the last six months. It was also the clothes, though. Last time Bennie had seen Ray, he had been clad in bright-orange jailhouse coveralls with a big white "P" on the back and an almost equally large one on the front. Now he was dressed in an exquisite dark-charcoal-gray suit, as were the two others accompanying the president. For perhaps the tenth time in the last thirty minutes, he discreetly touched his right pants pocket to make sure the small package he had prepared was there. He was pretty sure Ray had not seen him yet, screened as he was by the group around Alberto.

Ray and a hard-looking older bodyguard casually headed off to different corners of the room, taking up stations along the perimeter. Only a tall, serious, intelligent-looking man, who Bennie figured must be Raul Ortega that Alberto told him so much about, continued with Alvarez toward the other officials near where Bennie was standing. Ray was in the far opposite corner and likely still had not seen him. The group of officials all turned toward Alvarez and his lovely wife as they approached, and greetings and handshakes were exchanged. Each official would slowly drift toward where the receiving line was to be formed after having exchanged a warm personal greeting with the president and his wife. Only Alberto lingered, and then, taking Alvarez lightly by the elbow, he turned him and brought him the few steps over to Bennie. Alvarez had a very warm smile on his face, a sincere smile, Bennie thought, but there was curiosity in his eyes as Alberto made the introductions. Raul Ortega, an unreadable neutral look on his face, kept his position several steps behind Alvarez but was observing him closely. *Intelligent but wary eyes*, Bennie thought. It took all of his focus and concentration not to look across the room at Ray, who, now that the crowd had dispersed, surely must have spotted him, as he and Alberto were the only two standing and speaking with the president and his wife.

"Mr. President, Senora Alvarez, may I present Mr. Benjamin Santiago, a special representative of the American DEA. Mr. Santiago, it is my honor to present Jacques Pablo Alvarez, our president, and our lovely first lady, as I think you say in America. In addition to being my president, I would like to believe he is also my very old friend. Mr. President, Mr. Santiago came to us with some very important information of mutual interest considering our plans this weekend, and in gratitude, I invited him to stay through the sad events of today and join us in our discussions tomorrow—with your consent, of course."

"Most certainly, Alberto. Mr. Santiago, a pleasure to meet you. May I present my wife, Senora Salena Olivia Delarosa Alvarez. You are, I take it, one of Mr. Theodore Mills's appointments? I had the pleasure of meeting Senor Mills several months ago when he visited."

"That's correct, Mr. President. May I first offer my condolences to you and the Mexican people?"

"Thank you, Senor."

"Director Mills and I go back over thirty years, Mr. President. We came into the DEA at the same time. I'd like to think he considers me a close personal friend as well."

"And what are your duties, Mr. Santiago?"

"I'm what you might call his special representative and special projects director. I try to quietly take care of problems that Ted needs solved with little attention or fanfare."

"Your Mr. Mills is very wise, Mr. Santiago, to have such a friend. Please let me introduce you to Senor Raul Ortega. Among the many duties and services that Senor Ortega provides me, he also does for me what it sounds like you do for Senor Mills."

"Mr. Ortega, a pleasure, sir," Bennie said with a nod.

Raul stepped forward. "The pleasure is mine, Senor."

Firm handshake, never loses eye contact, thought Bennie. *This is a formidable man, a dangerous enemy.*

Senor Delgado, who was standing to one side, cleared his throat. "Excuse me, Mr. President, but it is that time."

Alvarez smiled at the deputy head usher. "Of course, Senor Delgado, thank you. Mr. Santiago, duty calls. Let's have a drink a little later. Alberto will get us together."

"I would consider that an honor and a pleasure, Mr. President, Senora Alvarez." The first couple of Mexico and the ever-present Raul Ortega turned and walked off.

"I too must go, Bennie. What do you think of our president?" Alberto asked quietly.

"Jesus, Alberto, can charm the socks right off you, can't he. If I didn't know what I know, I'd be in awe. A very formidable enemy, my friend."

Alberto squeezed Bennie's shoulder. "Very formidable indeed. Did you see your young Ray?"

"Yeah, I'll keep my distance until the crowd really gets here, and then I intend to make a try."

"Yes, that is good. Be careful, my friend."

Alberto went off to join the forming receiving line, leaving Bennie standing alone. Without really looking at Ray, Bennie looked casually about the room. He was gratified to see that Ray appeared to be doing the same thing. Bennie slowly raised his hand and ran it through his hair. In his peripheral vision, he saw Ray casually do the same thing. The unrehearsed spontaneous acknowledgment had been understood. Bennie would keep his distance but would be very cognizant of where Ray was at all times.

Raul was standing behind Alvarez as he was speaking with the chief justice of the supreme court while the formal receiving line was taking shape. He was surprised to come upon the American who had been a subject of curiosity the day before at this reception, but it also had answered some questions. Raul did not like loose ends no matter how small. To have this unknown American "diplomat" staying at the Rodriguez home, but not appearing on any of the official rosters, bothered him. Raul disliked mysteries, especially when they concerned their most dangerous enemy. Now that this Mr. Santiago's position had been made known to him, he could put the American out of his mind. No doubt Rodriguez, in his role as principal planner and leader of this Saturday's attack, had his reasons to have contact or coordination with the American DEA and to have him thought of as a "diplomat" and not the drug enforcement executive he was. This was where he would now shift his focus as it related to the American. What information had he delivered, and what, if anything, did it have to do with the upcoming operation? He reminded himself to talk with Baca as soon as this reception was over and see what he had as far as DEA intelligence on the man.

The receiving line was at last in place, and the formally liveried presidential ushers opened the large double doors to the prefunction space, where the arriving dignitaries had been collecting. A pecking order of sorts was understood by all as the assembled guests began to enter the receiving line. Heads of state, presidents, and prime ministers came in first, followed by vice presidents and then by the ambassadors and other official representatives. A second set of double doors was opened, and other members of the Mexican government who were not involved in the receiving line started filtering into the large hall. Bennie was grateful that others were filling the space, as he felt decidedly exposed standing all alone as he was against one wall, even if all eyes were following the goings-on at the front of the room. Like his operatives, he wanted to disappear into the background, and standing all alone against one of the ivory-colored stone walls, he felt like a neon sign saying "secret agent" or something.

He noted with interest the entry of the new head of the Federal Police, Alejandro Quito-Perez, and Hector Garcia Ramirez, who was now the head of the AFI, or FBI, as Bennie thought of it, under Alberto. Alberto had pointed both men out to him at his office but had not introduced them the day before. To think that both men could be working for the Condor reminded Bennie once again of their daunting task to expose Alvarez. Much closer to home was this question: Who else in the room was a traitor? Bennie had to operate on the premise that all were and try to make his contact with Ray with that thought in mind. Any transfer had to go unseen—tough, under the circumstances, with all others suspect. Bennie accepted a glass of champagne from a passing waiter and tried to appear nonchalant, almost bored in his posture and demeanor, but he felt the opposite. His eyes never strayed too far from Ray, who was staying by and large where he was, though Bennie never looked directly at him.

Bennie was uncomfortably aware that Alejandro Quito-Perez was walking directly toward him, no doubt with the intention of introducing himself. Alberto and he had discussed that possibility beforehand so as to have an agreed-upon story as to Bennie's appearance in the capital.

"Senor Santiago, isn't it?" The smiling new head of the national police said as he extended his hand. "I am Alejandro Quito-Perez. I'm sorry we did not have a chance to meet before now. The secretary has told me of your visit. Welcome."

The secretary hasn't told you shit, Perez, and he told me so himself. Careful here, Bennie.

"Thank you, Senor Perez. My condolences to you and your people."

"That is appreciated, Senor—truly a tragic event. Your vice president seems especially sensitive to the fact that it was an American aircraft, but accidents do happen, and we understand this."

"You have determined it was an accident, Mr. Perez?" Bennie asked.

"Oh, the official report will not be issued for months, and that will give the conspiracy theorists around the country, maybe even the world, time to foment all sorts of devious plots, but it is clear from the initial investigation that it was simply a tragic failure of a very small but important part of the aircraft. I am curious, Senor Santiago; you had doubts that it was an accident?"

"No, not really, sir, it's just that with the war you are currently engaged in with the cartels, and given my years fighting the same bastards, I sometimes see devils behind every tree. Call it institutional paranoia."

"No, I agree, Senor. My first thoughts were also that it must be another attack, but the evidence is clear this was simply an accident. The secretary indicated that you came bearing very interesting information?"

Liar—Alberto said he told you I was here in an official capacity to coordinate certain efforts and nothing more.

"Forgive me, Senor Perez, if I defer to the secretary here, but he indicated to me that our conversations were to be privileged. I'm sure he didn't mean that his principal subordinates were not to be included at some point, but I took his request to mean that he—not me—should discuss my information with you."

"Not to worry, Senor. I respect your discretion and expected no less of you. I'm sure if what you know is relevant to upcoming operations, it is likely we will discuss it tomorrow evening at the president's residence over some of his extremely fine collection of tequilas and whiskies, not this average champagne, eh, Mr. Santiago?"

"I have never had the privilege of sampling the president's hospitality, and it was mentioned that I may be joining your discussions, but I will readily admit, Senor, to a certain weakness for old and excellent whiskey, so I look forward to it."

"Well, I hope we have occasion to speak again and soon. In the meantime, it was a pleasure to meet you."

With that, Perez walked off and joined another group. As if choreographed, Bennie was then approached by Hector Garcia Ramirez.

This is no coincidence. These boys are two-timing me in a planned way, or my name ain't Bennie Santiago.

Their exchange was as amicable, but there was no denying that at its root was the same curiosity. Who are you, why are you a guest of the secretary, and what information do you possess that we would be interested in? Ramirez also left unsatisfied, Bennie judged. Bennie was an expert, he liked to think, at reading people. There was no question in his mind that Ramirez was less than honest somehow, a bad quality for the presumptive head of their FBI. Bennie thought him disingenuous and shallow, a likely traitor, given Alberto's views and the circumstances. Quito-Perez, on the other hand, was much harder a character to decipher, clearly a smart, tough guy. Had Alberto not shared his concerns with Bennie, Bennie would have not thought the new head of the police a potential criminal. He seemed like a cop—a smart cop at that; given Alberto's suspicions, that made Perez that much more dangerous, much like his possible puppeteer.

Alberto had said the reception would run several hours. The room was full now that all the guests had made their way through the receiving line. Bennie knew that it was likely the president would want to speak with him again, if not as a courtesy to Alberto then out of curiosity about Bennie's mission. He wanted to try to contact Ray before any more attention was placed on him by a possible extended conversation with the new president, so with a glance around the room to see where the known principal participants to his dangerous game were located, he began to drift toward Ray's quadrant of the room. He was lucky in this regard because the displays of finger foods were in Ray's area, so a large number of people was drifting in and out of that part of the room all the time. The president and Alberto were in a large knot of people near where the receiving line had been, with the ever-alert Raul just behind them. The two possible traitors were nowhere near the food tables, so Bennie casually went over. To his great relief, he saw Ray make a small, subtle, but important adjustment to his position, moving more forward and toward the perimeter wall near the end of the serving tables, so that if Bennie wanted to, he could actually stand to the side and slightly behind Ray and observe the crowd while edging closer, as would be necessary. It was as if Ray knew Bennie wanted to contact him beyond a simple sighting.

Smart kid, Bennie thought. *He sees me for the first time in months and allows for the possibility that my appearance here is not just a coincidence but likely tied to his note to Alberto. Based on that, he suspects some sort of contact beyond just a casual one. Good kid.*

Bennie had been right. Ray had not seen him at first when he had followed Alvarez into the reception hall. He had spent the entire day sitting around his casita and the mansion waiting for this afternoon. He had another prepared note in his pocket telling Bennie and Rodriguez about Alvarez's plan to slip out of his mother's estate in Baja and go north. He would decide later just how to contact Bennie further. If necessary, he'd try just walking out once they were in Chihuahua. He knew Carlo would take him whoring if he asked, and he would. Once in town, he'd walk off while Carlo was busying himself and call Bennie immediately. That was as far as his thinking had taken him. One thing he was sure of was that if Alvarez pulled the visit off and was able to get back to his mother's undetected, he'd do so without Ray. One way or another, the end, whatever it turned out to be, was in sight. He was never returning to the capital as part of the deception.

They had arrived at Los Pinos only a few minutes before entering the diplomatic reception room. Raul had gone over their assignments such as they were before they had left the Alvarez mansion. There were no security worries; Raul was only interested in passive intelligence gathering and wanted extra eyes on the room in general. Ray's position in the back corner of the hall near the tables where the food was displayed was as far from the receiving line as was possible, but was in a very good position to observe a lot of people during the reception. It also offered him his best chance to get near Bennie if he showed up. Bennie would have to come to him, but if he saw him there, the old pro would figure something out, of that Ray was sure.

As he had taken up his position, he had glanced around the sparsely occupied room and had not seen Bennie, although he had seen Rodriguez in a group across the room. Alvarez must have also, as he had made a beeline right to the small gathering. Ray had been careful to keep his expression neutral and also to appear interested in all quadrants of the room, but he never had really taken his eye off the gathering that Alvarez was now a part of. Several officials had walked away after obviously making their manners, and it had been then that Ray had seen Bennie on the far side of the group against the wall. He'd manage to get Alberto to get him here. Thank God!

Ray had a feeling of relief go through him that he had not experienced in a long time at seeing Bennie in person. His gamble had paid off; now it was up to Bennie. Ray had been sure Bennie must have noticed him, as alone as he had been in his area of the room. Bennie had shaken Alvarez's hand and then Raul's. Ray had to somehow get Bennie the word on that little complication as well. The note in his pocket said nothing about the sudden interest that Raul now had in Bennie. Raul had brought up the unknown American to him and the others again at lunch and voiced his concern and desire to find out who this American was and what he was up to with Rodriguez. Ray knew Baca was already working on this mystery. This was a decidedly unwanted little sideshow, thought Ray, as if he didn't have enough to worry about. The last thing he needed was a spotlight on Bennie just when it seemed possible that some sort of contact could be arranged.

Christ, if wasn't one thing, it was another, Ray had thought as he stole the occasional glance in Bennie's direction. After a few minutes, Ray had seen that Bennie was mostly alone as the doors were officially opened and all the bigwigs formed up the receiving line. Ray had been pretending to watch the receiving line while watching Bennie out of the corner of his eye when he had seen Bennie run his hand through his hair. *A signal, maybe?* Ray had thought. He had decided to mirror Bennie's actions just in case, and he swore he had seen Bennie nod his head slightly as he raised his champagne glass to his mouth. OK, they were maybe on the same page. It was now in Bennie's court to work his way over.

Ray had known Bennie would be patient and wait until the room had filled. Raul had been at Alvarez's side near the receiving line that had formed. Miguel had been the nearest to him and looked plenty bored. Ray knew he was lucky; Miguel was a formidable man, intensely loyal to Alvarez, and that was where his attention was focused: watch all near the new president. The minutes had dragged on, and Ray had watched anxiously as Bennie had stayed basically put. He had observed Alvarez's two most highly placed traitors, Perez and Ramirez, as they had each joined Bennie. Ray had no doubt that had not been mere social mingling. Someone, probably Raul through an intermediary, had made a point to tell the two traitors that Bennie was someone they had an interest in.

Just fucking perfect, Ray had thought. He'd have to keep an eye on them as well, in addition to Raul and Miguel. It had been a good thirty minutes before Ray had noticed Bennie starting to move around. This was it; there was no question that while Bennie's movements seemed casual and aimless, he was closing the distance on Ray. Ray would watch the others as Bennie made his move. He'd be the eyes and let Bennie do his thing. If they were being watched, he would warn Bennie off with a look, something. Bennie strolled slowly through the room with his right hand in his pocket, his left holding some champagne. A passing waiter with an empty tray gave Bennie the chance to dump the champagne glass.

The hors d'oeuvres spread had been set up with the plates set in the middle of the long serving table and identical displays of food going toward the ends. Therefore, there were two shorter lines of people serving themselves instead of just one long one. Bennie took a small china plate from the stack with the green, white, and red colors of the Mexican flag glazed into the center, and he selected a number of the delicate foods displayed. As he browsed the available delicacies, he was slowly moving to his left directly toward Ray. With his plate in his left hand, he drifted past the end of the buffet; passed Ray, who was toward the wall; and turned to face the room.

Ray made a subtle, very subtle, nod as he walked by. Bennie was certain he was signaling all safe or all clear; there was no warning in his eyes. He knew he was in a position where there was no one behind him—only Ray to his front left several feet away and then a reasonable crowd to his right screening Ray's associate there. He and Ray were lucky; the guests in line were partially screening him and Ray from a great deal of the room. It was only a question of making sure that those in line were people who had no interest in or knowledge of him or Ray.

Bennie put his right hand in his pocket and stood there with the plate in his other, simply looking around, as if taking a breather from eating. When he brought his hand out, he had his package palmed, and then he seamlessly transferred the plate to his right hand as well, holding the cell phone and transmitter against the bottom of the plate. He moved the package to his left hand as he moved toward the end of the table, where some dessert cakes and other sweets were displayed, as if to select one. The nearest gentlemen in line approaching the end of the table were both short Asian diplomats and seemed enthralled with a very attractive tall blond woman in line behind them who appeared to be Scandinavian. Bennie drifted the few feet toward Ray and slipped the package into his outer suit pocket as he went by. Like Ray, Bennie was not schooled in espionage tradecraft per se. He was winging it, and had his mark been someone he was trying to slip something to without his knowing it, he'd have failed miserably.

Ray knew immediately what Bennie had done. Bennie made a quick selection of a small cake and then moved to his right as if trying to get out of people's way as they exited with their plates. Bennie glanced at Ray's associate nearest them in the corner and could see he was completely uninterested in anything but what was happening immediately around Alvarez across the room. He started to stroll casually through the crowd when Senor Delgado surprised him out of nowhere.

"Senor Santiago, are you enjoying yourself? Is there anything that I might do for you?"

Jesus Christ, where did he come from? I swear I didn't see him before the exchange! Was he behind me?

Bennie quickly gathered his composure. "No, thank you. I'm fine—just trying to stay out of the way."

"Very good, Senor; I am at your service if you need me."

With that, Senor Delgado simply nodded and moved off to his duties. Once his pulse started dropping, Bennie's intuition told him that Delgado was nothing more than he looked to be: a good professional usher simply doing his job. Bennie made it back to what he thought of as his spot and turned to face the center of the room. Ray was in his peripheral vision to his left once more. As Bennie quickly located all his known enemies with his eyes, he relaxed a bit, for they were all to his right and across the room. They had been as far from him and Ray as was possible in the large reception room, with nearly a hundred people in between. Out of the corner of his eye, he saw Ray slowly and naturally run his hand through his hair. Bennie did the same a second later. Bennie was sure Ray had just given him the high sign; all was well. With that, he started breathing again.

The next half hour passed by in a blur. Bennie was happy and excited at having made what he believed was a successful pass. He had a glass of champagne when offered, but all he wanted to do was get out of there and get back to his room at the Rodriguez mansion. With the instructions he had written for Ray, it was a certainty that he would contact him tonight via text message at a minimum. Bennie had no idea what the sleeping arrangements were for the team Ray was involved with, but if nothing else, he could be alone in a toilet.

The way the burst transmitter of the special cell phone worked was that instead of a steady radio signal being transmitted, which was how typical cell phones worked, Ray's phone would compress and store thousands of characters of a text message. Then, with a push of the transmit button, it would send an extremely short burst of a signal. The most one would see if sitting in front of a radio signal scanner and staring at the signal-strength meter might be a jump in the needle for a fraction of a second, but nothing more. Background static would make such a monitor jump during natural atmospheric events. As for vocal transmissions, the small silicon chip in the phone's brain scrambled the signal and made it sound like dense static to the untrained ear. An expert in modern communications would, with considerable effort and the necessary sophisticated equipment, likely be able to isolate the static stream, but unless he had three such technical stations and could apply the concept of triangulation to try to isolate the source of the signal, he really had nothing. Bennie was lost in a thought when he became aware of Alberto coming up to him. Alberto, his back to the room, raised his eyebrows questioningly as he walked up. Bennie smiled and nodded, as if greeting him.

"Enjoying the reception, Bennie?" he asked softly, now standing beside him.

"Best damn reception I have been to in, say, three months, Alberto. Thank you."

"That is excellent; I'm happy for you. Why don't we go say hello and good-bye to the president and return to my home? I have been seen enough, and the president knows I have much to do before Saturday; he will understand my leaving early."

"Lead the way, Alberto; I can't blow this joint fast enough."

Their brief conversation with Alvarez and his wife was very pleasant and uneventful. Alvarez said he looked forward to seeing and talking with Bennie tomorrow evening at his residence. He added that he would be honored if both he and Alberto would take a late supper with him after the conference. Both said what a privilege they thought that would be and would look forward to it. Bennie in truth had real concerns about dining with the president, but there was no way to decline the invitation. A dinner with a nation's president under most any circumstances was an honor. This invitation was Bennie's first, and he was already not looking forward to it. With that they made their way out to the foyer, and a palace guard radioed for their car. Roberto was out of the front door even before the car stopped and had the back door open as they descended the steps. Alberto simply nodded his thanks to Roberto, and he and Bennie climbed in. As if by an unspoken agreement, they said little for the short drive back, talking only about the social aspects of the reception in case Alberto's car had been compromised somehow. It was nearing six o'clock; they would have plenty of time to discuss the afternoon's events once they had finished their discussions with Alberto's men and enjoyed a dinner with his sister. They arrived back at the mansion and went immediately to Alberto's study as Roberto went to locate the others. Alberto waved Bennie through the electronically controlled door and then closed it behind them. There were things to say only between them, and then there was the see-tee to fire up.

"Now we can talk, Bennie. Here is your package back. Tell me what happened at the reception."

Bennie gave him a short, detailed rundown of the drop. He was very sure that no one had seen him do it.

"What happens now?" Alberto asked.

"A couple of things; first, I don't think there is any doubt that as soon as he is alone and free from the others, Ray will at least text message me. I told him in my note to do as much, if for no other reason than to see if everything is working. From there, who knows? Maybe he gets in a place he can actually call me. Secondly, he will fire up his GPS locator. We need to track Ray, and that little device makes it possible. We will want to make sure that system is up and working as well. Ray's phone is also GPS capable, and anytime he uses it, we will have a fix on him that way as well. The small GPS device is our backup."

"Good, good. It seems we are off and running. Establishing safe communications was a big first step. What Ray has to tell us will obviously dictate our future movements. Let's contact Manny and see if he has the information you requested. I will want Colonel Portillo and Major Garcia to start planning an operation against Alvarez's lieutenants as soon as possible. The more I have considered it, Bennie, the more I want to strike out against him—and in a fashion that leaves him wondering who has done this to him. The timing is crucial here. If we attack him soon after we attack the Gang of Four, there will be great doubt in his mind as to where the attack on him has come from. That can only work to our advantage. In the very least, it will do great damage to his organization."

"I agree; sounds good. Anything you can do to Alvarez's organization also helps Ray I think. The more Alvarez and his people are looking outward, I have to believe the diversions help keep Ray safe. I hope so anyway."

Alberto nodded his head. "Yes, I agree. Until we can work out how to get Ray safely back, we look for ways to keep the pressure on our president. Now, let's see what my cousin has been up to."

18

A lberto and Bennie managed to establish contact with Manny on their first attempt, and he was as excited by the successful contact with Ray as Bennie was. He transmitted a file that the sergeant major had supervised in putting together with the senior lieutenant now running the surveillance. Manny explained that the team was told their captain had been pulled off for another classified assignment but would be back if the surveillance ran for any length of time. In the meantime, CID had three other soldiers under discreet surveillance who were known to get their drugs from the same character that Captain Irwin had. So far it appeared that no one was wise to the fact that Irwin was under lock and key in his own private area of the brig. In other words, they felt like they had containment of the captain's arrest. Manny said Colonel Romero was working on a plan that could start feeding the Mexican national some disinformation that could manipulate the cartel in a way to help with Alberto and Bennie's plans, whatever they turned out to be.

"What's Colonel Romero got in mind, General?" Bennie asked, a strain of concern in his voice. There were always dangers when you poked a bear, always the possibility of unintended consequences. Bennie had enough to worry about without having to think about what Manny and his counterintelligence efforts might be.

"One thought, Bennie, was to narrow the locations that these people move around to. For example, if we have Captain Irwin pass along in his next meeting that we are looking for this Carlo in the Monterey area, say, maybe that restricts their movements to the other two locations, which are easier for us to observe."

Bennie was relieved. That was a simple idea, one he would have thought of in time, he liked to believe.

"That's damn good thinking, General. I'm for it. Will Captain Irwin play ball?"

"Yeah, I think so. He's a very broken man. I don't think he ever had much fortitude or inner strength, and once Romey started talking to him, he opened up completely. He's obviously worried a lot about the consequences of his acts even as he was doing them. The prospect of a long prison term scares the living shit out of him—almost as much as the thought of getting whacked by the folks he's ratted out. He thinks the people whom his dealer is working for have such a long reach that he doesn't even feel safe in the brig. Someone has put the fear of God in him long before we did."

Alberto explained to Manny what he was going to have his people start planning. Manny agreed that strategically, anything that you could do to enemies that confused and disrupted them was always a plus. There was always the possibility of unintended consequences, but in this case it was worth the risk, in his opinion, because with Ray on the inside, he could give them a heads-up on responses—assuming, of course, that all the equipment worked and that Ray could find the safety to communicate.

With the basic elements of a plan forward in place, Alberto and Manny signed off. Alberto pushed an intercom button on the phone on his desk and asked that his other guests, except his sister, join him in the study. It was only a matter of a minute before the others were buzzed in by Alberto. Alberto spent that minute downloading the file that Manny had provided onto a disc for his commanders. He turned the disc over to Colonel Portillo with instructions to start planning an assault on the Chihuahua estate indicated as soon as practical after the assault on the Gang of Four on Saturday. The colonel nodded his acceptance of the order.

"Vicente, is all ready for Saturday?"

"Yes, Mr. Secretary. Major Garcia's reconnaissance team is already in place and has the monastery under surveillance. Antonio will be joining his team with the balance of his strike team by early morning. They are waiting just outside the city and will fly to the coast as soon as we leave here, and then they will helicopter to the drop zone. They'll rest the balance of tomorrow once they are in camp. A question, Mr. Secretary: Do you have other federal forces doing as we are? By that I mean setting up well in advance of the meeting?"

"No, Colonel, I do not. Our other reconnaissance units are not scheduled to be in place until very early Saturday morning and none in that area."

"Then we are not the only ones there early, Mr. Secretary. Today one of our observation posts watched the arrival of a number of vehicles and a dozen men, who spent the day preparing what appears to be a concealed exit strategy for someone. As you know, the old hall at the seminary overlooks a lake. Our team in position watching the rear of the old hall is at a distance of eight or nine hundred feet east across the lake near the crest of a hill. The lakeshore and road are not visible from the hall because of the orchard that runs down the hill to the lake. From what our team reported, there appears to be an old catacomb or grotto leading from beneath the hall down to the road at the lake. These men cleared the undergrowth, and there is an old stone archway of some sort there. This exit way, if that's what it is, cannot be seen from the hall as you look down toward the lake. All the normal entries to the hall are located at the front or the sides, and I know you have units scheduled to cover these during the raid. The rear of the hall has none, and as I understand your deployments, sir, you have no units at the rear."

"That is correct. We have that lower road covered, of course, but where it meets the highway to the north. My chief planner explained that as there was no escaping from the rear, our troops on the flanks would be sufficient."

"Under normal circumstances, Mr. Secretary, I would agree. But it seems someone knows something about the architecture of the old hall that we do not. They have set up a concealed camp of their own near the exit. There was no mistaking their actions according to the sargento mayor in charge of our team. They laid out fields of fire aimed at the exit before setting up camp."

"What do you conclude from this activity, Vicente?" Alberto asked.

"Only two possible scenarios make sense, Mr. Secretary, given their fire planning. Either they are there to make sure someone gets away and the fields of fire are to provide cover fire after someone has exited the grotto, or they are there to allow no one to leave by this exit and then they themselves get away. As this team of men is not part of any of your plans, Mr. Secretary, they can only be associated with one or more of the cartels to be present."

Alberto looked at Bennie, and Bennie looked back. Both were thinking the same thing. "You will have to deal with this potential threat, Colonel," Alberto said.

"We have already revised our plans to do so, Mr. Secretary."

"Fine, then we will not keep you further. I need to have a word with my sister, but under the circumstances I think we should cancel our dinner and allow you to return to your people. You will be back soon, and I will look forward to a future dinner. Thank you, gentlemen."

Alberto showed everyone out and embraced his sister, and they left.

"My offer of dinner still stands for you, of course, Bennie. Please, let's go in."

They sat down in the formal dining room, both at one end of the large table. Alejandro and his staff had already removed the place settings for the others who had left, and he began their food service after first pouring them each a glass of wine. After only two nights, their little dinners together had already become a pleasant ritual. When they were alone, Alberto asked, "Is there any doubt in your mind that Alvarez is somehow responsible for this strange group at the rear of the monastery?"

"None, Alberto, but the big question is, what are they up to and why? Is it a way out for people he may have inside the other cartels, for instance? That was my first thought. My second was that perhaps one of the other leaders knew of this grotto and has plans to use it as a backup if all hell breaks loose. If he shared this with a lieutenant, and some traitor has tipped Alvarez, then he has some of his people there to make sure no one escapes.

Unlike you and your people, the president wants no survivors. But who are we kidding; the possibilities are endless. But those are my best guesses."

"I agree, Bennie, but I believe it is a combination of your two thoughts. It is entirely logical to assume that Alvarez has the other cartels as penetrated as he does the government. He has shown a great talent for patience, especially when it comes to intelligence gathering. He must have people in with the other cartels. That is how he knows of this meeting in the first place. It stands to reason that he would want to save his people if they are in the entourages of the others. This escape route allows his people to get their leaders out of my fire but leads them right to the slaughter. Alvarez kills two birds with one stone. The question is, what do we do?"

"The Alvarez goons, if that's what they are, are probably nothing more than soldiers. The folks who try to use that escape, on the other hand, would likely be high-value individuals from an intelligence point of view. Your guys may have to take out a bunch of the goons to be in position to perhaps capture others."

Alberto was sadly shaking his head. "A great loss of life to be in position to capture anyone, but I am afraid there will be a great loss of life anyway come Saturday. There will be no less than eighty to a hundred of the Gang of Four when you take into account their entourages. All will be well armed. We assume that many of the soldiers will be posted outside, and we will take them there. But our intent with the principals is to capture and bring them before our justice, not just elimination. If they resist, which is likely, there will be terrible bloodshed—a terrible business."

Bennie, who was looking at Alberto, nodded in agreement and then asked, "I'm curious, Alberto: a monastery? I haven't heard you mention that before."

"The greatest of ironies, apparently, Bennie, that we have an opportunity to deal with the six or eight worst criminals in our history in what may turn out to be a quite terrible fight at a place of God—Saint Thomas of Aquinas on the Lake, near Los Mochis in the state of Sinaloa. It may be that one of the Gang of Four is a financial patron saint of the seminary. There has been a monastery there not far from the coast overlooking a beautiful inland lake since the fifteenth century. The Church began a seminary there in the 1920s, and it has persevered all these years, although with diminishing numbers. Still many of the priests that serve all over not only our country but in Central and South America took their education and their ordination at Santo Tomás de Aquino por el Lago. Our Church leader here in Mexico, Cardinal Elvira, was a student there.

"The seminary is located on the grounds of the old monastery. There is an old building there—very lovely really, set apart from the main campus—that was probably a retreat at one time but over the years was turned into a community building or meeting hall. Like several of the other important structures, it sits on the edge of a bluff overlooking a lake. Our informant told us that the Gang of Four has used this site before in their infrequent gatherings. It is perfect for them—I mean, a monastery, for heaven's sake. It would be the last place you'd think to look.

"There is an airport not far away at Los Mochis, a major highway runs by within a mile or so, and the ocean is but ten or twelve miles away. The bandits can use many different forms of travel to get to or out of the area. Once there, they simply drive to the rear areas of the seminary and conduct their business in private. It is a good mile from the highway back into the monastery grounds on the main entry road through relatively dense woods. Very easy for their entourages to observe and defend. We knew, of course, from our aerial photos that there was this lower access road to the lake that comes off the highway to the north. We intended to stage some of our teams there, where this road meets the highway, and will still do so after the major has dealt with this new threat."

"Jesus, Alberto, a complicated and dangerous business, I'm afraid. How many men will you be using?"

"In total, about two hundred and fifty. My Los Pueblos Fantasmas, as was mentioned, is already on site reconnoitering for the main forces, which will be quietly put in place by tomorrow night. Our forces will bivouac in the woods on the grounds and try to go undetected for the fourteen or sixteen hours we must wait for the cartel leaders to arrive. My other forces will only be told of the presence of a special reconnaissance force under my command tomorrow night. We anticipated that the cartels would also be sending in advance security parties, just not as early as they have apparently started to do, and Los Pueblos Fantasmas will deal with them silently. We have no idea if the Church officials have any idea who exactly they have allowed to reserve their meeting hall, and we will not make contact with the seminary leaders until just before we attack.

"I am using our best forces, Bennie—the top units from our national police's counterterrorist units and the best company of our army's special forces. We executed what they believed to be a surprise operational-readiness drill on them and have had both units at a remote training camp outside of Ciudad Obregon for a full week. Only General Lozano, our secretary of national defense, and I knew of the real purpose of the drill. In training exercises of this nature, all are told that no personal communication devices are allowed, except by certain senior officers. We then performed both inspections and security screenings to make sure this directive was followed once they arrived at the camp. We found about a dozen men with cell phones and not only removed these soldiers but placed them in the brig at Camp Diaz near Hermosillo until this operation is complete. Several have very insufficient stories as to why exactly they disobeyed a serious order. Four of the twelve are officers, including the executive officer of the company. We suspect that we will ferret out a number of cartel informants when all is said and done. General Lozano, who is an old friend from the south and whom I believe is reliable, began briefing his troops only yesterday on the real purpose of the various training exercises and maneuvers they have been running. He gave our two top field commanders the plan, and he reports that morale is high, and there is great anticipation from his command. The actual plan is mostly Manny's, although Lozano thinks it is mine, so I have confidence in its success."

"Well, given that the plan was from the general, I'll bet your general Lozano was impressed."

"Indeed he was, Bennie," Alberto said with a small laugh. "He said that I may have missed my true calling as a strategist and that he could not have crafted a finer basic plan himself; most gracious, really, of the general."

Bennie nodded, his smile turning to a concerned, determined look.

"Jesus, Alberto, I don't want to seem all paranoid here, but in our business, it seems to be an occupational reality that trust is a very valued and elusive commodity. I take it you really do trust the defense secretary?"

"I realize given the revelations surrounding Alvarez, a friend of many more years than Salvador Lozano has been to me, that it is hard to trust. But I have no reason to doubt Lozano. He has commanded troops that have battled the cartels and been wounded on several occasions over the years. And think about it for a second; if he is compromised by one of the others, I would think Alvarez would know. And if he is working for Alvarez, he will be doing his bidding, and that means helping me kill or capture as many of the bastards as we can anyway. But like my family, Lozano comes from old money, so he is less susceptible to bribes or other influences. I think he is an honest man."

Bennie started to say something, but Alberto smiled and raised his hand to stop him.

"Yes, my friend, I know; I know what you are thinking. Alvarez is one of the wealthiest men in the country, and he appears to be a criminal of the highest order, and that is most disturbing. Perhaps second only to confirming who was responsible for Emilio's death, that is the question I most want answered by Pablo Alvarez. Why, given his personal history, has he become this monster? These are questions, my friend, that I am very anxious to have answered."

With that, the two new friends finished their dinner. They had grown very close over the last several days. The circumstances that had thrown them together seemed to demand it, but they would have become friends under any circumstances. They were of like minds and personalities despite the differences in their countries of origin and their personal histories. It was near nine o'clock when they finished dinner, and they had still not heard from Ray. As they retired to their respective suites to turn in, Bennie promised Alberto he would alert him if and when he did.

19

I t was after seven before Alvarez and his inner circle returned to the mansion. Alvarez and his wife were hosting a small private dinner for several of the heads of state, so Ray and the two others took a simple dinner in their private dining room and then left by way of the kitchen to return to their casitas. After they had first arrived in Mexico City from the Alvarez home in Baja, where Alvarez had made the transition from the Condor to himself, Ray had spent several hours over several days after moving into the casita casually checking his room for electronic surveillance devices. He was sure there were no CCTV cameras to keep watch over him, but he was less sure about listening devices, so he would text only. He read the note that Bennie had included on the operation of the cell phone and the clever GPS device and felt comfortable he could properly operate them. It was easy, really, but so like Bennie to lay everything out in detail. His sense of relief at seeing Bennie and finally being able to communicate with him had lifted a great weight from his shoulders. He'd been feeling so lost, so guilty at not being able to stop the assassination and prevent the deaths of so many innocent people. He had been certain his failures during his mission would see him dismissed from the DEA if, somehow, he could ever get back to his country. But the closer he got to Alvarez and Raul, the deeper he was absorbed into the cartel, the more the possibility of returning home seemed nonexistent. And then there was the nobility of Alvarez and Raul. What they were trying to do helped so many people, saved so many lives, and in the end, was good. He could see a life with purpose helping his friend Raul, but with Bennie's presence and note, that now was all changing again, and he found himself sinking even deeper into an emotional quandry.

He sat up against the headboard and, using only the light of the glowing touchscreen, tapped out his first message to Bennie:

Very glad to see you thanks for
phone. Confirm you got my note.
Alvarez's dad longtime cartel leader
Vargas bros Chihuahua. Alvarez
learned of this at 38; assume you
know background. Given choice
arrest dad or join, joined dad.
Dad later betrayed and killed by
Traitor working for gang of 4.
Alvarez discovered who and
personally killed assassin.
Dad's true life plus his death
affected A deeply. Alvarez deeply
religious. Conflicts between
long held beliefs and dad's true
identity hard to handle.
Best guess Alvarez insane, also
smart and very dangerous. Sees
saving his people by eliminating
other cartels as path to salvation.
That's motive to be president.
Refer Plato, philosopher king.
Alvarez and Raul not evil.
That's a problem for me.
See chance to act if we must.
Alvarez plans last trip to see

Vargas bros mon or tue.
Will travel to family home in Baja
Then move to Pena estate thru secret
tunnel then from Baja as Pena to
Chihuahua estate as condor.
Must get him in north when exposed.
Alberto deputies Garcia and Ramirez dirty.
I need to know if we are good.
I've killed 2 men, didn't stop assassination
am I jammed up?

There was so much more to say and report, but Ray was satisfied with the start. He hit the Send button, and the message was encrypted and transmitted. The phone went back to the ready screen in an instant because of the programming on the small bit of silicon at the heart of the sophisticated but simple-looking device. There was nothing to do now but wait for a response, and he knew he would not sleep a wink until he heard back from Bennie. Suddenly returning to his old life didn't feel as impossible as it had just a few days ago.

The Rodriguez estate was only a couple of miles from Casa Rosado, but it might as well have been two thousand, as isolated as Ray had felt when he had first understood that Bennie was staying there, and there was nothing he could safely do about it. As short a distance as he was physically from Bennie, the path of the electronic signal Ray sent was as far. The burst of condensed and encrypted radio signal found the nearest ground-based cellular antenna and then was transmitted straight up. The signal bounced off the designated satellite and returned to Earth to be picked up by a special dish antenna on the roof of the DEA headquarters in Washington. It shot down through a fiber-optic connection to a mainframe computer that analyzed the signal and the encrypted command code that then directed the signal to retrace its path back to the designated receiver—in this case, the cell phone and laptop of one Bennie Santiago.

Meanwhile, across the great Chapultepec park, Bennie was standing in the bathroom in his boxer shorts when the message came into both his laptop and his new fancy cell phone. His laptop was in the other room, but the phone was sitting on the glass shelf above the stone vanity as he stared mindlessly into the mirror, brushing his teeth. He had never received a text message before with this new device, so the strange ringtone and vibration surprised him at first. He stopped brushing and picked the phone up.

The touchscreen instructions were simple, and he followed them to retrieve the text message the onscreen alert said was waiting for him. It had been three long months and many sleepless nights, but there on the screen in the simple keystrokes of the text message, in the shorthand so easily understood by ten-year-olds, was his first direct word from Ray. In the simple note was the beginning of understanding, the truth becoming clear as he glanced over the abbreviated words and phrases. Alberto thought it possible that his old friend Alvarez was nuts, and Ray's explanation and speculation seemed to go a long way to confirming it. Bennie thought back and could not recall Alberto saying much about Alvarez's father. It seemed he had been raised by his mother only. This now also was explained. Who the hell had his father been? He had to ask Alberto that one.

Bennie walked to the desk in his bedroom and sat down. He selected the Reply button and touched it and then slowly with his somewhat chubby thumbs typed out his reply to Ray:

Alberto got note contacted me.
Good job on passing it.
Who was alvarez father?
How did you get so close?
How does alvarez become pena?
How does pena or condor get north?
We have chihuahua and hermosillo
house under safe surveil
from overhead. Alberto best of good
guys and already working on raid in

chihuahua with goal of getting vargas
bros alive. Vargas bros at chi house now.
Understand ramirez, Garcia, and baca
dirty. Who else?
Heads up on possible leak our side
army in el paso. Word is out dea looking
for carlo in the south. You not
compromised in leak but be careful
as the carlo being sought is one who
busted jail el paso. Because you
with him others may take notice.
If you suspect as much, bug out.
Need you alive to help make case
against alvarez. actions don't
exonerate his trafficking and murders
no matter how noble they appear.
He is enemy number one, you must
believe. Need you out alive you
not to blame and not jammed.

It took Bennie forever to hunt and peck out the message to Ray with his thumbs. He no sooner sent it, it seemed, when Ray quickly responded. Clearly the kid had smaller thumbs and had texted a lot before this.

Thank you for believing in me.
I'm torn, Raul Ortega a good man
doing bad things for just cause.
When does good end and evil begin?
Alvarez dad armando vargas
chihuahua but also octavio pena
baja salt company. Salt and cruise
lines big path for drugs to north.
Dad mastermind behind multi

identities. Did it first with success for
years. Alvarez mom's family name.
I'm bodyguard and friend to carlo so too
close to call and communications
monitored 24/7 by baca team.
Last week saved alvarez from
assassination attempt by vasso and
barega by chance. Killed assassin
no choice. Vasso and 2 bodyguards
dead. Alvarez sees me as savior
part of God's plan to help him with
long time goal to be prez and get
gang of 4 who were behind death of
father and attempt on him. Alvarez
has gang of 4 deeply penetrated.
Oldest friend in alvarez inner circle
killed in assassination attempt.
Me named to replace now have to
be extra careful as always around
others in circle. Bad news leak el paso.
These people very smart, especially
raul ortega and ed vargas.
Ed has extensive intel network.
Baca and aide lorenzo key.
Baca knows all and has access
to everything in gov. Do not use gov
computer he sees all. Lots of small fry
in gov dirty. Baca key to getting this info.
General ramos of palace guard dirty, do
not know who else. tunnel connects
alvarez guest house with pena guest
house baja. Pena security dirty, knows
alvarez secret as do pilots of plane.

That and inner circle and ed all who know
truth. 11 total. P200 plane takes condor
to north in black flights under radar fast.
As pena he flies out of la paz private.
Could bug out before baja trip early next
week but not easy and deadly if I fail.
Should iI try? What raid in chihuahua?
Maybe I bug out in confusion if good
guys don't shoot me? How army
involved? Am running out of luck.
Time to get me the fuck out, boss.
Alive sounds good. Beers on me.

Jesus, Bennie thought as he read the message, *what a mess. An assassination attempt and Ray saves the guy. If he doesn't, he's probably dead. No choice, it sounds like to me. Wait till Alberto hears about that. And what the hell is the reference to philosopher kings? What the hell does that mean? Alberto was right on the money with his guess on the two Baja estates next to each other. Sounds like only eleven people know the truth about Alvarez. That also explains how he has kept such a big secret so long. Still, amazing no one has ratted him out all these years. Such loyalty makes them dangerous. At least Alberto has his confirmation on Ramirez and Garcia as dirty and General Ramos too. That helps.*

As Bennie read the second text message and began to grasp what all Ray was telling him, he admitted to himself he could not imagine what Ray had been put through. The message explained much, but there were many unanswered questions. Bennie was deeply troubled by the "God's plan" reference and to the personal conflicts Ray was obviously experiencing. His admiration of Alvarez was probably a touch of the Stockholm syndrome he'd been suspecting, but he didn't know what to do about it. The more he learned, the more he was convinced that Alvarez was a total loon. History was full of countries with lunatic leaders, but this was too close, and this was now. He needed to respond to Ray and get with Alberto immediately, regardless of the hour. He picked up the telephone and punched in the two-digit extension that Alberto had given him. Alberto picked up the phone on the first ring.

"Yes?"

"Alberto, it's me. Sorry to disturb you, but I have some news—we need to talk."

"Come to my suite, Bennie, just down the hall. We may speak freely here."

"Five minutes, thanks." Bennie tapped out a message as quick as his thumbs would allow:

Do not bug out yet unless you
feel imminent threat to life or
exposure. Understand why you
had to kill. Not to worry
I'd done same. Also understand
your feelings cant answer
good versus evil question wish
I could. Lets bring you in. the rest
We will sort out together.
Our army part of team.
Alberto cousin is our general
in charge at our border. His assets
watching houses in north. Great
intel. Alberto has special force
unknown to Alvarez that will target
vargas bros and can cover your
escape from chi as long as we
can stay talking and coord.
Hold on for now we will get you
out next week at chi house or wherever you go.
Call when you can 24/7
fucking thumbs too fat for this
texting shit. I buy all beers.

Bennie punched Send and then quickly went back through the messages and wrote them out for his discussion with Alberto. He grabbed a bathrobe, his phone, and the written messages and headed to Alberto's suite.

Back across the Bosque de Chapultepec, Ray read through Bennie's last message and then reread them all several times. He was hesitant to keep them or delete them. If the others found the phone on him, he could see no way of talking himself out of the discovery. If that happened, he'd be dead and would not want the messages to fall into Alvarez's hands. He took a few minutes and explored the programming of the phone and found where he could make operating it a password-coded function, so he did that for now. Baca was a genius—he probably could defeat any password-protected programming easily—but that was as much as Ray was willing to do tonight. Reading Bennie's words was the greatest comfort Ray had felt in a long time. Just having them made him feel as if his nightmare was about over. He'd wait and do his job for just another week, maybe. He would carefully watch and listen for any interest in the search for Carlo. *What the hell was that all about,* he thought. Bugging out of the heavily guarded presidential home was no easy task; he would do it from Los Pinos if necessary. It may also be possible if he did not have to accompany Alvarez. Everyone relaxed when Alvarez was somewhere else. He knew what Bennie was asking about making a lawful case against Alvarez. He'd be the star witness, no doubt. But he was not about to die trying to keep that goal possible.

Bennie lumbered down the richly carpeted hall in his bathrobe and bare feet, the soft scalloped glow from wall sconces lighting the way. Alberto, who had put on an undershirt and slacks, was also barefoot, standing in his doorway to let him in. Bennie simply nodded and walked in while Alberto closed the door behind them.

"I take it we can speak freely in here?"

"Yes, I have the entire house swept regularly by my special friends, but especially my suite and library. While we were at the reception earlier today, the colonel did so. In addition, they have also placed those clever little electronic jammers about the room. There and there," he said, pointing them out on the shelves.

"That also means that your special phone also likely does not operate in here if Ray should happen to call. Please, sit down."

"That's a bummer about my phone not working in here, but I don't think I'll hear from him again tonight. He did contact me, and I need you to know what I know."

They sat down on the couch in Alberto's sitting room, and Bennie spread his notes out on the coffee table. Bennie showed Alberto the messages as they appeared on the touchscreen and then the written copies he had made. Several times as the hunched-over Alberto read and reread them, he raised an eyebrow or muttered "good God" under his breath. Finally, after a few minutes, he looked up at Bennie.

"My first two thoughts, Bennie? Your Ray is someone I really wish to know as a friend. His courage and intelligence are extraordinary. The entire assassination-attempt story is chilling but does explain his rise in the organization. I am glad to hear that Vasso is dead; he was about number seven or eight on my list of people to get. Next time you have the chance, how about clearing up the status of Barega? It is a little unclear from Ray's message. He's also in my top ten. Secondly, can there be any doubt that my old friend Pablo has lost all sense of reality? He must have, for he is giving us our opportunity, as I am sure you read. I cannot believe Alvarez is doing something as stupid as visiting his cousins. That he believes he can get away with slipping out of what is now the presidential retreat in Baja unseen, with all the media and protection that will be there that he does not control, is further evidence in my mind of just how out of touch with reality he has become. He appears to feel he can do most anything he wishes. And Ray's reference to Alvarez as a philosopher king—that also explains much but also reinforces my view that he is quite insane, as Ray suggests."

"I know I'm revealing my ignorance here, Alberto, but I have no clue what this 'philosopher king' crap is about."

Alberto smiled warmly at his new friend. "You are one of the most intelligent people whom I have had the privilege to work with in our field, Bennie. It is just that in the typical curriculum that leads us to law enforcement, we have less need for the formal study of philosophy. I only did because it was required in my studies at the Jesuit schools that Alvarez, Emilio, and I attended. The Jesuits have a very classically based curriculum. Latin, philosophy, classical literature: they all were required areas of study. We also were required to study theology and ethics, which, given the behavior of my old friend Pablo Alvarez, would seem to indicate that he has forgotten everything the Jesuits tried to teach us. Philosopher kings are a theme from Plato's great work *The Republic*, in the utopian city-states he wrote about. In such cities only those kings who were indeed philosophers, as Plato defined such men, or philosophers who were elevated to kingship had the goodness and the wisdom to rule. It was really Emilio's and Pablo's area of interest, not mine, but you run in the same circles, and you become part of the discussions. I haven't thought about it in years, but it all strangely makes sense."

Alberto paused for a second, just staring into space, as if thinking about himself and Alvarez in their youth, before going on in a melancholy tone.

"Pablo Alvarez was always deeply interested in religion and philosophy as it applied to our personal lives, to our history, and to government, for that matter. I recall a debate I attended at the university during a history seminar on the subject of republican government versus dictatorship. I don't know what you know of our history, Bennie, but in our distant past, we had the occasional problem with dictators as presidents. Jesus, this is years ago in school and is something I would have never recalled if not for this philosopher king reference. Surprising everyone in the seminar, including our professor—old Father Calles, I think it was—Pablo took the position that it was not the dictatorships that were necessarily wrong, just the men who became the dictators. What made them bad was that they did not possess the cardinal virtues required to lead justly. He won the debate by convincing our professor that as long as the dictator ruled with the virtues found only in the truly good, then the people would follow and be best served. Utter nonsense, of course, but he carried the day. I remember Emilio arguing until he was blue in the face in defense of republican government, but it did not matter. It was all about the basic tenets of virtue."

"And just what are these tenets of virtue that Alvarez apparently believes he possesses?"

"I forget my Plato, but best as I can recall, they were wisdom, courage, and justice, and the fourth was…what…moderation or temperance, I think. Given Ray's mentioning of Alvarez personally killing the man who murdered his father, I guess in his case he means justice as in the eyes of the beholder. Hardly an attribute for a leader of a democratic country—and certainly not the actions of a virtuous man."

"I don't know a damn thing about Plato or utopias, Alberto, but I do recognize tyranny when I see it. More evidence than ever that we need to stop this guy."

"I agree. It seems my old friend has visions of being a modern-day Napoleon, but one who possesses the cardinal virtues—only like Napoleon, he clearly does not. He just thinks he does. In Plato's utopia, it was thought better to have a government with one flawed human being who at least retained the cardinal virtues, rather than a republican form of government comprised of deputies that lacked such virtues. The mere fact that Alvarez believes he is virtuous and therefore believes he can become a philosopher king and justify his actions as long as they are for the good of the masses—there can be no greater an indication of how truly mad he has become."

"So you agree with me, Alberto, that the man is a raving lunatic."

"That he is, Bennie; that he is. Only I fear that it is even worse than you suspect."

"What do you mean, Alberto? How in the living hell can it possibly be worse?" an exasperated Bennie asked.

"It is in Ray's reference to his saving Alvarez from assassination being part of God's plan. Pablo was always the most devout of us all. Emilio and I thought he may well end up at the seminary. His mother certainly wanted that. He was a true believer in the best sense—not fanatical but very sincere. To discover his father's apparent deceptions and criminal past and then fail to do the right thing and arrest him, followed by avenging his father's murder with one of his own, well…it is contrary to everything he was brought up to believe, contrary to his very essence as I knew it—or thought I knew it."

Alberto paused and slowly rubbed his hand through his mussed hair while shaking his head slowly. "Belief is all about faith, Bennie, and to have discovered what he did and then to have sinned as he apparently has, his faith must have been all but shattered. How else to explain the lawlessness in one I thought I knew so well? It is hard for me to imagine a Pablo Alvarez without his faith; it would be as if a ship has lost its rudder. He appears to still be devout; at least he goes through the motions each Sunday with his family, but how can that be with all that he has done? The hypocrisy is staggering.

"Then there is an event, an assassination attempt on his life, and he is apparently saved when it seems he should have perished. I can just hear him talking of God's plan. He has done that since we were boys, always wondering what God had planned for each of us. You see, Bennie, I am certain the fact he was not killed will be seen as a justification or confirmation of the righteousness of his path: save the people of the country from the merciless marauding of the cartels, and gain redemption for his sins. Oh, yes, Bennie, my old friend is certainly quite mad. We must act next week when he attempts to see his cousins. If we fail, I will have no choice but to have him killed, which means I may, in the end, be no better than he is."

Alberto paused again. "This is all so deeply troubling," he finally said as he slowly shook his head again, staring down at the messages.

"Hold it, Alberto, how in the hell can you possibly compare any of your actions to those of this madman? You're being way too tough on yourself. I don't know diddly shit about philosophy, but I recognize good and evil when I see it, and you're good, and he's evil. End of fucking story."

Alberto looked long at Bennie, a terrible sadness in his eyes. "Have I not violated the laws of my country, my constitution, and detained citizens against their will? Have I not sanctioned the murders of those I suspected, maybe even knew, to be criminals, if in the course of capturing others, I felt it was necessary—without benefit of warrant or due process? I suppose the only real difference I see is that Emilio and I indeed are not profiting from our vigilantism, but Bennie, vigilantism it is, and for what reason, what end? To destroy the cartels and save the people. How different are Alvarez and I really?"

Alberto's questions again reminded Bennie of Ray's personal conflicts. These were indeed muddy waters, he thought. He looked hard at Alberto and went on. "There are differences, Alberto. I know he was your friend for a very long time, but he is a criminal in every civilized country in the world as a result of trafficking. I don't care how many of the other cartels he kills off in the process. That's just acquisition and consolidation. He's a criminal; you're a cop—and a damned good one, remember that. Most I'll ever say on the subject is you have had to use unusual methods, maybe even extraordinary methods, to enforce the law. Leave it at that. Your breaking of the law in order to fix it was necessary because of the terrible circumstances down here and only because nothing else would work. The system is busted down here, for Christ's sake. 'Desperate times require desperate measures'; didn't someone famous say that? Your motivations and goals have never been more noble. Don't compare them to Alvarez's, no matter how similar you may think they appear. I thought the general and I got you all squared away on this thinking."

"Yes, yes. Manny said many of the same things you are. Forgive me my detour into self-pity. We really had no choice. And if faced again with the choices we made, I would do so again."

Alberto sighed deeply. "Even Emilio said that, and there was no more honorable and lawful constitutionalist in the country. But now that I have bared my soul, I realize something else Manny said is also true. I can never allow what I have done and am about to do with Los Pueblos Fantasmas to ever come to light. There would be many who would not understand. If we indeed can take the initiative over the cartels with our operation this Saturday, my admitting my own malfeasance would only cloud and diminish our gains. Perhaps this is nothing more than my own justification for my actions, but for the sake of Emilio's memory, I will do as Manny suggested and fold that tent quietly. And as I said, if I do not want my personal legacy to be that of an assassin, we best expose Alvarez for what he is, what he has become, and bring him to justice."

"Now you're talking, Alberto. Manny would forgive me, I think, if I passed on to you something he said to me about you. He told me that he could not look himself in the mirror and honestly say he had an ounce of courage when compared to you, and I could not agree more. It took a lot of balls for you and Emilio to organize and try what you did, and Emilio paid for his courage with his life. Don't lose yours. You are good, and that son of a bitch Alvarez is evil. I don't know much, but I do know that."

A suddenly very emotional Alberto Rodriguez simply looked at Bennie and nodded. He was grateful for the words from his new friend and did not trust himself to speak for several seconds. His thoughts of his brother and Bennie's reference to Emilio having given his life in their quest for justice had made him lose his carefully maintained facade of control for just a brief moment. Alberto cleared his throat with a small cough and then asked quietly, "May I keep your notes, Bennie?"

"Sure, just keep then tucked away somewhere safe, my friend."

Bennie and Alberto stood up, and Bennie said, "I don't know about you, but I'm bushed. See you for breakfast?"

"Certainly. I look forward to it," Alberto said as he walked Bennie to the door. "Is seven too early for you? I must get into the office and finalize the plans for the raid. You may sit in on all the meetings, if you wish."

"Seven's fine, Alberto. Better I go in with you than sit around all day waiting until we go see *el presidente*. Imagine, my first private dinner with a head of state, and I wish I could avoid it. Says something about the mess we got on our hands."

"Indeed it does, Bennie; indeed it does. Good night, my friend, and thank you."

20

Valentine Corro was sitting at the kitchen table. Alonzo and his wife had left the day before to visit several of their grown children in Albuquerque. He had suggested it, and Alonzo had understood his meaning. *Get lost for a few days.* He was frustrated and a bit afraid. Eduardo Vargas had sent him up here to find out who was looking for his brother, and so far his questioning of the various distributors and retainers in America of the Vargas family business had yielded no results. Val knew he was missing something here. Eduardo had not been able to hide his concern when he had ordered Val on this mission. It wasn't like the Vargases were unknown to the authorities and not occasionally watched. So why all the sudden concern about Carlo? He was an escaped inmate from the American jail; it only made sense that they would want him back. He had to admit that the Americans searching in the south was new, but there were many such new procedures and attitudes at the border, especially after all the chaos related to the deportations. But an order was an order, so as he was instructed to do, he called on Thursday night to give Eduardo an update but had nothing to report.

Eduardo had only barely concealed his dissatisfaction. That was what put the fear into Val. He was a valuable and loyal soldier to the Vargases and had been for a very long time, yet he knew what the Vargases were capable of. He knew what they had done with the Mendoza brothers, and they had been business associates, if not actual friends, of the Vargas family for a very long time. He had a different relationship with them, he realized—perhaps even a better one, he hoped. After all he was not only loyal and productive for Eduardo, but he kept a very low, very quiet profile, characteristics he knew the Vargases appreciated, unlike the foolhardy antics of the Mendozas. He owed Eduardo, for he had done what Valentine had always wanted to do to avenge his son.

It had taken all day Thursday to arrange to get the three men he was currently waiting to see to Las Cruces and the safe house. All three were key people in Eduardo's network and the most knowledgeable on the subject of Carlo, his escape, and the surveillance that had Eduardo Vargas so nervous. If they knew nothing and that was what he had to report, Eduardo would be very unhappy, and Val would be very worried. The first of the three was Alejandro Guerro, his eyes into the sprawling US Army base and the operative who was running the soldiers on the base who were, in one form or another, betraying their country in exchange for drugs. The second was his highest-ranking informer within the El Paso division of the DEA. The third was his only remaining informer on the El Paso Police Force. His top informer, the special services lieutenant who had helped the very careless Carlo Vargas escape from jail the first time several months ago, was the chief suspect in the escape case and had already been arrested and arraigned on suspicion of aiding in the escape. The two policemen had had no prior knowledge that the other was involved with the Vargases until the escape had revealed this.

The three arrived in separate cars within minutes of each other. Alex arrived first and was greeted on the porch by Val and told to go on in. As the other two arrived, Val went to each separately and told them to wait in their cars until he came and got them. Val would have preferred they not meet, but because of their jobs and the scrutiny they were under, this early-morning time frame had been the only one that worked with their schedules and his.

Alex had no idea who the other men who showed up as he watched out the kitchen window were. For DEA agent Paul Archuleta and Detective

Edgar Diaz, it was a little different. Both recognized the other, as their units from time to time worked together. They did not know each other well and, until this moment, had no idea that the other was involved in the sordid side of their occupations. Both were surprised on the one hand and, in a strange way, relieved. Each, in his own moment of initial recognition, thought that the other may be someone he could turn to if he were faced with a difficult problem that he could not discuss with anyone else. Believing himself to be the sole traitor in an organization, with the specter of being revealed and prosecuted for his crimes, weighed heavily on both men. The added money that was the motivation behind their treachery was good in and of itself, but even that aspect had been more difficult and less enjoyable than each had imagined. Flashing money around that would be hard to explain and do nothing but draw attention was out of the question. Having the stashes of unspent cash around was more a constant reminder of their criminal activities rather than a relief from some of life's more troublesome financial burdens. They were no good to their cartel if they left their law enforcement organizations, and staying in their organizations handcuffed their freedoms to spend what they earned. It was difficult to spend some of your hard-earned cash on fancy vacations or expensive toys when you only got two or three weeks of vacation a year. And given their occupations, new cars or houses would make them stand out, and that was exactly what they could not risk.

Each knew that the answer lay in leaving the organization sooner rather than later and leaving the community. Only then, in a different city, state, or country, would they be able to finally spend what they had been accumulating. If only their illicit employer would let them. Just recently Paul Archuleta had informed his contact, who in turn reported to Val, that he intended to resign from the DEA so he could head south to Costa Rica and spend the next thirty years fishing, only to be told that they would tell him when he could leave and not before. To leave early would see his DEA office called with a tip on an informer and where he could be found. The same message had been passed on to Edgar Diaz. Both men would remain for the time being in their respective positions and continue to report everything of interest they came across. Of course the cash payments would continue; after all, it was a business relationship, but no one was skipping out, not just yet.

Val came in from the porch and sat down at the modest linoleum-covered kitchen table opposite Alejandro. "Coffee, Alejandro?"

Alex was very uncomfortable. He had not seen his recruiter since the day he had left the small farm in Mexico to begin his new duties in Juarez. The man had snatched him from a potentially life-threatening short stay in prison to a life of ample riches, creature comforts, and an endless supply of college coeds. He was certain that from time to time, he had recognized his voice over the phone when he passed information along. But the last words the older man had spoken to him personally before he left the farm were these: *For security reasons, we shall not meet again. Do your job, and do it well, and you will live a long and profitable life. Fail, and you will not.*

"No, Jefe, no coffee. Jefe, why am I here, and why have you violated security? I have done everything you have asked."

"Yes, you have, Alejandro. You have done well. So well, it seems, you have come across some information that is very important to some very important people. There is more information our employers require, and it is believed you have it or can get it. The need for this information is what required this meeting. I'm truly sorry."

Alex ignored Val's attempt to make him comfortable. "What information, Jefe? I know only the schedule where the American drones will be searching at the border, and right now, I do not even know that!"

"Relax, Alejandro," Val said as he sipped some coffee before going on. "In your last communication, you said that your man who provided the schedules was temporarily working on another assignment, and that assignment was to find an escaped Mexican national named Carlo. This Carlo is important to our employers, and they want to know who is looking for him. Is it the US Army, and if so, why? That is something they typically do not do. Especially on our side of the fences. So, Alejandro, tell me what you know."

"I swear, Jefe, I do not know more than that! I expected to get schedules and locations from my source, not the little information I did."

"Do you think your source was telling you everything he knew?"

That question was one that had been bothering Alex since Monday. He was certain that Danny had held considerable information back. That had been his gut instinct at the time. But what his jefe or anyone else could not know was how you had to play your sources to keep them in the game. Danny was an addict, and he was weak, but he was not stupid. Quite the contrary. Alex could only push him around so much without pushing him over one of several edges. It was sickening how weak Danny was, and keeping him propped up was almost a full-time job. Alex had pushed as hard as he felt he could on Monday. He knew in time he would get more out of him, but it required finesse.

"No, Jefe. He knows more, but he is weak. He is my best source, so I must be careful."

"I thought so, Alejandro. I think I know what you are going through, and I am sympathetic. But the stakes, for reasons unknown to me, seem to be very high, and I must have more information. That means you need to get with your source and get me more."

"Jefe, I am not due to meet him again until next Tuesday, and even then, with his new assignment, he said this was not a certainty. He said he would contact me when he could meet again."

"I'm afraid this will not be sufficient, Alejandro. How do you contact him?"

"By cell phone, of course, but only rarely. Once we set up our regularly scheduled meeting, there has been no reason to contact each other. In fact, he has only done so once, and that was because of this new mission business. We have no idea how good or extensive the army's or the other authorities' intelligence organizations are, so we must be careful."

"I appreciate that, Alejandro, but it is necessary we try. Call your friend; tell him you wish to meet and meet today if possible, but certainly this weekend."

Alex looked long and hard at his boss, and then slowly pulled one of his two cell phones out and began texting.

"What are you doing, Alejandro? I said call him."

"That would not be wise at this hour, Jefe. He is likely at his job on the base. He said that the job was important and that he was subject to even greater security. If, as most people who carry cell phones to their work do, he has silenced his phone, it will still alert him to a message. He then can call me when it's safe to do so. It must be done this way, Jefe." Alex tapped out, "Call me now, Alex," and hit the Send button. "All we can do now is wait."

Val was very unhappy with how this was going but recognized that his operative was correct in his caution. He got up and told Alex to come with him and wait on the porch while he spoke with the others. He waved at Paul Archuleta, motioning him to join him in the house.

Alex sat down in one of the old wicker chairs on the porch and watched the unknown man as he came up on the porch and went into the house. He wondered who exactly the other two men were and what their roles were in the organization. Alex could overhear parts of the conversation from the kitchen, but there was really nothing of interest other than the man had something to do with the DEA. This did not surprise Alex. Jefe was asking the other man exactly what he had asked him. Whoever the other man was, he also professed to know nothing on any search for a Carlo. The only piece of information he could offer of even the most remote interest was that there had been a senior agent from Washington running around the El Paso division from time to time over the last four or five months, and he seemed to be involved with projects over and above what was being routinely conducted. He had shut down some existing operations and had started others that seemed very routine, but to Paul Archuleta's eye, more often than not, no one had any idea what he was up to.

The rumors going round were that he was on a witch hunt trying to ferret out the informers in the division. Paul had taken these rumors seriously and was very cautious in his actions for all the obvious reasons. He knew of the reputation of SAC Bennie Santiago and knew that discovery was a real possibility. Jefe wrote down the name Paul had been given and told Paul to specifically keep an eye and ear out for any information regarding the escaped inmate Carlo. He further instructed him to discreetly ask around about it, an order that Paul knew immediately he would ignore. He would lie to Jefe long before he actually started kicking the bushes about an old escape case. Val walked Paul to the door and shook hands with him; then they went out onto the porch. The two informers on the porch glanced at one another, but then each looked away.

The third man left his car and came to the house and went inside with Val. Alex did not know this one either. The man had a scared look in his eyes as he walked into the house, ignoring Alex. Alex made an effort to listen to the conversation going on around the kitchen table, but again, judging from Jefe's hard questions and dissatisfied attitude, there was little information of value to Valentine. What was of value and interest to Alex was that the man was a detective on the El Paso Police Force. He filed the face and name away, thinking he should learn more about the man. The one thing he did hear the detective tell Jefe was that there was some sort of mystery surrounding the escape of a Carlo and another inmate three or four months in the past, but the detective did not know the details. He only knew what he had overheard his captain telling another detective at the time, but he had paid little attention, as it had not concerned him. He did not know the inmates that had escaped, nor had he ever been asked to look into them before.

Diaz had been very surprised at the escape—like everyone else on the force—and by the discovery that another relatively senior officer was now implicated in aiding this Carlo's first escape. This fact had not been lost on Edgar Diaz. It meant that some cartel, maybe even the one he was working for, also had sources inside the department. Diaz wondered how many others there were. The El Paso Police Force was not all that large, and after ten or fifteen years, you knew practically everyone on the force. It wasn't just through the work but through the softball and bowling leagues that were organized to promote group relaxation and team building.

Val instructed Diaz to carefully ask about the mystery. He wanted to know everything he could find regarding this case, and he wanted the information now. To do so this long after the escape could only arouse suspicion if the wrong people were asked, and both men knew it. Like Paul Archuleta, Diaz said he would look into it, but the truth was he would think twice before asking anyone anything. Edgar Diaz had done a lot of boneheaded things in his life, the dumbest, no doubt, being suckered into his role as an informer. He'd made some personal financial mistakes and had needed a way out for his family. He's been approached one evening by a man he'd talked with on several occasions at his favorite bar to help a kid from Mexico who had become involved in narcotics. He'd been told that the boy's concerned, wealthy family in Mexico was willing to pay generously for anything he could do to help their son. All he had to do was provide some relatively benign information in return for payment, and he had done it. It had all seemed so harmless at the time. What he had not thought through in a moment of desperation was just how slippery that slope was. Edgar was dumb but not stupid. He had been "handled" brilliantly, as he now thought back on it. The kind of information he had initially passed on, while it had been wrong to do so, had had little detrimental value to either the force, to operations, or to the actual crime rates. That was how his reasoning or rationale had gone. Only when the drinking acquaintance from the bar—his handler, as it turned out—had first asked him for some really serious information on undercover operations, and showed him a record of all that he had done that would be turned over to the police if he did not cooperate further, had he realized the depth of his involvement and mistake. Once the hook was set, they, whoever they really were, had you. So he had gone along. What was so very unique, almost ironic, about his illicit relationship, he thought on many occasions, was even though they had him cold turkey, the payments continued and even got more generous. It was as if an honorable business relationship existed between him and those who required his information. A strange reality, he had thought.

Diaz, with Val trailing, walked out of the house, never looking at Alex; walked to his car; and left. Val stood on the porch looking off into the pecan orchards to the south, obviously deep in thought, until Alex said, "I got a text message from my source."

Val turned. "And?"

"He says he will call me during his lunch; that is all."

"Well, that is a start, I suppose. Do not underestimate how important getting information on this subject is, Alejandro. It would be a mistake to do so. Whatever you had planned today, I suggest you change it. I want you here when this informant calls back. He is the one who has generated all the interest in those who employee us, and they take their business seriously. Understand?"

Alex simply nodded, thinking that as was usually the case, things had been going too well for too long, and his life was about to change again… and he had absolutely no control over it.

Less than sixty miles away at the sprawling base northeast of El Paso, Colonel Romero was on his way to the brig to visit the sequestered Danny Irwin. The buzzing cell phone on the corner of his desk had startled him at first, as he had not heard its electronic announcement before. He had been holding on to the captain's cell phone since his arrest just for this opportunity. He, the general, and the sergeant major had discussed just what they would do if Irwin was contacted, so he was prepared. Over the last several days, in sessions with the now totally broken captain, they had also told him what was to be expected of him. He would talk with his Mexican national contact, and he would say what had been rehearsed. This would hopefully lead to a meeting at their greasy spoon, where Danny would be wired and watched and could start disseminating the false information that Colonel Romero had cooked up with Bennie Santiago's help.

The first piece would be as they originally talked: let the Mexican know that the army was looking in the Monterey area. With what little they knew of the plans the general's cousin was cooking up for the following week, the team wanted to try to limit the movements of the Condor and his entourage to the two central northern estates. That could only help. Colonel Romero was also working on the details of more disinformation, but this was a start.

At 12:20 p.m., back at Alonzo Martinez's farm, Alex's private cell phone rang. With Val watching and listening, Alex answered. "Yes?"

"Alex, Danny."

"Danny, I need to see you. Can you meet me today?"

"Christ, no, Alex. Not with the security I'm under in this new project. What's wrong that you need to see me?"

Sounds very scared, Alex thought. *Jefe and those who control him have no idea how weak this man is. He can be pushed only so far and so fast.*

"The people we work for are very interested in your new assignment, and they want more information now, Danny. These are dangerous people, for the both of us. They asked me if I thought you knew more than you told me last time, and I had no choice but to say yes. I knew you were holding out on me but decided to give you a pass. What you did tell me, these people have an interest in, and they do not care who they burn in the process. So you must give me more."

"I want to, Alex, but security on this assignment is high. I even had to take quarters on the base. We are all being watched by CID, our base police. I can probably get away tomorrow morning early for breakfast since it's Saturday, but we have to be careful."

"Tomorrow is fine, Danny. Harry's at seven?"

"Sure, Alex. Look, I have to go—even this call is dangerous. How do I explain this number if CID starts checking phone records or something? We will have to work out something else, some other way to talk."

I have to give him something, thought Alex. "Relax, Danny. I will bring you a new phone that no one will know about. One you will use only for me. There will be no records. We will not talk again on your phone, so relax. Tomorrow at seven, and Danny, you better have some information for me."

Val was happy with the exchange. He would be contacting Eduardo tonight and pass on the few things he had learned today. Just having the prospect of more information would satisfy Eduardo that he was doing his best and making progress. He hoped.

The atmosphere in Interrogation Room 2 of the Fort Bliss brig was somewhat different. A shaking Danny Irwin disconnected from the call and promptly threw up in the wastebasket beside the table where he, the colonel, and the sergeant major were sitting. He could now add the humiliation of them witnessing that to everything else that had gone wrong in the last week. He used the sleeve of his orange jumpsuit to wipe the spittle from his mouth and looked pleadingly at the colonel. "I can't go through with this, sir. I want to, but Alex will see right through me."

"You will go through with tomorrow's meeting, captain, so start thinking about getting your shit together. The next twenty or forty years of your life are riding on it. Think about that next time you want to blow lunch. Your contact will not be surprised if you're uncomfortable and nervous tomorrow. Focus on the message, and he will be satisfied. We will have people close watching, and of course we will hear everything. Now, let's get started…"

With that, the colonel spent the rest of the day preparing his messenger. Colonel Romero had spent a great deal of his career in intelligence, but little of it had been spent with counterintelligence. Still, he thought he had a feel for it. Big things were brewing in Mexico, and this little operation might contribute to the success of those missions. He'd get this mousy little shit ready to do his part if it was the last thing he did.

21

I t had been a long day, and Alberto decided they should leave the office at four. He needed a drink, and he needed to quietly check in with Major Garcia. One of the really difficult aspects of covertly dealing with his Los Pueblos Fantasmas strike team leader was that their communications had to be protected in ways that precluded just dialing him up from the office. Like the arrangement Bennie had with Charley Willis back in Washington, Alberto had a different phone with which to communicate with the major, and he did so only from his home.

Bennie had sat in on the day's coordination and planning sessions for the raid and had hardly said a word. It had not been expected that he would. He had been identified by Alberto to his team, including the traitors in the room, as a DEA observer. Bennie had offered at one juncture that the DEA had raids of their own planned in several American cities to coincide with tomorrow's attack. But he had had to admit that he was not even sure whose distribution networks they would be hitting, only that they existed and that they had Justice Department clearance to proceed. Bennie had promised to have interrogation results to Alberto as quickly as they could be developed. Alberto and Bennie had taken lunch together in his office but had used the time only to speak of the upcoming raid and the myriad of planning details to be ironed out as aides had come and gone.

After leaving the office, they made the short drive from the Zocalo to the Bosque de Chapultepec in silence, as was their custom. The ever-professional Alejandro was there to greet them, somehow alerted to their arrival, and they went directly to Alberto's inner sanctum. They had to be at the Alvarez mansion at six thirty for the informal briefing for the president and whatever other staff he would be including. For sure his two highest-ranking traitors would be there, representing the Federal Police and the Justice Department. Alberto went to his desk to make his calls and also to touch base with Manny in El Paso. Bennie headed for the comfortable seating area in front of the fireplace, for he had his own calls to make. There was a voice mail from Charley asking him to touch base, and he also wanted to check for any updates from Ray, although he expected none. He was sure he would hear from Ray later that night. Bennie grabbed his iPhone and speed-dialed Charley's personal number. He heard the standard clicking as the encryption system did whatever it was the clever programmers in the Technical Branch wanted the signal to do.

Charley answered on the second ring. "Hey, Bennie, hang on a second. I'm on my way home, and you caught me in the car. I don't know what's more dangerous: the cartels or these Northern Virginia commuters."

"Sure, Charley," Bennie responded.

There was a pause of several seconds before Charley came back on. "OK, Bennie, I'm off the 95 now. I should be able to talk and not kill myself. I hope your day was better than mine."

"Mine was boring, Charley, and tiring. I had to look interested for hours during meetings in which I contributed nothing and really was not. With what all Alberto has told me about his plans, I already knew the drill front to back, so it was like fingernails on a chalkboard to have to sit through it again today. What was so bad about yours? No disasters, I hope."

"Maybe not a disaster, but some real concerns, Bennie. I have been on the phone with John Walker in El Paso. First, let me say I think his choice as your deputy down there was brilliant, even though he can't understand half of what people are saying in their Texas twang, and they can't understand his Brooklynese. He has a real hard-on for the cartels and seems very good at finding out things without leaving any tracks. He's been quietly keeping tabs on the Condor's people who are coming and going from the safe house Ray discovered, and this has led him to people who are beating the bushes down there for information on who's looking for Carlo. He says that a player showed up at the safe house night before last and is obviously a key figure. We have identified him through his car as one Valentine Corro out of Juarez. He cleared the border legally Wednesday night. He's ostensibly a car-parts salesman for one of the large manufacturers down there. I'm going to have some of the guys up here look into that in the morning."

"Don't, Charley. If I am guessing right, what you will find is that the company is probably owned by either the Alvarez or Pena families. Let's not dig into anything that could get back to Alvarez. We need to respect the talents of the Baca guy who is Alvarez's information guru. Alvarez is apparently curious enough about who's looking for his cousin. Let's not go and give him anything more to think about."

"Sure, Bennie—sorry. I must be tired or jetlagged out from the hops back and forth to El Paso. I should have thought of that."

"Lighten up, old pal—with what little we know about what all the Condor is into, we just need to tread lightly for another week or so. Best guess is that we will find that this auto-parts supplier is also one of the Condor's mechanisms for getting drugs into the country. I assume you got my voice mail on my contact with Ray. We have even more leads what with the Baja Salt Company and the Alvarez cruise lines. Ray is giving us a motherlode of intelligence, Charley, and that was in just one exchange last night, for Christ's sake."

"He sure has, Bennie. Your plan is working brilliantly."

"Let's not give each other reach-arounds just yet, Charley. We need to get Ray out first, and we need to nail Alvarez. Tell me, what's Johnny found out that has you concerned?"

Charley went into the entire surveillance of the Martinez farm and the fact they had now identified one confirmed DEA informer and one from the El Paso police. In addition, there were at least a dozen other operatives working the distribution end of the Vargas organization who were being watched. Also, a nerve of some sort had been hit, Charley said, and he was pretty sure he knew what that was. Bad people were beating the bushes—quietly but with a sense of urgency—looking for information on anyone who was looking for Carlo Vargas and why.

"Bennie, we have confirmed that this Corro character has spoken with no less than a dozen people around El Paso, and we do not have the manpower on your covert team to track anyone else these dozen are then talking with. What I'm saying here, Bennie, is that given the depth and breadth of the Condor's intelligence-gathering apparatus up here, we have no earthly idea who else is involved and whether there are people out there who can compromise you or Ray."

Bennie was saddened when Charley mentioned that the one confirmed DEA informer was Edgar Diaz. It wasn't as if Edgar had been a bad agent. He was lazy, for lack of a better description, and others had worked far harder for advancement and moved up and out. Edgar had been pigeon-holed because of his own character traits.

"I'm goddamned sorry to hear that Edgar Diaz has gone bad. I never figured him for something like this."

"Once we had him meeting this Corro guy, John's team didn't have to look too far today to find out he's had some financial problems we were unaware of that have mysteriously disappeared. He was always a plugger—unimaginative and lazy, maybe, but I always thought him reliable. I'm not looking forward to the day we've got to book him."

"Neither am I, Charley. So you have no specific concerns, just the possibilities that there are people out there who can hurt us?"

"That's right."

"Well, that has always been a possibility, hasn't it? I've given the leak a lot of thought, and what's the worst that Alvarez can find out if the general and his team have their traitor bottled up, as they say? Maybe they find out the DEA is involved with the army, but that's hardly news."

"I think you're overlooking one very important piece, Bennie."

"What's that?"

"You. I'm worried your name will come up down there. Diaz for one knows you have been in and out of town for months. Alvarez knows there is some kind of extraordinary surveillance underway, and you just happen to show up in Mexico. It's no secret that Alberto and the general are cousins.

I'm worried that Alvarez and his key people will start connecting the dots much like we did."

"Hmm, I hadn't thought about me. But what did you tell me in DC last week? Let's not take counsel of our own fears or some such poetic shit. It's almost logical to think that the new secretary of public security would tap in to all the resources he can to combat the cartels, including his very close cousin the general. And I have already been introduced to the president as Ted Mills's traveling troubleshooter. They still have no real connection between our search for Carlo Vargas and what we are really up to. In a way, some of the scenarios they could envision actually act as a diversion. Let's stay on course and get this over quick, and we'll be fine."

"Maybe you're right, Bennie, but let's all be extra careful. I suppose you've heard that right after meeting with Corro this morning, that Guerro guy who has been running your captain Irwin made contact?"

"No, I hadn't heard that yet. But Alberto is on the horn right now to the general. What went down?"

"Guerro wants to meet with the captain tomorrow morning, and Colonel Romero is making it happen. They will feed Guerro the line of crap about us searching in the Monterey area."

"That's a good thing, Charley; glad to hear it. More diversion."

"Well...maybe. I hear the now-remorseful captain is an eyelash from being a basket case. Only time will tell if this will work, but if Alvarez and his band of psychopaths get an inkling that they are being jobbed, they will know more than a simple search mission is underway. So watch yourself."

"I trust the colonel, Charley. Listen, I need to go over some things with Alberto. I don't know what your dinner plans are, but I'm off to the new president's place for a quiet private dinner. Keep on top of things up there, and I'll try to do the same down here. Next time, we can go over some of the incredible intelligence Ray has given us. For now, let's hope Alberto's raid comes off, and he gets the Gang of Four. With them gone as well as the Mendozas and now Vasso, it will have been a very bad week to be a cartel leader. Even more so if we can catch that bastard Alvarez on the fly next week."

"That it has been, old friend. You watch yourself down there. Alvarez is likely to have people trying to figure you out. He may even do so himself over your oh-so-special dinner, so don't underestimate the guy."

Bennie chuckled. "Will do, Charley."

Alberto had finished up his conversations with his major and his cousin a little before Bennie finished his with Charley, so he had overheard the last part of the conversation. They exchanged information on Colonel Romero's scheme, and Alberto updated Bennie on the actions of Los Pueblos Fantasmas. Theirs would be the first action in the early-morning hours of Saturday to silently eliminate the rear guards who had been quietly set up by one of the cartels, in addition to the guards at the grotto entrance. It appeared to the major that two cartel leaders did not trust the others and had made their own arrangements to have back-up retainers in the area. All told, there were a total of twenty-five enforcers in two camps on the back-side of the seminary. The men of the first camp at the grotto were aware of the other and were watching it closely. That made taking the watchers the major's first action. The men of the second camp had taken care to conceal themselves in their location upon arriving but apparently had assumed that there was no danger around the not-too-distant curve in the lake road. A simple reconnoiter and they would have discovered the other camp. A further reminder, Alberto said, that while armed and certainly dangerous, the cartel enforcers were not in any sense a trained force.

All told, the Los Pueblos Fantasmas strike team totaled thirty men in three squads of ten. They had set up a camp to hold prisoners on the east side of the lake and would try to keep the killing to a minimum, but no one really believed that would be possible. The enforcers would go down fighting, for the most part, so that was just too bad.

Alberto and Bennie had their ritual five o'clock cocktails and then went to their suites to rest and clean up before leaving at 6:15 p.m. for the president's home. They both wanted to be rested and sharp while in the lion's den later that night.

22

The presidential motorcade pulled into Casa Rosada at six o'clock. President Alvarez and his small personal group of aides and security men entered the Alvarez family mansion by the front doors as various other security elements of his now-official entourage moved off to prearranged parking and posting areas. The president was running thirty minutes late, according to the official schedule that was prepared every morning by elements of his new staff. With a small party of invited guests showing up at six thirty for a security meeting, there was not a lot of time available to freshen up or simply grab a long-overdue drink at the end of another busy day. For those who knew Pablo Alvarez personally, they could see a real bounce in his step. For all the long hours he was working in his new job and all the very significant national events that had occurred in the past week, he was buoyant of spirit, and he could not conceal this.

The last twenty-five years of his life, as viewed through the prism of the present happenings, seemed a hazy blur. Alvarez had been truly happy in this house, especially twenty-five years ago when beginning a law and government career that to an extent he had avoided at first, given his deep interests in the performing arts, philosophy, and religion. He had had a real satisfaction in prosecutorial law, he had come to find out, and this had surprised him. Because he was a child of privilege, his mother had instilled in him a reverence and sincerity to his religion and all the good that it stood

213

for, while his father instilled in him a sense that he was obligated to help others of lesser circumstances.

His parent's life lessons had evolved into much more than simple acts of Christian charity or philanthropy but rather into greater accomplishments on a much larger, wider stage. In his first two years in the attorney general's office, he had come to realize that one of the core philosophies that he believed in—Plato's "Any man may easily do harm, but not every man can do good to another"—could be fulfilled on a grand scale when one had political power coupled with the basic tenets of the cardinal virtues he felt his mother had instilled in him. He had not been at the Justice Department but for a few months when he had begun to realize what could be achieved for his fellow citizens in the arena of public service.

As he had begun his justice career, he had realized that his other interests in life had actually prepared him for what he was destined to do: help his country do better for its people. His enthusiasm and dreams had been all but shattered on the night his father had come down from the north and told him of his family's true legacy. He had thought he would not survive that night, learning his family was deeply involved with the trafficking and given the terrible choice he had been forced to make, but he had.

In the ensuing years, from his important and sensitive position in the government, he had supplied his father with the information he required to both overcome their enemies and also avoid detection and the actions of the lawful government. His father in turn had provided him information that allowed the government to effectively crack down on others involved with trafficking. It was during this period he had slowly started to regain some of his lost idealism as he realized, in ways he could have never imagined, that he could still get some of the worst of the criminal traffickers that existed. Eliminating the worst of the traffickers was in both his family's and the government's interests. But unlike the government, whose strategy at the time had been to align themselves with the biggest and most heinous of the offenders who continued to kill anyone and everyone in their path, Alvarez's father took on only the terrible and never the innocent. The difference might appear slight to more lawfully minded observers, but it was the fingerhold in a piece of morality that allowed Alvarez to survive himself. *There is a difference between us and them*, he rationalized on many occasions. It had been enough to get him by in the early dark days of self-hate and doubt that hung over him.

His father, he had slowly learned, had built a vast, largely undiscovered organization that in its own way was accomplishing a lot of good. Certainly the root business was morally wrong, but what was being accomplished and what could yet be accomplished were not far removed from what he had dreamed he could do when he had realized his calling and joined the Justice Department. That his family would profit from these actions was something he neither acknowledged nor denied; it was what it was. He did what the emotional limitations within him allowed him to do; he simply ignored the moral implications of his trafficking profits and laundered them into legal currency with which he could continue his father's legacy of philanthropic giving. To think on the moral implications led to dark places within himself, and he would not revisit the places he had been that first night when his father had exposed him to the terrible truth. He had barely managed to escape that place once and feared that he would not be able to do so again, if ever he went down that dark path.

The assassination of his father had been a giant step back at first, as he had not truly realized just how emotionally dependent he was on the father figure he had seen so little of as he was growing up. While his father may not have been around like other fathers, when he was, his impact on Alvarez had been enormous. All he had ever seen in his father was a giant—a man of great wealth and power who was quiet and kind and used the family wealth for nothing but good, or so it had seemed. That bubble of goodness had been shattered with his father's revelations, and the emotional bubble that had still existed had been shattered by his father's violent death. There had been times during that period when he was certain he would not survive his grief. As ironic as it was, the emotional force that had kept him going; that had made him go north and assume the identities of Nicolas Pena, Pablo Vargas, and the Condor; and that allowed him to get up each day and just *do* was the prospect of avenging his father's death. For all the years of devoted attendance to his deep faith, it was not that faith that had seen him through his lowest moments but the knowledge that he had the means and the power to find and kill his father's assassins.

He had been frustrated at times in his role at the Justice Department in just how difficult it could be to marshal a case through to trial and actually get the conviction that he knew was the right and just outcome. He had many cases stall out because of disappearing evidence and vanishing witnesses. The first time it happened had been a real eye opener for the young prosecutor to the depth and power of the forces he was fighting.

There had been no such frustrations in his father's case and no months of tedious procedural steps. It had not taken him long to learn that it had been the two Tijuana cartels, the genesis of the Gang of Four acting loosely together, that had been responsible for his father's murder. The individual chosen to betray his father and carry out the gang's wishes had been easily discovered and just as easily shot to death by his own hand. What was not so easily killed was a growing desire to get those who were truly responsible. As the then-forty-year-old Pablo Vargas had begun to plot just how he might take that revenge, he also began to see just how the dreams he had had at thirty could still be realized. He could never truly make amends for what his family had been involved with in their long past, but he became determined to do so much good for his country and his people that one day he could face them with the truth. That was his most deeply held secret and desire and one that he had not even shared with his closest friends or family. One day he would tell his story, and he and his family would have the forgiveness of a grateful nation. And it was that belief, if ever revealed, that was all the evidence anyone would ever need to understand how truly mad he really was.

As an interim president serving out the remaining four years of the original Castillo presidency, by Constitution, he could then run for his own six-year term. In all, he intended to be president for ten years, a tenure that had not been seen for decades, since the times of endless revolutions and dictators. In that time he intended to lead a reformation of his country second to none in the world, growing a viable middle class and raising the standard of living for everyone. He realized that he could do more from the position he had created rising out of his father's illicit and immoral world than he could ever have done in the lawful and politically hazardous landscape that existed in Mexico. His path was imperfect, and he knew this, but his deeds would far outweigh what had been required, or so he believed. He truly revered the cardinal virtues and the whole abstract notion of benevolent utopias served by philosopher kings. In his mind's eye, he could see those abstractions being transformed into reality. Deep down, in his soul, he believed he could truly be a philosopher king, and he would leave a far better country than what he had inherited—and the people would in time forgive him and his family.

Raul Ortega followed his old friend into his private study with only young Ray in trail. Raul made out the assignments for the inner circle and was glad he had assigned Ray to him. He was considering making it a permanent assignment. Not only would Ray learn the essentials faster with Raul showing him the ropes, but truth be known, Raul much preferred Ray's company to Miguel's. As Pablo started looking over various files on his desk, Raul paused and thought about the circle, how good it had been for so long. He and his brother Manuel had been the first selected by Pablo's father to protect his son when he was twelve and sent from Baja to the city to start his formal education. Miguel had been the third, then Arturo Medina. Both had been friends and guards to Pablo's father at first. When Armando had been killed and a young Pablo had taken over the cartel, their inner circle had become complete. Arturo had been the first of the circle to die protecting Pablo, who had replaced him with Arturo's son Luis. That had been a terrible mistake, as Luis was not the man his father was, and Raul had always known this. But Pablo was an emotional man, loyal to the memory of Arturo, blinded at times by his deep emotions, and he had elevated the unworthy Luis anyway. Raul had always known that Luis would have to be dealt with at some point, as his sick obsession with young girls became more and more a problem. It was sad that Ray had had to be the one to eliminate Luis—Not that Luis would be missed but rather because of how it had seemed to affect Ray, who appeared to harbor feelings of guilt for having killed him. Raul regretted that events had played out as they had during the assassination of the ex-president, but what was done was done. Ray was a good man; preventing Luis from raping one of the young daughters of the man they needed to place the bombs on the presidential jet was something he would have done too. With the inner circle now reduced to just three, Raul was forced to consider whether their very close-knit group should be expanded, but he'd set those thoughts aside for now.

He liked Ray and looked forward to building a long mentoring relationship with him. He knew Pablo was of a like mind, and the three of them would be close friends, he was sure. His old friend Miguel was hard of hearing, said little, and was getting moodier with each passing year. Much like Carlo Vargas, Miguel was a fist. You would want no other by your side in a fight, but there were fewer and fewer fights. Miguel was not much more intelligent than Carlo but had more personal pride in his bearing and his responsibilities. Time spent with Miguel passed slowly and in quiet. It may have been vanity on his part, but to Raul, the bright, interesting Ray Espinoza reminded him of himself at that young age. Truth be known (and Raul knew the truth—if nothing else, he was the supreme realist of the inner circle), he knew Ray was innately far more intelligent and accomplished at twenty than he had ever been. But Pablo had seen something more in Raul years ago, and through insistence and constant but gentle pushing, Pablo had made Raul the man he was today. The idea of ever graduating secondary school, much less the university, had been something he could not have imagined at twenty.

Today he was a driving force in the running of a country. Pablo hardly made a move where he did not seek out Raul's wisdom and guidance. Pablo had mentioned to him the idea of moving him over to the leadership of the Federal Police, maybe even the secretary of public security, in the second administration. That was a foolish thought now, but who knew—maybe in four years, that would be possible. It would mean getting rid of the popular and very well-known Alberto Rodriguez, but that would be a good thing, and he would consider it. He'd be in his midsixties, but with that age would come more wisdom, he thought.

The greatest decision that would be made in the next ten years was just who would follow Pablo as president. Castillo would be long dead by then, and the power of the party would be Pablo's. He could name his successor. It would not be either of the traitors, Alejandro Quito-Perez or Hector Garcia Ramirez. Pablo intended to reveal them as informers for the Condor within the year as the "investigation" that would follow tomorrow's raid on the Gang of Four was wrapped up. There were some good young people in the government who had never consorted with cartels who could be brought along, especially in ten years. Pablo would see that the country was left in good hands. A compromised president wasn't necessary. Pablo would still have Geraldo Baca in his place.

Ray was the last to enter, and he closed the study door behind him as Alvarez walked to the bar to make their drinks. Similar to the ritual that Alberto and Bennie had evolved over the stressful and eventful week, so had Alvarez, with the members of his circle. It was an anchor in a way, a reminder of their friendship and the camaraderie that had long existed between them and recently with Ray.

"Raul, who all is to be involved in this conference?" the president asked as he started to make their drinks.

"In addition to us, there will be Quito-Perez; Ramirez; General Lozano of National Defense and his aide, Attorney General Farias; and of course Secretary Rodriguez and his American DEA guest. I have had the bar in the formal living room stocked so that we may serve ourselves during our discussions and keep this informal, as you requested."

"Good, thank you. Have we learned just what information Alberto's American guest thought was so important that he felt the need to deliver it in person?"

"No, not so far. I suspect you will have to ask him yourself at the conference. I still do not like this man just showing up here. I feel there is more here than meets the eye."

"Perhaps so, Raul. Has Geraldo been of any help?"

"Not yet, but he did message me earlier that he wishes to see us as soon as possible."

"Let's get him in here. I know our guests will be arriving soon, but we shall have them entertained. We have as much time as Geraldo requires, and I would like to know whatever he has come up with on this American before I have dinner with him."

Raul nodded his acceptance of the order and went to the phone on Alvarez's desk and dialed the appropriate extension for the security room. Lorenzo answered and relayed the president's request to Geraldo.

The security office was just down the main hall from the president's private study, so there was but a brief moment before Geraldo was buzzed through the electronically controlled door into the study. The entire conversation about Bennie made Ray extremely nervous. He felt strongly that Geraldo, despite all his wizardry, would not trip to why Bennie was really down here. Bennie simply was too careful for that, and the number of people who knew of Ray's involvement was just three, as far as he knew. If Ray knew anything about Bennie, he knew he was definitely into other schemes as well—some real, some diversionary—and he was grateful for it. All that would serve to do, if Geraldo could pick up on these other missions, was distract Alvarez and Raul from Bennie's primary one. Ray knew there was safety in diversion.

The always sour-looking Geraldo came quickly in. Everything about his mannerisms had always struck Ray as twitchy. As he walked by Ray, the look on his face was as if he had just sucked a lemon—more sour than usual.

Alvarez turned from the bar. "Ah, Geraldo, good to see you, my friend. What can I fix you?"

"Nothing for me, Jefe; thank you."

"You look upset, old friend. Are you the bearer of bad news? Does this concern my friend Alberto's houseguest, our mysterious DEA representative?"

"Perhaps yes, Jefe, but maybe no; that is what is troubling. More like inconclusive news that raises more questions than answers, I fear. We have heard from Eduardo."

"And what has my cousin told you that has upset you, Geraldo?"

"Am I free to speak, Jefe?" Geraldo asked as he glanced with nervous eyes toward Ray.

"Of course, Geraldo. I have no secrets from Ray. Ray, do not be offended by Geraldo's caution. He and Eduardo are involved in many sensitive areas that you have not previously been made aware of. Now you will be."

"No offense was taken, Jefe. I respect Geraldo's caution."

Geraldo nodded thanks to Ray, and there was almost a hint of a smile at the corners of his puckered-up mouth.

"Continue, Geraldo," Alvarez said pleasantly.

"Jefe, Eduardo heard on Wednesday from his operative on the military base near El Paso that gives him the flight plans for their spy drones that watch the border. A part of that group that Eduardo's informer works in has been tasked to locate an escaped trafficker named Carlo. And more alarming, the US Army is looking for this Carlo down here. That is, they—"

"Did they say our Carlo, Geraldo?" Raul interrupted.

"Raul, please," Alvarez said. "Let's let Geraldo make his report, and then you can ask your questions."

"Excuse me, Pablo," a very concerned Raul answered.

"Go on, Geraldo," Alvarez said, with a casual wave of his hand.

"As I was saying, Jefe, the Americans are flying their spy drones into our airspace looking for someone who has only been identified as Carlo. And no, Raul, none of the information has said Carlo Vargas, but it can only be our Carlo. The information references the escape three months ago. The American army has apparently turned over the control of these spy drones to the American DEA. The operation is being run by a senior agent named Smith, but our operative believes this was a false name. The project has the interest of their commanding general, our man says, and he believes the operation is not a joint operation with any of our agencies. When Eduardo found out about this Wednesday night, he immediately sent one of his key people to El Paso to find out more."

"Who did he send, Geraldo?" Alvarez asked calmly.

"Corro, Valentine Corro."

Alvarez nodded his acceptance and apparent agreement with the choice.

"Corro was instructed to carefully talk with anyone and everyone we have up there, if necessary, to find out who is looking for Carlo and why.

Eduardo specifically wanted Corro to find out why the sudden interest in Carlo after all these months. Corro contacted Eduardo earlier today and reported the following. Our operative handling the informer on the army base believes his man was holding back information and knows more than he has said. Our man has set a meet with this informer for tomorrow morning to press him further. Corro also has information from one of our sources in the DEA that says the only unusual occurrence he has observed recently is that there has been a senior man from Washington in the southwest off and on for the last three months and that he is apparently involved in operations that others in the DEA, like Eduardo's men, know nothing about. The senior agent mentioned by our DEA contact is currently the houseguest of Alberto Rodriguez, Mr. Santiago. Also, I do not believe I need to remind you, Jefe, who the secretary's cousin is."

"No, Geraldo, you do not. That is an interesting connection, is it not?"

"'Interesting' is not the word I would use, Jefe. I think 'dangerous' would be more accurate."

"Go on, Geraldo," a still very calm and neutral Alvarez said.

"Corro has one man left in the El Paso police. Our principal informer is himself in jail suspected of helping Carlo to escape, which of course he did. We have lost him, and he has no doubt told the authorities everything he knows. We cannot overlook the possibility that the authorities' renewed interest in Carlo is in some way a result of their interrogations with our man. Fortunately, the way that Corro has this particular string set up, it was entirely one way. Our lost police lieutenant reported what he knew via cell phone after he helped Carlo to escape the El Paso jail, and had no idea who was on the other end. Corro had not met face to face with him in several years, and the policeman has no idea who Corro really is. There is no path to us. All our burned informer knew about Carlo is that he was ordered to help this inmate he did not know escape, and in the process, he compromised himself. What our remaining man in the police has told Corro that is of interest it this: he recalls overhearing a conversation at the time of Carlo's second escape from the federal jail that would seem to indicate there was some sort of mystery surrounding it. Just what that mystery is—or was—is unknown to our man. Corro has ordered him to try to find out.

The information that concerns me the most, however, has come from another source Eduardo has in the DEA whom Corro is not involved with. An informer we have in El Paso reported yesterday that he discovered that some of his DEA colleagues passed on information this past weekend to the army. This information alerted them to a connection between Corro's man running the informers on the base and our informer there. Corro's man, as you may know, acts as this officer's dealer and exchanges drugs for information."

"Yes, yes, go on, Geraldo," Alvarez said kindly. "What is it about this last piece of information that concerns you, other than the obvious, which is that Corro's officer on the base is likely known to the authorities and therefore we are soon to lose this source of information? It would not be much of a loss, Geraldo."

"It is not that, Jefe. What disturbs me is that the army authorities are now aware of our informer, and yet Corro's man arranged a meet with him this morning for tomorrow. That can only mean two things. At a minimum the army authorities will be watching their traitor and maybe even orchestrate a way to hear what is discussed, or worse—"

"Or worse," Raul interrupted as he looked over at Alvarez, "they have already detained our source, and the meeting is nothing more than some type of setup."

"That is correct, Raul," the very serious Geraldo said.

"A setup? For what purpose, Raul?" Alvarez asked his old friend evenly. "I can see that it is a certainty that Eduardo has lost this particular source. Given this new search mission they apparently were beginning to conduct and the fact that it likely involves Carlo, that is unfortunate; I will acknowledge that. But why think this is any more than what it appears—that the army authorities have discovered yet another soldier with a drug problem?"

"If the authorities have our soldier, then they will also soon know he has already let someone know here in the south of this new spy mission in our airspace. Their clandestine search, such as it was, is blown. That would make their operation ineffective, would it not? And that would be good for us, not a threat. I respect your views, Raul, and of course yours, Geraldo, but so far, I do not see this as much of a threat."

"It is more than that, Pablo, because of several facts that I think we have no alternative but to put together," the obviously concerned Raul explained. "We have here in the city, staying as the guest of Alberto Rodriguez, this Senor Santiago of the American DEA, who, according to one of our DEA sources in America, is spending much time in the southwest. Doing precisely what, no one is certain. We have this joint DEA military spy operation in our airspace, a first against us. To our knowledge, the secretary is running no such operation in cooperation with the Americans, and I would think we would know. That makes this incursion a unilateral action on the American's part. That is a serious thing to do and unprecedented. The drones are commanded by the American general Rodriguez from their base in El Paso, who is the close cousin to our Secretary Rodriguez. As I understand the family relationship, General Rodriguez was very close to both Alberto and Emilio Rodriguez, and Emilio was recently murdered in what was no doubt a trafficking-related action. So this general now cooperates with the DEA and institutes this unilateral search at this time? All to locate Carlo, we are told by our source, three months after his escape from their jail. Why Carlo, and why now? Do they somehow think Carlo was involved in Emilio Rodriguez's assassination? We know that to not be the case, but what has happened recently that would initiate this incursion and this search for Carlo?

"No one involved with the authorities really knows anything about Carlo, or at least that is what we believe. Has something else happened that somehow can be connected back to Carlo? Except for escaping their jail, what has Carlo been involved with—or is involved with—that could warrant their attention? What I am driving at here, Pablo, is that I see no logical reason that Carlo should be attracting this attention now, yet he is.

"What have you told me on countless occasions? Never underestimate your enemy. Well, I suggest we do not start now. This search with their aircraft makes no sense, not now. So what is the American DEA really up to, and why is the American general helping? It does not seem possible to me that this general would be involved in such an action without his cousin knowing about it. That can only mean that Secretary Rodriguez does know yet has not seen fit to advise his president of this operation. Why would he do such a thing unless this action was in some way directed toward you? If it were directed at anyone else, surely your secretary for public security would have advised you."

Geraldo was nodding in agreement as he looked at Alvarez. "Jefe, I agree with Raul. There is also this report that there was some mystery surrounding Carlo's escape. Add to that the report that the American army authorities acknowledge they are dealing with their soldier, our informer, yet he is set to meet with our handler tomorrow. What are we to make of that?"

Alvarez looked at his technical wizard and then to Raul and then to Ray. He turned his attention to Geraldo. "Geraldo, was there any mention in any of this of Ray? Are the authorities looking for both escapees or just Carlo?"

"Nothing about Ray. Just Carlo, Eduardo told me."

Alvarez turned to Ray. "Ray, this may sound like a strange question considering the circumstances, but was there anything about the escape that you found unusual?"

Jesus Christ, I do not like where this is going. I don't like any of it. I have to give them something, Ray thought as he fought to keep a blank look on his face.

"Nothing, Jefe. One moment we were driving down the street, and then we were hit and crashed. There was confusion, and the guards were stunned; we grabbed their weapons and forced them to give up the keys, and we quickly left, never looking back. We were gone within a minute or two of the crash. The only thing I ever wondered about was the truck that hit us. I do not remember seeing it or the driver after we stopped or at any time during our escape. I am not sure he even stopped. Could that be it, Jefe—that whoever hit our vehicle never stopped?"

"Perhaps. It could be a simple hit-and-run accident. Maybe even likely the other driver could have been in America illegally and could not be part of any police report. Were there others in the van, Ray?"

"Yes, Jefe, four other prisoners that I did not really know, but they had to be important if they were being moved to the new prison, as Carlo and I were."

"Perhaps, Raul, the crash was intended to free one of the other prisoners?"

"Possible, Pablo. That is not an idea without merit, but it's almost likely if one of the others was an important man in one of the other cartels. My mind would rest easier if we had the names of the others being transferred that morning. Maybe we would know of them."

"I will agree with you, Raul, and you also, Geraldo, that I do think it is telling that the authorities are only looking for a Carlo and not both men. That does seem to indicate that Carlo is someone special to them for some reason. Geraldo, did Corro say when his people would be following up?"

Ray's stoic outer appearance belied the huge emotional turmoil that was coursing through him. *My God*, thought Ray, *I'm glad they're considering my lie, but they are missing so obvious an alternative—or what seems to me to be obvious. But maybe I'm not thinking clearly. Be objective, asshole: Is it obvious to me only because I know the truth that the whole incident was staged? If I did not know that, would I think of me? Jesus, they are so close to the truth.*

"No, Jefe. I am sure Corro put great pressure on them to perform, but under the circumstances, they all must be careful, or they will do nothing more than draw attention to themselves."

"Yes, I am sure you are right. Geraldo, see what you can find out about Carlo and Ray's actual escape—news stories, any follow-up stories, that sort of thing. See if you can find out the names of the others in the van that morning and any other mysteries this informer says he overheard others talking about. Raul, I appreciate your view of events and the questions you raise. We should and will take them seriously, but let us also not attach a greater significance to them than the facts warrant. Let's allow Corro and Eduardo to do their jobs. For our part, we shall have Geraldo here continue to look into the issues. Also, we shall continue to watch both Alberto Rodriguez and his guest. During the course of the evening, perhaps at dinner after our guests have helped themselves to some wine, I will ask some questions with the intent of gaining additional information on the interesting Senor

Santiago—without, of course, revealing anything we know. Best we see how they both act and react. I will have a private word with General Lozano about increasing our air patrols in the north and also increasing our radar awareness. Alberto need not know of this. Besides, what can the American drones actually see as they fly around? Is it even possible to find one man? Frankly, that strikes me as pure science fiction."

"With respect, Jefe," Geraldo said, "these aircraft are very effective and quite extraordinary. Our air force is to receive a squadron of these from the Americans soon as part of our earlier joint-border agreements. They are older versions of what the Americans are now using, but if you knew where to look—a specific area, for example—and had clues to know what to look for—say, a known pattern of movement—you would indeed be able to identify a single person."

"Thank you for the information, Geraldo. But I still do not think we have much to worry about just yet. Raul, update Eduardo on your thoughts, and for the time, let's have Carlo stay close to the Chihuahua area until we know more. No sense in having him attract any attention. And Raul, tell Eduardo to watch Carlo carefully without insulting him. In other words, let's help Carlo stay out of trouble if he should visit his women, OK? Also, have Eduardo have some of his men watching for any unusual aircraft or over-flights of our estates. I do not believe Alberto is any closer to me than they have ever been, even with the help of his cousin and this Senor Santiago. But we shall not underestimate our adversaries, Raul, as you so wisely counsel. Also, I think we should move up our schedule to depart for Baja to Sunday afternoon, assuming all goes well tomorrow. I will give a nationwide address tomorrow night to summarize our victory over the Gang of Four. It will be a triumphant end to what has otherwise been a very stressful and tragic week for the people. I think our victory will go a long way to bringing our people out of their grief for Fernandez. Our leaving the city on Sunday afternoon so that I may visit my ailing mother will be seen as a perfectly reasonable thing to do. We can then move to the north Sunday night. Eduardo has to keep Carlo under control for only two days, and then we will be there and he with us."

"Yes, Pablo. I will see to the arrangements."

"Fine." Alvarez looked at his watch. "Six forty. My guests are no doubt here. Geraldo, one last question. What have you discovered about Mr. Santiago thus far?"

"Jefe, I have read as much on the man as is available in the databases we may access without attracting attention. He appears to be exactly what we have heard: a long-tenured, highly decorated investigator with an enviable record of achievement. He was offered the post of deputy director of their DEA for operations, the third-highest position in their organization, but turned that promotion down to remain a field agent. He evidently is not a man concerned with politics or power. He is, I feel, Jefe, a man of great talent and integrity. He has perhaps his two closest friends in the top positions in their DEA and therefore has the freedom and support to pursue whatever agenda or goals he wishes. That makes him dangerous in my view, Jefe."

"I would agree with you, Geraldo—a man we should certainly respect. Ray, my guests are most likely having drinks in the front living room; would you please go tell them that I am running a few minutes late and will join them directly? Then you may go and have your dinner and take the rest of the night off. Thank you.

"Geraldo, you know what to do; you also may go. Thank you for your report, and please tell Eduardo we have spoken. Raul, please stay for a moment."

After Ray and Geraldo had closed the door behind them Alvarez looked at his old friend. "Now, Raul, tell me what I feel you could not bring yourself to say in front of the others."

Raul smiled a small, knowing smile, acknowledging Pablo's intuition. "How could you tell?"

"I can always tell, old friend, when you are really worried about something. Do not be concerned; no one else could see this concern in your eyes."

"Pablo, I am worried. I have no doubts that Secretary Rodriguez, this Senor Santiago, and General Rodriguez of the American army are somehow working together, and whatever it is, Alberto Rodriguez does not wish you to know about it. I also suspect that the catalyst for this alliance, if that is what it is, is not Carlo at all but the assassination of Emilio Rodriguez. One thing we have not mentioned tonight is our failed attempt to coerce Alberto last month. The Condor makes a direct attempt to subvert the head of the national police with the threat on his family. But the attempt fails with the daring helicopter rescue Alberto somehow arranged for without our knowing, removing his family as a possible pawn for us—another mystery, by the way, I have not been able to figure out, and I must. Soon after, Emilio is killed. If it were my brother, I would have blamed the Condor. Carlo's only connection is that he is a part of our organization, a fact we believe is unknown to the authorities. I realize I am speculating here, but what I think has happened is that the Rodriguez brothers knew more than we were giving them credit for, and the remaining brother has solicited help from that part of his remaining family that is in a position to help him get his brothers' killers. I think we must assume the worst case here."

"And the worst case, old friend?"

"That Alberto Rodriguez, or more likely his brother, has or had discovered some connection from Carlo to the Condor that we are unaware of. If not the Condor, then certainly the Vargas family of Chihuahua, which puts them one step closer to you. Rodriguez knows something, Pablo; I feel it. And he is pursuing it outside his official duties with the help of the others."

Alvarez looked long and hard at his old and close friend. He was never surprised by Raul's intelligence or deductive reasoning skills. Raul had come so far from the simple guard his father had selected to protect Alvarez all those years ago. For the first time in a long while, he felt a little trapped. Should he tell his old friend what Emilio Rodriguez had revealed to him that night, just three weeks ago, regarding the connection to the Pena alias that had resulted in his murder by Manuel's hand? Or just let it go for now? He hated the idea of deceiving his old friend, especially when he was right—or at least on the right path to figuring it all out. But his instincts told him to keep the information to himself for now. *Why?* he wondered. *Why not just tell Raul? He will tell me that it was the right thing for Manuel to do, just as Manuel did when he asked for my forgiveness for having killed my best friend. But it seems so clear that God would have never taken Manuel as he did, therefore protecting the secret of Emilio's assassination for all time, unless there was a purpose that was part of God's plan.* He would not tell Raul.

"My feeling is, Raul, that you are right in some way. So let us watch and learn. Let the others reveal to us what they are about and what they are up to. There is no connection to me here in the city; I am confident of that. I also feel that making a connection to me through Carlo is very unlikely, and of course there is no connection between us and Emilio's unfortunate assassination. Has there been any progress by our police?

"We, not the police or Rodriguez, know who the shooters were. They were mercenaries we have also used. They do not know who was behind the contract. They were approached by an unnamed source with a great deal of money, and they took the job. I'm afraid that's a dead end."

More dead than you know, old friend. Your brother had the cutout killed. And with Manuel's untimely death at the hands of that despicable Vasso, that trail is also dead. Best we leave it at that.

"Pablo, there is another topic we must discuss."

For the first time in the last twenty or thirty minutes, the countenance of Alvarez changed. The upbeat, confident, nonplussed president suddenly looked very sad. "I know, old friend."

"If I am right, and Alberto Rodriguez does know more than he is letting on, it is necessary to your long-term plans that we eliminate that potential threat."

"I was afraid you might mention this, Raul. Perhaps I am more a coward than I realize; I have refused to think about that possibility. Alberto and I have known each other for so long. We were never as close as Emilio and I were—I know this—but think what you will of me, I love Alberto like a brother. I have known only six dear friends in a full lifetime; it seems so few. Your brother and Luis's father have both died that I may live. Emilio was murdered, and you, Miguel, and Alberto Rodriguez are all I have left. Am I to murder one of my three surviving friends so that I may fulfill my destiny? I think not. I have been deeply troubled for the last several years, uncertain if my actions are indeed God's will. I know you do not believe as I do, but young Ray's deliverance has helped me to believe that they are. My fate, whatever it is, is now in God's hands. Alberto is not to be harmed."

Raul merely nodded his agreement. *He gets so sentimental, but am I to think less of him because he does have a conscience? I may have to save you from yourself, old friend, and endure whatever punishment you feel is necessary.*

"You are many things, Pablo, but a coward you are not. It will be as you wish. I must speak with Geraldo; then I will join you in the living room." He turned and left the president of Mexico to consider his beliefs and future events alone.

Alberto and Bennie arrived precisely at six thirty and were shown into the large formal front living room of the lovely mansion. Also there were the traitors, as Bennie had come to think of them, Quito-Perez and Ramirez, and Attorney General Farias, secretary of national defense General Lozano, and his aide, Colonel Saynez. The seven of them were easily swallowed up in the large space and, as happened at most such events, gathered informally around the bar. They were standing in a loose circle having their first drink when Ray walked in. Bennie could barely conceal his surprise at seeing him up so close and with so few people around. He just wanted to turn and embrace him in the worst way, excuse himself from the others, and walk Ray right the hell out the front door of the president's residence. Bennie could still not get used to his appearance. Apparently for close aides to the president, there was a dress code. Not unlike his appearance the day before, Ray looked very sharp in what was clearly an expensive dark-charcoal-gray pinstripe suit that made Bennie feel a little self-conscious about his own. Bennie wasn't a clothes hog by any stretch of the imagination, but he did recognize tailored suits when he saw them, and Ray's fit him like a comfortable old glove, by the looks of it.

Ray walked up with the confidence and bearing of a man quite comfortable in his surroundings and place and approached Alberto, who, as secretary of public security, was the most senior of the cabinet-level ministers in the room. Attorney General Farias; Quito-Perez, as head of the national police; and Ramirez, as head of the AFI, while technically listed as members of the president's executive cabinet, were nonetheless department heads and senior deputies to Alberto. General Lozano, of course, was the second most important cabinet secretary in the government hierarchy after Alberto.

"Senor Secretary," Ray said with a small bob of his head, "the president sends his regrets for the delay required by his attention to several small matters. He will join you shortly. Is there anything at all we may provide you in the meantime?"

"Thank you—Senor Ortega, isn't it?"

"Yes, Mr. Secretary."

"We all appreciate the responsibilities the president bears. I believe we have everything we need here, gentlemen?"

There were several murmurs of yes. "We appreciate your letting us know that the president will be joining us soon," Alberto said pleasantly, as he thought, *I look forward to the day we can indeed share a drink together, young Ray.*

"Will you be joining us, Senor Ortega?"

"I will not have that pleasure, Senor Secretary. If you will excuse me, gentlemen."

With that and another nod to Alberto, Ray walked past the attended bar and through the servants door into the butler pantry and the kitchen beyond. He had not once looked at Bennie, not trusting himself to do so. Dealing with Alberto Rodriguez like he had done had been hard enough, knowing that Alberto knew who and what he was. He intended to get a message off to Bennie as soon as he safely could, letting him know just how close Raul Ortega seemed to be to figuring out the truth and the change in schedule for the trip north.

The group made small talk for several more minutes and then turned to the entry from the foyer as the president came striding in. Alberto was the one man in the room who could detect the confidence in his former friend as he entered. It was a strange feeling for Alberto to have had that thought: *former friend.* For all the great and often tragic events that had transpired recently, it was the first time he had thought of Alvarez in those terms. Even when discussing strategy recently with Bennie, he was certain that phrase had not entered his consciousness. He had seen Pablo Alvarez in their lifetime together at emotionally low times and at high times, and the man was riding high—that much was evident. Alberto wanted to disabuse him of the high he was on as soon as humanly possible.

After making sure his guests all had fresh drinks, the discussions around the bar became casual and were for the most part no different than those you might find in the gentlemen's bar at any upscale club as the members gathered after a tough week. It was as if Alvarez was putting everyone at ease in his presence, addressing those he knew by their Christian names and inquiring about their families or asking them how they were adjusting to their new responsibilities. All but the attorney general and General Lozano had been in different positions only a week before. He made references to common events in their shared pasts or told quick anecdotes of Alberto or of Ramirez from when they had been in college together. He engaged Bennie in a pleasant conversation about his law enforcement career and reminded him how much he liked Director Mills when he had met him several months before. All in all a tour de force performance, Bennie thought, for in spite of the man's huge character flaws, he never missed a beat, sounding and looking not only presidential but absolutely sincere with everyone. Bennie mostly watched and listened as he sipped the fine old scotch whiskey that Alvarez had available for his guests.

I want to say this man is a four-star phony, Bennie thought, *but in a way he really isn't. He seems off his rails enough to really believe in what he's doing, and that makes this happy horseshit genuine and not an act. I have to remember that. This man is, in addition to everything bad we have discovered about him, a first-class politician who will continue to win the people over with every passing day. When he goes on national television and reports that he has all but wiped out the major cartels in Mexico, the people will be in his pocket. We can't act fast enough, and our evidence has to be irrefutable to trump the goodwill he will be carrying.*

It wasn't until the president suggested that they move to one of the seating areas available in the large room that the discussions turned to the business at hand: the planned raid set for noon tomorrow, which was the scheduled time that an informer had said the Gang of Four was to meet. Unknown to the others, of course, was the fact that Alberto's Los Pueblos Fantasmas had been in place for almost thirty hours and would be initiating their first strikes within hours. Bennie had sat in on Alberto's discussions planning and fine-tuning the raid, and also the planning for the aftermath, on two occasions so far this week and was not really listening to the briefing but rather thinking about Alvarez's upcoming trip to his mother's. He mentioned to the group while they were standing around the bar that if all went well tomorrow, he planned to have a national address early in the evening tomorrow night. With that complete, he planned to go to Baja on Sunday afternoon to see his ailing mother, who, he was sad to report, was not doing well. All the others had been sympathetic at the mention of this, but Bennie knew Alberto, like him, was harboring all kinds of emotions at the thought of Alvarez's trip, but sympathy was not one of them.

Alvarez moving up his schedule would mean that Alberto's skilled young major would have to shift immediately from the very dangerous tactical operations they were engaged in at the seminary to the planning and execution of yet another, hundreds of miles away. And this assumed that the major and his troops would be in a condition to do so. Bennie had never served in the military, but he had read enough to understand that any combat action was at best unpredictable, no matter how good the advance planning. As he was thinking about this, Bennie suddenly subconsciously realized that the president had directed a question at him. He refocused on Alvarez and said, "My sincere apologies, Mr. President, I was thinking about an aspect of what Alberto said about the plans for tomorrow and missed your question."

"Nothing to apologize for, Senor Santiago. I simply asked what the information was that you felt was so important that you saw the need to come down here in lieu of communicating or passing it through your liaison officer at your embassy."

Bennie looked at Alberto and then returned his attention to Alvarez. They had discussed the likelihood of Alvarez asking such a question and were prepared.

"Mr. President, as you may or may not be aware from your discussions with Director Mills several months ago, we have certain security problems in our southwest division out of El Paso. That division is our largest and our most important in our fight to interdict the trafficking—our front lines, to use a military metaphor. One of my jobs for the director is to try to find out who the informers are in our organization. It is not, however, my only area of responsibility. I also am in charge of running our special operations in the entire southwest United States.

"One of my operations has netted us some very high-value Mexican nationals who were residing illegally in my country. As a result, we have been able to obtain very good intelligence on some of the cartels in your country. It is from one of these sources we were able to confirm that two weeks ago, all three of the Mendoza brothers from Chihuahua were executed. The youngest brother, Federico, was actually killed in my country. We have recovered his remains for evidentiary reasons. As there are likely very few people who actually know the Mendozas are dead, and if the wrong people found out that we know, it would be possible in my view that the cartels responsible would be able to figure out who it is we have who gave us that information. And that is the kind of information I wish to keep from our enemies. Frankly, sir, I am not sure just who I can trust in our southwest division, but I wanted your Federal Police, and specifically Senor Rodriguez here, to know what I know. So I hopped on a plane, and here I am."

Alvarez showed no emotion or unusual interest as Bennie told him his story. What Mr. Santiago had just told him made sense and could well be the truth. He, of course, had ordered the Mendozas' execution as the Condor and, once the deed had been carried out by Eduardo and Carlo, had not given it another thought. He had not even wondered if his head of the national police had heard. He turned his attention to Alberto, who was sitting to his immediate left.

"Have you heard about this through your sources, Alberto?"

"Some rumors only, Mr. President; nothing we could confirm. It is something we have been working on, but as you realize, we have been occupied with higher-priority investigations as of late."

"So no idea about who has done the country this favor?"

"No idea yet, Mr. President, but in time, especially if we can take a great number of prisoners tomorrow. As you are aware, we want as many of the Gang of Four alive as we can, for the intelligence potential."

"Yes, I agree. Well, Senor Santiago, on behalf of my country, thank you for bringing us this information. I of course value life but am not saddened that we are free of the Mendoza brothers."

While they were discussing why Bennie was down here, Raul Ortega had quietly entered the room and stood off to one side and observed the conversation. He had heard Bennie's explanation and thought it bullshit, but there was nothing he could do about that at the moment. The conversation continued for another hour as they moved from details of the upcoming action to the many mundane details that would be required to jail all the suspects they hoped to capture and to the process for further investigation, compiling the evidence, and subsequent prosecutions. Attorney General Farias could expect to be very busy next year, they all agreed. The discussions concluded when the president stood and thanked everyone for giving up a significant part of their Friday evening to attend the briefing. The others were aware that Secretary Rodriguez and his guest were staying on for dinner and quickly made their way out, escorted by Raul.

Alvarez led his two remaining guests into the formal dining room, where three place settings were arranged at one end of the large, polished wood table. It was if they were dining on a Baldwin grand piano, the near-black finish was so deep and lustrous. For the next two hours, the three men shared what was, to all appearances, a wonderful dinner with warm and comfortable conversation. For all three men, each in their own way, the reality of the situation could not have been more false, their thoughts more different.

For the cop in Bennie, in spite of the many hours he himself had been undercover in similar situations as this dinner, he was still a mess inside knowing what he knew as he sat within a few feet of Alvarez. He recognized, as he had tried to make Ray understand, that the safest way to conceal your feelings while covert was to keep the lie you were living as close to the truth as possible. This trick served Bennie well, and he knew it. Any difficulties he may have had trying to disguise his true feelings as he sat next to Alvarez were easily masked by the natural and expected outward appearances anyone would be expected to exhibit dining with a head of state for the first time. He was sure Alvarez was none the wiser to his true feelings or his discomfiture with the dinner. Bennie, however, could not imagine the stress on Alberto as he sat there over dinner participating in more stories of him and Emilio and Alvarez as they had done this or that in school. The worst part of the evening for Alberto surely was when Alvarez had solemnly looked at the two of them after the first several toasts and made one to Emilio with the incantation, "To old friends not with us tonight, who sacrificed so much that we may be in a position to do justice for so many." Bennie would not have been a bit surprised nor blamed Alberto had he taken up his steak knife and stuck it in the deceiving bastard's eye.

For Alberto, the last several years of dealing with just whom to trust and whom not to trust had galvanized him in some way such that he could look normal, even relaxed, to be in the company of who was now his former friend. He ironically maintained his poise and an appearance of warmth in his eyes by keeping the image and memories of his brother near him—that, and he had the knowledge deep down inside that one way or another, he would have his revenge and soon. He hoped to do it publicly by bringing his narcissistic, psychopathic host to trial. But if that turned out to be impossible, he would simply have Los Pueblos Fantasmas deal with the son of a bitch. He could live with that, and then he would toast to Emilio and to justice—and mean it.

For Pablo Alvarez, his demeanor and attitude during the pleasant dinner were in fact sincere. He had questions in his mind about Bennie Santiago— maybe curiosity was a more accurate description—but he did not feel threatened in any way. Alberto was different. He was a threat, but Alvarez had no doubt he was in a position of strength so great that he could deal with it, whatever it was. As Raul probably speculated correctly, his old friend was most likely aware of the drone flights in the north being conducted with the assistance of his cousin. That meant Alberto was involved, no doubt, and that made it likely that something was in the works, and it probably had to do with Emilio's death. Alvarez could not escape the nagging feeling that Emilio probably shared with his older brother all or part of the information he had discovered that would eventually lead to Nicolas Pena, even if Emilio had said he had not.

Emilio had always been the cleverest of the three old friends, but it would be a mistake for anyone to underestimate Alberto. Alvarez certainly would not make that mistake again. In his heart, he knew what Raul had suggested was probably the thing to do, but he had to draw the line some-where. He simply would not kill everyone. Alvarez had realized that early on and had initiated the failed coercion attempt on Alberto for that reason. Co-opting was so much more preferred to killing. Having the Condor threaten Alberto and his family had been a bluff, but Alberto had perceived it as a serious threat. He too was curious how Alberto had so quietly and expertly arranged their extraction from their estate tennis court and their subsequent relocation to his cousin's army base near El Paso in the United States, which effectively put them out of reach. Not that he'd ever harm Alberto's family; he wouldn't.

He'd privately wept when he heard that Emilio had been killed, for he knew it had been Manuel's attempt to protect him. With a word to Manuel, he knew he could have prevented it, but he had stayed silent, and he would regret that for the rest of his life. He could try talking with Alberto, tell him the truth man to man, old friend to old friend about his family's history and the terrible choice he had been given. He could try to make Alberto understand what he was doing and why, but that was a fantasy, and Raul would have none of it. No, his old friend Raul, like his older brother, would have Alberto killed long before he could ever have such a talk.

His intelligence network was deep, and he had resources he had not used so far, deep, reliable sleepers who had not been activated and would not be for the time being. Not for several more weeks, anyway. He would wait until the raid was successful, wait until his primary enemies were taken out. He wanted dearly to see Eduardo and Carlo one last time, and he wanted to see the look in Barega's eyes as he told that fat, simple bastard he had failed in every way and was going to die. Raul would have his vengeance as well for his brother. No, for now the country needed heroes, and it needed to be lifted out of the fear and despair that had permeated all aspects of Mexican life for so long at the hands of the other cartels and for the grief over Fernandez's death.

By this time tomorrow, he thought, *I will have made Alberto a national hero. He will get most of the credit for our success tomorrow, and his popularity and profile will be raised to unprecedented heights for him. And this is a good thing.*

Their dinner finished and the next day's pending action weighing on all of them, Alberto and Bennie expressed their deep appreciation at the president's hospitality and left. It was not far to Alberto's home and only took a few minutes. Not a word was said, but looks were exchanged that bridged the silence and seemed to confirm each of their feelings. They had to get Alvarez. They returned home about nine and parted for their separate suite of rooms, each to deal with his own personal thoughts.

It was after eleven. Bennie was in his bed but nowhere near asleep when his phone alerted him to an incoming message. He grabbed the phone without turning on the light and scanned the message from Ray:

Baca talking with Eduardo.
Eduardo's man is one running
informer at army base that spilled
beans. Eduardo man corro sent
north to find out who is looking
for carlo. Check safe house las cruces.
He spoke today with informers in dea
and el paso police. Dea traitor gave
them you as being involved in
actions unknown to el paso dea.
Raul believes you and general
cousin involved with some action
with alberto and knows alberto not
sharing info with alvarez. That makes
alberto action suspect. Alvarez thinks
all to do with Emilio death.
Police informer has told of some
kind of mystery surrounding my
escape. When asked I said only that
other driver did not stop.
Very worried about Raul. Is on
road to truth and missing what
seems to me the obvious.

Need your perspective should I bug out?
Do not underestimate Raul.
You and alberto need to grab
baca as soon as possible.

On the one hand it was unbelievably gratifying to be once more in touch with Ray, but the messages tempered greatly these emotions. Bennie read and reread the message and thought about calling Alberto and sharing with him, but could see no reason to add to Alberto's burdens tonight. There was nothing they could do this evening to better understand the message much less deal with it. Better to let Alberto get some much needed sleep. It would keep till the morning. He looked at the message once more before sending Ray a short response:

do not bug out. carlo story and
questions still a good diversion.
big leap to think of you. hang tough
we will act in a few days in chi town.
stay in touch, we need to talk soon.

What was it Raul was close to knowing? Bennie's reply was the hardest thing he had done on this operation since having Ray incarcerated five months earlier. Big picture, he needed Ray to stay where he was and was gambling that the truth was still out of Raul Ortega's reach. But on a personal level, he felt like a hypocritical shit. He'd come down here with only one goal in mind—get Ray the hell out now—and here he was telling him to stay put. He hoped he was making the right call, for he knew he could never forgive himself if things blew up somehow, and Ray was exposed and killed. *A damn shitty business*, Bennie thought as he put his phone back on his nightstand, *damn shitty*. He lay back on his bed, wide awake in the knowledge that there would be no sleep again tonight.

23

Santo Tomás de Aquino por el Lago
(Saint Thomas of Aquinas on the Lake)
Los Mochis, State of Sinaloa
Saturday Morning

O stensibly, the planned government raid this day was technically a police action. In all, the government had outstanding warrants on some
forty known members of the various cartels that supposedly would be showing up today—everything from drug trafficking and murder to unlawful
intimidation and escape from incarceration. It was the government's intention, therefore, to try to serve those warrants. Other than the principals
that an informer said would be there, the government had no idea who else
would be part of the entourages.

The Federal Police, supported by special units of the country's military,
in addition to serving the warrants they possessed, were ordered to "detain
and arrest for questioning on suspicion of firearm violations" all members
of the cartels that showed up for the planned summit. This was based upon
the certainty that all the members of the entourages would be armed, in
violation of the laws of the country. That was the order as written: detain
and arrest.

To the fifty members of the Drug Tactical Unit of the Federal Police
that were actually involved and the two hundred troops of Company
A, First Battalion, Special Forces Air Mobile Group, the GAFE (Grupo
Aeromovil de Fuerzas Especiales) of the Mexican National Defense Army,
the detain-and-arrest portion of the order was both amusing and no doubt

some cover-your-ass legalese written by some government lawyer in the capital. It had to be. Anyone in the government who thought for a second that the heavily armed entourages of the four cartels scheduled to be at the summit would allow themselves to be "detained" had shit for brains. During their joint training and team familiarization and rehearsals over the last several days, the Federal Policemen and soldiers all agreed that the cartel retainers might indeed allow the Federals to "detain" them, just a second or two after the last available round of ammunition they carried was spent, and their empty Kalashnikovs or American-made M16-A2s, or the popular compact Israeli Tavors—to name just three of the many light assault weapons available to and known to be carried by the cartels—were locked on an open, smoking breech. But likely not one second before. This was going to be the shootout, they all believed, and not like the fucked-up operation against the Mendoza cartel a month or so before that had gone so badly.

The officers and commanders of the combined strike team made a point to tell the troops that the security on this op was ironclad, and it would be the cartels that would be surprised this day and not the Federals. No one outside of them and a very small circle in the government knew where the joint-action team was or where they would be going and when. If ever there was a black op, this was it. The men of the combined strike team knew nothing about the source of the first-rate onsite intel they had been receiving in their updates in the last forty-eight hours, but their confidence in what their officers were telling them was boosted by the stream of updated information. There were clearly informers in with the cartels and recon boots on the ground at the seminary, as well as other units on the federal highway north and south of the seminary.

Alberto's Los Pueblos Fantasmas, of course, was handling the seminary onsite intel, and four ten-man recon squads from Company D, First Battalion, had been quietly dropped off at points along the federal highway, two miles north and south, in positions to report on all traffic movements that may be of interest and to interdict any reinforcements that the cartels might call in. The two northern squads also were in a position to observe the small local road that headed west to the ocean and the public beaches and small marina located there. Trouble from the sea had also been planned for.

The intel from the recon GAFE assets on the highway was communicated directly to the major in command of the morning's assault at his communications center onsite. The intel from the ghosts was communicated to Alberto, who then relayed it to his top Federal Police tactical commander in overall charge of the operation, who in turn relayed the information to the major commanding Company A. The army was the sledgehammer, while the police commander had the responsibility of enforcing the country's laws. The strike team commanders knew they were facing a lawless group of criminals this day, but an attempt had to be made to observe the laws and legal procedures of the country; even the cartel bastards had rights. It was made clear to all in the attack force that an attempt was going to be made to minimize bloodshed and to in fact detain all those who showed up. To the special forces troops, that meant take prisoners. The men of Company A had rehearsed the likely scenarios and the required fire discipline that was built into the fire plan. But if the cartel entourages responded as many felt they would, it would get deadly exciting very quickly, and the resulting mess would take weeks or months to sort out.

The government raid to try to capture or kill Ricardo Arellano, Ramon Fuentes, and the two Felix-Contreras brothers from Tijuana and, from the east coast, Armando Caro and Jesus Qiuntero—or the Gang of Four, as they were collectively known—began very early on Saturday morning in that quiet, still, serene cusp of time between the late night of the spent day and before the dawn of the new one.

Colonel Portillo and Major Garcia had had extended conversations with the secretary regarding their initial assault. First the guards and then those sleeping at the grotto entrance needed to be taken in silence. If in the course of the attack on the grotto group, the ghosts were detected and the alarm sounded, this would alert the second group, and no doubt the word would go out that there were other armed cartel or government forces in the area, and that would be enough to blow the entire operation. Because of where the cartel groups had been located, the planning group had finally concluded that both camps were escape alternatives for at least two of the cartel leaders. This was the only logical conclusion. They were not advance scouts in the traditional sense, for they could see nothing from their positions. They were there to get their principals out if the shit hit the fan, and whoever they worked for would know to escape to the east. All in all, a simple backup if the main road in was compromised.

The strike teams of Los Pueblo Fantasmas broke into two groups, with the larger team A going for the group of infiltrators at the grotto entrance because there were twelve cartel soldiers there, and they were watching the second cartel group on the lower lake road, who had no idea their arrival had been seen by so many. After observing the grotto group, as they were thought of, from the first night they had arrived, Major Garcia and his sergeant had their guard rotations and patterns down pat. By three in the morning, there would only be a pair of guards watching the other encampment and another pair on duty at their own. The eight others would be asleep.

Dull, boring routine takes its toll on the untrained and undisciplined. This was especially true in the very early-morning hours, when the body's internal clock said it was time for sleep. The two guards at the camp were anything but alert and in fact were taking turns napping while on duty. The two watching the other cartel camp were more alert—there was no napping here, as there were armed men not three hundred feet away who were thought of as the enemy. The lake access road that came south from the federal highway meandered through dense woods for a half mile before meeting the lake below the seminary, and then it traced the shore ten to fifteen feet above the water's edge. The grotto camp was the southernmost around a long, gentle curve as the road followed the shore, out of sight from the second camp. Both camps had made attempts at concealing their vehicles and their camps with the use of what looked like fish nets that liberal amounts of long grasses and leafy branches had been added to. Why the second group that had arrived had not thought to patrol around the curve was a mystery to the colonel. The most they had done was station a guard at both ends of their camp, clearly believing they were the first and only backup group in the area. Their ignorance or arrogance, whichever it was, was wrong twice, and they would pay for it.

There was cover near the lake for the well trained, and the ghosts of Los Pueblos Fantasmas were nothing if not superbly trained. The camps and therefore the guards were tucked up against the side of the road at the base of the hill descending from the seminary above. Where the meeting hall was located, the long slope to the lake and lake road was covered by an old apple orchard that still produced the occasional fruit. While the lake was clearly visible from the top of the bluff, the road was conveniently screened from view by the orchard and the sloping hillside itself as it rolled gently downward toward the lake. Because the two encampments were concerned with possible action from the direction of the top of the hill first and then secondarily the possibility of someone else coming down the road from the north, that was where their focus was trained. They had set up their camps and the security routines, such as they were, to meet those threats. They simply had not imagined an attack from across the beautiful, tranquil Lake Aquinas.

The black six-man rafts Alberto's ghosts used were made of a special material that seemed to devour any light and not reflect it. In the predawn darkness, the quarter moon that rose in the early evening was mostly finished with its predictable journey across the clear, star-filled night sky, and the shore road at the base of the hill was once more consumed in total darkness. The warm bodies of the guards, both those sleeping and those supposedly on duty, were clear green spectral shapes in the sophisticated night vision equipment the ghosts wore. Their plan assumed that their targets would also have such equipment, but none was in evidence, as viewed through either the personal devices the stalkers wore or through the incredible night vision scopes many had attached to their weapons. To a man, the ghosts of Los Pueblos Fantasmas preferred night actions. With their equipment and training, they always felt they had a major advantage over those they attacked.

Team A approached from two directions. One six-man squad circled the lake from the south and approached up the road, descending to the lakeshore in the final several hundred feet to ensure their invisibility. The rest of team A, twelve men in all, and all of team B, another twelve men, came silently across the lake in their low-slung black rafts, invisible on the tranquil inky-black surface. Once making the shore, they split up into their attack groups and silently crept into position. All the action was being directed and watched by Colonel Portillo and his two spotters from the command's concealed perch east of the lake. Each of the three had high-powered night scopes that could read the numbers on the license plates of the mostly hidden vehicles the cartel bands had arrived in. Every inch of the far shore was being watched carefully.

For Alberto's ghosts, the only truly reliable weapon the stalkers had for silence was instantaneous death. They had discussed nonlethal alternatives in the interest of minimizing casualties, but in this scenario, they had no choice; the unlucky guards who had drawn the midnight-to-four watch had likely seen their last crescent moon traverse the sky. Once the guards were dealt with, only then could they use the Taser weapons they also carried. It was one thing to Taser a man in his sleep and another to try to get close enough to do so to a heavily armed guard, no matter how drowsy he may be. But Alberto's ghosts would try.

From the lakeshore, two teams of two crept silently up the bank toward the two targets watching the northern camp. One man of each team had a handheld Taser, the other his compact and lethal Belgian-made FN F2000 assault rifle with sound suppressor and laser sight. The shooter of each team would stay in his fixed, concealed position just off the road, his targeted guard a mere thirty feet away and in his sights, while his partner made an attempt to approach. The stalkers would try to silently creep up from behind to within the ten to fifteen feet necessary to make an ultra-accurate Taser shot. The latest versions of their weapons were capable out to thirty feet, had laser sights, and, in the hands of a professional, were highly accurate. The two Taser stalkers wanted to close that gap to get a 100 percent shot. If at any time their partners in their concealed positions thought the targets detected the attack about to blindside them, they were free to take out the guards lethally. It was the squad leader's call, and his finger was on the trigger.

Both of the guards were sitting in the grass having a whispered conversation, their attention on the camp a couple hundred feet to the north. The two ghost stalkers, in their special soft-soled all-weather boots, were as silent as the death the two guards would surely experience if they realized too soon what was happening. The stalkers got to ten feet and, with a double click in their headsets from their squad leader, took their shots. Both guards went down, twitching and writhing uncontrollably but in relative silence as the neuromuscular incapacitation characteristics of the low-voltage devices overrode the brain's command and control systems to the muscles. The stalkers quickly gagged and bound the incapacitated guards.

The two teams of stalkers to the south at the grotto camp were not as fortunate. Given their positioning, there was no sneaking up on the guards from behind as they watched the road to the south, for that would have meant coming from the campsite itself. The squad leader felt like he had no choice but to have his two shooters take their single silenced shots. It was over so fast that the unfortunate guards had no idea what had hit them. With all the guards taken, the twelve-man main body of team A silently crept into the camp. Each ghost targeted on a single cartel member, and they Tasered them in their sleep. The two leaders were found soundly asleep on cots in the grotto itself, an empty bottle of Jack Daniels nearby. In a matter of minutes, all the incapacitated retainers were bound and gagged. The four stalkers of team A returned to the lake and moved north to join team B, which was already in position to take out the only two guards standing watch at the second camp, one at either end. In less than ten minutes, team B had taken the second camp with only one guard killed.

In less than an hour, the ghosts had silently eliminated the threat, killed three, and taken twenty-one prisoners. The next few hours were devoted to the task of clearing the field and returning the captured retainers to the prepared detention sites across the lake. In the meantime, as the captured cartel soldiers regained their senses, a squad from the intelligence division of Los Pueblos Fantasmas began a series of intensive interrogations of the suspected camp leaders. For the almost twenty-four hours that the intelligence elements of Los Pueblos Fantasmas had been watching the camps, they had clearly identified the leaders. It hadn't been hard. With the attempts at camouflaging their vehicles and their camps came manual labor, and it was easy to see who was giving the orders and who was doing the grunt work. The leaders had also been on their phones a lot. Maybe to their bosses, maybe they were just chatty—who knew. But now that the ghosts had them, they needed to know if there were all-clear codes or other communications to be sent, and that meant getting the information out of the leaders. It was hoped that the muffled screams of the leaders being aggressively interrogated could not be heard through the dense woods surrounding the base camp a half mile to the east of the seminary.

With the grotto entrance secured, one squad from team A reconnoitered the hidden passageway for its entire length. It was remarkable what they found. The old tunnel had been carved out of the dense clay soils many years before and then lined with stone slabs on the floor and up the side walls until the stone met the smooth, arching plaster ceiling. There was evidence of old wall pockets that had clearly been designed to hold torches or lanterns, but these had been replaced with surface-mounted metal conduits and industrial-quality electric light fixtures. The stone floor was nothing more than a series of endless steps that marched up into the darkness, leading, they suspected, to a basement under the old hall. The squad was using only their night vision equipment and low-light battery-powered lanterns to make their way. At several intervals on the climb up the hill, the steps ceased, and there was a larger cavern-like room about thirty feet on a side with a level floor. Each of the two rooms held huge stockpiles of weapons and literately bales of plastic-wrapped American currency. Whichever of the Tijuana cartel leaders who had organized the summit and suggested the seminary as a meeting place was obviously a chief benefactor of the seminary and somehow knew of this space. Whatever currency could not get laundered or sent offshore was evidently being kept in this "bank" beneath the seminary. The squad continued its climb and indeed discovered that the grotto terminated in a hidden room off a small, dark, musty storage basement beneath the front portion of the hall. The door that they had pushed through from the grotto side was nearly invisible to the naked eye from the basement side. Anyone from the seminary routinely visiting the basement would never see the passageway. Given all the cobwebs the ghosts saw, no one was using the basement very often. The old wooden stairs from the main floor above looked like they had not been used in years. The door to the stairway was from a pantry off the simple but large kitchen where catered meals could be organized for those using the hall. Someone had taken great pains to conceal the old grotto from the basement. And that someone had to be one of the principal cartel leaders.

The combined police and army force had begun staging for the upcoming action forty-eight hours before in a bivouac about nine miles from the seminary. Located beyond the rolling hills to the east in an unoccupied wooded area, the some 250 troops and Federal Police officers, along with their equipment, had first moved from their remote training camp outside of Ciudad Obregon to the staging area by helicopter, and then they had made the move to the seminary on Friday afternoon into the night on foot from the east. No one at the seminary had any idea that so many heavily armed Federal troops had arrived and were now bivouacked in the woods between the federal highway and the manicured grounds of the seminary itself. Their line of march had been carefully reconnoitered and mapped for them prior to the staging. The skilled special forces teams of Los Pueblos Fantasmas had reconnoitered their lines of march to bypass the two surprising cartel encampments established ahead of the planned summit. Of course, the Federals had been completely unaware of this shadow group or, for that matter, the small encampments of cartel retainers. They would not find out about these until after the attack, if then.

The Federals had arrived near eight o'clock Friday night after the relatively easy nine-mile march and set up their bivouac at the preplanned location deep in the woods confirmed by their handheld GPS devices. The encampment had been carefully selected to be far from sight or sound of all of those living, studying, and working at the seminary but close enough to stage to the killing grounds. There was a decently large clearing in the center of their bivouac area that could accommodate several helicopters if necessary, but to the untrained eye that might happen to be taking a nature walk through the woods, the troops were all but invisible in their camouflaged, prepared positions. Totally concealed surveillance posts had been established to watch and control all access in or out of the seminary at the one main entry road and at the secondary access road to the lakeshore. Careful, skilled patrols had been sent out to reconnoiter the ground for the next day's planned assault. Actually, the onsite commanders had been reassuring themselves and their troops that there would be no cartel ambushes awaiting them. The planned action would not be a repeat of the Mendoza fiasco a month earlier. The government had had what they believed to be reliable intelligence on that op as well but had become the ambushed when they had attacked. Clearly, someone within the government involved with the Mendoza raid planning had been working for the cartels. Whoever that was had not been exposed, so they were taking no chances.

Their top commanders and planners, headed up by the secretary of public security Alberto Rodriguez himself, had relayed to the troops that independent reliable recon teams had already scoured the grounds, and all was as planned. Several hours of patrolling had satisfied the onsite commanders that was indeed the case. The Federals seemed to have the advantage. While the cartels might have picked the location for their summit, the killing ground had been selected by the Federals. If their intel proved to be correct—always an unknown going into a fight—they would have the cartels outmanned, outgunned, and outpositioned. The fight would be very one sided. If only.

24

Santo Tomás de Aquino por el Lago
(Saint Thomas of Aquinas on the Lake)
Los Mochis, State of Sinaloa.
Saturday Morning

C ompany A of the First GAFE had been selected for the mission not alphabetically but because they had been judged the best of the regiment. Though the regiment was normally commanded by a captain, the regimental colonel, on orders from General Lozano himself, assigned the battalion operations officer, an experienced major, to take command in the field with the company commander serving as his executive officer. The company's regular XO was sitting in a brig cell being questioned on just why he had violated orders and brought a personal communication device on the training op the previous week. His answers thus far had been far from satisfactory. The mission was too important to leave in the hands of a captain, no matter how excellent his reputation, so the major had been placed in temporary command.

The company was organized on classic infantry lines with each of the six thirty-man tactical platoons commanded by a first or second lieutenant. The twenty-man headquarters platoon, while responsible for the overall command, logistics, medical, and intelligence functions of the company, could fight as effectively as the tactical platoons. Each of the line platoons was made up of three ten-man squads commanded by a second lieutenant or a first sergeant. While classified as light infantry, the company of special forces was particularly lethal and would be in a position to wreck total and complete havoc on the cartel entourages.

251

There was no doubt that bands of streetwise criminals armed with the latest in automatic weapons were dangerous and could appear quite lethal, especially to unarmed citizens, but they were nothing when compared to the highly trained special forces troopers. It was expected that at least one of the Tijuana cartels used as its retainers former special forces members. That was a sad day in the military's history when one of the first highly trained units, some fifty men, had deserted en masse and sold their services for big money to one of the Tijuana cartels. But that had been seven years ago, and things were different now. Alberto and his onsite commanders knew that the traitors would likely be involved and were ready to deal with them. They would be the last to lay down their weapons, and they would put up the most effective counterfire. They'd be easy to spot as a result, and there were contingency fire plans to deal with them.

The intel said that the cartel caravans were to arrive independently and meet on the main athletic field of the seminary, and from there, only the leaders were to move further up the main road to gather at the old community building turned meeting hall high on the gradual rise that overlooked Lake Aquinas to the east. According to the informant's intel, each leader was apparently allowed four retainers only at the meeting hall. That meant about twenty armed men at the old hall. The remaining eighty to ninety armed retainers of the combined entourages would remain at the field, and presumably, no one would get itchy and start World War III among them. All of the germane details had been provided in the intel briefing report that had been distributed to the assault teams. The intel was so detailed about how the cartels were to conduct themselves that the troops—and most of the commanders—had thought it had to be pure bullshit. How could anyone know such detail? The question had been asked and answered: the Federals had a reliable source in a cartel camp that was feeding them all the intel. All would have been flabbergasted to discover that the traitor in one of the cartels was in fact a longtime member of the Condor's cartel, and the Condor was their new president. As the cartels did not trust one another, the details of how the summit was to be organized had been necessary and agreed to in advance to satisfy the leaders. With the confirmation by the nighttime patrols that only the Federals were on the grounds, while still highly doubtful of the accuracy of the intelligence they were receiving, the troops were nonetheless confident that they had the upper hand.

The Federals had eight hours to rest up from their night march, eat, and review their individual small-unit plans for the last time. Just before dawn, they would quietly move through the woods and take up their various concealed attack positions. The bulk of the forces were to surround the large open athletic field with the light infantry company from the First GAFE assigned to this task. Their job was to contain and capture the large retainer forces that would be waiting for their leaders to return from the summit at the old meeting lodge. On three sides of the field were woods where the special forces troopers could set up easily concealed positions. It was here that they established most of their light machine gun positions and carefully laid out the fields of fire that would bring the entire field under a withering crossfire yet not expose any other team to the same fire.

The fourth side of the field was open and a part of the general campus, with lawn areas and old shade trees the principal features. Set back from the field on this side was an old brick pump house and maintenance building that two squads of Federals quietly occupied in the night. There would be several light machine guns placed here, as well as a squad with 40mm grenade launchers to cut off the only avenue of retreat to the highway, through the central seminary grounds. These squads, plus the endmost squads from the deployments at the west and east ends of the field, had the added task of flanking and cutting off the entourages if they made a break for the seminary. Under no circumstances could the combined police and army units allow this, for that would mean potential hostages for the cartels, and that was a leverage the planners were determined to deny them.

The army company and their national police colleagues were armed to the teeth. At a minimum, every soldier in the company carried the FX-05 assault rifle or heavier. The FX-05 was known as the Xiuhcoatl, from the Aztec language for "fire serpent." The Mexican-manufactured assault rifle was based on the design of the German made Heckler and Koch G-36V but did have differences. The receiver, or stock, was a carbon-reinforced polymer, and the barrel was made of an advanced stainless steel. The model the GAFE troops used had a thirty-round detachable box magazine and fired the hot NATO 5.56 x 45mm round. With an effective rate of fire of 750 rounds per minute, the 150 troopers of the company surrounding the field carrying fire serpents could pour a combined hundred thousand rounds per minute into a kill zone. No armed group could survive that kind of fire if their only cover were their expensive SUVs, no matter how well armored. In addition to their base personal weaponry, each platoon had a special-weapons squad that was armed with two gas-operated air-cooled M249 light machine guns and three HK G36 assault rifles with the AG36 single-shot 40mm grenade launcher assembly. Each of the ten M249s squad automatic weapons available to the company, or the SAWs, as they were affectionately called by their handlers, was capable of a withering thousand rounds per minute using the same NATO 5.56 x 45 ammo as the standard assault rifle, only in linked belts. When the guns were placed in concealed, prepared locations, as the ten SAWs had been by the major in command of the company, not much would be able to survive the highly accurate crossfire that had been set up to cover the soccer field. If the cartels did as the intelligence said they would and all gathered on the field, the amount of fire that could be brought to bear would be devastating and decidedly not survivable.

The fifteen G36/AG36 grenade launchers of the company would be used initially to make a point if the major's call for the immediate disarming of the entourages failed and was met with return fire. The company had four high-powered digital radio megaphones that could be linked, and three of them were located with lieutenants on different sides of the field. When the major made what everyone hoped would be his surprise announcement to the entourages, revealing to them that they were surrounded and outnumbered by the national police and the army, the message would be blasted over the field from all four devices simultaneously. The one great hope of the plan was that a call for their immediate surrender would be met with the practical realization that this was simply not their day and that they'd not elect to shoot it out, having heard that they were completely surrounded and realizing that they had been driven into a trap. The troopers of company A also had a good laugh at that piece of wishful thinking. One of the senior sargento mayors had gruffly commented at their last unit dinner before their march that the planners relying on such hope should wish in one hand and shit in the other and see which one filled up faster. The young troops had had a good laugh at that.

If, as the major sadly expected, his call for the armed retainers to lay down their weapons was met with an unholy release of fire from the cartels, his grenade launchers would be his first response. He intended to unleash a rapid fifteen-round volley targeted to take out as many of the vehicles as possible and to shock and awe the retainers. The concussion of a single exploding 40mm grenade, even if you were spared from the hot ballistic fragments, would be physically devastating to anyone not behind solid cover. Eardrums would shatter, and brain concussions were possible, causing not only pain but disorientation. To have fifteen near simultaneous explosions all aimed at a specific target area—referred to by the planners as TOT, time on target—as well as the likely secondary explosions from the vehicles as fuel tanks exploded once penetrated by hot shrapnel would result in a devastating first strike without a shot having been fired from an assault rifle or SAW. The grenade attack would be accompanied by a short, clearly visible blast of tracer fire from the light machine guns over the heads of the entourages from all four sides of the field. There would then be a ceasefire, and the major would demand again that they lay down their arms. It was anticipated that there likely would be a lot of wild return fire from the retainers, even at this point, but this had been discussed with the troops, and fire discipline would be observed. There would be no return fire until the major made his second demand. If the major had no choice but to give the "fire, return fire at will" command, he knew he would have the massacre that he and his superiors did not want.

The major had ten men in his medical squad spread throughout the company, but they would be overwhelmed by what would surely be the sixty to eight, maybe even a hundred casualties in need of immediate help if things went very bad. This contingency had been planned for to an extent, and there were six medevac choppers at their base camp nine miles to the east that could be on the scene in minutes once the special forces had the field under control. The hospital at Los Mochis was small but modern and would be alerted to a potential influx of gunshot victims after the attack had begun.

While the sledgehammer of Alberto's—really, Manny's—plan was dealing with the entourages at the field, Alberto's tactical police unit would be dealing with the principals at the meeting hall. Here, Alberto had fifty men to deal with about twenty that their informer said would actually be involved with the summit. His police were armed with the same assault rifles as their special forces counterparts. The grenade launchers they had would be firing nothing more than concussion canisters and tear gas through the side windows of the hall. The police units designated to go in, protected by their gas masks would then enter. The object of the police unit's part in the overall plan was to try to capture all the principals alive. Their role was particularly dangerous because to simply surround the hall and pour thousands of rounds into the old stone and timber structure was not an option and that meant going in after them. Here the tactical units' dress deviated from the camouflaged summer utilities and floppy hats the soldiers were all wearing. All members of the tactical unit wore body armor and Kevlar-lined helmets. They would enter the hall from three directions simultaneously, just after the half dozen concussion grenades had followed the tear gas through the windows.

Because the meeting hall sat as it did, on the crest of a hill overlooking the lake to the east, with some open grassy parking areas and a more park-like setting on the other three sides, there was not as much opportunity for concealment that the woods surrounding most of the soccer field offered. This required the police, with their GAFE advisors, to prepare camouflaged positions during the night that could not be readily seen by even the alert observer. This required digging shallow positions in the open areas during the night that could then be covered over with their ghillie blankets and appear undisturbed. The ghillie blankets, with their mat-like structure, were laced with native grasses and other local vegetation so as to all but disappear into the surrounding landscape. These preparations had taken several hours before the police units could settle in and get some rest.

The battlefield communication systems being used by the forces were top shelf. All squad leaders had voice-activated headsets that kept them in constant communication with their overall commanders. Even the police, laying low in their prepared positions, need not look out or keep watch and perhaps reveal their positions, as a steady stream of information came into them from spotters in other concealed positions in the adjacent woods.

After the principal cartel leaders were in the hall and into their meeting, it was anticipated that there would be a few guards stationed at the outside. While regrettable, it would be necessary to silently take these guards out so the police units could then approach the hall unseen. This meant snipers, and their fire would be silent and lethal. An eight-man squad from the regiment, attached to the police, would have this task. Each of the highly trained shooters had his spotter. They were arrayed in concealed positions from three hundred to six hundred feet distant from the hall with two sniper positions positioned to take out anyone in the front side of the hall, and then one team each covering the south and north sides. The main doors to the hall, of course, were located on the front, and there were exit doors on each side toward the back. The rear wall was nothing but a wall of glass that afforded those meeting inside with a beautiful view of the lake to the east but no access. Unknown to the tactical police units, Los Pueblos Fantasmas had the east covered. The plan called for the snipers to initiate the action for the entire force on the go order from the police commander at the scene. With their long barrel-silenced American-made M110 SASS (semiautomatic sniper system) sniper rifles, the four shooters chosen for this action were the best the military had to offer. Each could shoot a half minute of angle, which meant they could put every 7.62 x 51 mm NATO round through a half-inch circle at three hundred feet or the equivalent one-inch circle at six hundred feet. They would not miss.

The semiautomatic characteristics of the specially made sniper rifle made it very easy to get the telescopic sights back on the target about the time the first slug hit. They would take out any outside guards, and then the police units would quickly approach the hall from their carefully concealed positions the moment they received the all clear from the spotters. The fifty-man team would take up their locations at the outside and then hit all doors and the side widows at the same moment. The tear gas grenades crashing through the side windows would hopefully be the first indication to the cartel leaders inside that they had been betrayed. This was to be followed by the concussion grenades and then the assault itself. Once the police units initiated their assault, that was the signal for the major to announce the presence of his force to the assembled entourages at the field some five hundred yards away, although it was likely that the more observant or alert of the retainers who had some combat experience might recognize the distant, muffled echoes of grenades going off—at which time, it was hoped, all hell didn't break loose.

The reverend monsignor of the seminary had been visited the day before and briefed. Alberto's office had thoroughly vetted the priest and was certain he was reliable. As Alvarez secretly wanted the Gang of Four at least as much as Alberto did, he did not fear there would be any breach of security to allow this. It was important that the monsignor be aware of just what was going to be taking place on his campus. When approached, he had been shocked to learn that the philanthropic foundation from Tijuana he believed was using his meeting hall for their annual meeting was in fact the country's worst cartels. The organization had made very generous donations in the past and was thought to likely do so in the future. The monsignor had taken the deception badly at first but then worked hand in glove with the senior police commander to invent a subterfuge that would keep the students and faculty away from the north end of the campus and the hilltop meeting hall. At the evening meal Friday night, because of the sad events that had occurred in the country in the last week, the monsignor had ordered that the next day be a day of silent and personal reflection. This would keep the seminarians in their rooms for the day. To the faculty and staff, including the maintenance staff, he had called for a general meeting of all those who would typically be on campus on a Saturday to be held in the chapel at 11:30 a.m. This would get most everyone inside and away from the targeted sites. Several undercover officers from the police would remain at the monsignor's side throughout the noon hour to keep him apprised of the situation. He would be told by the onsite commander when he could tell his staff the truth, although if things got ugly quick, it would be relatively self-evident.

With all preparations made and the combined police and army units in place by dawn, there was nothing more for the police and troops to do for the next six hours but to wait. For the soldiers who had been training up hard for an action and then spent the early-morning hours taking up their positions with the anticipation of a nasty fight on their minds, a down period of six hours of quiet nothing was the worst part of the mission. Six hours to think about what all could go wrong—but it was necessary. It was the worst for the police units in the open surrounding the hall, dug in as they were in their shallow camouflaged traps. If the cartels sent watchers in the hours before the arrival of their principals, if they somehow eluded the recon outposts, they had to see nothing. Of greater concern was that the cartels had people in the seminary already—a maintenance worker or one of the faculty. Some co-opted soul could tip them off to the Federal Police's presence. It had been Manny's insistence to Alberto that the cartels could be expected to do the unexpected. However hard it was on the troops to have to sit it out an extended period of time, the tactic was necessary. Alberto knew that the presence of the two cartel encampments to the east constituted the realization of this threat, and his Los Pueblos Fantasmas had dealt with that during the night. If the cartels had eyes on the campus already, they would see nothing undisturbed or unusual as the dawn broke over the quiet, serene seminary setting.

Unknown to Alberto or his combined force was the fact that Manny was correct. Ricardo Arellano, who had organized the Gang of Four and whose idea it was that the two previous summits be held in this idyllic setting, was from Los Mochis. He had made his reputation and connections there before moving to Tijuana and building his empire. His father and several cousins still worked for the diocese, much as Ricardo had in his youth. His elderly father had no idea his son was who he was. He was as good a man as Ricardo was bad—one of God's ironies, one could suppose, in the balancing of good and evil in the secular world. But his two cousins tipped the family balance to the bad, as they were on the payroll. Each of the cousins, during the morning hours, on foot or in one of the seminary service vehicles, had made his routine rounds, setting sprinklers here or taking one of the mowing crews there, with every move observed by the Federals. But the cousins had seen nothing out of the ordinary. It was simply another beautiful morning in a very spiritual place tucked in the woods overlooking the lake. They made their calls; all was normal and clear.

At 11:40 a.m., the recon team from Company D covering the highway approach from the north reported that a five-vehicle caravan of black GMC Denalis had just gone by their position and would arrive at the seminary within minutes. On cue, the Company A recon team in their concealed position at the main entrance reported that the caravan had arrived, turned in, and was proceeding up the main seminary road at a very slow and cautious speed. These reports were transmitted over the net, and the entire strike force was in the know. The same recon team in the north made a second call several minutes later, announcing a second four-vehicle caravan approaching. This was followed quickly by the southernmost recon team watching the highway, who reported the third caravan, this from the south. The first caravan arrived at the field as the intel said they would, only instead of parking in the general area of the middle, it parked more in the southwest corner of the field. The first on the scene, this caravan unknowingly picked the location of greatest challenge to the Federal forces. Clearly whichever cartel this was had at least one person among them who recognized the location that would give them the fastest way out if there were problems.

The second and third caravans arrived within a few minutes of one another, passed by the first five vehicles, and took up positions along the mostly west and north sides of the field facing the first. The last caravan, also five vehicles and strangely the only one with all-white luxury SUVs in lieu of what seemed to be the standard black or dark gray, came from the north also and made its way slowly onto the field, parking more at the northeast end facing all the others. The disposition of vehicles was in a long arc from the southwest to the northeast, everyone in a position to watch the others. All told there were eighteen SUVs on the seminary's soccer fields—all heavy, all luxurious to be sure, and all likely armored in some way.

The major in tactical command mumbled *shit* under his breath and quickly evaluated the disposition of vehicles and altered his firing plans accordingly. All could still be brought under some level of crossfire, but not nearly as effectively as if they had gathered in the middle of the large field. There went the first hope down the drain. He needed some of his troops at the east end to move to the west, and he needed some of his west-end troops to move as far south as their cover would allow. The troops had to move quickly and do so without being seen. He quickly gave a sit rep and the necessary orders over the command circuit, and also ordered the squads in the pump house to make the first five-vehicle caravan their initial target. It was imperative that any avenue of escape to the south be cut off. Hustling through the woods as quietly as they could, his troops made their moves to their new positions and sighted in their targets.

In the meantime, as the major was dealing with his tactical challenges, a single man from each caravan got out and walked toward the center of the field. From the beginning, when Ricardo Arellano had first proposed that his counterparts meet with him, because of their long histories of butchering one another, some means had to be developed that would allow them to come together safely. This counsel of four men—the ambassadors, as they had come to be known—was the answer. Each man was a known senior subordinate to his leader. They were the ones who met and exchanged ideas on how and where to meet and how to do so in a way that everyone would feel safe. This was their fifth meeting face to face, although they communicated by cell phone frequently when the times called for it. There was no camaraderie here; in fact, all to some degree hated the others for all manner of reasons from their pasts. But like their sponsors, they all knew that it had become necessary to stop killing one another and focus on defeating the increasingly disruptive actions of the government. That, and there was a dangerous, powerful force out there, the Condor de Muerte, that was growing stronger and required their combined attention as well. They would have invited this Condor to join their loose alliance, but no one knew where he was or really who he was. He was as much a phantom to them as he was to the Federals, only he was poaching on their men and transshipment routes, and that had to be stopped.

The four senior lieutenants stood in a loose circle in the middle of the field and nodded their greetings. Arellano's man spoke first. "Our people here say all is well. We are alone."

One of the others smiled and then spoke up. "Ours also say all is clear. What? Do not look so surprised, Fernando; you think you are the only ones who have eyes here?"

With smiles and nods of respect around the circle, all four men got on their cell phones and speed-dialed numbers. Almost in unison, they all said, "All clear."

Arellano's cousins of course had called in their all-clear report earlier in the morning, but so too had the backup team for Jesus Qiuntero, the Butcher of Brownsville from Matamoros. His trademark for years had been to leave the heads of his victims on six-foot spikes in public spaces, be it kidnap victims, business rivals, or police and judges he had had to take out. He also was not shy about crossing the Rio Grande into neighboring Brownsville, Texas, and leaving his mark there, therefore his name. Of the Gang of Four, he was by far the most ruthless, the most cautious, and perhaps the most intelligent when it came to his safety. The second encampment that Los Pueblos Fantasmas had taken out in the night had been his. His had been a smart move—to plan for an early reconnoiter and also to have a back way out. The problem was that he had assigned the wrong men to the task. The men he had chosen were indeed loyal but had become arrogant and careless after years of dominating the defenseless, the weak, and the innocent. In the end, they had been weak themselves.

About five that morning, when the electric shocks being applied to his testicles had become too much for him to bear, Qiuntero's camp leader had told the intelligence chief of Los Pueblos Fantasmas what his instructions had been. Early in the morning, he was to get himself in position to watch the hall, and if by eleven o'clock, all was still safe, he was to call a number and give the all clear. The man had been given a choice: make the call and do as he was told, or he would be executed right here in the camp—not by gunshot, quick and painless, but rather by excruciatingly slow electrocution, hanging from the tree as he had been during his interrogation, the shiny copper clamps attached painfully to his balls, the current alternating between on and off.

The grotto camp, it had been learned within five minutes of the intelligence major attaching the copper clamps to the still slightly hungover leader, had indeed been there at the instructions of the Condor de Muerte. Their job: kill everyone who came out of the grotto but one, someone called Fernando Mateos. The leader had been carrying a picture of him in his shirt pocket so he could identify him. Mateos was Ricardo Arellano's man on the field who had told the others all was clear. He also was the Condor's man in the Arellano camp and the chief source for all the information that had been passed to the Federals. After ten long, dangerous years of doing the most vile and despicable of acts for Arellano, Mateos had proved himself beyond a doubt and had risen to chief lieutenant. He had cemented his position by accepting the very dangerous role as one of the four ambassadors who had initially met and forged the loose alliance. The life expectancy for an ambassador was judged to be measured in hours in the beginning, but all four had survived, and with his survival, Fernando Mateos had raised himself above all suspicions. He knew that the Condor was going to take down Arellano in time, and he was counting the days when he could return to his boyhood home in Chihuahua and put the last ten years behind him.

With the all-clear signal given from the ambassadors in the field, one SUV from each group slowly pulled out and, with the white one in the lead, turned onto the main interior road of the seminary and headed east for the hilltop meeting hall. The police units there were made aware of the movement. When the vehicles arrived, one by one, the men got out. From the lead white Cadillac Escalade and the nearest black one, Ricardo Arellano and Ramon Fuentes got out with their four bodyguards and went to the front of the hall and turned and waited. From a third SUV, the two Felix-Contreras brothers got out, followed by their guards. They greeted the other two with smiles and handshakes. Armando Caro, also from Matamoros, and then Jesus Qiuntero, each with their four guards, joined the others in front of the hall. They appeared to be discussing some point or other and then turned and entered the hall. One man from each camp stayed outside, evidently the result of the conversation just held.

Earlier that morning, Colonel Portillo, from his vantage point on the hillcrest four hundred yards to the east, had watched through the optics of his high-powered spotting scope with interest, as a priest from the seminary had directed several of what looked like the custodial staff in the setting up of the room for the day's guests. Long wooden tables had been placed in an open square with four seats to a side. White fabric tablecloths had been placed over the tables along with some small floral arrangements. All in all, as viewed through the tall east windows of the hall, the room had looked very nice. It was a shame that wouldn't last for long. At about eleven, the priest had returned, and he had opened the overhead counter door between the main room and the kitchen. He had taken out of the refrigerator what looked like, for lack of a better description, party trays of snack foods along with a variety of bottles of juices and sodas and had set them up in shallow ice-filled trays. His work done and the man apparently satisfied, he had left the hall and headed for the chapel for the meeting called by the monsignor.

There were additional chairs along the wall, but they would not be necessary. Each of the cartel leaders took a seat at the table, with one lieutenant from each group also taking a seat. Three guards from each of the four cartels took up stations standing against the walls. The four ambassadors joined the six leaders at the table.

There in his high-powered spotter scope were the principal enemies he had been fighting for more years than he cared to remember, gathered together in one room. Colonel Portillo had the frequency for the command net that linked the major commanding the special forces with the overall commander from the Federal Police. He had listened in on the net but had not transmitted; he soon would. In his many years with the Federal Police and the last two commanding Los Pueblos Fantasmas, he'd often dreamed of the day he could participate in an action that would rid the country of the pestilence that was the cartels. Dreamed, yes, but in his heart and mind, he had never really believed the government could succeed, until today.

25

Saint Thomas of Aquinas on the Lake
The Meeting Hall
Noon Saturday

P olice Commander Genaro Molinar, a veteran of many police actions against the cartels and Alberto's handpicked overall commander of the operation, had also dreamed of a day such as this for many years. He and Major Ruiz, as the two onsite tactical commanders, had been told there were recon assets on site that had reconnoitered the seminary ahead of their infiltration and also had laid out their lines of march. Thus far, everything this unknown recon force had done had been spot on, as far as Molinar thought. Any curiosity he had about just who they were was long dismissed; he really didn't care as long as he got accurate information. He wondered at first, when going over the plans initially with the secretary, just what all the secrecy was about, but he had grown used to the compartmentalization that Alberto Rodriguez had instituted when head of the Federal Police and now agreed with it.

Molinar was watching the hall through his field glasses from his concealed position a hundred feet to the south, although his view was limited through the three fairly small windows on the side. Unlike the large peaked windows to the east that allowed those in the hall a grand view of the lake below, the side windows had a more practical use and were there for ventilation purposes only. From his position, he could just see the front of the hall and had an angled view into the first side window. He watched, fascinated to see the clearly recognizable faces of the six notorious men he had been trying to get for so many years enter the hall. His oldest son had followed him into the national police, and his bodiless head had been discovered on a steel spike alongside a country road outside of Matamoros four years ago, a victim of the Butcher of Brownsville. He had agreed with Alberto Rodriguez, when asked, that it would be better if the leaders could be captured alive and brought before public justice for their crimes—everyone but Jesus Qiuntero, that is, but he had kept that desire to himself. If Qiuntero were alive when Molinar got in there, he would be dead soon after. Molinar was taking no chances with the Justice Department and the cartels obvious deep penetration there. Qiuntero had no more than a few minutes to live, one way or another.

Through his spotting scope, Commander Molinar could see some of the interior, but not much. About the time he was wishing he had a better view, there was a double clicking on his command-net headphone, and a voice he had not heard before but one that sounded vaguely familiar broke in. "Commander Molinar, this is recon asset one. We have line of sight into the hall. Targets are arrayed as follows…"

With that, Commander Molinar unbelievably got his wish: a detailed description of what waited for him inside. He tapped his transmit switch. "Recon one, whoever you are, thank you. Be advised we are initiating in two minutes."

He tapped his police force net circuit and communicated what he learned to his entire team, including the snipers.

"Shooters, select targets at front. We are a go in one minute. Advise when acquired." One by one his shooters, communicating on the police team net, called in their target selections and the fact they were on target. Commander Molinar switched to his group-wide net so that all commanders and squad leaders on the net could hear him. "Group, this is Commander Molinar. Shooters are on targets. Major Ruiz, are you ready?"

"That's an affirmative, Commander; we are ready at the field."

"Gas and shock teams, are you ready to move forward?"

"Yes, Commander," came the calls from those squads.

"Shooters, confirm on targets."

"Shooter one on target; two on; four on target; three on target."

"All units, on my mark. Shooters are weapons-free, ready, mark!" The words had hardly left his mouth when Commander Molinar saw the four guards at the front just drop, almost simultaneously. This was real, not theatrical, not acted. This was life and death at its most basic. There was no dramatic clutching of the chest or last-second pleas for help or perhaps forgiveness. One second as he watched, the four hard-looking men were standing casually about, talking, three of them smoking; the next second they just dropped to the ground. They were all, no doubt, the victims of a single high-velocity steel jacketed bullet shot through their personal ten-ring, that small, aptly named one-inch circle representing the dead center of the full-torso targets his police shooters and the military used on their ranges. *Christ*, he thought, *those men can shoot.*

"Target down," came the calls from the four different shooters.

"Grenade teams, Molinar, *go, go, go!*"

From both sides of the hall, from what appeared to be a grassy depression here or a small area of native shrubs there, the eight grenade shooters popped out of cover from their concealed positions placed nearest the hall and ran the very short distance toward the side windows, knelt down, aimed, and unleashed their gas shots. Before they had, several of the police swore later they had heard someone from inside yell a warning of some kind. An alert guard—no doubt one of those standing against the wall, perhaps just idly gazing out the window opposite him—had no doubt seen someone running toward the window. But it was too little, too late. The grenade shooters quickly reloaded with their flashbang variants as the interior of the hall already was beginning to fill with the CS gas and smoke. Eight of the flashbangs flew through the shattered windows, instantly exploding with the blinding six-million candela flash and the ear shattering 180-decibel blast. Molinar's main attack groups hit the front and side doors a split second after the flashbangs blinded and disoriented most in the main hall.

Through his high-powered spotting scope, Colonel Portillo saw the attack begin and also watched as one of the guards along the wall started to move, no doubt the one who had seen the attack coming a second before the tear-gas canisters had shattered the six side windows. As the room quickly filled with smoke and gas, the incredibly bright white light of the flashbang grenades made the colonel turn away and blink and close his eyes for several second. As he turned back to his viewing scope, he saw one of the large east windows shatter, blowing outward in thousands of small shards of glass. The colonel thought it was caused by a flashbang, but then his logic immediately said this was not possible, as the delay between the flashbangs detonating and the window blowing out had been too long. Someone was trying to shoot his way out. No sooner had the thought gone through his head than three men came running out the shattered opening.

Probably Qiuntero, the colonel thought. *He thinks he has backup down the hill; too bad.*

One of Molinar's men on the north side nearest the east end saw the running men, turned, and released a quick burst of automatic weapon fire as the three men went over the crest of the bluff toward the orchard. He saw a man drop, amazed at his shot, not knowing he had missed badly. There were two concealed ghost teams of two men each lying hidden in the tall native grasses of the orchard to cover this avenue of escape. They were close enough to the top of the hill to have seen and heard the large rear window being shot out and had seen the three men come racing out. Their assignment was to keep anyone from escaping toward the lake. Taking them alive was preferred, but given the action and the circumstances, none of the four members of Los Pueblos Fantasmas wanted to reveal themselves. All four were holding their version of the FX-05 Fire Serpent with a thick, round sound suppressor attached to the muzzle. The shooters wanted controlled, deliberate fire if it came to it; there were just too many friendlies up the hill to risk full auto, and they had therefore set their Serpents to semiauto. Each got off one round within a second of one another. The lead guard took two slugs to the chest and was dead before he hit the ground. Qiuntero and the trailing guard each took nonlethal but debilitating hits to their torso mass and dropped in their tracks, losing blood rapidly. If attended to within the next ten or fifteen minutes, they would survive; if not, they would die. It just wasn't going to be their day.

All told, the action at the meeting hall was over within less than ten minutes after the front guards had dropped in their tracks and the gas canisters crashed through the windows. The main force had hit the front doors and found Armando Caro and his four guards in the front hall trying to get out that way. Caro had been sitting closest to the front door and had turned and dived toward the front hall as the gas had gone off. He and his guards had mostly had their backs to the main hall when the flashbangs had gone off and had not been as debilitated as most of the others. But before they had been able to reach the front doors and potential safety, the doors had come crashing in along with shouts of "Drop your weapons!" Caro had instinctively dropped to the floor to give his men a clear field of fire, but the multiple bursts of automatic weapons from whoever had been coming through the front had dropped all four of his men before they had gotten off a shot. Two had died; two would live to see the inside of a courtroom and serve out their sentences in a federal penitentiary. He had been quickly pounced on and cuffed before he had really known what had been happening as more armed men had rushed by him.

Ricardo Arellano had been on Caro's left and had been overwhelmed both by the gas explosions and the flashbangs. He had not been able to see and had been in a daze from the concussions in the room and choking badly on the gas. His best and strongest bodyguard had been together enough to drag him toward the kitchen, and then, physically picking him up, had tossed him through the counter opening where the snacks and drinks had been sitting. He had slid across the narrow kitchen counter, splattering everything that had been set up, and landed badly on the floor. His guard had dived through as well and grabbed his leader and had half dragged, half carried him toward the pantry that led to the stair and the safety of the grotto. They had not made it. To the guard's dismay and angry cries, the door he had personally checked a week before would not budge. It had no lock but would not open, and his conscious mind had not been allowed the time to try to figure out why. As the main force had come through the front doors and into the entry hall, several officers from the left-hand side not engaged with Caro's men had gone deeper down the hall and turned into the kitchen as planned to clear this room. Others on the right-hand side had been do-ing the exact same movement to clear the closets and bathrooms located on that side of the hall. Arellano's guard, a former senior sergeant of the National Army's Special Forces, had gotten off several shots, wounding one officer before he had been dropped for all eternity with a countervolley of automatic fire. The dazed and stunned Ricardo Arellano, the Terrible Tyrant of Tijuana, as many in law enforcement and the media called him, lying on the floor stunned and partially blind, knowing but not understanding how something had gone terribly wrong, had lost control and wet and soiled himself right there on the seminary's spotlessly clean linoleum floor.

For the two Felix-Contreras brothers and the remaining mix of body-guards, they had been easily apprehended, having unluckily been sitting or standing in such a way as to have taken the brunt of the grenade blasts. All were found in varying degrees of agony on the floor, both blinded and stunned by the attack, choking on the CS gas. They had been quickly cuffed and contained.

Now, the attack complete, Commander Molinar entered the room, looked around, and approached his most senior deputy on the scene, Commander Diaz, and asked who all was not accounted for.

"Qiuntero and two of his men managed to get out through the win-dows, but they are down just outside."

Molinar walked out the shattered window and saw several of his men attending two wounded men who were down. A third was apparently dead, as no one was paying any attention to him.

"You two," he ordered, "carry that man to the clearing, and call for a medic."

They looked at their commander and did as they were ordered. Molinar looked down at the conscious and ashen-faced Jesus Qiuntero and asked, "Do you know who I am?"

Qiuntero nodded; he knew the face and at least a portion of the life story of every senior police official he had come in contact with. "Know your enemy" was something he had learned at a very young age.

"Do you remember my son, Guillermo Molinar of Matamoros?"

Understanding slowly dawned on Qiuntero as he recalled the name as the older officer started to point his Glock at him. He nodded and tried to speak, the sounds raspy but coherent. "Yes, I remember your son. He cried like a woman just before I cut his fucking head off."

Tears streaming down his craggy face, Genaro Molinar started pulling the trigger and did not stop until the breech slammed open after the last shot from the magazine of his Glock G17. The bloody mess that had been Jesus Qiuntero was unrecognizable above the shoulders. Slowly and methodically, the emotionally broken Molinar replaced the spent magazine in his Glock with a fresh one, raised his gun to his head, whispered a short prayer of forgiveness to his wife, and pulled the trigger.

Meanwhile, back at the field, Major Ruiz reacted to the tactical problems presented by the unpredictable manner the cartels had parked their vehicles as best he could. The redeployments took a full fifteen minutes, for the men had to move themselves and equipment through the woods so as not to be seen. Lines of march between the widely dispersed platoons of the company had been marked during the night as his troops had set up. He knew that his four top sargento mayors would lead the troops the quickest way possible to their new locations. It was a nerve-wracking fifteen minutes as he watched the conference and then the four principal vehicles drive off. He knew he had no more than five or ten more minutes before Commander Molinar would initiate the attack. His men had just reported in when Molinar made his two-minute call. They were ready. He called his grenade squads and ordered them to target the seven mostwestern vehicles first and then the ones more to the north. He knew if all hell broke loose, the four Denalis were in the best position to make a run for it. He wanted them stopped dead in their tracks, followed by the second group and so on. All his squad leaders responded in the affirmative to the revised targeting orders.

Over his command circuit, he was listening in to all the traffic going on around the hall. He was as surprised as Commander Molinar must have been to hear the report from the as-of-yet-unidentified recon one asset. *Who in the hell else is in on this*, the Major had wondered. When Molinar gave the *go, go, go* command for the assault on the hall, it was the major's cue to make his announcement. All told, there were a total of fourteen SUVs and by his top sargento mayor's count and eighty-two armed retainers on the field. There were few weapons in evidence, and most of these were being held by men sitting inside the SUVs. It was apparent that efforts were being made between the cartels to look nonthreatening out of fear of accidentally starting a shootout where none was desired. Everyone was playing nice for the moment. The major tapped his mic and announced to his command, "Making the call." A quick check of the radio megaphone system confirmed all four were online. He triggered his device.

"*Attention.* Lay down your weapons. You are surrounded and under arrest. Repeat, lay down your weapons."

The announcement blared over the field. Everyone easily heard it, and it caused an immediate reaction on the field. Some of the men looked nervously about, but most of the retainers dove for their vehicles and the weapons they held. The major gave it another try. "Lay down your weapons. You are surrounded, and you are under arrest."

As he had feared, the retainers' first reaction was to start shooting. From rolled-down windows in the vehicles and after men started pouring from the SUVs, there was wild fire in the direction of the woods. Some of the senior cartel members had the sense to realize that if there was threat out there, it was in the woods. The amount of fire was fierce but inaccurate. Mostly the rounds were flying wildly high.

The major let the fire continue for eight to ten seconds and then muttered, "Fuck it. Grenade launchers free," he barked into his headset. Immediately there were the telltale puffs of smoke from the fifteen launchers spaced around the field, and almost as immediately, vehicles began to explode in spectacular fashion as the 40mm high explosives found their targets. The carnage was far worse than the major had imagined it would be. The seven southern- and western-most vehicles had been double targeted and suffered double impacts. They were nothing more than burning, smoking pyres in seconds. It took his grenade launchers only a second or two to reload, and they turned their attention to the remaining seven SUVs, three of which had spun out and were attempting to flee the killing ground. They never made it. The seven expensive luxury SUVs remaining also were hit with multiple grenades and erupted into flame as windshields and windows blew out. Already there were secondary explosions from the obviously full fuel tanks, and this began contributing to the mayhem. In his awe of the carnage before him, the major failed to order the machine guns to demonstrate their awesome warning fire as planned. It was not until his XO, the captain whose command he had taken over, had summoned the nerve to call it in and ask if the SAWs were weapons-free did the major's focus come back on the present.

"Negative, hold fire." The major made his second megaphone call. "You are surrounded! Lay down your weapons, and move to the center of the field. This is your final warning."

The fire from the cartels diminished as the vehicles started exploding all around them, and the retainers dove for what little cover they could find. But as the major gave his second warning, a heavy outpouring of fire erupted from the survivors on the field. The major decided to improvise.

"Command, hold your fire. I say again, all troops hold fire," he yelled over the command circuit for all to hear. "SAWs only—repeat, SAWs only—open fire. Fire at will."

It wasn't as if the major was squeamish about death or casualties in battle; he wasn't. But he did have a conscience, and he also had eyes and a brain. He knew he was in a tactically superior position and had his wounded enemy in the open and in the sights of a crossfire. To order his 150 troops weapons-free would have annihilated any surviving cartel members. Once they started, his troop's blood would be up, and it would be very hard to get them under control. On the other hand, he only had ten SAWs. That many he could control.

For the soldiers of fortune or family members or just unlucky petty criminals, whoever and whatever they were composing the entourages that had joined the cartels and now remained on the field, they were, after all, human beings, and they were largely defenseless and had no place to hide. The major was acutely aware of this fact. Their only defensive cover, the vehicles, were smoking hulks, spewing dense, toxic black smoke and tongues of flame as every possible part or fluid that could burn did so. That required they separate from their only cover. This left the remaining fighters with… nothing, no cover whatever. The only possible alternative was the prone position on the field, as if they flattened themselves low enough, there would miraculously be safety in the blades of grass. As the ten SAWs opened up, that misguided notion was horribly, horribly disabused as the combined ten thousand rounds per minute poured into the field. It was over in seconds as the NATO rounds chewed up the field like a swarm of locusts, and the major knew it. He gave the field a five-second burst before he started yelling, "Cease fire, cease fire," into his mic. It took the SAW teams an additional five to ten seconds to calm down and stop. The few surviving retainers were lying flat on the ground, arms raised as both evidence that they had laid their weapons down and a plea for the hell on earth to stop. The major ordered all on the field to raise their arms, or the shooting would continue. Most who could were already complying, but here and there was the single arm raised, as if that was all the strength that the individual could muster. The major ordered his troops onto the field.

In spite of his best intentions to avoid a massacre, as the saddened major toured the field, the captain at his side, he was nauseated by the results. He had held the fire of over 150 troops with automatic weapons, and the terrible death from the several thousand ballistic rounds was still everywhere. His platoon leaders had been ordered to divide up the field and rapidly assess the numbers of dead and wounded and report to the XO. He called Commander Molinar, but could not get him on the circuit, so he ordered the six medevac choppers to the field on his own. There was an additional medic with each chopper, and they could assist the ten he already had trying to save the few wounded they found. His top sargento mayor took a squad and was marking landing zones for the inbound choppers. Already the wounded were being laid nearby in anticipation of being moved to the hospital in Los Mochis. He kept telling himself that he had used restraint, but the torn-up bodies he saw were telling him the opposite. He tried to raise Commander Molinar once more, failed, but finally heard from one of the police subcommanders, who simply said the commander was a casualty and unavailable. As the operations order specified in the event of the loss of Commander Molinar to injury or death, the major announced on the net that he now had overall command and ordered his communication section to alert the hospital in Los Mochis to the pending arrival of a great deal of wounded. His XO, who had been strangely cavalier in the moments leading up to the start of the fight, as if they were involved in some sort of elaborate training exercise, walked up to him looking grim for the first time since the shooting had stopped and made his preliminary report.

"Sir, first count we have thirty-three wounded survivors, eight of which are critical and may not survive the medevac. We have eight unwounded cartel members under arrest, and the intelligence team is trying to ID them right now."

The Major was too numb to do the elementary math in his head. "And the dead, Captain?"

"Forty-one confirmed dead sir."

Forty-one—half—in what, ten seconds of actual firing? The major simply nodded, took one last look around, and then grabbed his military cell phone and speed-dialed the general. He had assured the general when he was given the command that he would do everything in his power to capture as many of the criminals as possible. In every briefing leading up to today's action, he had been reminded that this was a police action, a police action, a police action, until he was sick of hearing it. Well, he had tried, but what it was, was a massacre.

26

A lberto, Bennie, and General Lozano were set up to monitor the entire action planned at the seminary over the command circuits, both audio and visual, as they were broadcast into the Situation Room on the fifth floor of the Department of Public Security and Justice building on the Zocalo. They, along with the traitors, Quito-Perez, in his role as head of the national police, and Garcia Ramirez as director of the AFI, plus limited senior staff, began gathering at just after eight o'clock Saturday morning. The attorney general was in his office in the adjacent building but was represented at the Situation Room by his top deputy for criminal prosecutions. The president and his immediate staff were at his offices in Los Pinos. The president and the AG were to be advised by telephone of the actions at the seminary when they occurred. All total, including aides and essential staff to run the communications and other such related tasks, only twenty government people not actually participating in the raid were aware of the potentially titanic events to take place on the tranquil grounds of one of the oldest monasteries in the country.

Of the twenty, Alberto and Bennie alone knew that at least six were cartel members themselves headed up by the president. It was the most supreme of ironies that the only man who perhaps wanted the day's events to be successful more than Alberto and Bennie was their principal enemy,

Alvarez. One thing they did not know was if any of the Gang of Four had been as successful as Alvarez in penetrating the upper reaches of the federal government. They hoped not but were taking no chances. Alberto, with the consent and support of Alvarez and General Lozano, had kept the planning for the raid known only to a very few. Commander Diaz, the national police commander for Sinaloa, who had been the recipient of the original tip from the Condor on the summit, had called the day before and advised the secretary that his source had called again and said the summit was still on for noon on Saturday. Diaz was now serving as one of Commander Molinar's deputies on site. Diaz's source, of course, was Alvarez. Alvarez's source was Ricardo Arellano's ambassador, Fernando Mateos, operating deep undercover, and Arellano was the driving force behind the Gang of Four.

The Situation Room, or the Center, as it was referred to by those who worked on the fifth floor, was a large windowless room located almost in the dead center of the fifth floor of the historic building. The room was sandwiched between the central elevator, stair, and mechanical cores that had been retrofitted into the building over the years, and the pale-blue walls had banks of electronic equipment, computer terminals, and high-resolution flat-screen monitors lining three of them. The low, arching plaster ceiling had the latest in recessed LED lighting that emitted very little glare. All in all, the interior architecture gave the room a cool, somber tone matching that of the operators who now sat before the monitors and banks of keyboards, dials, and knobs. The room was staffed and used for all manner of natural and unnatural events, from hurricanes and earthquakes to major police actions. Any significant event that affected the public security or safety of the citizens was coordinated from this space. All of the government's departments had feeds into this room, and all government databases and communications could be accessed by the special staff working for Alberto with a few keystrokes. The entire setup had been one of the enormously successful projects organized and executed with great care by the government's top systems and IT expert, Geraldo Baca. The only technological center as good, perhaps even better, was that at Los Pinos being manned by Baca and his assistant, Lorenzo. Whatever information, be it digital, audio, or visual, that went into the Center, it also went to Baca, wherever he was—only no one else in the government, including Alberto, knew this. Alvarez did not require phone calls from Alberto in the Situation Room to monitor events as they happened; he had Baca. But to keep the illusion of operational secrecy intact, Alvarez had been clear with his old friend and subordinate: "Call me just as soon as you know something, Alberto."

The communications technicians and other staff present were briefed on the pending operation only after they had arrived as ordered to the Center. Each had to pass through a metal detector just inside the electronically operated Center door that could be set off by the wrapper on a stick of gum, so attentive to security Alberto was determined to be. For those working in the Center, it was the second such security screen they had been required to pass through this morning, as one could not gain access to even the public spaces on the first floor of the justice building without passing through metal detectors in the central lobby. Within the Center were two lavatories, a small kitchen, and one small glass-enclosed office at one end of the center. A large executive conference table and chairs in the middle of the room dominated the space.

Two armed security people were standing outside the Center door in the corridor, and two were on the inside. They wore black and dark-green soft cotton/nylon ACUs with a digitized camouflage pattern and black berets, and they carried holstered sidearms along with the compact Belgian assault rifles slung over their shoulders. They had no markings or patches that identified their units, nor did their utilities have name or rank badges. The ten armed men on the floor were Los Pueblos Fantasmas. All were of average height and had closely cropped hair and stonelike faces. Except for the occasional "Yes, sir," or "No, sir" or "Speak with the secretary," no one could get anything out of them. General Lozano was told only that the security was being provided by a special tactical unit of the police and nothing more. If he had questions, he did not ask them.

Only Alberto and whomever he invited had access to the private glass-walled cubical in the Center. Bennie, at any time, and occasionally General Lozano had been the only ones to accompany Alberto to the private space.

Alberto, Bennie, and General Lozano were the only three in the Center who had retained their individual communication devices. Bennie and Alberto each had two. Any reports from Colonel Portillo were coming to Alberto on his special phone, and Bennie had his special phone in case Ray made contact. Alberto heard often from the colonel that Bennie had gotten nothing from Ray, but he really did not expect to.

Alberto and Bennie had arrived at eight thirty, and soon after Alberto convened a meeting of senior staff. This included all his department heads and their chief deputies. All told, there were twelve men in Alberto's conference room in addition to him and Bennie. The staff that had arrived that morning at nine on the orders of the secretary had been surprised to find armed special forces officers in fatigues and carrying personal weapons standing in the lobby as the staff got off the elevators. Before passing through the metal detectors, all cell phones were removed, tagged, and placed in a large plastic box as the puzzled—even angry in some cases—executives and staff members were treated in a way some felt was beneath their dignity. Several of the twelve who were directed to the conference room intended to make their displeasure known at having to be at the Zocalo on a Saturday morning with no prior announcement and then to be treated like common criminals, in their opinion, as they arrived at the top floor of the government building. Most had been in their beds sleeping or having leisurely breakfasts with wives or girlfriends when, beginning at seven thirty, they had received calls from either the secretary himself or Quito-Perez and Garcia Ramirez to report to the office precisely at nine. No other information had been given despite the questions from those senior officials who felt they should be made aware of the reasons before they arrived to work.

Once they had arrived in the conference room, Alberto had greeted them seriously but warmly and had asked them to forgive him for the secrecy and the security, but an event of great national importance was in the works that required the utmost of security. It was necessary, Alberto explained, that no unapproved communications be sent out, which necessitated the removal of their cell phones. Finished with his preliminaries, he asked all to follow him to the Center.

The technicians at the Center were already there, having been ordered the day before to report at seven for a surprise system-wide readiness drill. None were surprised, as such drills happened about once every three months, and it had been at least that long since the last. All in all, quite routine. Their attitudes all changed when the secretary himself, followed by his American guest and General Lozano, arrived at eight and told them this was no drill. Each was handed several pages of an operation order on which were listed the frequencies and other control information they would be required to contact to follow the communications from the field once transmissions began.

The government officials followed Alberto and the others to the Center, and one by one were allowed through the Center door. Once inside, they had to pass through yet another security screen. The aide to Alberto's chief of staff, a clean-cut young man in a nice-looking suit, was very surprised to be required to go through another screening as he entered the room and stopped dead in his tracks before the walk-through metal detector.

"Please, sir," the intimidating armed policeman standing to one side said. "Pass through."

The aide did and immediately set off the alarm. An officer on the other side had a hand wand and quickly located the cell phone the man was carrying.

Alberto heard the commotion and walked over. "What is this about?"

"Mr. Secretary," the officer with the wand said, "this man was carrying a cell phone."

Alberto turned to the now quite petrified little bureaucrat and asked, "Your phone was taken from you when entered the floor. Where did you get this?"

"Mr. Secretary," he stuttered, "I keep a spare phone in my desk in case something happens to my regular one. I stopped by my desk and picked it up. I apologize, Mr. Secretary; I wasn't thinking clearly."

Alberto looked coldly at the young man then turned to the officer. "As soon as everyone is in, take this man to detention, and hold him there." Alberto then turned away, ignoring the pleas from the aide as he was quickly led from the room. There was no actual detention facility in the building, so an interior janitor's closet had been set up just for this type of occurrence. The now-handcuffed aide was taken there and cuffed to a pipe than ran vertically through a corner of the small room. His mobility was decidedly limited, but he could sit or stand as he chose, only he could go no farther than an arm's length from the pipe. One of Alberto's ghosts took up position outside the door for the duration. When the clearly scared young man said through the closed door that he required the use of the facilities down the hall, the guard, without opening the door, told the miserable little shit to use the slop sink near his feet.

The others in the Center, who were either standing around or sitting at the executive table, shock evident on their faces, had watched silently as the young aide had been handcuffed and led out of the Center. Alberto walked back to the conference table, sat down at the head with Bennie on his left and General Lozano on his right, and asked everyone else to also sit. He looked around the table and said, "Gentlemen, what you just witnessed was a likely cartel operative, in defiance of my security speech not ten minutes ago, attempting to place himself in position to report to his handlers on what all goes on here today. I assure you that we shall eventually get to the bottom of that particularly sad episode."

He then went on to tell them in great detail what would be happening at noon today. To a man, the others who had not been involved with the planning were flabbergasted to learn of the opportunity the cartels were presenting the government and the comprehensive plan that had been prepared in great secrecy to deal with it.

"Gentlemen, let me go on to say that my office is very aware that certain cartels have infiltrated the highest levels of our government. It is my sincere hope that all of you who are present here today are true and loyal citizens. For I assure you, I will find out in time if you are not."

Alberto Rodriguez had been known to all those around the table both professionally and, for many, personally for many years. He was respected as an intelligent and gifted professional but also for his mild manner and great sense of civility. The last statement he gave was so filled with a quiet menace and determination that even those who were guilty of nothing felt a shudder go up their spines. For Ramirez and Quito-Perez, it was all they could do to keep their faces impassive. They knew the Condor was not a part of today's raid, but that didn't mean there weren't others who might know something that could throw light on their association with the Condor. So compartmentalized was Alvarez's intelligence measures that neither Ramirez nor Quito-Perez had any idea the other was a traitor, nor of course did they know that their employer was Alvarez. Each was left to wonder if somehow Rodriguez's warning was somehow directed at him. It was only 9:20 a.m., and there was almost three hours until the raid was set to begin. Alberto opened the table up for questions and discussions regarding the planned events.

Everyone wanted to know about the source of the intelligence that had obviously come into the secretary's hands, but Alberto said that all such sources would remain closely held secrets for the obvious reasons.

"Let me just say that Senor Santiago here from the American DEA is more than just my houseguest and leave it at that."

All eyes turned to Bennie, who sat impassively, revealing nothing with his look. Alberto had raised the idea to Bennie of saying such a thing early this morning as they shared breakfast. The idea of disseminating a completely false line of thought had come to him the night before. The traitors in the room no doubt felt they knew all about Bennie and what information he had brought with him. Saying something like this might just make them scratch their heads and wonder what Bennie knew that had not been shared. Bennie loved the idea, calling it "enlightened bullshit," which had elicited a chuckle from the otherwise very serious Alberto.

"Let it be just one more thing the traitors think they have to worry about," he had said with a chuckle. Alberto, still chuckling, told Bennie he was going to file away his delightfully American description for the tactic for use at another time.

After the group's initial curiosity had passed and what questions that could be answered had been, the discussions got down to the nitty-gritty of all that would be required following the raid—everything from an after-action review to be conducted by General Lozano to the nuts-and-bolts procedural requirements necessary to prepare the known worst offenders for trial. There was even some discussion about just where the worst of the cartel leaders would be incarcerated when it got to that point. In this discussion, Alberto deliberately misled the group again and did not mention the true location he had planned for the worst of them. Better that any allies they may have in the room not get a head start on any planning.

There was a new military brig with two new cell block buildings on one of General Lozano's bases outside the city that had been constructed over the last eighteen months, with funds buried in the military appropriations for just this occurrence. Modeled after the highly modernized and electronically secure US maximum-security federal prisons, each of the two small concrete buildings, with their twenty-four individual cells, could be securely operated with only a force of four guards, such were the modern electronic security systems in place. Twenty-four such guards had already been vetted and trained to operate the facility on a twenty-four-hour basis, and the guards were even now showing up for work every day to sit and watch the two empty facilities. That would soon change. They were being paid very well and had access to significant bonus monies to report any unlawful contacts if ever they were approached by criminal elements, much like the arrangement Alberto had with his ghosts. An experienced American contractor with several US federal penitentiary projects in his resume had quietly been doing the work on the base, and all was ready. All anyone on the base or the general's staff knew was they had a new, very good-looking jail facility in a remote corner of the base.

The minutes dragged by for the remaining hour until the attack. Bennie joined Alberto on several occasions in the glass cubicle to receive updates from Colonel Portillo, who was watching the hall from his hillside observation perch. Portillo had updated Alberto earlier in the morning, before he and Bennie had had their breakfast, on the success of the ghost's mission during the night. He had called back an hour later to report on the results of the interrogations and to confirm for Alberto just who those in each camp were working for.

At eleven o'clock, com checks were run, and contact was established with Commander Molinar and Major Ruiz. In addition, several of the HD monitors on the wall began receiving video feeds from both the police and army forces. There were two such camera-carrying men in each group, with small helmet-mounted and handheld devices. The cameras would be able to provide real-time imagery from the field with any audio commentary the camera-toting soldiers and police would care to provide. All conversations over the team com links and the command circuit were also being piped into the room. Those not involved with the planning had no real idea what they were seeing. Most knew of the monastery and the seminary located there, but none had ever seen it. All the transmitted images showed were several very tranquil, almost pastoral settings, with no human activity evident. Nevertheless, most eyes were riveted to the monitors.

When the call came in through the overhead speakers from one of the recon units watching the federal highway that a caravan was en route, the tension in the Center increased tenfold. For the honest government servants in the room, who, like Alberto, had been fighting the fight against the cartels for years, the hours they had had to sit around waiting for the raid to begin were excruciating as the magnitude of the operation sank in. The cartels could be dealt such a crushing blow that all realized they had perhaps a once-in-a-lifetime opportunity to begin to take their country back.

All those sitting around the conference table listened and watched the monitors as the caravans of matching SUVs began arriving. When the four ambassadors emerged and walked to the center of the field for their brief discussion, one of Major Ruiz's cameramen had a good sight angle and took his handheld camera and zoomed in on the four.

Quito-Perez spoke up. "That is Arroyo, Torres, and Villalobos. All known associates of one cartel or the other. Very senior, all very bad. Their warrants are among the forty we have on site. I do not recognize the fourth, who seems to be doing most of the talking; he is a new face to me."

The others never took their eyes off the images on the monitors as he spoke. It seemed too surreal to believe that they were watching the country's worst enemies in real time. The conference on the field over, the men rejoined their particular caravans, and Alberto and the others watched as one vehicle from each group drove off toward the meeting hall, just like the informant had said they would. Whoever was doing the spotting and the televising for the tactical police units at the hall caught the four SUVs slowly coming up the road and parking in the open grassy area in front of the beautiful old stone-and-timber hall. As the men were getting out of the vehicles and heading to the front doors, Quito-Perez once again started rattling off the known faces. "That's Arellano and Fuentes. Those next two are the Felix-Contreras brothers…the last one, that's the Butcher, Jesus Qiuntero. All six showed up, Mr. Secretary," Quito-Perez said in an excited voice.

Alberto just nodded. He didn't need anyone to tell him who was who. He had wanted these men for more years than he cared to remember. As the leaders and their guards went inside, leaving four to remain outside, Quito-Perez mentioned that of the twenty-six who were at the hall, they had warrants on the six principals plus at least eight other recognizable faces, including three of the four who had met in the center of the field and now accompanied the leaders inside.

As there were no cameras inside, and all the camera at the soccer field showed was a few men milling around the vehicles, for the next few minutes, those gathered in the Center watched the monitors and listened to the military chatter as the commander at the field seemed to be adjusting some of his units. The overall commander meanwhile could be heard alerting his command to when the attack would begin. Even those not familiar with police or military jargon could follow along. Everyone seemed to lean toward the monitors a bit when the command to the snipers was given. One of the police spotters shooting the video was focused on the four guards at the front. To the astonishment of those watching, without so much as another sound, all four just dropped to the ground in total collapse.

"Four kills," muttered General Lozano, just loud enough for all to hear. He had handpicked the shooters, and while his face did not show it, he was happy and proud at their marksmanship.

The second spotter position was off to one side and seemed a fair distance from the hall. In the corner of the image being broadcast, the group could just see the guards at the front drop, but the second cameraman seemed to be focused on the open area adjacent to the hall. As Commander Molinar shouted his next commands, armed men started rising seemingly out of the ground, firing their weapons through the windows. Others appeared and started rushing the doors. The attack at the hall was over so fast that those who had shifted their focus to the monitor showing the field didn't realize it had happened.

The major's demand for the entourages to lay down their weapons could be heard clearly over the open mic of one of the camera-carrying soldiers. As Alberto had feared, the armed enforcers produced automatic weapons from everywhere and started firing wildly in all directions. The image of the field was lost for a bit as the one soldier broadcasting from the wooded area clearly ducked for cover. A communications technician touched a button, and the monitor switched to an image of the field being shot through the open window of the pump house. The men in the Center watched with fascination as the scene played out, and all were startled when the SUVs on the field started blowing up. No one could count the number of explosions; there were simply too many too close together. Bodies seemed to be flying everywhere, some moving of their own accord, others thrown through the air as a result of the horrific explosions. Immediately, dense black smoke obscured portions of the field as a second burst of explosions was picked up by the first cameraman on a second monitor. Commands were shouted, and then the field seemed to be raked with weapons fire, easily visible as every fourth or fifth round was a tracer round. And then there was silence.

The SUVs were still pouring black smoke, but the field was mostly visible. The bodies were everywhere, some moving, most not. Armed camouflage-wearing soldiers began appearing out of the woods in large numbers. They were the only men standing. A hush came over the room as the firing stopped. In the background, they listened to the commands being barked over the military and police circuits. General Lozano recognized the voice of the major he had put in charge calling for the medevac choppers. Alberto turned to Quito-Perez and ordered him to place the call to the hospital in Los Mochis and alert them to what they would shortly be receiving. Perez seemed to be in shock, and Alberto had to tell him twice. There were six military doctors with the medevac unit, flown in from all over the country as part of another false readiness drill. Not until they were mated with the medical evacuation squadron in the woods east of the seminary the day before had they been told of the mission.

Bennie watched the entire raid having never said a word. A part of him was rejoicing inside. The cartels had taken a dreadful beating, and the flow of drugs into his country would no doubt decrease as a result. It had to. He had never been in the military, but he had been part of many armed raids. Even he was amazed at how much destruction had been created so fast. Bennie knew from experience and his reading of history that most battles turned on the killing ground: who had it, and who did not. Largely as a result of the decisions the cartels had made—where and how to meet being the most important—in their desire to avoid being trapped or surprised by one of the other cartels, they had chosen to meet in the open. The cartel groups, both those in the hall and those on the field, had unknowingly positioned themselves for intense crossfire from multiple concealed locations. *Shit, maybe not since Custer*, thought Bennie, *has a group been more stupid or arrogant about the setting of an event.*

Bennie got up from the table and went into the glass cubical and called Charley on his second encrypted phone and gave him a brief rundown on the results. He told him he would get back when he had captured and killed lists. Charley could barely keep the pleasure of Alberto's success out of his voice. When Bennie got back to the table, Alberto was on one of the landlines, updating Alvarez. He made much the same comments to the president as Bennie had to Charley. *Will get back to you when I have more.*

Both Quito-Perez and General Lozano were talking with their people in the field and at the hospital. The first medevac chopper took five minutes to reach the field and another ten to reach the hospital. The situation at the seminary was beginning to sort itself out. Alberto had worried during the planning about the potential for a massacre. Manny had told him that was something he could not control, so he shouldn't worry about it. The cartel shooters would either lay down their weapons or they wouldn't—"And if they didn't," Manny had said, "then your people will have to make them, the hard way." Major Ruiz reported to General Lozano that he had taken no casualties at the field, the fight had been so one sided.

As he had been quietly told to do, Commander Diaz reported in to Alberto personally and told him that they had three wounded, none serious, and one dead. The fatality, he was saddened to report, was Commander Molinar, apparently by his own hand. Diaz said his men had found his body next to that of whom they believed was Jesus Qiuntero. Alberto asked Diaz to keep the circumstances surrounding Molinar's death to himself for now and to make sure any others of his command who might be aware of it to do likewise. That was an order. He reminded him to report in occasionally and privately, outside the chain of command.

Alberto ended the call and looked down and just shook his head. Molinar was one of his most experienced and trusted commanders and would have been one of his choices to lead the assault based on merit alone. But he felt he owed him for the personal loss he had suffered at the hands of Jesus Qiuntero, and that had made his selection to lead the raid easy. Molinar had always been so professional and had told Alberto on several occasions how much he looked forward to seeing Qiuntero at trial. It had all been a lie, and now his old comrade was dead. His grief for his murdered son had overridden his senses, and Alberto realized he had missed it, and he felt bad. Yet another senseless casualty of the fight against the cartels. He got up from the table and walked slowly into the kitchen. Sensing his new friend was hurting, Bennie got up and followed.

There was much serious work to do in the days ahead for the men in the room, but for now there was a celebratory spirit growing as smiles and optimistic discussions were occurring all around the table. Many men were dead, and there were murmurs about how tragic that was, but to a man, those around the table were thrilled at the apparent success of the operation. It was not yet known whom they had in custody and whom might have been slain during the raid, but the cartels had been hurt, probably very badly, and this was a good thing, and they showed it. In front of the inevitable media cameras and reporters, they would show restraint and solemnity, but not here. Several even pulled out cigars but refrained from lighting them in deference to the secretary, who was known to not smoke.

General Lozano looked around the table with something akin to disgust on his face and suggested to the assembled gentlemen that perhaps they should wait for the preliminary after action report before celebrating. Most of the men around the table secretly thought he was a pompous, too-serious, self-important officer. Alberto did not care what their opinions were; he liked and respected Lozano the most, above all the others around the table.

A communications center had been set up in the now-smoke-cleared meeting hall, complete with a two-way televised setup. A communications sergeant announced that the commanders had arrived and would be speaking shortly. The men in the Center waited the few seconds it took for Major Ruiz and Commander Diaz to arrange themselves on their chairs and check their monitors. One of Alberto's technicians had set up a tripod and had his camera focused on the secretary, who had returned to the conference table.

"Mr. Secretary," Diaz said, "can you see and hear us, sir?"

"Yes, Diaz, we can. Please report."

"Mr. Secretary, consider this our preliminary report, but I also say that I believe it to be very accurate. Our forces took four casualties—three wounded from gunshots, none seriously. One dead, Commander Molinar himself, sir, who was fatally shot. I know he was your friend, Mr. Secretary; please accept my condolences at this time."

"Thank you, Diaz. Please, go on. The leaders, what of the leaders?"

"Yes, sir. Jesus Qiuntero is dead, by the hand of Commander Molinar, it would appear on first examination. All the others we have in custody are relatively unharmed. Caro, Arellano, Fuentes, and the two Felix-Contreras brothers are en route to the detention area as we speak under heavy guard. We have forty-six cartel enforcers confirmed dead."

This number brought audible murmurs from several at the table that several minutes before had been smiling broadly.

"That number is likely to rise. We have treated thirty-six enforcers at the site for wounds, and the most seriously wounded are already on their way to the hospital in Los Mochis. Our chief medic believes that four will not survive; their wounds are simply too great. I will follow up on this aspect. We have twenty-two enforcers in custody unharmed. They are being detained at the field, and we will be moving them to the detention facility just as soon as we have use of the choppers. Our intelligence section has identified a total of thirty-two known cartel members whom we have outstanding warrants on. Of course, one of these, Qiuntero, is dead. A great many of those in the company of the leaders appear to be just retainers, soldiers. We will make a great effort to identify all of them. We are in our investigation mode. Both the field and the hall have been cordoned off, and our forensic troops are in the process of marking and tagging all the evidence as it lies. The photographers and video people are continuing to document every centimeter. That photography, plus what was taken before the shooting started, should be powerful evidence at the individual trials. Forensics will be fingerprinting all weapons in the hopes of matching up individual weapons with the unknown shooters we have in custody. Our hope, of course, is to be able to bring the more serious charge of attempted murder to bear over and above simple weapons charges and resisting arrest. Clean-up teams will begin their work as soon as we have finished gathering evidence. This concludes my preliminary report, Mr. Secretary."

"Thank you, Diaz. Good report." Alberto turned to the others at the table. "Any questions for Commander Diaz, gentlemen?"

Assistant Attorney General Hinojosa, a good man, Alberto thought, asked, "Mr. Secretary, where will those being arrested be held in detention? We will want to begin our interrogations as soon as possible."

Alberto looked around the table. "Gentlemen, please do not take this as any sort of negative reflection on your character or honor, for none is intended, but the specific detention facility will for the time being remain a closely held piece of information. Those with a need to know have been told or soon will be. I realize that there are some of you here who take exception to some of the compartmentalization protocols I have instituted. We have no idea who the cartels have inside the federal government, nor do we know to what level they have us infiltrated. But I assure you, gentlemen, they do. And until I can get to the bottom of that, need to know will be the standing order. I will not risk a breakout attempt by one of the cartels to free their leader because some low-level administrative or staff person on the payroll of the cartels comes across the name of the facility. The less you know, the better, for now, Senor Hinojosa."

Hinojosa simply nodded.

"Commander Diaz, I am appointing you overall commander onsite to take Molinar's place. You have my full confidence. General Lozano and I must report to the president. Please keep Director Quito-Perez advised on your progress." The monitors went black, and Alberto turned to the others.

"Gentlemen, this has been a significant day, and there is much work to be accomplished from this point forward. I expect your best and will not accept anything less. Nothing you have seen or heard in this room shall be discussed with other staff or the press until after the president does so."

With that blunt statement, Alberto, Bennie, and the general and his aide left the Center for the short trip out to Los Pinos. Alberto called the president as he had been requested to do, and Alvarez asked him to please come out to Los Pinos as soon as his duties permitted, but no later than two. It was now one thirty.

27

For any national leader, no matter how large or small the country, there was never enough time in the day to do all the work required. Presidents, prime ministers, or whatever title they went by were constantly faced with the press of their official duties from the trivial, ceremonially, or purely political to the truly important and sometimes history defining. It went with the job. As much as Alvarez wanted to be at the Center and watch the events he had orchestrated unfold, beyond watching the ten or fifteen minutes of the live feed that Baca had pirated, from the time the actual shooting started and stopped, it was necessary for him to devote his time to a myriad of other Executive Department issues. He looked up from the large antique desk that seemed to dominate the president's official office as Raul came into the room, looking decidedly unhappy. Alvarez simply raised his eyebrows in question as Raul sat down in one of the upholstered side chairs.

"Pablo, no matter what we try, Geraldo and I cannot make contact with our people at the seminary. Both Icaza and Martinez had their instructions, and neither has reported in since last night, nor do they answer their calls today. I believe, therefore, that we must assume they have been taken out in some action, that they did not get Arellano as we had hoped would happen, and that we have probably lost Mateos. We clearly saw him enter with the others. He was supposed to get out with Arellano through the basement, but…"

"Yes, yes, Raul," a grim-looking Alvarez said as he sighed deeply. "I hope Fernando shows up, but I expect the worst. They must have been discovered and removed from the scene, and that is most regrettable. I now will have his life on my conscience as well. God knows he deserves so much more for all his sacrifices. Alberto will likely have any details; he is on his way over to make his report."

"We have the onsite commander's full preliminary report saved, if you would like to see it beforehand."

"No, that's not necessary. I will receive it from Alberto, but I will want you here. I deeply regret the loss of Fernando, if that turns out to be the case, but we have scored a great victory here, Raul."

"I agree, and if Rodriguez was not due in the next several minutes, I would suggest we toast to it."

"I believe we will do just that when Alberto gets here, but plan on a private celebration tonight, just the four of us—say, at dinner. Continue to see what you can find out on our men at the seminary, but now is a time for a tempered celebration, old friend."

"Perhaps when we see Eduardo and Carlo, we can celebrate properly."

Raul turned and left, the deep concern on his face returning. He had hoped to hear from Rodriguez that their men had been discovered and eliminated. If that was not the case, it was back to being a mystery, and Raul hated mysteries.

Alberto and Bennie were pulling up to the front of Los Pinos about the time Raul was leaving the presidential office suite. They had been expected by the ushers and were shown directly down the corridor that led to the executive offices. As they walked, Alberto said to Bennie, "Best you wait in reception until I call for you. We must treat this as purely Mexican business at least initially."

"I agree, Alberto. I need to use the can anyway. Then I'll rustle up some coffee. Don't worry about me."

Alvarez's appointments secretary was standing in the large, handsome outer office waiting for the secretary. "Mr. Secretary, the president will see you."

Alberto walked through the door, and Alvarez stood up and came around the great desk to embrace his friend. With what looked and sounded like sincerity, Alvarez said, "Congratulations, Alberto, on what I believe will go down in our history as the day this government took the country back from the cartels. I am so grateful for all that you have done."

"Thank you, but perhaps we should wait for my police's final report before we celebrate. My commander on the scene said that of the forty warrants we hoped to serve today, we will successfully enforce thirty-two of them. That means of the worst known cartel members, there are eight out there on whose whereabouts or activities we know nothing as of now. Yes, we have hurt them, perhaps set them back a year or two, but I fear they will come back under new leadership. There is simply too much money at stake for others not to want to try to fill the vacuum."

"I agree, Alberto, of course, and promise as president that we will step up all our efforts to root this evil from our country. When I return from my mother's, we shall talk more of that. Like you, I want to hit the remnants of the existing cartels very hard. I suspect that your interrogations of the survivors have the potential to be a great source of intelligence. With the information you acquire, we will be able to do even more. I will support any actions you desire, for you have a great friend in the executive branch."

Alberto simply nodded in what could have been thanks. Raul Ortega entered quietly through a side door and nodded hello to the secretary.

Alvarez acknowledged Raul with a look and went on. "Tell me what details you have thus far. I would like to hear the breakdown of who we have, casualties, everything."

Alberto went through his notes on the report that Diaz had made. "If I may, Mr. Secretary?" Raul asked. "There were forty-one dead from the field and an additional five at the hall itself?"

Wondering where your execution squad is, eh, Ortega? Well, keep looking and wondering. You will never find or hear from them again.

"Regrettably, no, Senor Ortega. That total will go up. Commander Diaz said that there would likely be three or four additional dead as a result of the wounds they received at the field. The total will be near fifty."

"Thank you, Mr. Secretary," Raul said with a small glance at Pablo. Both were thinking the same thing: *Where are the others? Mateo had no less than a dozen men.*

"Forty-six, fifty, that does not matter to us now," Alvarez said with a dismissive wave of his hand. "What does is how we follow this up. My press office is at this moment alerting all the networks and the major print media that I will be issuing an important government announcement today at five. I have had the Justice Department's office of media relations contact all the television news outlets as well and advised them that under the emergency broadcast provisions of the law, we will be interrupting all programming from five until five thirty. I intend to make a detailed statement regarding this action today, and when I do, I will want you and General Lozano at the news conference with me. I will take no questions but will introduce you two, and we will allow no more than ten minutes of questioning from the press before I end it. We will solemnly report today's action, but it is also a celebration of a great victory of the people over the cartels. The last thirty years have been a great national nightmare, and today was a great victory, your victory. I will want to exploit this fact given all the very bad news the people have had to endure this week. We need to lift the spirits of the people, Alberto; there is much grief over Fernandez's death, and this will do it."

"Of course, Mr. President. I am at your orders," Alberto said, dreading the thought of the upcoming circus.

"Come. You two are my very oldest friends," Alvarez said as he stood and came from behind his desk, "and I want to toast your success, Alberto."

"It was the men, not me; they were the ones in danger. They were the ones facing the guns. Genaro Molinar, also a friend of many years, is dead."

"It was your plan, Alberto," Alvarez said as he very kindly grabbed Alberto by the shoulder, "and because of its brilliance, our casualties were few. I will mourn Molinar's passing, but you were the architect of this action, and whether you like it or not, old friend, you will become a hero to our people. I know you are somewhat depressed. I can sense it, and I understand, but one day in the not-so-distant future, you will come to look with pride on this day."

They had moved to the bar built into the bookshelves along one wall, and Alvarez poured the drinks. "Here, take this. You also, Raul. Gentlemen, I give you Genaro Molinar and all the other brave police and soldiers who delivered this blow to the worst criminals in the land."

"Hear, hear," Raul said.

Alberto said nothing but was thinking, *Yes, I will celebrate this victory. When it's complete. I will get you, you malignant son of a bitch.*

He forced a small smile and drank down the fine whiskey that was offered. They spent the next several hours going over the statement that Alvarez intended to read and continued to receive updates from Commander Diaz. It was clear to Alberto that Alvarez had been working on the statement for some time. He went through the motions trying to keep his thoughts from drifting to next week and the next "brilliant" action he was planning.

We shall see how brilliant you find me next week, Pablo Alvarez.

Press Room, Los Pinos
Bosque de Chapultepec
Late Saturday Afternoon

The press started arriving at the basement press room of Los Pinos in large numbers about three thirty. There were always a few reporters in attendance, the senior correspondents for the major Mexican networks that covered the president, but few others. Once the heads-up had gone out to all the media outlets around two thirty, there had been a feeding frenzy of fruitless, annoying communication from reporters of every government contact they knew to try to be the first one to break the story of why the government was taking over the airwaves. "A national address of great importance" was all any reporter could come up with. One of the big Mexico City stations, Transmita Dos, had a lead but was too busy or stupid to follow up on it. One of the news editors had a cousin whose son wrote for the local paper in Los Mochis, who called and said that some incident had occurred outside town, resulting in many injured people being treated at the local hospital.

But all the editor had done was send his Hermosillo-based reporter and camera crew down there to follow up on that local story. The crew would get to Los Mochis at six, and the story would be all over the country by then.

Saturday was a big day for television viewing in the country because of all the interest in the national sport, soccer. Every region had its favorite team, and most played games on the weekend, many of which were televised. Most of the larger television and radio stations around the country began thirty- or sixty-second spots alerting their viewing public that the president was to make a national address at five and to stay tuned. For two hours the major media in Mexico frenzied itself into a lather trying to discover the topic of the upcoming address. There were rumors of ex-President Castillo dying, until an enterprising young reporter had risked being shot and scaled the wall surrounding the old president's estate and photographed him tending his flowers in his greenhouse. Another rumor to make the rounds was that there was a heightened outbreak of the influenza at the camps. Again, this proved false. The Mexican media raised so much fuss that several of the larger foreign news organizations got into the fray. CNN and FOX from America had their own crews at Los Pinos, and others joined in a pool service being conducted for a group of smaller news outlets.

At ten before five, Alvarez's press secretary walked into the overflowing press room to make a few remarks about what was about to occur and also to give the television broadcasters a ten-minute heads-up on the president's arrival. Most of the more sophisticated and financially solvent stations and networks interrupted regular programming to conduct introductory news and commentary lead-ins to the president's address. On most every channel, there was a common thread of discussion. None of the commentators could recall a recent presidential address where the topic wasn't well known beforehand. The mystery was what made this a big story. Other commentators reviewed the week's events, and one station even speculated that they would not be surprised if the president was going to announce that President Fernandez's accident had in fact been a deliberate act. A rumor to that effect had made the rounds about four, but no one had anything to go on, so it was mostly disregarded.

By now across the country, the citizens' curiosity was greatly aroused. All over the country, a great many of those citizens who were not at home gathered at cantinas or other such public places where the broadcast could be watched. The press secretary walked to the front center of the room and announced, "Ladies and Gentlemen, the president."

All told, there were tens of millions of eyes watching as those members of the press who had been sitting stood as the relatively young, handsome, and yet not completely well-known new president made his way to the lectern. Alberto and General Lozano followed, taking up positions behind and on each side of Alvarez.

"Good afternoon; please be seated." Alvarez waited until the din in the press room quieted down before going on.

"My fellow citizens, as a people we have suffered many setbacks and losses recently. We mourn greatly the tragic loss of President Fernandez earlier this week. Also, many of our citizens continue to suffer from the problems on our northern border with the return of so many of our countrymen from the United States and the unfortunate and unnecessary hardships as a result of this government's failure to respond quickly and effectively to the worsening crisis there. More tragically, however, we have seen so many in our country over the last several decades murdered; others forcibly taken from their homes, many never to be returned; and the loss of thousands of members of our brave police and justice departments in the States and the federal government as a result of the unchecked lawlessness of the drug trafficking controlled by the large and powerful cartels that have been ravaging our country. The rise the past several years in the cartels' illegal and dangerous activities was nothing short of a criminal insurgency designed to defeat our lawful government and deny to us all the rights and protections we should enjoy in our representative republic. Earlier today, a great many of those responsible for that lawlessness have answered for their acts. Through confidential information provided to Secretary Rodriguez in his role as director of our national police force, he was alerted to a high-level summit to be conducted by the four largest, most powerful cartels in our country, sometimes referred to in the press as the Gang of Four. For the last several weeks, Secretary Rodriguez, with the assistance of General Lozano, our secretary of national defense, planned and organized and today executed a brilliant raid on this Gang of Four as they arrived at what they believed to be their secret meeting place. In a most cynical and sinister act, which could be expected of those who care so little for humanity or the sanctity of all we hold dear as lawful citizens, this group of criminals chose the grounds of one of our country's most revered places, the seminary of Saint Thomas of Aquinas on the Lake near Los Mochis, in the State of Sinaloa, as their meeting place. They reserved the meeting facilities there under false pretenses, deceiving the Very Reverend Monsignor Luna and his staff with the belief that the facilities had been reserved by a benevolent and generous private foundation. Nevertheless, we today have dealt a crippling blow to the worst of the drug traffickers in our country…"

A buzz had gone throughout the room like an electric shock from the moment that an understanding of where the president was going with his remarks became clear. He went on describe the raid and to spell out in general terms the judicial processes that would be taking place over the next few months as the federal investigation of the events at Saint Thomas of Aquinas on the Lake was concluded and the procedural steps toward trials for all those captured could take place. He finished his remarks by saying, "My fellow citizens, I personally and we as countrymen owe my old and good friend and our secretary of public security Alberto Rodriguez a great debt of thanks for his intelligence and skill at having planned and executed today's raid. That concludes my statement. I will not be answering any questions today, but Secretary Rodriguez and General Lozano have graciously consented to taking a few of your questions."

Cries of, "Mr. Secretary! Mr. Secretary!" rang out in the room as the worked-up reporters jumped to their feet to get recognized. All told, Alberto had to endure almost twenty minutes of questioning before the president's press secretary announced, "Last question!"

Office of the President
Los Pinos
Bosque de Chapultepec

Alberto and General Lozano had, at the invitation of Alvarez, followed him back to his office. Bennie was waiting in the outer office, where he had watched the press conference, and was greeted warmly by the president and invited to also come in to his office. The press secretary closed the heavy door behind them, and they followed Alvarez once again to his private bar, where, after asking each man what his pleasure was, Alvarez poured four tumblers full and passed them around.

"Mr. Santiago, would you join me in saluting these two fine public servants who today did more for their country than I think they realize?"

"It would be my honor, Mr. President."

"Gentlemen, we salute you." All four drank down a portion of their drinks. It was obvious to Bennie that Alvarez was just managing to keep what he could only describe as a sense of euphoria from just shooting out of his every pore.

Goddamn, Bennie thought, *he has this day become the single largest and most powerful trafficker in this country, maybe even in the world, and, in the process of monopolizing the trafficking, killed off those responsible for the death of his father and the attempts on his life, if Ray's information is accurate. What a kick-ass day for him. We need to get the hell out of here and finalize plans for next week.*

"Salvador," the president said, turning and looking at the general, "if I may ask you to excuse us, I have some more police business to discuss with these two."

"Of course, Mr. President. Thank you." There were handshakes all around, and the general left.

"Mr. Santiago, how did your raids go today?"

"Fine, Mr. President. I will be leaving the city here shortly, probably to-morrow, and going to Los Angeles to meet with our people there and get an accurate accounting of everything, but may I first say, as one police profes-sional to another, how terribly impressed I am at what you all accomplished today. I know Director Mills will be speaking with our president in the next day or so and will be briefing him on just what your success means for my country. No doubt the cartels will try to reconstitute themselves under new leadership, but that will take time, and you now have some very valuable information sources to develop further that will no doubt allow you fellows to do even more damage to the bastards, if you will pardon my vulgarity, Mr. President."

"I could not have said it better, Mr. Santiago, and I thank you," Alvarez said with what appeared to be a very genuine smile on his face. He knew that Raul was very uneasy, maybe even worried about what Alberto and this American may be plotting, but he saw no great threat here. And with the announcement that the American was leaving the country, he was even less worried. He would need to settle his old friend Raul down a bit on their trip north.

"As to our raids, Mr. President, I have received preliminary information only from Director Mills's office, but by the sounds of it, we did very well. No one was killed today, I am happy to report, and it appears we have taken into custody some thirty or forty people and an impressive haul of drugs, currency, and some records. I will of course be sending the secretary a full and detailed copy of anything I come up with. Also, we intend to conduct very thorough and aggressive interrogations of everyone we have in custody, and I will also be sending extracts of that information as soon as we develop it."

"Excellent; my congratulations on your accomplishments. I will look forward to hearing from you through Alberto here. Gentlemen, it has in-deed been a most unusual and hectic week."

Alvarez turned to Alberto and placed his empty hand on his back in a personal and affectionate way, "I cannot believe, old friend, it has been only seven days since we were speaking in my office at the Zocalo about my pending resignation." Alvarez turned and looked at Bennie. "I probably should not have said that, Mr. Santiago; forgive me. If I have your word of honor not to repeat anything I say, I will complete my thought."

"Of course, sir; you have it."

"On second thought, there is no reason you should not share this with Director Mills, who will of course share it with other senior members of your government. If you could just tell your people that before anything is made public, you allow us to make this public in due course and in our own way."

"Absolutely, Mr. President. I will make whatever you say a code-word-file subject, and that will limit it for the time being to just Director Mills, our intelligence director, and me. It doesn't have to go any further than that."

"Thank you, Bennie. Is it OK if I call you Bennie?"

"Again, an honor, Mr. President."

Asshole. Only my friends get to call me that, and you're no fucking friend.

"It seems, Bennie, that our recently deceased president had been embezzling oil revenues and diverting them to his private accounts offshore. One of our auditors discovered this and made me aware of it as the then secretary. Given his duplicity, and also for his dreadful handling of the immigration mess and the postponement of elections, I felt I could no longer in good conscience serve in his administration and resigned my office a week ago Friday effective this past Monday. I appointed Alberto here as my successor, and we met last Saturday to begin the transition. But as the world has seen, there was the unfortunate air crash on Monday, and I had no choice but to stay in the government. Our people took a terrible emotional hit with the unexpected death of a president. I saw no reason to add to their misery by also announcing that he was likely a cartel-connected criminal. After we hold the elections and have improved conditions in the north, then we will put out word that there were certain financial improprieties. But not before then."

"I understand and agree, Mr. President. Nothing is served by telling your people everything now."

"Alberto, my press office will be putting out as part of the routine schedule announcements tomorrow morning that I have advanced my planned trip to the coast and that I will be leaving tomorrow at two for my mother's in Baja. Will this affect any arrangements you are making?"

Alberto thought about it for a second before answering, but he shook his head slowly and said, "No, not really, Mr. President. Preparations for the press and staff camp across the road from your family home are nearly complete. All the parking, temporary power, and housing structures provided by General Lozano are in place as well as the large community dining facility and field kitchen. The press people will have to make their own housing arrangements. We are only providing spaces for your presidential guard and my Federal Police, who will be providing security. The communication and sanitary facilities are also complete—or complete enough, I should say—so that you may visit your mother. Anything we need to finish up can be done over the next several days without jeopardizing your safety."

"Thank you, old friend. I cannot tell you how much safer I feel tonight after what you accomplished today. I will sleep easier knowing those bastards, as Bennie so correctly called them, are in your jails. I would invite you, Alberto, to go with me, but I am afraid it will not be that pleasant for you. My mother is not doing well."

"I appreciate the thought, Mr. President, but I also have made plans. I have not said anything to Bennie about this yet, but after all that has transpired, I thought I would go south to Campeche and visit my sister and her family, who are vacationing there on the gulf, and invite our American friend to join me. Maria and the children are still in America, so I need some company. How about it, Bennie—would you care for a couple of relaxing days on the beach with part of my family if I promise you no business?"

"Sounds great, Mr. Secretary; it would be my pleasure to join you." They finished their drinks and left the obviously very happy and satisfied president and headed to Alberto's home across the great Chapultepec park. Once they were in the safety of Alberto's home, Bennie asked him, "Are we really going to your sister's, Alberto?"

"No, Bennie. She is indeed at her home there, but you and I are going to our family beach home at Zihuatanejo on the Pacific side. We call it La Casa de Campo del Sol Poniente—the Villa of the Setting Sun. It is a very beautiful place, and I really could use some rest. But it is also a very good place to meet with Colonel Portillo and Major Garcia. They and two squads of their men are already on their way, the officers to meet with us and the men to provide security as we make our plans for this coming week. We must act fast, my friend. We will wait until Alvarez leaves the capital at two, and we will leave soon after. We will go to Salvador's headquarters outside the city, where I have arranged for one of his helicopters to take us west."

Bennie just smiled approvingly at Alberto's scheming. He liked it. He'd have told him he agreed with the old "limp leg" maneuver he just had just given Alvarez, but after a previous attempt during one of their dinners to explain the nuances and differences of American football from his version—not to mention the slang—he decided to not head down that amusing and frustrating path again. They had several drinks and then their ritual dinner, just the two of them, served expertly as usual by Alejandro after they had successfully raided Alberto's cellar once more. Even the reticent and ever-professional Alejandro had said as he was pouring their first glasses of wine, "My congratulations, sir, on the events of the day." Bennie could see that Alberto was letting off some emotional steam, and he was determined to help him.

Halfway through dinner, Quito-Perez called to advise the secretary that there was a huge spontaneous outpouring of people gathering at the Zocalo, singing and dancing to celebrate the defeat of so many cartel leaders at once. Alberto asked if it was peaceful, and Quito-Perez said yes, so there was nothing really to do but have the capital police watch over the demonstration of joy.

After the very excellent pork loin concoction Alberto's chef had prepared, washed down with several bottles of a very nice Monterey County, California, pinot noir, they called it an evening around nine and, with a little bit of a wobble in their walk, made it up the curving stairway to their respective suites. Bennie had just slipped under the covers and closed his eyes when his special phone buzzed and vibrated on the nightstand. The sudden adrenaline rush snapped him out of his slightly inebriated state, and he went from pleasantly satiated to nervously alert in a microsecond. *Jesus Christ*, he muttered, *my old ticker can't take much more of this shit.* As he opened the text message from Ray, he realized that he had gone perhaps two hours tonight while at dinner with Alberto and not once thought of Ray. The thought disturbed him a bit. Ray's message was to the point:

> Alvarez very pleased with
> himself and overconfident.
> Raul very concerned
> still about your mission and
> albertos holding back info.
> Alvarez not worried and said
> they will revisit with edurado
> on monday or tuesday. Alvarez
> told Raul you leaving town.
> whats the scoop? Raul may
> have people watching so be
> careful. Raul a bulldog when
> curious and bugged. Eduardo
> source las cruces is making progress
> after operative met contact
> at base today. Believe I have until
> tuesday before Raul makes
> Alvarez listen hard and targets
> you and alberto. What is plan
> for chi town? Getting warm
> here need info and plan.

Shit, Bennie thought. *I need to reassure him, and I'm so goddamn unsure of everything.* Bennie slowly pecked out his response to Ray, his thumbs and the wine making it difficult.

Leaving town with alberto to
meet troops that will make
raid in chi town. targeting tuesday
or wednesday. earlier if plan
allows. Al told alvarez we were
going to gulf big fib. From now
till raid alvarez to have no idea
where we are so not to worry.
whatever the leak at base told eds
guy is misdirection so not to
worry about that either. Our
general running that end of show.
Eds man las cruces soon to be
out of action, my turn to fuck
with them. stay cool cavalry
on way. call first chance any
time 24/7. I will update you
on specifics as they are finalized
we will get these bastards.

A quick minute later, Ray shot back:

thanks boss sounds good.
Will chill and do my part just
let me know what that is.
Need to end this mission.
Lines between me and them
not as clear as they once were.
Condor and Raul basically good.
Don't want them killed but
don't have an answer about future.

Ray's last few comments made Bennie pause. *Shit, that charming bastard Alvarez is working on Ray. And I suppose I can see why Ray feels like he does. In a fucked-up way, I can see that what Alvarez is trying to do will actually help some, especially down here. Goddamn, more than ever need to get Ray out. No matter how noble he believes their cause, they are still criminals. I have to make Ray see that.*

Troubled by Ray's last thoughts, Bennie tried focusing on future plans. He thought Alberto's taking out of Alvarez's backup team at the seminary was inspirational. With everything that this Raul Ortega seemed to be dealing with for Alvarez, having more men go missing had to be a mystery that surely messed him up just a bit more. Bennie thought it was high time he got into the act. He wouldn't bother Alberto tonight; the poor bastard had earned a good drink and a good night's sleep. But at breakfast tomorrow, he'd let him in on his idea. It was time that this Eduardo's guy in Las Cruces went missing—not arrested, not killed, but plain missing. He had given that possibility some thought today and could see no downside. Worst case Alvarez might start to realize that they were being targeted, but if they did not know for sure who, what the hell. What would Eduardo Vargas and Raul Ortega do when their key man no longer returned their phone calls? Drive the bastards crazy, he hoped. Johnny Walker could probably pull it off, but Bennie was sure the general had counterterrorist troops on his base who could do a snatch and grab on the quiet, and no one would be the wiser. Plus they had the jail cells handy where a guy could be stashed for a couple of days before the law kicked in. He'd run it by Alberto in the morning and maybe give the general a call.

It was time to really start kicking these guys in the balls. With that as his last thought, he fell sound asleep and got the best rest he'd had in a couple of weeks.

28

Bennie woke up at six after sleeping hard for eight hours. He had been living in one of his two suits for the last week, freshened daily by Alejandro, to look like they had come straight from the dry cleaner's. He had a single pair of comfortable old khakis and a polo shirt stuffed in the bottom of his battered suitcase that he had not yet dragged out, and given it was Sunday, put them on. He sat on the couch of his sitting room and jotted a few ideas in his notebook. Finished with the thoughts that had been bugging him, he headed down to the kitchen, where he knew there would be someone from Alejandro's domestic staff who could rustle him up some coffee. He always thought a little clearer after his first couple of cups. Ray's text last night had momentarily put a damper on what had otherwise been a decent buzz, and the good night's sleep had done wonders, but he still needed some caffeine or a couple of aspirin to dull the small headache at the base of his skull. As he entered the kitchen rubbing the back of his neck, he was thinking, *Jesus, I'll never learn. Malt whiskey with a red wine chaser can be a bitch.*

A chef's assistant named Javier was sitting in his white uniform in the kitchen reading a paper when Bennie walked in. Javier handled breakfasts and lunches for the chef and assisted on all the important dinners. He stood up and smiled; it was not the first time that the North

American had wandered into the kitchen early in the morning. He rather liked Senor Rodriguez's guest. The first time he had come in early unannounced, he had stuck out his hand and said, "Morning, name's Bennie. Can I trouble you for a cup of coffee?" Javier wasn't used to Senor Rodriguez's guests even being aware that he was alive, much less coming into his place of work and introducing themselves. He liked Senor Santiago and understood why Alejandro was very insistent that he be treated well by the staff.

"Morning, Javier. Could really use some coffee."

"*Si*, Senor Bennie. I just made some; let me get it for you. If you will pardon me for saying this, if the empty bottles tell me anything, it would seem that you and Senor Rodriguez had a very good dinner last night."

"Jesus, are those still lying around? How many did we kill?"

"Just three, Senor. It is my responsibility to keep the records of the wine cellar. The maids keep the bottles for me until the next morning so that I may record what was taken out. That way Alejandro knows what to replace."

"Well, my apologies for keeping you so busy this past week. I know we've made a dent down there. Whatever the hell we had last night was outstanding, if my badly beat-up memory serves me correctly."

Javier simply smiled and walked over to the coffee urn and returned with a cup.

"It is good to see Senor Rodriguez has a friend, Senor Bennie. He misses his family. Here is your coffee, and please, take the paper. There is much in it about what Senor Rodriguez did yesterday; I am very proud."

Bennie thanked the young cook and went to the dining room with copies of *El Universal* and *El Heraldo de Mexico*. Both papers had huge headlines regarding yesterday's raid. The picture covering the top half of the front page of *El Universal* had been taken at the press conference and showed a determined-looking President Alvarez making a point with Alberto watching him from the background. *El Heraldo de Mexico* had a large photo of the crowd at the Zocalo, estimated at one hundred thousand people, that had gathered at the huge public square in the Centro to celebrate. It had the appearance of a candlelight vigil given the thousands of points of light that could be seen in the long-exposure photo, likely from all the illuminated cell phones in use for calling or photographing in the dimly lit great square.

There were extensive biographies and pictures, mugshots mostly, of the leaders of the cartels and a few of their identified followers who had been killed and captured. There were also stories on Alberto and General Lozano. Bennie flipped from the first couple of pages to the editorials, which were positively glowing in their summaries of the big event and what the country may expect in the future as a result of what they described as the Alvarez government's "bold and decisive" action. Bennie largely ignored most of the papers but did read with interest an article by one obviously enterprising reporter who had managed to get his hands on a list of names of the thirty-two captured yesterday whose previously prepared outstanding arrest warrants had been served. It had been discovered during the night, as more and more of those captured had been identified, that an additional twelve of those arrested also had outstanding warrants on a variety of charges. A few of those in custody would get some sort of immunity from prosecution if they provided high-value information leading to additional arrests.

Javier came in and asked Bennie if he'd like some breakfast, but Bennie said he'd wait for Alberto. He was on his second cup of coffee when Alberto, also casually dressed for the first time since Bennie had been there, came walking into the dining room.

Bennie looked up from his reading and smiled. "Your national media is saying nice things about you this morning, Alberto."

He and Alberto had discussed what a colossal pain in the ass the media usually was for law enforcement officers, wherever they lived, just the other night at a dinner. "You're a national hero this morning, my friend."

"You know what you can do with that national-hero business, Bennie. Coffee, *por favor*." Bennie poured while Alberto glanced at the front pages. "I will be receiving a written progress summary by ten of whatever the investigations, identifications, and even some interrogations have turned up thus far."

"I think at least portions of your progress report are in the paper already. *El Universal*, page three."

Alberto flipped to the page. "Damn," Alberto said, disgusted. "It appears you may be correct. I see no real damage to the integrity of the investigation with this obvious leak, but I intend to try to find out just who did this."

"I understand and commiserate, but it's probably a waste of time. Likely someone in your organization either got himself laid or picked up a few bucks for sliding a little information over. I see the byline is a woman reporter, so my guess some guy on your staff thinks he's scoring points with the senorita by leaking this stuff."

"You are probably correct, but I must put a stop to it nonetheless."

Bennie shrugged his shoulders as Alberto read on. "Listen, I heard from Ray last night."

This got Alberto's immediate attention. Bennie went on to show him the text exchange and tell him his idea for picking up the Corro guy in Las Cruces.

"I agree, Bennie. What is that phrase you used—no harm, no foul?"

"That's the one."

Alberto smiled at his friend and then went on. "Let's have our breakfast first and then call Manny. I don't know about you, but I am not quite myself this morning, and some food will no doubt help. I apologize for my excessive celebration last night."

"First of all, there is no need for an apology. You earned the right, as far as I'm concerned, to run naked through the yard and howl at the moon if you wanted to," Bennie said with a grin, in spite of the dull, throbbing pain at the base of his neck.

"A most disagreeable image, my friend, on several counts," Alberto responded, also trying to muster a smile through his hangover.

It was nine before they entered Alberto's study and contacted the general. They had spoken to him last night to update him on the raid and to receive his report on the setup they were running with Captain Irwin. Danny had been very shaky but overall had done as he was told and passed along the disinformation they had agreed to—specifically, that it was believed by those looking for this Carlo that he lived and worked in the Monterey area.

But that was all he had overheard or been told when asked to search where they directed. Danny had reported back that his handler, Alex, had seemed pleased. The disinformation was now working its way through the pipeline to Eduardo Vargas.

Alberto first called Manny on his private number, saying only after he picked up, "Can we have a serious conversation?" That was their code phrase for firing up the see-tee if an initial attempt failed and using their regular communication devices was necessary. Manny had taken to carrying the see-tee to his quarters at night just in case. Alberto caught him out at breakfast with Beth, and he said he would call him back. Twenty minutes later, on the screen of Alberto's open see-tee, came the now-familiar "Safety One for Ghost One." Alberto logged on and activated the secure two-way visual communication system. After an exchange of pleasantries and congratulations, Alberto got down to business.

"Manny, Bennie wants to poke Alvarez some more. He has told you of this man Corro sent to your country by Eduardo Vargas to try to locate who is trying to find one of his bosses."

"Yeah, right, Al—what about him?"

"We want him to disappear. If Bennie put you in contact with his deputy there in El Paso, could you arrange for Corro to be picked up without anyone seeing or hearing anything about it?"

Manny paused for a second, as if considering a thought, and then said, "I suppose so. I assume Bennie is nearby?"

"Yes, he's right here."

Bennie leaned into the camera's view. "Morning, General."

"Hi, Bennie. A question: Why me? Is there a security problem with your guys?"

"Not at all, General. It's just that they are more of investigative 'knock on the door and arrest the bad guy' types. We need this guy to go away and no one be the wiser. Your basic snatch and grab. My thinking was that my guys could provide the intel but that you have the troops experienced in this type of action, and you have a place to keep this guy out of sight for a while before we need to start processing paper on him."

Manny thought it over for a second and then said, "If you were to have your man contact me regarding a joint action to detain a known or suspected criminal illegal alien, I'd be well within my basic orders and responsibilities to have border corps personnel assist the DEA. Tell him to call me, Bennie."

"His name is John Walker, General, and I will brief him in as soon as we are done here. Thanks."

"Manny," Alberto said as he rejoined the conversation, "We are off to Zihuatanejo to meet with my Los Pueblos Fantasmas commanders. Alvarez is going to Baja at two. Based on a message from Ray last night, he will be in Chihuahua tonight as the Condor. I will want to mount an action to take Alvarez and his entire brain trust no later than Tuesday, if it can be done. I have had Colonel Portillo thinking about this since Friday, but he went directly from the seminary to Zihuatanejo last night, and I am unsure how far along his thinking is."

"I'll tell you right now, Al, that Tuesday is cutting it close. He may be able to move his men around the country in that time frame, but there will be logistics issues, and more intelligence will be needed. Even some time on the ground in the neighborhood would be useful. Maybe Wednesday, more likely Thursday would be more reasonable."

"Perhaps more reasonable, Manny, but not practical. We have no idea how long Alvarez intends to stay in Chihuahua, and it is imperative we catch him there. I have been toying with ideas on just how to reveal the truth about our president to other senior officials in the government, and believe I know how I will do this to ensure believability and make our case, but we cannot take the risk that he will cut his stay short for whatever reason. We know, or at least we believe, he will be in Chihuahua into Wednesday. In my mind, that means we take him on Tuesday."

"OK, Alberto, I agree with everything you say; it just means it will be more of a tactical solution on the fly—but what the hell, that happens in battle all the time. You will just have to do the best you can. Let me know what I can do to help."

"One thing we require as soon as it can be accomplished is to have your drones find us a staging area close to but out of sight of the Condor estate near Chihuahua. I'm told we require an area capable of handling several helicopters without revealing our presence. Can this task be done today?"

"No problem. I'll have the sar major get over and get the kids looking for a place. He will know what you're looking for. What else?"

"There is one last thing that I need you to consider, Manny. If Colonel Portillo requires more than his forces to complete his task, despite my complete trust in General Lozano, I am reluctant to involve people from our own national police or army, not knowing who all Alvarez has in place in those organizations who could betray us and alert him. Any traitors in those organizations would not have revealed themselves in our joint action yesterday because we, meaning Alvarez and I, were fighting a common enemy. However, that will no longer be the case when we go after him. If I needed it, what help could you provide?"

Manny looked long and hard at the camera, obviously mulling it over. "Well, Alberto, I'd be lying if I said I haven't already been giving that some thought. I felt that there was a possibility that at some time, you just might require a little muscle from a secure source. The simple answer is, yes, I will help. The more complicated one is that depending on the forces we are talking about, I am starting to push a threshold here. But what the hell. I never planned on being in uniform the rest of my life anyway. I'll do whatever is necessary and then explain it up the chain later."

"Thank you, Manny."

"General, it's Bennie. I would understand if you had to go up the chain. I appreciate the risks you've taken so far and do not want to be the one responsible for torpedoing a fine career. So a question for you. What if the head of the DEA came to you and asked for your help on an emergency extraction of an embedded agent in Mexico? Say an extraction in force. What would that require?"

"I see where you're going, Bennie, and I like it. If Charley, for example, called me and said he had an agent in harm's way and needed my help immediately, I would do so and follow up with the paperwork and reporting later. Assisting the DEA in covert actions is part of my responsibilities. I had Romey look this up the other day; nowhere does it specifically say just in

US territory or not south of the border. I'm to lend help where and when it's required using the assets available to the border corps and using my own judgment. I'm sure the policy wonks in Washington intended the language to mean in our territory, but they were not as precise as they should have been, so screw 'em. And Alberto, I would never send an extraction mission out that wasn't able to defend itself, if you get my drift. My sons of bitches would be lethal."

"Thank you, Manny. This could work. Getting Bennie's man out and back to the United States is critical to our mission. I will discuss this with my colonel."

"General, Bennie again; anything new from the surveillance?"

"Several things, one good, one maybe not so good. Our bad guys, the Vargas brothers, seem to be staying pretty close to home. Not a lot of moving around. Unless they have been smuggled out—and we have had eyes on every vehicle in and out of the place in the last several days—they are still at the Chihuahua estate. The one disturbing thing we've seen is what looked to us like spotters. They have put out a couple of people with binoculars scanning the sky. Problem with that is it's very hard to be a spotter from a concealed position. Their people are out in the open. We pulled the birds back to ten thousand feet and have been using max zoom on the lenses. So far I think we have seen their spotters, but they haven't seen us. It may be coincidental, or maybe someone heard something, and they're looking for the birds. No way of knowing."

"Shit, not coincidence, General. That's Alvarez or those around him being smart. He gets word we are looking for Carlo in Monterey with drones, and as a precaution, he has people looking for us from the other estates. Smart guy, Alvarez. Did you see the same thing happen in Hermosillo?"

"Yes, we did, Bennie so your analysis is probably right on. I don't think that will hinder us, though. That data we sent down was really detailed, so Colonel Portillo has what he needs for planning purposes. As time and tactics warrant, we can always spool the birds in for a closer look. They're a bitch to spot at a mile even if you have good optics and know where to look."

"Manny, please deal with Corro as soon as you and Bennie's man can get together. Bennie and I were going to leave for the coast after two, but I think we will go as soon as possible. Ray has warned that Alvarez may be having us watched. It will do him no good once we enter the base from which we depart. If he has people watching my sister's home, and we do not show up, he will think to look in Zihuatanejo. We shall take steps to make it appear we are not there. However, the sooner we meet with Portillo, the sooner he can stage in Chihuahua."

"Sounds good, fellas. Let's hook up again later today. I'd like to hear what your Colonel Portillo has to say."

They signed off, each having plenty to do for a Sunday. Alberto and Bennie stayed around the mansion just long enough to pack up and for Alberto to receive his update on the raid. It was a shade past ten thirty when Alberto's motorcade headed for Camp Zaragoza southeast of the capital. They'd be at the house in Zihuatanejo in time for lunch. Alberto called Colonel Portillo from his secure cell phone to have him meet them at the alternate landing site and not the beach. He and Emilio had had contractors cut in a landing zone and an access road a mile away in a densely vegetated part of their land holdings so no one would see helicopters come and go. Alberto did not underestimate the possibility that Alvarez had people watching for them in Zihuatanejo, despite the misinformation he had given him. Typically, when he went there, they landed on the beach below the house. That was where Alvarez's people would be watching. He wanted the plan for the Vargas raid worked out by tonight so that Portillo, Major Garcia, and the men could rendezvous with the rest of their people in the Chihuahua by this time tomorrow. He was determined that the raid would be on Tuesday.

29

This was Pablo Alvarez's first trip on the presidential aircraft. Even though he had held cabinet-level appointments for the last two presidents, circumstances had never come up where it was either necessary for him to travel with the president; neither had he just been invited along. For the most part, prior to Saturday's raid, the upper echelons of the government had traveled fairly secretly, except for the president, and not often in groups. It just made them too high value a target. Because of the crash of president Fernandez's aircraft, Alvarez was required to fly in the old Mexican Air One, a twenty-year-old Boeing 757. They would fly to La Paz and then take the official presidential helicopter—a Sikorsky 70A Blackhawk variant, not dissimilar from the aircraft Alberto and Bennie had flown to Zihuatanejo earlier that morning. The media covering Alvarez's departure from the official presidential hanger was about triple that of a regular trip. The country was celebrating this Sunday in a big way, and even though Alvarez had thrown the lion's share of success for the raid toward Alberto Rodriguez, the people loved him. The story on the raid was reaching a worldwide audience. While all eyes were fixed on the president as he mounted the forward stairs, Ray and the other members of the inner circle, along with the press members invited to fly to Baja Sur with the president, were mounting the rear stairs. The circle would move to the front of the plane while the press idiots rode in the back.

Raul had gone over the general plan at lunch at the mansion: arrive La Paz at three thirty and then the family estate before four. Pablo would visit with his mother, and then he and the circle would move to the Pena guest house via the secret passageway, where Alvarez would alter his appearance to that of Nicolas Pena and, with the help of the Sanchez brothers, take the two Pena Land Rovers to the maintenance area for a black flight out. Pablo had vetoed driving back to La Paz and taking the Pena jet located there to Chihuahua. The security checklist the presidential guard was operating by had been mostly prepared by Raul and showed the thoroughly vetted Senor Pena and party leaving for destinations unknown via the north gate at about nine, not to return until Friday. Once the two Land Rovers cleared the north gate of the residential community, there would be no further security checkpoints or government interest in Senor Pena. Departures made through the north could circle back to the road to La Paz or simply get to Mexico Route One and head north. No one would be interested in where the reclusive Mr. Pena was heading. After sunset, no one would be able to see their departure from the maintenance area's airstrip. If the winds were out of the northwest, a rare occurrence, it was possible someone, perhaps the nearest police or presidential guards at the north gate, might hear the sound of a distant aircraft to the north carried on the breezes, but only for a second or two before Alvarez's pilots executed a hard low turn to the northwest out over the ocean. The aircraft would never come closer to a mile from the gate, and at an altitude of a few hundred feet, would not be seen past the low hills even in the bright light of day.

Pablo had spent the morning with his wife and children and then had begun receiving congratulatory calls from most of the heads of state in the western hemisphere. The most satisfying had come from the American president. They were of a similar age, and Pablo looked forward to meeting him again, this time as president. The American president had suggested that their staffs start working on a timeline and an agenda to meet in the near future, and Alvarez had readily agreed.

Ray's morning had been anything but comfortable. At their regular staff breakfast with just the three members of the inner circle present, Raul had asked Miguel to help Geraldo with anything he might require while he and Ray attended to a few tasks out of the mansion. At eight thirty, Ray had followed Raul to the large parking area of the mansion, and they had taken one of the cars and departed through the back gate away from the press and had driven toward Reforma. Ray had recognized that they seemed to be headed for a nightclub that Alvarez owned called the Blue Light Club. Raul had taken Ray there his first night in the city, only this was a Sunday morning, and the club would be closed. They had pulled off the nearly vacant side street the club was located on, driven slowly down an alley, and parked at the rear of the building. A man whom Ray assumed was the manager had been standing inside the rear door to greet them, which he had done with a nod of his head and a nervous smile. With the manager leading the way, they had gone down the dark back hallway and turned into a very large, nicely appointed, well-lit office. The manager had offered to bring them coffee, which Raul had declined for the two of them, and then had excused himself, closing the door behind him.

Raul and Ray had been alone, and for the first time in a long while, Ray had actually been very nervous. Why had Raul brought him here? Had Raul learned something about him? Something that required Raul to get rid of him? Ray had checked his HK to make sure it was accessible as Raul had made his way to the desk at the end of the room.

"Have a seat, Ray; we have a few minutes before our guest is to arrive."

Raul had sat in the high backed executive chair and appeared lost in thought, a very serious look on his face, before refocusing on Ray.

"We have a problem. I say 'we' meaning the three of us who are charged with protecting Pablo. Perhaps our most difficult task is to protect Pablo from himself. Do you understand what I am saying?"

OK, relax; this has nothing to do with you. He's talking about a threat from Alberto.

"I think so, Raul. Sometimes Jefe may not want to do what is best for his safety, and we must do it for him."

"That's correct. In this case, I am referring, of course, to his friend of many years Alberto Rodriguez, who—along with his cousin in America, a very powerful general in their army, and I believe this DEA man who has been staying with Rodriguez—are on to Carlo somehow, and that could lead to Pablo. He sees no danger or at least thinks it is not a real threat, not yet, but I think it is a mistake to think that it is not very serious. I believe that Alberto may believe that Carlo somehow was involved in his brother's death. Why else to involve his cousin—the American general—and the use of his spy drones? What makes this threat so ironic is that we of course had nothing to do with the death of Emilio Rodriguez, yet something has these men looking for Carlo, and that means they could stumble onto information that would lead to Pablo. We cannot have that."

Goddamn, do I dare ask the obvious? Or does it get Raul thinking about something he has not thought of, or by asking the obvious, do I make my position more secure? Gut instinct, Ray.

"May I ask a question, Raul?"

"Of course."

"Is Jefe in danger from Rodriguez because I am around?"

Raul had smiled. "You ask very good questions, but no, Ray, I don't think so. You are very valued here with us, but I do not believe you are anything to the Americans but a lucky inmate who happened to get away when Carlo escaped. They have no idea where you are. I had Geraldo check, and other than a warrant out for you and a general alert to other law enforcement offices that you may be in the northern part of their State of New Mexico in or near Albuquerque, there is nothing on you since the escape, and Geraldo would know. To them you are just one of thousands of young men they were trying to prosecute. With the way you are growing your hair and with the sunglasses you wear in public, even if you did appear in the background of a photo or on television, I think you would be unrecognizable to anyone who may remember you, and like I say, I do not believe anyone is looking for you."

Thank God for Bennie again, Ray had thought. *He no doubt planted that bulletin somehow. And thank God Raul thinks linearly. If the great Geraldo's computers say I've gone north, he will no longer think about me in the south. I think I'm OK.*

"I believe we need to take steps to deal with Rodriguez and eliminate the threat. Pablo would tell me to stop if he knew we were here and why, but he is blinded right now by both the success of yesterday's attack and his friendship with Alberto, especially since his brother was so recently a victim of those we now have defeated."

"Did the Gang of Four kill the brother?"

"I know who killed Emilio; we are not yet certain just who hired him. Likely we will never know. In my mind, it had to be either Arellano or the Butcher. They are the only ones of that group with enough balls and, to be honest, the brains to try something like that. I would rather not be here this morning, but events require this in order to protect Pablo and give him the time he needs to do all that he wishes to accomplish. The man who will be meeting us is called a cutout, Ray. He will be my contact with the small group of ex-military special forces that hire out for assassination. Alberto Rodriguez must regrettably be eliminated, and that means we must go against Pablo's wishes and do this for him. I have asked you to help me because as distasteful as this part of our job may be, it is sometimes necessary, and you need to learn how to operate like this. Also, if something should ever happen to me, I will need you to explain to Pablo what my motivations were. He will listen to you. I am doing this to protect my friend. Alberto Rodriguez is a good man, a just man. The idea of having to order his murder goes against all that Pablo has taught me, but I am trapped—trapped between trying to be the man Pablo has made me and Pablo's dreams. If we do not stop Alberto, he will stop Pablo, as surely as the sun rises."

"I will do whatever you ask, Raul." *More evidence of the man's conscience and goodness but also of his corruption, if I can call it that. Whatever the good of his and Alvarez's goals, they are corrupt. Alvarez has done this to him*, Ray thought, saddened again by the entire mess and what he knew he would eventually be required to do to stop it.

"Thank you. We will be meeting with Eduardo, probably tomorrow, and he will be a part of our group. He also believes there is more going on here than we know. What I have in mind is for Eduardo to conduct a series of assassinations against some dirty police, prosecutors, and judges we have been paying for years, as if the Gang of Four is taking their retribution on the government for our attack. After several weeks of this, they will strike in the capital and get Rodriguez. Like me personally, the country will mourn his loss. We will of course crack down on the criminal elements that are still active, and we will all breathe easier. I will, when the time is right, tell Pablo what I have done. He will not be happy at first, but eventually he will see the necessity of this action. Listen when the cutout gets here. I will not introduce you. I will give him his assignment, and we will set up our next contact when we return from the north. OK?"

"Whatever you ask, Raul, I will do."

I need to nip this in the bud. First chance I get, I let Bennie and Alberto into this little scheme. At least I'll have a description of the cutout for them that maybe can lead them to the bastards who got Alberto's brother. I'd like to do that for Alberto.

The meeting with the cutout was short and to the point. As a police officer, Ray was delighted with whom Raul was working with. The most frustrating thing that could happen to an officer when canvassing a crime scene and talking with witnesses was when the perp they described looked so typical. A witness who looked like every other person walking the street was like having no witness description at all. The man who arrived to meet with Raul was well dressed but had two very distinguishing features that made him stand out; first, he was a very large man, tall, and he must have weighed near 350 pounds. Second, he had a very nasty scar on his neck that ran from near the bottom of his left ear to his shirt collar. How anyone could have survived such a wound was unbelievable in itself. Surely if a man with his looks existed in the police databanks, they would know whom to watch.

After the brief meeting, at which Raul ordered the assassination of Alberto Rodriguez, the exact date of which would be provided in the near future, they returned to the heavily guarded Alvarez home, now the presidential mansion. The entire trip to the Blue Light and back took barely an hour, and Ray was grateful for whatever relationship he had developed with Raul that had put him in a position to watch and report. He wanted desperately to have a friendly beer with Bennie and hoped that Alberto would join them, and they could toast an end to this nightmare. They had a couple of hours before they had to leave, so Raul told Ray to go grab some rest and pack and be back at the mansion at 1:15 p.m. Ray did a quick double-check of the casita and the grounds outside and sent his quick text:

> Raul this morning put contract
> out on alberto. I was there and
> am his second in the planning.
> Action is unilateral on Rauls
> part. Alvarez not aware of plan.
> Shooters are ex mex military
> Special forces. Probably same
> group that got emilio. Raul using
> cutout as go between. Stands out so
> easy to i.d. Mex about 6'3" and at
> least 350 with 4 inch scar left ear
> to lower neck. Plan is to begin
> what looks like pay back attacks on
> police and judges in north for
> saturday raid and after several
> weeks go after alberto.
> We leave at 2 for baja and then
> at 9 direct black flight to Chihuahua
> estate as condor. Barega coming
> for lunch tomorrow at which time
> he will be killed.

The presidential party departed the capital on time, and the trip was quick, comfortable, and uneventful. At La Paz, the helicopter was ready to spool up as soon as the president was onboard. There were only twelve seats on the chopper and no room for the press. They would make the almost fifty-mile drive on their own, most eating the dust of the car or SUV in front of them.

Most of the major news outlets already had other crews on the scene at the president's mother's estate in anticipation of the president's arrival.

The newly constructed helipad was located across the road from the Alvarez estate near the new temporary quarters and hospitality village that had been constructed by the army on the barren site. The big black Sikorsky took twenty minutes to make the trip. Video and photo journalists were there to record his arrival. Even though it was only perhaps three or four hundred feet from the pad to the front gates of the Alvarez mansion and then several more hundred feet down the private drive to the house itself, there were several big black Suburban's to take the president and his party to the inner areas of his estate, and Ray and Miguel were the ones tapped to do the driving. No one but the president and his closest aides would get through the twelve-foot-high gates of the estate. Despite all the planning, the posted rules, and the large number of national police and presidential guards in attendance at the new support compound, there was still a zoo-like atmosphere generated by the unruly and professionally competitive members of the press.

Alvarez relented to their requests and took a few questions that would make all the television stations by their five and six o'clock news broadcasts: Yes, he was pleased with the progress of the investigation, but it had been barely twenty-four hours since the raid, and he asked the country to be patient. They had all the criminals in custody, and they would be brought to trial in due course in the proper and legal manner. No, he would not reveal the jail or prisons the captured criminals were being held at. No, the media and therefore the country would not get to see those arrested until their public trials. Yes, he was very proud of Secretary Rodriguez and the success of his plan and also to be able to call him an old friend. He only wished that the action of yesterday could have taken place a few weeks earlier and that his brother-in-law and the younger brother of Alberto Rodriguez, one of the real architects and leaders in the fight against these terrible criminals, might be with them today to share in this victory. No, the investigation into Emilio Rodriguez's assassination was still ongoing. It was his personal hope that through the police's interrogations of those captured yesterday, perhaps some additional information could be brought to light on that case. No, he was sorry, but no press would be allowed inside the walls of his mother's home. He would hope they would understand his need for privacy, not so much for him but for his mother, who was not well. Yes, he was looking forward to seeing his mother, and on that note, if they would all forgive him, he wished to begin doing that now. With that, the news conference was over, and he climbed into his SUV with its darkly tinted windows, and they drove off.

The large gates through the walls surrounding his family home were opened electronically by Miguel, who was driving the lead SUV. The members of the presidential guard tasked to guard the gate did so from their own black government Suburban that was pulled across the gates to block access to them after the gate had closed. Teams of governmental protectors were located at each corner of the walled estate, and others still were watching the beach. When the presidential party arrived at the front of the rambling mansion, Alvarez was the only one to get out of the first SUV and go in the front doors. Raul, Ray, and the others pulled around to the side into a parking area and began carrying the few bags they had—and the equipment Geraldo Baca was required to always have with him—down the path to the guest casita overlooking the ocean. Ray couldn't help noticing again the setting for the small guesthouse, sitting as it did in the clearing overlooking the ocean. Anyone coming upon this scene would never suspect that from the lower level, you could pass through a hidden door and be in the guesthouse of the neighboring estate in a matter of a few minutes.

For Ray, Raul, and the others, including Geraldo and Lorenzo, they spent only enough time in the casita to make their way next door through the tunnel. Geraldo and Lorenzo, of course, went to their electronic cubbyhole, while Raul invited the other three of the circle upstairs for a drink. He pointed out that they would need to stay off the patio and deck of the Pena guesthouse so as not to be seen from the ocean side by the security people on the beach. They'd do their drinking inside. The Sanchez brothers had made sure the casita's refrigerator was well stocked with a variety of foods and were there to warm up a simple dinner for the group. The plan called for Pablo to join them after dinner with his mother, then the Sanchezes were scheduled to bring the Land Rovers down at nine, and they would depart for the maintenance area. The sun would be setting about then, and it would be dark enough for them to fly out soon after. Alvarez showed up unaccompanied at seven, and it was clear he was saddened by the visit with his mother. There was really nothing more to do until nine but wait.

In spite of Raul's concerns, Alvarez insisted he was all right. Eventually Raul was able to draw him out of his funk with an updated report from Alberto's office on the progress of the identifications and early interrogations. Ray was listening to that, very interested, if nothing more than out of professional curiosity. Alvarez slipped back a little when he asked Raul about someone named Fernando Mateos, a name that Ray had not heard discussed before. Raul said he was sad to report that he was indeed on the captured list, meaning he had not escaped as planned. That was the good news; they could do something about Fernando if he was alive and they knew where he was. As for the others, Raul said, they were on no list, captured, wounded, or dead.

"They cannot just have vanished, Raul. Have you considered sending in some knowledgeable people to check?"

"I have thought about it but have not done so yet. I was going to suggest that perhaps the head of the Federal Police should go see the site of such a great victory, especially if the Condor should order him to."

"Yes, yes, a good idea. It would not appear unusual for him to want to see how the fieldwork is progressing. It's not like Quito-Perez likes to get too far from his office, but in this case, it's necessary. I will contact him tomorrow," a clearly reticent Alvarez responded.

At ten till nine, the Sanchez brothers arrived with the Land Rovers, and they packed up and drove to the secondary of the two Pena gates. As they passed out the gate, they could look to the south and see in the gathering darkness a mob of people and bright lights burning three or four hundred feet down the road at the new support and media camp. If anyone at the camp noticed their departure, it didn't show as they turned north and headed off into the relative darkness. At the north gate, the officer in command noted that as per the security schedule he had a copy of, the two-car caravan belonging to one Senor Pena, neighbor to the new president, was slowly approaching. Having earlier left the new security compound to take up his post, the officer could hardly blame the man for wanting to leave the circus that accompanied the new president and go elsewhere. He had his two men open the gate, and they stood to one side as the vehicles passed by. Ray had expected them to stop the vehicles and match names on a list or something, but nothing of the sort was done. He supposed their thinking was that anyone heading away from the presidential compound was not a threat. From that point it was a reverse of what they had done a week before when they arrived on Ray's first trip on the plane as part of Alavarez's inner circle. They pulled up to the warehouse/hangar building and then boarded the unique-looking aircraft that was parked just inside.

The pilots spun up the engines, turned off all interior and exterior lights, and eased the aircraft out of the hanger as the large motorized hanger doors closed behind them. It was necessary for the pilots to taxi all the way to the northeast end of the paved road/airstrip because of the typical winds. Ray recalled their arrival flight when the plane had landed on the mile-long straight piece of road easily; he wondered if taking off was as easy. The pilot in command stood on the brakes as the engines were throttled up, and when he released them, they shot down the road with amazing acceleration and were airborne in seconds. It was dark, but Ray, his face pressed close to his window, still could see ground features from the light of the rising sliver of a moon. The plane was still very close to the ground, perhaps only a couple of hundred feet, when the pilot made an almost ninety-degree turn to the northwest away from the residential community and the Alvarez home with all its attending security. In seconds they were over the black ocean and headed out to sea. Ray was not looking forward to the flight, but at least this one would only last an hour or so. The mere fact the duration was shorter made the thought of it less uncomfortable, but still they would have the gut-wrenching climb up and over the Continental Divide just before they dropped into the Chihuahua area. Carlo would be meeting them in a prearranged location south and west of Chihuahua. Alvarez had been right about one thing: the radical maneuvers did not bother him as much this time. Maybe the darkness helped. With the soft cabin lighting now on and reflecting off the window beside him, it was nearly impossible to see the ground racing by as Ray looked at his own reflection and wondered about the planned attack on the Condor's Chihuahua estate and his chances for survival.

30

La Casa de Campo Del Sol Poniente
Zihuatanejo, Mexico
Sunday Afternoon

Bennie and Alberto arrived quietly and without incident to the beautiful seaside home of the Rodriguez family. They were accompanied by Roberto, now dressed in the camouflage fatigues and rubber-soled boots he preferred to a business suit and wingtips, along with their two army chopper pilots. Colonel Portillo and Major Garcia met them at the clearing landing site with the two Range Rovers from the estate and drove the men through the dense coastal foliage to a well-disguised rear security gate and into the walled compound. The main access road off the public highway was the only widely known way to approach the beautiful estate from the nearby towns and resorts. The secretly cut in road from the rear wall of the estate to the secondary landing area led only into the dense underbrush and coastal forest. No one other than the Venezuelan construction company that had completed the work was aware of it. The pilots, two of General Lozano's best, were shown to their own casita and told to relax and take advantage of all the estate had to offer, from food and drink to a dip in the pool. The only rules were no alcohol, no leaving the compound, and no outside communication with anyone. Before leaving Mexico City, both had been told that they were now part of a classified follow-up to the highly successful cartel raid of Saturday and asked to give up their personal cell phones. They were told the phones would be returned to them when they got back to their base south of the city. They had no way of knowing that it would be several days before this would happen.

Alberto, Bennie, and Roberto, now once again Captain Rodriguez of Los Pueblos Fantasmas and aide to Colonel Portillo, met in Alberto's study to review the situation. Major Garcia wanted the secretary to know that he had ten two-man teams scattered about the native undergrowth around the estate on a twenty-four-hour basis. They had silently scoured the entire area on three sides out to a quarter mile and were certain that no other forces or individuals were anywhere nearby. Nor could a force, the major went on to say, infiltrate the grounds of the estate undetected. His teams, all concealed and invisible in the almost jungle surrounding the estate, would note the attempted passing of anything larger than a small dog. The fourth side of the estate overlooked several hundred feet of the native landscaping as it tumbled down the dune from the main house, which sat perched on the highest edge of the low sandy bluff, before the lush green cover gave way to the wide-open beach and the tranquil blue waters of the Pacific. Here, the Major reported, there was a different situation.

The estate, or what little could be seen of it from the ocean side, was definitely being watched. His troops nearest the beach on the west side of the estate were keeping track of what they thought of as an overly inter-ested fishing group. A small outboard fishing boat was trawling a four- or five-hundred-foot path back and forth off the beach several hundred feet to seaward, and a close visual inspection of the boat from his team, which could watch them clearly from concealment with their high-powered spot-ter scopes, could see that at least one of the two men ostensibly fishing periodically looked the main house over with a pair of binoculars. Last night, one of his teams in the bush had spotted a lone man who had literally skulked down the beach and took up a position in the undergrowth below the house and within thirty feet of his team. The lone man had kept watch until about two in the morning and then departed after being replaced by another skulker. At dawn this morning, the fishing boat had showed up again and began its routine of motoring slowly first south and then back to the north, and the skulker had left. In total, the major believed that a team of no less than four men was watching them on a rotating basis. As long as the secretary stayed off the terrace, there would be nothing for the watchers to report, other than that the domestic staff members who lived at the estate were periodically visible. Indeed, the four-man team hired by the Condor through Raul's contacts in the area was watching the house and reported that the secretary was not there. They would continue to watch and report as ordered. *Why not*, the local thugs thought. The money was too great to pass up, and they were breaking no laws.

Colonel Portillo outlined the basics of his planned assault on the Condor's Chihuahua estate. The estate was a walled area roughly eight hundred feet square located in the gentle hills southwest of Chihuahua. The entire property sloped from the high side on the west down to the main hacienda, located more or less in the center of the walled area, and then sloped more steeply to the front wall on the east side, where the one and only heavily fortified gate was located. The entry gate was at the lowest point of the estate. The two-lane paved road leading up from the valley floor passed by the entire front wall of the estate and a portion of the south wall before turning away from the estate in an uphill curve that led further up into the hills. The west and north sides faced nothing but the dense brush and a thin forest of scrub pine and other assorted pine trees common to the area. The occupants and visitors to the estate, once allowed to pass through the guarded entry drive, proceeded on the private drive as it snaked up the moderately steep hillside until reaching the near-level clearing of the central grounds, where the main house was located. The private drive ended in a circle drive in front of the modern but classically designed main mansion.

In addition to the main hacienda, there was a total of ten smaller casitas on the property. All were located against the tall outer walls as if attached. Four casitas each were in the rear corners of the compound uphill from the main hacienda, with two others along the southeast wall; one seemed to house the domestic staff, and another appeared to be a storage building. The walls of the estate must have cost a fortune, the colonel offered. Judging by the shadows cast at specific times, he guessed their height at ten to twelve feet and their width at something just under two feet. The casitas appeared to have lean-to or shed-like roofs whose high point was where they met the outer wall. He wondered, as he told Alberto and Bennie during the briefing, if there might not be the occasional undetected door from a casita through the perimeter wall. When Alberto asked why, he said simply that for a man as smart as the cartel leader they were trying to capture obviously was, it seemed to make no sense to have only one avenue of escape, that being the front gate. Bennie and Alberto looked at each other, both thinking the same thing—a grotto.

The colonel went on with his report. From a not-yet-located base of operations within reasonable marching distance of the estate, his force would close on the fenced compound from the uphill or west side. From the photos and video supplied by the drones, it was clear that the security defenses were of a perimeter nature and that the twenty-four guards they felt they had identified were focused on a frontal assault from the direction of the narrow paved country road that passed by the estate on the two lower sides. Typically, it looked like twelve guards manned positions along these two sides at any given time with four of the twelve near the front gate. The videos from the drones confirmed that all carried assault rifles of one kind or another. The remaining dozen off-duty guards typically were either in the main house, where it was assumed they ate, or in their own casitas. From the patterns they could derive from the videos, most of the guards were housed in the eight casitas in the back corners of the site. Colonel Portillo proposed to infiltrate the perimeter defenses from the high ground of the west side at night and then deploy and conceal his teams until dawn. He wanted to wait until after the shift change that occurred at six each morning and then catch the nighttime guards in their beds. When asked by Alberto, he explained why he had considered and disregarded a total nighttime assault.

A night assault could succeed, but if at any point, surprise was lost, the ghosts would be at a disadvantage, and the prospects of capturing the Condor and the key members of his brain trust alive went down. With the first goal of the mission being to take this man alive, the colonel had decided to mount an early-morning raid at a time picked by him when a large part of the guard force would be tired, not alert, and could be silently defeated. He first wanted to eliminate nearly half of the known opposition. He then proposed to create the appearance of a frontal attack at the gate, which would force a response by the remaining cartel enforcers to that location, which, as he explained, was also the lowest part of the estate. He would then split his forces, with half taking up a blocking position near the front of the main house where they could effectively keep the bulk of the remaining enemy forces pinned down on lower ground, while the other half of his force conducted the main attack on the hacienda from the rear. His capturing force would use tactics similar to what the secretary's national police had used on the hall at the seminary, a gas- and concussion-grenade attack where the principals would be located with minimal protection. While his capturing force was executing their mission against minimal resistance, his blocking force and the four-man diversion force would mop up the armed resistance at the gate. Extraction would be by helicopter from the rear-yard clearing.

What he required most urgently, the colonel said, was a site located from which he could stage and mount his attack and, if possible, more intel on the layout and the personnel within the main hacienda. It also seemed impossible to him that given the attention to security the cartel seemed to employ, they would not have some sort of perimeter warning or defensive systems on the backsides of the property, especially from the high ground. There had to at least be electronic systems there, if only for advance warning. In addition, he wanted to know if there were backup forces in Chihuahua whom those in the hacienda could call upon once under attack. His diversion force would be equipped to keep any help from coming up the road for a time; they would have four grenade launchers with them, in addition to their personal weapons, that could devastate anyone coming to the rescue. But extraction of his forces and their prisoners would be threatened if significant numbers of other cartel forces could be brought to bear.

"Colonel, thank you. You and Roberto and the major go get some lunch. Bennie and I will join you shortly." Roberto opened the study door for his superiors and closed the door behind them.

"Bennie, let's get Manny on the see-tee and see if he has come up with a staging area. Also, I think it is time you contact Ray and see if he can provide answers to the other questions the colonel asked. I admit I had not considered the idea of reinforcement. I also am worried about the idea of a grotto or some other means of escape other than through the front gate."

"We're cops, Alberto. Let's leave worrying about the army stuff, like reinforcements and defenses, to Manny and the colonel. You talk to the general; I'll text Ray and see if we can't get some answers." Bennie had turned off his phone before the flight down and, knowing that Ray would be airborne to Baja, had seen no reason to turn it back on before now. Seconds after the software booted up and the encryption software loaded, the device told him he had a new message. He quickly glanced over the text from Ray and then looked up at Alberto, who was watching him.

"From Ray, seems you've pissed Raul Ortega off. Got him a little worried. He put a contract out on you this morning. Here, look."

Alberto carefully read Ray's text. "It seems you are correct, Bennie. This is very helpful. It would seem I have some time before I must worry about this threat, and in the meantime, we will be able to strike first. Once we have Baca and the traitors in the city, we can conduct a search for this large man with the scar. Perhaps we will get lucky, and we will get these ex-military assassins as well."

Over the next half hour, Alberto spoke with Manny, and Bennie composed and sent his text message, remembering to give Ray a little pep talk about his confusing feelings he had passed on:

Got your message Al being
careful. Planned attack of Chi
estate firming up for tuesday
maybe earlier if all goes well.
Need more on site intel as follows;
what are condor patterns in
morning say 7 or 8? Who all in
house at that time and where?
Can see defenses at front walls
and gate but what of back sides?

No guards there but has to be
something, electronic maybe?
Are there condor reinforcements
that would respond to
a call for help? Seems to us
someone as smart as alvarez
would plan for back way out
if attacked from front but
nothing visible from xlent over
head images. Must be an escape
plan. Try and find out but not
to point you attract attention.
Eds man in north soon be gone.
We will need close contact
with you during assault so you
safe and not accidental casualty.
We need you, alvarez, baca alive
in that order. Others if possible
not likely if they fight back.
Understand the blurring of lines
that has you thinking. Not to
worry. Remember who you
are, you are good and alvarez
bad despite the results.
Respond as soon as safe to do so.

Manny was very helpful and sent them overhead imagery of a possible staging area just two miles from the Condor estate on the other side of the hills. It would mean some humping by the ground troops but nothing they couldn't handle. Alberto reviewed the basics of Colonel Portillo's plan with Manny, who approved.

"The colonel's plan is fine for dealing with those bad guys we know about and, I agree, gives him the greatest chance of getting the people you want alive. The timing is critical, however, between the parts. The minute he opens up with his diversion at the gate, it will have two reactions; the other guards will likely do as he's planned and reinforce the gate, but those in the house will also be alerted and ready for the attack."

"I agree that Alvarez and his inner circle will be alerted, Manny, but Ray has told us that Alvarez is feeling very full of himself right now. His people around him, the true bodyguards, will no doubt be nervous and anxious, but Pablo Alvarez will not be. If he were to receive reports that no vehicles or attackers have entered the site, human nature says that they will relax a bit. That is when the colonel's capturing force hits them, but from the opposite direction, the more open and accessible rear of the house. When his guards call for men to leave the gate, they will have to move uphill, and of course the colonel's blocking force will have them at a distinct disadvantage."

"Could go like that, Al. Like I say, I like the plan. The guards at the gate will soon find themselves in a crossfire, and I'd hate to be in their shoes. The success of this mission all depends on what Ray can tell us about any electronic defensive systems and if he can tell us who is where in the house before and especially during the attack. At some point, your guys will need to know where the high-value targets are so they can specifically target them. I don't think it's necessary that the troops know exactly who it is they're after—just that it's the leadership of a powerful cartel, and they need to grab alive or kill as many as they can. But what I'm suggesting, Bennie, is that you need to tell Ray that at some point, he needs to get himself into a position where he can feed Colonel Portillo real-time intel during the action."

"I understand, General. I will send him a second message."

"Oh, and Al, I know this is the hard part, but sometime very soon you, and Bennie will need to let the colonel and the major know that you have a source inside the target, and it should be before the attack begins. They have to know who Ray is and where he is, or you risk getting him killed. I know, Bennie, that Ray's identity has been your most closely guarded secret for months, but the troops need to know."

"I realize this, Manny. Should we do so today, now?"

" I would, fellas. Just tell the officers for now; they can inform their troops when they get there. You look pained, Bennie, but it has to be done."

"I know, General. I'll get over it. It's just that…well, you know what I mean."

"I do; believe me. By the way, guys, the op to grab that Corro guy is laid on for tonight. I will call later on and update you on how it goes."

"Thanks, Manny. Just hold on to him, and keep him away from everyone."

"Will do, men. Once last thought, Al. This is more down your line of work than mine, but have you given any thought to documenting this raid? What I mean is, if you pull this off, you will have the president of the country in a place he's not supposed to be in the company of known or suspected criminals who are his relatives. I'd think that some video of this would go a long way to helping you convince folks down there that their president is the fucking bad guy we all know he is."

"Jesus, Manny. I'm embarrassed to say I had not considered this. I have been thinking in terms of a military action and not a police one. The entire estate and everything in it is evidence, of course. We will have members of our force document as you suggest. I was planning for my national police units in Chihuahua, Hermosillo, and Monterey to enter and secure the estates at some point, but not until after I had Alvarez in custody and away from the estate. My plan, such as it is, was to fly to the capital and then brief just the leaders of the legislature, the Supreme Court, and Castillo of what I know all at once in an emergency meeting. My trump card was to then order the presidential guard and my national police to enter the Alvarez home in Baja. After I arrest Ramos and announce it, I will replace him with his deputy, Colonel Mariano Cordova, who is not only a fine officer but reliable. Our combined units there will be told to secure the Alvarez estate, and I will allow a media team to accompany them and video everything. We will have our own media personnel there who will broadcast everything back to me in my control center. That is where I intend to bring the responsible government representatives. What my people will find, of course, and what Castillo and the others will see with their own eyes is an empty house where our president is supposed to be—with the exceptions, of course, being Senora Alvarez and some domestic help. Alvarez's absence will be all the proof I need."

"That's all great, Alberto, but I'd suggest also having a live feed, maybe from the staging area and the Alvarez estate showing their false president in custody."

"A good idea, Manny, I will arrange for it."

"One last thing, Al. I think your colonel has everything planned out well and that you will need no further help from me. But nevertheless, I wanted you to know what I have in reserve if the shit hits the fan somehow and you need outside help. As you know, your government has been moving people out of those despicable refugee camps south of Juarez that popped up in the last year and forcibly getting folks to relocate south to the newer and better-organized camp in Miguel Ahumada. Your troops are stressed out and stretched out all along the border. As you are no doubt aware, we have been providing relief help when asked. Ahumada is only about 140 miles north of the Condor estate up your Highway 45. We have been flying and trucking logistical aid there as part of our agreement with your government for several months. Mostly we have been providing food and water convoys and other such relief supplies. Because of the history of cartel violence in that area and the hijacking of some of the earlier Mexican convoys, I insisted that we be allowed to ride shotgun on the convoys with both air and ground assets. Alvarez himself approved the protocols when he had your job, Al, along with General Lozano. So what I'm telling you is that I ran a convoy down there yesterday to replace the one that's already there and did not recall the first one. Instead of sacks of flour and wheat in this new one, I had mostly men and equipment; instead of all water-tank trucks, I have one with AV gas for the four choppers I sent along as cover. What this means is you have at your disposal two platoons of special forces, about fifty men, and they are armed and briefed on a possible rescue operation that they may be asked to provide on a joint US-Mexico antidrug operation. I sent Jeff Green along as the command sergeant major. A captain is in command, but he knows to let Jeff run the show. They have been cooling their heels in their own camp for twenty-four hours, and your civil and army officials there seemed to be glad to have them around."

"Manny, I do not know what to say, but thank you. Who is the army commander you have coordinated with?"

"Overall, it's Brigadier Lopez out of Juarez. The liaison officer that's assigned to the convoy was a Major Escobar, he and a squad of about five men."

"I will contact my friend Lozano and coordinate this, and Manny, I thank you."

"Fellas, I've got a concern and a suggestion," Bennie interjected. "Assuming that none of those bastards get wise to Ray's part in all this, I'm gonna want to get him out of the country as soon as possible. What's bugging me, guys, is that unless Alvarez and all his people think Ray is dead or missing, he's in danger unless every goddamn tentacle of that organization is caught or killed. And I don't think we can ever know if we have accomplished that. We need their people to believe he's dead and then get him home. I'd like to request that you send a chopper from wherever the hell you have them and pick Ray up, General. Could you arrange that?"

"Sure, Bennie. It's a little tricky only because we would need to come get Ray when Alvarez and all of his people are gone. But if nothing else, we can safely improvise this on the fly, I think. Al, I assume you're going to take Alvarez and all the others to the staging area and then haul their asses somewhere else for safekeeping?"

"That is correct; that was the idea. The staging area, then the base at Cuidad Obregon, then to Tampico."

"Great, then after you get Alvarez and his people out of the estate or even the staging area, I will send Ray a ride. If we sent a chopper down from Ahumada, we can have him back at my base ninety minutes later. Will that do, Bennie?"

"I couldn't ask for more, General."

"Alberto, it's about 140 miles from where my guys are to the estate; I had Romey check. Once we get the word, we could have a chopper at the estate in about sixty minutes if it was not already airborne. What I'm thinking is that I have, say, two choppers and a squad prepositioned someplace closer. You guys pick the time of the assault, and I'll have the two choppers take off and head north like they're headed for home and then loop them back to the south out of sight from everyone. We park someplace close by, and then when your people have cleared the site, we swoop in and extract Ray."

"That is a good idea. Here is what I propose."

Alberto told Manny that there was a reservoir southwest of Chihuahua north of Highway 16. If Manny's helicopters flew down the Rio Sacramento valley, staying just in the barren foothills to the west side, they would not overfly much as they worked their way around the west side of Chihuahua. The airport was to the northeast up another valley, and they would not have to worry about air traffic or much radar surveillance if they flew just in the western hills. From the north side of the reservoir, it was less than four miles to the Alvarez estate located across the valley on the opposite slopes. They would only be a minute or so by air from the estate.

"OK, Al, Bennie, leave it to me. We will have a drone check out the area and find a suitable place. Once we know what time you're scheduling the assault, we can schedule my troops to their standoff area in a way that doesn't alert anyone."

There being nothing else to say, they wished each other luck and went back to work on their part of the plans. Alberto got his officers back in the study and handed them the disc with the new information showing a possible staging area. After looking at the disc on his laptop, both Colonel Portillo and Major Garcia called it perfect. It was well inside the operating limits of their aircraft and a close enough march from the estate, and it seemed entirely isolated.

"Colonel, how soon can you have the strike team moved to the new staging area?"

"We can do so tonight, Mr. Secretary, just after dark. We have transportation from Tampico en route to Cuidad Obregon to take the prisoners back to our base. We will keep our secondary base at Cuidad Obregon active until this strike is complete. There is no reason the assault team cannot get there now, set up, and maybe even start conducting our own recon."

"Good, good. We are working on getting you the additional intel you have asked for. I would hold on any close reconnaissance until we learn more about possible electronic defenses. Also, you need to be careful with communications. We know that all communications on the estate are monitored."

Colonel Portillo and Major Garcia both raised their eyebrows at this. *How could they know that?* each thought. Alberto glanced over at Bennie, who was tight lipped and looked grim, but nevertheless nodded his head.

"Gentlemen, what I can now tell you is that we have an intel source within the compound, and we are in communication with him."

This produced some wide eyes and knowing looks among the three officers. Bennie noticed and answered. "Colonel, the man is one of mine in deep undercover. We managed to get a device to him recently, a kind of super cell phone. It's some sort of encrypted burst transmitter, whatever the hell that means. Does that help?"

Colonel Portillo nodded. "All our field communicators use encrypted burst equipment, so we shall be fine, I think."

"Gentlemen," Alberto resumed, "the courage this man inside possesses need not be articulated. If we fail, or if he is caught communicating with us, there will be no investigations, no second chances. He will simply be placed against a wall and shot. We have asked him to try to get us the information you have asked for, Colonel. Also, we are asking him to somehow get into a position where when you are set to launch your attack, he will be able to advise you on the locations of our targets. Given his role at the compound, getting into such a position could well be dangerous and destroy his cover, for we are asking him to do tasks that are contrary to his regular duties. Getting him out alive is our first objective. For the purposes of our plans, his code name and call sign will be Intel One. Colonel, Mr. Santiago will provide you a device that will allow you to communicate with Intel One when the time comes. Once it's in your possession, you will be able to monitor any communications between our source and Senor Santiago here. Your orders are to not use the device for anything more than monitoring until you are on the grounds and it becomes necessary to begin communicating directly. Is that understood?"

"Yes, Mr. Secretary. I appreciate the sensitivity of this man's position; we all do. I will be grateful to just monitor the situation and pick up any additional intelligence."

"Hopefully, Colonel, you will then be able to work out the necessary identification methods you and your team will need to keep from doing him harm."

"I am sure we will be able to do so, Mr. Secretary."

Bennie handed over the spare cell phone he had been carrying, and Alberto continued his instructions.

"For now, you gentlemen do what you must with the information we have provided on the staging area, and get our assault teams ready to go tonight. Colonel, how soon could you mount your assault once we have more intel?"

"Tuesday morning for sure, Mr. Secretary. Tomorrow morning is just too soon. I will want to get as much intel as possible and also do some of our own reconnaissance."

"We will talk with our source and get his input on our timing. We will meet again after lunch and whenever we hear from Intel One. Thank you."

There was nothing more for Alberto and Bennie to do until they heard back from Ray. There were now eleven people in the world who knew of Ray's existence and where he was. Bennie had not felt so hopeless in a long time, but on the other hand, he was more hopeful that events were building that would put an end to this nightmare once and for all.

31

In Random Airspace over Northern Mexico
Sunday Night

L ater that night, after Colonel Portillo had contacted the base at Cuidad
Obregon and transmitted his orders for the redeployment of the attack forces and the coordinates for the staging area, the electronically invisible flight carrying Alvarez, Ray, and the others left the level, comfortable
air space over the Sea of Cortes behind them and flashed over the coast
of the Mexican mainland just forty miles south of Cuidad Obregon. Near
Huatabampo, they began the twisting, turning, and climbing required to
navigate the uneven terrain features of the coastal foothills below them.
Except for the typically gut-wrenching high-G climbs and descents and the
occasional turn, the flight was quick and uneventful as they approached the
flight's termination and sensed the plane preparing for landing—or so it
seemed in the passenger compartment.

On the flight deck, it was a completely different story as the chief pilot
had to make some quick, unexpected, and exciting last second adjustments
to his landing approach. In fact, he had been required to turn away from his
programmed flight plan and then circle back for a second approach when
his short range on board radar had suddenly detected they were very quickly
overtaking other aircraft. A formation of three low, slow targets flying at
about five hundred feet altitude had suddenly appeared on his scope directly
on his flight path. *Shit*, he muttered. *Where the hell did they come from?* Since
he was only at four hundred feet and descending, had he not turned away,
he simply would have flashed under them at nearly two times the speed they

were going, but then they would have seen him. Given there would have only been a hundred feet of vertical separation between them, they would have also felt his wake turbulence as he'd blown by.

They were helicopters, obviously, given their flight characteristics and formation flying. What bothered the pilot was that his TCAS (Traffic Alert and Collision Avoidance System) had not detected anything out there in front of him from a longer range as they had raced down the eastern slopes of the central mountains, which meant that his bogies were not using transponders, the radio signals that his TCAS would have picked up. As he also was not using one, he was as invisible to the flight of choppers as they had been to him—even more so, as he had been overtaking them from slightly behind. That meant they were illegals or, more likely, a military flight on maneuvers, given their formation. It had happened before. His passive airborne radar had painted the slow-moving aircraft one time before he killed the switch in case the bogies had radar detection capabilities.

He had been fast approaching the formation from below and behind and turned away in plenty of time to avoid detection, he hoped, but it was an exciting minute or so. He made a wide 360-degree right-hand turn to the southeast that allowed the bogies to clear his area and then made his second approach. When his onboard GPS computer told him they were back at his landing initialization point, his copilot called in their arrival, and as if by magic, the road functioning as a landing strip jumped out of the darkness as carefully hidden runway lights lining the deserted section of road came on, defining the limits of his runway. He passed over the outer threshold, which in this case was a dark SUV of some kind with its lights now on, and set the high-performance aircraft on the paved road smoothly. All told, they had been airborne for an hour and fifteen minutes. As the pilot was standing in the cockpit doorway saying good-bye to his employer, he said nothing about the incident. No one was harmed, and they had not been detected, so he decided to just keep the entire near collision to himself.

In what was another of life's many unrealized happenstances, for a brief moment in time, the helicopters of Alberto Rodriguez's Los Pueblos

Fantasmas, the reception caravan of Carlo Vargas, and the sleek aircraft carrying Pablo Alvarez had all been within a quarter-mile circle. And as it happened, they had all been observed by a mechanically sophisticated device operated by borrowed men doing the bidding of Bennie Santiago.

Circling above the darkened unmarked piece of geography was a US Predator drone under the control of a senior sergeant some 260 miles away. A young lieutenant, oblivious to anything more than the evening's mission parameters, was standing and looking over his shoulder. Obeying their orders, they had followed the caravan as it left the targeted estate and watched on their monitors the transmitted images from a mile above as it drove into the remote high desert, the real time images as clear as a bell through the lenses of the infrared and low-light cameras aboard. From their lofty platform, they had been circling and watching the now-parked vehicles when the flight of helicopters had slowly entered the edge of their field of view from the south heading north, and then they had witnessed the near collision as the fast-moving twin-engine turbo prop had appeared out of nowhere from the lower left of the high definition image, turning away only at the last second with just hundreds of feet separating them. All the machines, those sitting on the ground and those moving through the air, had been clearly visible to the infrared camera as their hot engines gave them away in spite of the darkness. Even the rotors of the choppers had been visible, so hot were their leading edges from friction when contrasted to the cold earth in the background. As if ships simply passing in the night on a wide and fog-blanketed ocean, the passing of all the players went largely unnoticed. The pilots of the Condor's plane were aware of the other electronically invisible flight that had passed through the area but did not know—nor could they have conceived—of its significance. Nor did they know that they had been observed from above.

For Carlo and his men sitting in the dark on the little-used rural road, they would have at least heard the flight of low-flying helicopters as they passed so closely by their deserted landing strip had they not been sitting in their SUVs on the cool desert night or had the sound of the small portable generator that would soon provide the needed power to the makeshift runway lights not been humming just outside Carlo's Escalade.

The sergeant and lieutenant controlling the drone knew of the men in the vehicles and could guess that they were there to meet the twin plane after it landed, but they did not know who had arrived or why. Compartmentalization, having already robbed them of any knowledge of the raid being planned, had also deprived them of the explanation of the choppers and why they had lumbered by this part of the desert or for what purpose.

The most knowledgeable regarding the extraordinary events that were soon to take place were the pilots and men of Los Pueblos Fantasmas in their flight of helicopters, and yet they had been completely unaware of the presence of the sleek Italian aircraft that had turned away from them only at the last second or of the vehicles and armed, dangerous men on the ground just off their right side they had nearly over flown and ironically would soon be facing. And they had remained completely unaware of the near-invisible drone circling above them and now in their wake. Nature's veil of darkness that came recurrently as the earth spun on its journey through the void of space, exposing only a modest portion of herself to the omnipresent sun, had done its work.

Had any of the pilots or men of Los Pueblos Fantasmas been interested in looking out any of the numerous available windows of their craft into the dark night and peered just to their rear, the lighted section of road in the middle of nowhere was now as suddenly visible as the quarter moon high in the clear sky on their starboard side. They would have realized they were not alone in this barren patch of high desert south of Chihuahua. But even if they had noticed, perhaps nothing more than idle curiosity would have entered their consciousness, as they too would have been ignorant of the significance of the others. They landed uneventfully at their assigned clearing high on the side of the hills to the north as the caravan of luxury SUVs bisected the dark night on back roads on the high desert plain to their south, making their way back home, a home the ghosts would soon be attacking, the night's events just another example of the randomness that existed sometimes in life.

Perhaps if one or the other of the players in the random dance had been aware of all the circumstances and also possessed a love for literature, he might have reflected on the disparate events and recalled the prose of Longfellow: "Ships that pass in the night, and speak each other in passing: Only a signal shown, and a distant voice in the darkness; So on the ocean of life, we pass and speak one another, Only a look and a voice, then darkness again and a silence."

But none had.

The main strike team in the three helicopters that made up the total compliment of the secret air forces of Los Pueblos Fantasmas had no idea how close they had come to taking out the Condor and the majority of his brain trust...by accident. The chief pilot and commander of this flight of heavily modified Bell 412SP's was leading the V formation at 500 feet and a speed of 130 knots (150 mph) using his low-light night vision headgear, look-down radar, and GPS navigation computer to guide him in the darkness to his assigned landing zone. His copilot suddenly had said, "Whoa, what was that?"

"What," the pilot had asked sternly, never taking his eyes off the ground in front of him or his heads-up instruments.

"Nothing, Captain. I got what I thought was a hit on my detection monitor, but there's nothing there. It just spiked for a second."

"Check it again."

"Nothing there, sir."

"Have maintenance pull it when the mission is over."

"Yes, sir. Noted." The captain commanding the air assets of Los Pueblos Fantasmas was an older serious pilot and brusque and direct in his manner because of the mission parameters. Flying at night was dangerous in any circumstance, requiring every ounce of concentration a pilot could bring to bear, and doing it at near top speed and so close to the ground made it even more demanding. Like their illegal counterparts, the captain was under orders to deliver the thirty-man strike team to a specific location and to do so without being seen. This meant at night and nap of the earth, or nearly so, to avoid radar detection. This evening's flight from their base camp staging area outside Cuidad Obregon to the hilltop near Chihuahua had been thrown at him at the last minute. The base east of Cuidad Obregon had been established a week before, near another hilltop in an uninhabited area set among the scrub pines and shrubs common to the northwestern part of the country to support the raid at the seminary.

Out and back, it was a five-hundred-mile round trip to the new LZ, just inside their performance envelope without the necessity of refueling somewhere else. There would be a fuel truck back at base that would top them off, a three-man maintenance team with their truck and all the basic equipment to keep the birds in the air, plus food and shelter for the pilots and the other ground echelons of the command necessary to support them. Also at the hidden base camp were the detention and intelligence sections of their secret army to keep control of and do the interrogations on the prisoners they had taken in Saturday morning's action. Ground transport from the logistical section of Los Pueblos Fantasmas was headed north from the Ghost's secret headquarters near Tampico to take possession of the prisoners and return them to the main base. Something very big was up, the chopper pilot thought in the back of his mind as the ridgeline began to take shape at his front. Never had all parts of Los Pueblos Fantasmas been in the field at once. Something big indeed.

The strike team was heading for a near-level clearing on the south slopes of some low mountains located two and a half miles southwest of the Condor's Chihuahua estate. The clearing was near the crest of the small rugged range of large hills, while the estate was located several miles down the north slope. Manny's drone had carefully photographed and interrogated the site with its onboard systems and confirmed that it was perfect for Alberto's use, although the commander of the flight of three choppers had no idea where the GPS coordinates he was closing in on had come from. Each Bell carried a squad of ten men, fully packed and heavily armed ready for several days in the field. The senior officers were away, presumably working out the details of the actual assault, whatever it was. All the troops knew was they were headed to a staging area and they were to make a camp, lay low, and stay hidden until the commanders showed up. The senior officer present was a captain and Major Garcia's second in command, and he had

Sergeant Major Sammy Montoya, formally of the US Army and now retired, with him. Things would be done right. All the men were still jazzed by their successful actions of the day before and had been surprised when they were hustled out of their bivouac near the seminary and then flown north along with their prisoners back to their base camp, only to be told to repack their gear, resupply, and prepare for another action. What the hell, they had kidded. All in a day's work.

The command pilot of the lead chopper glanced at his GPS indicator and then confirmed visually he could see the clearing very well through his low-light gear. He triggered his short-range craft-to-craft communicator and said, "One to team, standard echelon formation landing on me."

"Two affirm."

"Three, Captain."

Came the clipped responses.

What Mother Earth had provided in the pushed-up sand-and-clay mountains that screened their arrival from the distant cartel estate was supplemented by the clever engineers at Bell. The Bells were fitted with the latest edition of the new soft in-plane flex-beam four-blade rotor with swept tips for reduced noise. When coupled with the offset twin stacked tail rotors and their muffled Pratt and Whitney turbo-shaft engines, the three black helicopters were nearly as quiet as they were invisible in the darkness. The captain flared his chopper in the center northern portion of the clearing so the two lieutenants flying on his left and right sides just to his rear had plenty of room to land. In the short hour it had taken for the air assets to return empty to their base camp at Cuidad Obregon, the ghosts of the strike team had established an invisible bivouac just into the scrub forest on the north side of the clearing. A com check confirmed they had reliable contact with their base. The men were all fed a hot meal before heading for the new LZ, so there was nothing more to do for now but to hunker down, get some needed rest, and wait for the senior officers with the plan and objectives to show up.

32

Vargas Safe House
Las Cruces, New Mexico
Sunday Evening

Valentine Corro watched from the porch as Edgar Diaz drove off and breathed a sigh of relief. He wasn't sure if he had the answer Eduardo Vargas had sent him up here to find, but he did have something. The wreck of the military transfer van carrying Carlo Vargas to his new jail had been no accident. Or at least that was what Diaz's captain believed. Diaz had been reluctant, he had admitted to Val, of even raising the question, but a softball game between Diaz's team and the captain's and the beer drinking in the parking lot afterward had given him his chance without appearing overly interested. Teddy had told him it had to have been a planned event, and that meant a cartel had busted Carlo, last name unknown, out of jail for a second time.

The captain almost had it right. Val had no idea who had helped Carlo to escape, but he knew it hadn't been his brother, Eduardo, and that was the only logical person who would have done so. He dismissed the idea of another cartel going after Carlo, and it was also possible that one of the other prisoners had been the object of the attempt, but he dismissed that as well.

It finally dawned on Val what the other possibility was. Who or what had the most to gain by Carlo being returned to his home? Or more specifically, Val thought, to his employer? It had to have been an American law enforcement agency that had planned the wreck, most likely the DEA. They had wanted Carlo to return—that was the only thing that made any sense, and if that was the case, why? To follow him was the only logical answer.

He Googled the story and went back through the news reports. That was when it slowly hit him—the second man, the young suspected murderer and cellmate who had also escaped. Was it possible he was a plant? It was the only thing that fit. And if what Val believed the truth to be *was* true, that meant that the Condor had been infiltrated for months now. Val had it all wrapped up in his mind, but one thing was really bothering him. If the Americans had the Condor penetrated, how was it the Condor did not know? He had the DEA and the other organizations so deeply penetrated that surely word would have gotten back. And also, there had been no actions taken against the Condor he was aware of. If the DEA were getting information, why had they not acted on it? There were some loose ends to be sure, but he was sure of one thing: the wreck freeing Carlo Vargas had been staged, and it was likely an American law enforcement agency had arranged it.

He went inside and made the call. He got the message-drop voice mail, which meant that Eduardo was changing up his phones and numbers again. Eduardo would use a new phone to access the drop and then call Val, most likely in the morning. What a relief; he had been sent up here by a clearly concerned Eduardo Vargas to get answers, and while this was maybe not the answer Eduardo wanted, it was something.

Val realized he was hungry. He was a good cook, and he had a decent wine in the refrigerator. He could relax a little for the first time in several days. He would call his wife too after dinner. He knew how much she worried whenever he came north, even legally. But she could stop her worrying, thought Val. *I'll be home soon.*

But she had reason to worry.

All told, there was an eight-man squad led by Manny's top counterinsurgency special forces sergeant major, along with Bennie's deputy John Walker and one of his men, in the planned snatch. The DEA guys were monitoring the communications that was being fed to them from their people watching and listening to all the electronic devices they had planted at the farm. Corro was alone. The old couple had called from Albuquerque asking if it was OK to return, but Corro had asked them to give him a few more days. To Johnny's people listening in, it sounded like the old couple was very happy to stay right where they were in Albuquerque. When Johnny was sure that only Corro was present and obviously fixing himself a nice dinner, by the sound of it, he gave the sergeant major in command the high sign, and the counterinsurgency troopers silently moved in. There were windows into the modest and homey kitchen area of the old house from the back porch and one from the side. The shooting team—one shooter, one spotter—would be taking the shot from the side widow with a Taser. The spotter silently slit the screen while Corro stood at the stove some twenty feet distant, his back to them, humming a song and preparing something that smelled pretty good to the troops.

The shooter carefully took aim and fired. Corro took the twin darts to the area between his shoulder blades, near the base of his neck. He spun around, only partially cognizant of what was happening, and very quickly fell to the floor, twitching and convulsing. The sergeant major and three other men went quickly in through the porch door and had Corro bound and gagged just as he lost consciousness. The squad's medic injected Corro with a sedative that would keep him knocked out for hours. With Johnny Walker supervising the efforts, the squad removed all evidence of the dinner and any sign they or Corro had ever been there, made his bed and cleaned up the bathroom, did the dishes, and included a nearly impossible-to-see repair of the screen that had been cut. They turned on the porch light, locked up the house, and left. Anyone, including the old couple whenever they returned, would find nothing to suggest anything more than that Corro had thoughtfully cleaned up the place and left.

About nine o'clock, a typical provost marshal van pulled into the sally port of the new maximum-security prison facility in the remote northeast quadrant of the huge US Army base, and, with only the few MPs of the facility, the counterinsurgent sergeant major, Colonel Romero, and Johnny Walker in attendance, carried the still-unconscious Valentine Corro to one of the unoccupied cells on the first tier. With its solid steel door completely segregating the prisoner from the random traffic in the hall, no one, inmates or other guards, would be aware of the inmate in cell 112. Colonel Romero had a word with the sergeant of the guard, and that would ensure that only a select few MPs would even have contact with the prisoner, and all were top soldiers.

Hours later, when Val woke up disoriented and thirsty, he lay still, opened his eyes, and moved nothing else, trying to recall where he was. He didn't know. He slowly remembered he had been cooking dinner and then there had been a shocking sensation, the terrible tingling pain at the base of his neck, as if he had stuck his finger in an electric socket. and he thought he remembered seeing a black face before everything had gone blank, but that was it. He raised his head slightly and looked around, and his heart sank. He was in a jail cell— there was no doubt of that—but of a type he had never seen before. He closed his eyes and thought of his little dove sitting at their home in Juarez worrying about him like she always did and whispered a silent prayer for forgiveness. One way or another, his life was over. It was possible he was being held by another cartel; he knew much of value, but that was not likely, he told himself. He would be in a far different and worse place if that were the case. No, he decided, he must have been picked up by the American authorities; that had to be it. They had a system of justice he knew and would not kill him. There was some solace in that. Perhaps he would live to see his beloved wife again. If not, he had paid his debt and got word back to Eduardo.

He sat up and slowly swung his legs off the low, hard bunk that seemed to just hang from the wall and noticed there was no window, just a narrow slit in the end wall where some outside light filtered in through the glass block. Through the front bars of his small cell, there was smaller space, and beyond that, a formidable-looking steel door. The small space was spotlessly clean. He listened for a few minutes but could hear nothing: no traffic, no screaming, or snoring, no footsteps, nothing. He was dressed in an orange fabric jumpsuit and there were some canvas slip-on shoes sitting on the floor but nothing else. There was a sink and stool in the corner and a cup he could use to get a drink, which he got up and did. His legs were shaky, unsure. He turned and saw, sitting on the small concrete desk opposite his bunk, a plastic tray with some prepackaged foods of some sort so he could feed himself. The metal stool that sat in front of the desk seemed to just grow out of the concrete floor. Nothing could be moved. The bed, desk, stool, sink, and toilet were made of concrete or stainless steel and seemed to have no joints or fasteners. He had dealt in auto parts for a very long time and thought he knew a thing or two about manufacturing, fasteners, and connectors. His cell was almost monolithic in that all the parts were part of the whole. Very discouraging, as far as those things went, he thought. A lot of money had gone into the design and construction of a space so cold in its properties and parts as to be totally depressing to the occupant.

It would be a full twenty-four hours before Valentine Corro would even hear, much less see, another human being. It was the longest, loneliest twenty-four hours of his life. He could never recall having gone so long a time and not have some sort of human contact, a sound or a sight that would reassure him he was not really all alone. His depression grew with each passing hour. Life's diversions and the touch of others, especially his wife, usually made it possible to get through a day without dark memories of his kidnapped son. Left alone as he was, with nothing but his own thoughts to keep him company, all he did was think about that awful day. He knew then that if he had to endure very much of this solitude, he would go mad. He had no way of knowing, but eventually, he would be moved south without ever having seen a US magistrate or a courtroom and held in a similar cell in his own country. As far as the world was concerned, he had vanished from the face of the earth. And his wife of twenty years would be left to wonder yet again in her sorrow what she had ever done so wrong in her temporal life to have offended God in such a way that she had lived to see both a son and now her husband just disappear.

The Condor Estate
Chihuahua, Mexico
Sunday Evening

Carlo's embrace as he had stepped off the plane nearly forced all the wind out of Ray's lungs. The smile on Ray's face was almost genuine at the realization of the great emotion he saw on the older man's face. While Alvarez, his false white mane and beard now back in place, climbed into the Suburban just at the plane's wingtip with Raul, Miguel, and Geraldo, Lorenzo and Ray climbed into the second SUV with Carlo and several of his guards. Carlo could not say enough about how good Ray looked and the quality of his clothes. Ray told Carlo he looked forward to having a private drink with his old friend when they got back to the estate. Carlo seemed to understand this to mean that anything to be said of any significance would be done so in private. Carlo was excited about the raid that had seen so many of their enemies either killed or caught and talked of little else on the rest of the drive. In passing, he mentioned to Ray that it looked like their old friend Barega would be joining Jefe for lunch tomorrow.

"I don't think he will like what we are serving up!" Carlo said before bursting into laughter at his own macabre wit.

Free to fly in a straight line, as Alberto Rodriguez's choppers had done, it was only about twenty miles to the estate from the makeshift runway, up and over the mountains to their north, but for the three-vehicle caravan on the roads they were forced to follow, it was over thirty. Nevertheless it only took about forty-five minutes before they arrived safely. Eduardo was outside beneath the porte-cochere when they pulled up. He warmly embraced Alvarez, Raul, and Miguel and then came to the second SUV and did the same to Ray as he got out. He looked and acted happy to see them, but Ray noticed real concern in his eyes. He needed to find out what that was about. Also, he needed to find some privacy and fast. He had taken to carrying the ultrathin cell phone Bennie had given him around in his front-left jacket pocket. It did not show and it made it easy to feel when the device alerted him to messages. He had turned it off for the duration of their traveling and wanted to check and see if Bennie had gotten his heads-up on the assassination contract. But he had come to know Alvarez and was aware of the deep vein of sentimentality that ran through him. There would be toasts and conversations with his closest friends first, before anyone went to bed and he could be alone in his room. Alvarez led Eduardo, Carlo, and the circle into the house and directly to the study. The doors were closed behind them, and Alvarez embraced Eduardo and Carlo once again. As Alvarez was still holding on to Carlo's arms, he looked to Eduardo and asked, "Did you tell him?"

A very emotional Carlo answered before his brother could. "Yes, Pablo, he told me. And I want you to know that I respect what you were forced to do in keeping your other life and identity from me. Eduardo explained how in doing the things that you required of me, I was often in places that exposed me to kidnapping by our enemies. I understand I could not give away what I did not know. I am so proud of what you have done and proud to have played my part."

They embraced again, and over Carlo's shoulder, Alvarez glanced at Eduardo and mouthed, "Thank you." Alvarez leaned back and looked at his oldest friend and cousin and said, "Carlo, I am filled with such joy. It is time you were welcomed to my inner circle."

"I must tell you," Carlo said with a big grin on his face, "after Eduardo told me the truth and I saw you on television, I felt like such a fool for not recognizing you sooner. There before me was my childhood friend, and I just did not look closely enough."

"I am just glad you understand, Carlo."

They had several toasts to Carlo, and he made a grandiose one to his cousin and the president of the country. Carlo told the group several stories of their last summer together as kids at the beach—stories they had all heard before but laughed at once again as if hearing them for the first time. They spoke of the raid and their success over the Gang of Four. Just what it meant for the future would wait until tomorrow, Alvarez said. They were interrupted only once when one of the guards brought a message in from Geraldo and handed it to Alvarez.

Alvarez glanced at it and then said, "An updated report from Quito-Perez; fifty-four are now confirmed dead as a result of our attack. The five leaders and twenty-eight others who survived are in custody, but Quito-Perez does not know where. This includes several of our men who have courageously been our eyes and ears into the other cartels for many years. My friend Alberto Rodriguez apparently does not think much of his new police commander; nor does he trust him. A check of the jails they were to be taken to reveals that no new inmates have been brought there. Now, where do you suppose they are, and what is Alberto doing with them?"

Raul spoke up first. "Pablo, you know how I feel about Rodriguez. He is dangerous and definitely doing things that we are unaware of. But if I were him and had managed to get my hands on the five most wanted criminals in the country, I also would be very careful about just where I held them and whom I told. He expects the cartels to hit back, maybe even to try to get their leaders back. In this case his caution and his actions are predictable."

"I agree," Eduardo said. "I am concerned about many things, but where Rodriguez is holding that pack of dogs is not one of them. I would hope we could get Fernando back. He is as responsible for our success as anyone."

"In time, Eduardo, in time. Alberto may be able to hide the truth from his subordinate, but he cannot hide it from me. What I wonder is why does he not trust Quito-Perez? Just his intuition in uncertain times or is there more to it? Does he actually know something?"

"Just one of the many subjects that has me concerned," Eduardo answered.

"Also a subject we shall go into more tomorrow, my friends," Alvarez said. "For now, Eduardo, let's focus on Barega."

"I have handled it just as you asked, and as you predicted he would, he has fallen completely into the trap. I met with him on Friday—on his ground in Hermosillo with just my driver, so he felt very safe—and I told him that there were great changes coming in our business relationships as a result of events you had orchestrated. He of course wanted to know what you had arranged for and what changes I was talking about. I told him he would find out this weekend but that all I could say about the changes was that his area of distribution would be expanded greatly and soon, and this could take place with our agreement and understanding. Of course what has limited his ambitions these past years is Arellano and the other Tijuana cartel. If he wanted to know more, I said you would entertain him for lunch here at the estate on Monday at one. By six o'clock on Saturday, he sent word through our man in town that he would be delighted to have lunch with you. He is so predictable, Pablo—always has been, except for the episode with Vasso. Since I showed up without a show of force, so shall he. It will be a matter of pride for him."

"So he is," Alvarez answered with a smile.

Ray was following the conversation and thinking about Barega's visit set for tomorrow and was worried. They had underestimated Barega once, and if not for his intervention, Alvarez and he and the others would have been killed. Bennie and Alberto's raid was probably on for tomorrow night—for sure Tuesday, by the sound of it. The last thing he needed was these guys fucking it up by not taking Barega seriously, maybe letting this guy get close enough with some support to do some damage, putting everyone on alert. That would make whatever Alberto and Bennie were planning that much more difficult. Ray needed "normal" so whatever Alberto had planned would have a greater chance of success. He decided to do something about it.

"With respect, Jefe."

"Yes, Ray, what is it?" Alvarez asked as he and the others turned their attention to their usually silent friend.

"Barega was involved in the planned attack by Vasso, and was that not a surprise?"

"Yes, he was, Ray. And you think he will use tomorrow's lunch to try again? Is that what you are worried about?" Alvarez asked.

"Yes, Jefe. I think it would be a mistake to think that Barega is not planning to try to kill you."

Alvarez glanced at Raul and Eduardo; they were all thinking the same thing: *Smart kid.*

"It is true that Barega did surprise me with his involvement with Vasso. We shall not make that mistake again. We will be alert tomorrow, and it is true that Barega also must think very highly of himself for having been involved with Vasso and believing that he has kept that knowledge from us. It will empower him to try to kill me, but not before he learns all he can learn from me. His curiosity and vanity will kill him first, Ray. I have no doubts he was very impressed with the raid on Saturday. He has visions of becoming hugely wealthy and powerful now that I have cleared the field for him in the west. He will want to know how I managed to arrange this. It all goes back to information, my friends."

Ray nodded his acceptance at Alvarez's explanation but still had a serious look on his face as he glanced at Carlo.

"Pablo," Carlo said to his cousin, "I agree with you about Barega, but I will make sure we are ready if he should be so stupid as to try something. How about I take Ray with me?"

Alvarez smiled at his cousin. He knew Carlo wanted to be with his young friend, ask him about the city, even the plane. They had discussed it on the flight in. The decision had been made that Carlo was to be brought in on everything now. Eduardo would still have him watched for his own protection, but he needed to know. Ray and the others had been told on the plane. Ray would be the one going back and forth from the south to the north. They were counting on Ray to continue to influence Carlo in ways that made him less a security risk.

"Fine, Carlo. Good idea, but let's keep it low profile, nothing to arouse Barega's suspicions in case he has his own people watching us, OK?"

Alvarez, Raul, and Eduardo had other subjects to discuss. Miguel called it an evening and went to his suite, and Ray followed Carlo out of the study onto the patio. He took out and lit one of the thin black cigars he liked so much. He asked Ray about the last week, and Ray told him. Carlo took particular delight at Ray's description of his flight on the plane. Ray decided to get the discussion on a track that might help Bennie. "I don't trust Barega. He wants Jefe dead, Carlo. How do we protect him?"

"Jefe is right; Barega will not try anything tomorrow, but we will not take any chances. He should only be traveling with his personal protection tomorrow. That means four to eight men. We will know long before he gets here how many men he has. The plan is to serve his men a nice lunch here on the patio while Pablo and Eduardo meet with Barega and whoever his second is these days. No guards will be present in the study. Once we have his men here, we will take them without bloodshed, I think. There will be too many of us, and they will not fight. Once I give Raul the word that we have his men, he and Miguel will go into the study and get Barega. And that will be that. All of our worst enemies will then be eliminated. There are still a lot of little cockroaches running around, but we will get them in time, or they will just go away."

"What if he brings more men, Carlo? We have, what, maybe twenty here at the estate."

"Twenty-four, Ray, and that's not counting Eduardo and me and you four. That makes thirty. Plus we have the men at the garage if we need them."

"The garage, Carlo?"

"You have passed it a dozen times, my friend," Carlo said, grinning, "where the road meets the highway at the bottom of the hill. There is a business, a construction company, with a fenced yard for its trucks and its buildings. We own the business, and it is a real one—good masons. They did a lot of work on the estate when it was built. The mason that runs it has maybe a dozen men who work for him. But each day there are about thirty men who show up for work. We have two dozen soldiers there in the maintenance garage all the time we are here. Two shifts. They drive old cars and trucks, and we have several large trucks there that can get them up here in five or ten minutes if I need them. We have even more in town on call if necessary. We are quite safe, Ray."

"This is good to know, Carlo."

"Jefe is important, now more than ever. He will be safe here. I always have a few surprises up my sleeve."

"Are there more than the men at the garage?"

"Yes, but we won't need them; what I do with men, Baca has done with his fancy toys. The entire estate is watched with his cameras and other shit." Carlo started laughing. "You should have been here when we first moved here. Baca thinks he's so smart and tells Pablo that his security system is the best that money can buy. The first week we lived here, no one got any sleep, as his alarms kept going off every time an animal bigger than a small dog ran by the estate. The hills are full of bucks, and we knew every time one was close because one of Baca's motion detectors would see it and set off an alarm and turn on the emergency lights."

"I have never heard one at night. Did he take them out?"

"Naw, just changed some things. Moved shit to the walls like he should have done in the first place. We don't care about what's up in the trees; it's men trying to get over the walls, so that is where he should have put his shit to begin with. Bucks don't climb walls, so everything has worked since then. The reason Baca has two people at each estate is they are the ones who watch the cameras and the fancy lasers and keep them fixed. Haven't you ever noticed the first thing Baca does every time we get somewhere is head to his little room and check everything out? That is another one of his jobs for Jefe. Making sure all his electronic shit works. Jefe is safe here, Ray, or at any of the other estates as well."

"Thank you, Carlo. It was stupid, I know, but I was worried."

"Not stupid, Ray—smart. You are a good friend and a cautious one. It is one of the things I admire about you, always have, but we need to get you some fun too. Let's have a drink. I want you to tell me about the women in the city."

"Carlo, you would not believe how many there are," Ray said as they headed inside, and Ray thought, *Well, it isn't much, but maybe this will help Bennie.*

In the study, Raul and Eduardo were going over the information they had on what they were calling the Rodriguez threat but making no headway with Alvarez. It was now after ten, and Eduardo added another piece to what he thought was a growing case for alarm and action.

"There is one more reason we should deal with Rodriguez and the American, Pablo. My man Corro, the one I sent north to try to find out who is looking for Carlo? He has not called in tonight. I told him I wanted an update every night at nine, and he's late."

"It is what, ten thirty, Eduardo," Alvarez said glancing at his watch. "Perhaps he is just doing his job. Give him time before getting concerned."

"His instructions are to call at nine. I have sent him two messages in the last hour. Never has he taken more than a few minutes to get back to me. I think something has happened to him. I don't like it."

"Leave it to the morning, Eduardo. If you haven't heard from him by then, have someone check it out discreetly."

Eduardo nodded his understanding but glanced at the grim-looking Raul. Raul had already let him know they needed to talk. Pablo would go to bed soon, and then they could get together and figure out a way to deal with the problems that their friend and cousin would not see.

For Eduardo, as preoccupied as he was with the many tasks he was orchestrating, he had simply forgotten that he had changed phones and did not think to call the message drop he had set up to see if someone called during the time he was switching his phones over. Corro had his direct number, so he never called the drop. Eduardo would eventually remember to call, but not until Tuesday morning.

33

The Condor Estate
Chihuahua, Mexico
Sunday Evening

I t was after eleven before Ray was able to gracefully get rid of Carlo and head to the privacy of his suite. If he had it to do all over again, he'd have had Bennie get him a device that could scan for electronic bugs. This assignment had driven Ray to the edge of paranoia. He quietly went around checking for bugs, but the truth was he knew so little about all that was available he wasn't even sure how or where to look. He closed and locked his door and only then reached into to his jacket pocket and took out the precious slim communicator. The minute it loaded up, he got a notice he had a message from Bennie. He downloaded it and then scanned the text. His first thought was, *Well, I guess it's true what they say about great minds thinking alike. At least I have something to tell him.* Ray thought about what he wanted to say for a few minutes and then sent his text:

Tuesday would be good, tomorrow
barega comes for lunch will be
killed. People will relax by night
once that is done. Alvarez ed
Raul and circle meet for
breakfast 730 to 800 usually.
Always in main dining. Baca,

lorenzo plus two others will be
in security room across hall from
alvarez office. Assume you have
basic layout of house from air.
south wing rooms for ed carlo
two guards and key domestic staff.
North wing is alvarez suite on
end plus 4 suites for circle.
Center is alvarez office nw
alvarez dining sw, great room
between. Security offices ne
corner on front. Kitchen, dining
and great room open onto back patio.
Alvarez usually in office by nine.
In addition to domestic staff of
about six, there will be 2 to 4
guards in kitchen or hall out
side office. Guards on duty will
be at wall and front gate as you
say. Backside walls all have
laser detec system on wall,
repeat on wall. Woods clear.
Know nothing of back way out of
estate but was thinking what
about chopper? Backyard
looks like was leveled for just
that kind of thing. Alvarez has
men at mason business where
small road meets highway.
At least 24. More are a call away
in chi town. Give me heads up
on actual time of raid. Is my
phone my way of contact

with troops? Will you be here?
If not you who and how will they
know me? Send answers.

Tuesday morning, it sounded like. That's when they're coming in. Why not night?
Ray wondered. *Thirty-six hours. Now if only the Barega thing will just go
down smooth, and we don't move, and I don't get killed by accident, maybe this
is about over.*

Bennie must have been sitting on his phone because Ray was still holding his and thinking about the events coming up, and his phone vibrated
with the alert to the incoming message. He opened it and read,

Be careful tomorrow too bad
for Barega stay low. As of
now plan is to hit tuesday
morning about 9. Albertos
troops already near about 2
miles. Troops are the best
of the best. I will not be
there. Commander is col portillo,
second is maj garcia.
Portillo is on our net as of now.
Attack has many parts. Diversion
at gate to draw guards and
keep them pinned there. Main
body hitting house from behind
in flashbang and gas attack on
dining or office wherever you
tell us alvarez is. That is key
you need to supply location
if possible. Albertos troops can
handle fence defense and back up
guards. No worry there. You

alvarez and baca alive that's
entire goal. Need their locations,
that's critical, and yours. Sit tight.
Bennie.

Nine o'clock Tuesday. They must have their reasons, Ray thought. *What's it like at nine around here? The overnight guards will be in the rack; that's at least eight men. God knows I spent my fair share of time pulling that duty. I have to tell them that. Most everyone in the house will be either in the kitchen dining or the halls; some staff must clean our rooms.*

Hadn't thought of that. We should be in the office at nine. Diversion at the gate. That sure as shit will draw everyone's attention there. Carlo will most likely head that way. The guards in the house will also likely go to the front. But who can really know? Ray got back on his phone and sent the quick message.

Will plan on nine and try and
make myself useful. 8 to 12
guards will be in outlying
casitas off duty. Most will
be there sleeping. Betting
you know that. Remember
2 to 4 guards will be in house
typically in hall or kitchen.
Domestic staff 6 to 8 will be
all over but unarmed. Need
to minimize casualties in
that group if possible. All are
women. To col portillo if on
my net will try and be in
position to give you verbal
reports but text may be
necessary. Assume all know
what baca looks like.

Alvarez has long white hair
and beard. But that could
change in an attack. If
so he will be who he is. No
idea who will do what when
you hit gate. Baca lorenzo and
two others monitor all signals
in and out. Assume teams
attacking know this? How safe
are communications?

Ray was surprised when, as he was opening the return message, he received a second. First time that had happened. The first message was from this Colonel Portillo, whom he had never met but hopefully would have that pleasure:

Portillo for intel one.
All communications safe.
Do the best you can tuesday
morning. look forward to
meeting you. troops understand
objectives. out.

The second message was from Bennie, as he knew it would be.

Ray, need you alive so
take no chances when shit
hits fan. Hide in a closet
whatever it takes but stay
out of line of fire. Alvarez
alive is preferred, but I can
live with him and the others
dead. Al can make his case

to the country just as easy with
a body as the man. Do want
baca alive given what he
knows. Hunker down compadre
no heroics. That's an order.

Ray was in his bathroom the entire time he was communicating with Bennie and now this colonel, force of habit. He had the suite to himself, of course, it was just that old habits died hard. There were differences between this suite and the one he had experienced in Monterey, but they were small; it had been a wonderful set of rooms. He undressed, killed the lights, and crawled into the king-sized bed. His window blinds were not closed tightly as they always had been in Monterey. It had to be a clear night, for the light from the developing moon was shining through. No doubt one of the maids preparing the suite earlier had thought to allow some daylight in and brighten the place up for his arrival. Alone with his thoughts, he wondered if it had been someone like Maria, one of the housekeepers in Monterey, a silent lovely wallflower, who, like the rest of the domestic staffs, seemed to drift in and out, never making her presence known except through her labors. She had been terrified of him once word got around that he had knifed to death a man. The fear in her eyes still bothered him.

This was his first trip to Chihuahua since he had killed Vasso's assassin and been elevated to the circle. What did the staff here know? Would there be more like Maria with nothing but fear in their eyes? Ray still could not come to grips with how much that bothered him: her obvious fear and probably the assumption of evil. He hated the thought. Another part of his intellect invaded the emotional part that was feeling sorry for himself and seemed to remind him that it was that fear, the reputation he had unexpectedly created with his accidentally killing of a man, that was very much keeping him alive and above suspicion.

He realized he was bothered by Bennie's instructions to hunker down, hide, and stay out of the line of fire. In Ray's short career, he had been one of the guys through the door first. He was a leader and a team player, and going in first was what he had trained for on the force. He had never been one of the SWAT guys. More often than not, he was already on the scene of a bust, undercover, in the room, and prepared to take action. He had set up many a bust that way. To use Bennie's words, when the shit hit the fan, he had taken out more than his fair share of those who had resisted—surprised the hell out of the bad guys from within. Now he was being told not to do that, to lay low instead and let Alberto's troops do their thing. His police instincts said no way, but for maybe the first time in his adult life, he had very selfish thoughts about staying alive, whatever it took. He wanted to see his dad again. He wanted him to know what he had done, what he had been forced to do. It hit Ray hard that his last words to him had been so inadequate, like he was headed out for a round of golf or something: *See ya, Pop. Gotta run—will be out of touch for a while with this new job. I'll call you when I can.*

What had Bennie told his dad, if anything, the last six months? Ray was ashamed at the sudden realization. He hadn't thought about that until this moment—not while sharing the cell with Carlo in El Paso, not in the three months down here.

What does Pop know? What's he told Mom? He needed to know. He needed to live. In his twenty-six years, he had never gone six days without talking with his folks, and it had been six months. Dad would have contacted Bennie by now; he was sure of it. What had Bennie been able to tell him that would have kept him from worrying all this time? Dad would have told his mom even less or flat lied to her to keep her from worrying.

He had to get his mind back on Tuesday morning. He knew some of what was coming but not all. That made what he did know probably just enough to get himself killed. What if after the diversion at the gate, he found himself in the study with Alvarez and all the others looking the other way—six of them, one of him, and their backs to him? He had a twelve-shot Glock and was an expert in its use, although they did not realize this. To them he was El Cuchillo, the knife. They never thought in terms of Ray being any good with a handgun, but he was. Damn good, and he had proved it on several occasions. He liked Raul, even Alvarez, for God's sake. How twisted a thought was that? Could he shoot them in the back? He didn't think so, and that was very troubling.

A feeling of déjà vu came over him as he watched the ceiling fan slowly and nearly silently going around and around. Where had it been? What disaster had kept him up that night staring at the ceiling? He just couldn't remember; the days were beginning to all blend together, and he had to remember. What had today been? How long had he been under—day ninety-five, or was it ninety-six?

Jesus Christ, he thought, *however many, it's been too long. What was that bullshit idea we studied in that criminology class, kidnapped victims identifying with their kidnappers after protracted time periods—the Stockholm syndrome? These are not your friends, remember that. If they knew the truth, there'd be no understanding, no forgiveness. They'd kill me sure as shit without batting an eyelash, or would they? Given the turns Alvarez has had in his life, he'd probably understand if I told him the truth about me. Face it, you can't kill them, not like that. They'll no doubt defend themselves, but I can't let them kill Alberto's men; and I can't do any good hiding, but if I'm not, then I may have to kill Raul and the others. I need to be out of the room when all hell breaks loose. I need an excuse for not being there. When the shooting starts, I need to stay away from wherever Alvarez, Raul, and the others are and trust that Alberto's people are the best, like Bennie says. Maybe I secure Baca, make sure neither one of us gets killed. Not a bad idea, but how to arrange it? Better figure something out and fast.*

Rodriguez Residence
La Casa de Campo del Sol Poniente
Zihuatanejo, Mexico
Sunday Night

The three officers of Los Pueblos Fantasmas and ten of the twenty men had left early in the evening for the capital, where transportation was waiting for them that would get them to Cuidad Obregon by nine. They'd transport to the staging LZ near the Alvarez estate before dawn, and Roberto would return to Zihuatanejo with the chopper. Meeting the colonel and the others in the city were two officers from the intelligence section of Los Pueblos Fantasmas who had flown over from Tampico, bringing with them small digital cameras with satellite-uplink capability. The two would be the official video documenters of the second transfer of presidential power in the republic in just over a week. They would also be the source of the critical evidence Alberto would need to get Alvarez, short of a confession. Alvarez's presence in Chihuahua with known cartel associates would be unexplainable, especially after Alberto ordered the presidential guard and his national police into the Alvarez compound in Baja along with the media, where they would discover Alvarez missing. Add to that the information that Alberto intended to sweat out of Geraldo Baca, and he would make his case.

The images of the raid that these men captured would be sent to Alberto's personal encrypted laptop, and he had been told that the technicians at the Command Center at his office would be able to patch in and broadcast the pictures to any monitor in the room. The timing would be crucial. He had members of the antiterror unit (ATU) of the national police for the federal district discreetly watching all the important members of the government he would need at the Center to make his case. His officers had no idea why they were following the chief justice of the Supreme Court, the legislative leaders, old President Castillo, or any of the others, for that matter. They suspected that the secretary had important reasons, too important and too classified for them to know, so they just followed their orders. Alberto had spoken directly to the captain in charge of the ATU, whom he ordered not to divulge this surveillance to the new head of the national police. The captain had a hundred questions but did as he was told; after all this was the secretary giving the orders. Both Alberto and Bennie hoped he was reliable and not in Alvarez's web. Bennie had reasoned that Alvarez would have compromised higher-ranking officers and not a lowly captain. Alberto had smiled at Bennie's reasoning and had remarked to his friend, "I'll believe it if you will, Bennie." They had shared a few seconds of comic relief at that comment. Both knew there was no knowing for sure the allegiance of the captain. The captain's men would begin bringing those being watched to the

Center just before the attack was initiated. There and then he would make his case.

They had knocked back a couple of drinks at sunset sitting around the pool. It was a shame, Alberto said, they couldn't be on the terrace at sundown, but people were watching, and his people were watching the watchers. Alberto told Bennie about the last time he had enjoyed a drink on the terrace with Manny and how many pitchers of margaritas they had consumed. It made for more comic relief, and relief of any sort from the weight of what they knew and what was soon to happen at their hands was welcome.

Much as Ray was alone with his thoughts this night, so too were Alberto and Bennie. Alone in the guest suite that Alberto had showed him to, Bennie thought about how much he wanted to be in the north with the ghosts, to be there to identify and guide Ray to safety, but his presence was required in Mexico City. He had to be the American representative in the three-ring circus they were about to expose. He had long ago given up on his youthful faith in a God, plagued as he was by all the unanswered questions and terrible earthly events that seemed to dispel the notion of an all-caring, all-wonderful supreme being. He could never come to grips with the idea that the suffering that had resulted from some terrible event was all part of some greater plan, and there were lessons to be learned or some good to be realized by the living. All Bennie had ever seen was heartbreak, despair, and broken lives as a result of these plans. His emotions dulled somewhat by Alberto's fine whiskey, lying in bed in the dark staring at the plaster ceiling above, he whispered a prayer anyway: *God, if you do exist and you do listen, let me have Ray back safely, and try to forgive my ignorance for not believing. If you need a life, take mine, but let the kid survive the next thirty-six hours.*

In his own suite, Alberto also was having trouble sleeping. The thoughts keeping him awake ran in an unbroken circular stream. Any thought he had was just part of this storm going around and around in his head. Whatever subject his mind jumped to simply picked up the stream of thought from that point, and it always ended up at the same place and the chilling realization that if all went well—and it seemed so terribly obscene to him to use that word *well*—he would likely be the next president of Mexico. Perhaps never in his country's history had a likely presidential choice wanted the honor less. He could refuse it, but who else to fill the void at this important time? There were some good young men and women coming up in the government, but the men were either not yet ready, or sadly the country was not yet ready for the capable women. The older members in the party were either too old or too corrupt in some way and not fit to lead, in his opinion. He was willing to accept Bennie's appraisal that he was a good cop, perhaps even an excellent one. His leadership of the national police had required him to be more an administrator and policy shaper than a policeman. He had done well at it. He had no choice but to step into the breach for at least the remaining portion of Castillo's *sexenio* (single six-year term) and then one more, if he felt the country needed it.

There were politicians the world over, driven by personal vanity, hubris, or the simple cravings of power and adoration, who spent years scheming and maneuvering at any cost to be in a position to be elevated legitimately to the leadership of a modern democracy. Others were driven for good reasons, noble reasons, the true public servant who thought he or she had an idea how to do more or better than others and had had this belief and talent recognized by the people and rewarded with their vote. Others still stole the leadership of their country at the point of a gun or at the head of a column, and others still used a twisted interpretation of some holy writing that led to fanaticism and the oppression of the many by the few.

For Alberto, if he did what he must do and succeeded, a grateful people would hand the reins of power to him willingly. And he'd be forced by circumstance, honor, and conscience to accept, and he would dread it.

They would be leaving in the morning, back to the city. There were more plans to be made. The known traitors, Ramirez, Quito-Perez, and Ramos, would need to be picked up tomorrow night, but they would be easy. All he had to do was order them to meet with him on a matter of great importance. He'd have Roberto with him backed up by the remaining squad of ghosts. Roberto and his men would be carrying new identification marking them as "special agents" of the national police and written orders signed by him, their chain of command direct to Alberto. No one had authority over them. The cancer of the cartels had begun to be excised from the soul of his country yesterday. It would continue tomorrow and then, with God's help, be finished on Tuesday morning.

34

Estate of El Condor de Muerte
Chihuahua, Mexico
Monday Afternoon

In comparison with all the attention to the complex details and dangers of the many significant events that Alvarez had orchestrated over the last several weeks, the killing of Gerardo Barega and his lieutenant was uncomplicated and easy. Ray should have been prepared for just *how* easy it was to entrap and kill a man, having worked undercover for as long as he had, but the simple deception and swift murder that he was at least tangentially an accessory to still caught him by surprise.

Ray had spent most of the morning with Alvarez as Raul and Eduardo had gone through their concerns about Alberto Rodriguez and his American DEA friend and whatever scheme they were pursuing. There had been more fuel added to that fire this morning, as Eduardo had confirmed that his man in America running down the information search concerning Carlo was missing. Early Monday morning, he had called and ordered his man in charge of the intelligence gathering on the big American army base to go to the farm and find Corro. An hour later he had reported back that the farm was deserted, and it appeared that it had been deserted for some time. There was no sign of struggle; in fact, after having broken into the house, he found it neat and clean. The second report was from Raul, who told Alvarez that Rodriguez and his guest had not shown up at his sister's beachside home, nor had he showed up at his own. "As of this moment," Raul had said grimly, "We have no idea where the man is or what he is up to."

Alvarez always had subjects he could discuss with his principal secretary, so he decided to call his subordinate and ask him. After several attempts, there had been no answer. Calls to Ramirez and Quito-Perez also had resulted in nothing but questions without answers. They only knew that the secretary was out of town. Eduardo had been as agitated as Ray had ever seen him, exclaiming that it was becoming increasingly clear to him that Rodriguez and the American knew something about Carlo and that it could have no other possible outcome but to lead directly to the Condor. Raul had wholeheartedly agreed.

"Perhaps, Eduardo," a serious but unconcerned Alvarez had responded. "We shall continue to watch him. You both know the source of my reticence. I would hope we could resolve these mysteries without the death of yet another old friend. But there is much to what you say. So in the meantime, let's watch him closely for now, and we will address this again when we are back in the city. I have some ideas on how we might flush the game from the bush if Alberto is indeed up to something. Raul, have there been any results yet from my order to General Oberon to be watchful for these pilotless craft?"

"None yet. They have had the skies over Monterey watched now for several days but have nothing to report, or they are too stupid to see what may be there. I'm sorry, but I don't trust Oberon or think he is up to his job."

"We will replace him soon Raul, but for now, let's focus on Barega and what we must do to fully take over his group. I will want a minimum of bloodshed, but Eduardo, do what you feel is necessary; let's just keep our actions as silent as possible."

"Yes, Pablo."

The conversation had fallen into both long-term and short-term planning for filling the voids left with the capture or deaths of the other cartel leaders. The most interesting fact that struck Ray was Alvarez's decision that the amount of drugs going into the United States would be going down substantially. With less supply, there would be higher prices, of course, so profits would remain the same while they got rid of all but the cleverest of transportation and distribution schemes. Despite his feelings regarding the necessity of the upcoming raid and putting a stop to Alvarez's dreams, Ray could not help but be impressed by the unilateral action Alvarez was planning to reduce the flow of drugs into his country. This would be a major step forward in finally addressing America's drug problem. However, the thought also clouded his personal feelings, as once again he was left to question whether eliminating Alvarez was the right thing to do. Ray had often wondered if legalizing drugs would eliminate the crime. In his own way, that was what Alvarez was doing, especially when he gave back so much of the money through his father's philanthropic trust.

It was just after noon when Eduardo took a call and, after listening and saying nothing, disconnected and said, "Barega is on his way. Three vehicles, eleven men, and him. I guess I was wrong last night suggesting that he would show his courage by coming with fewer people."

"You may not be wrong, Eduardo," Alvarez said, smiling at his friend. "In fact, I will wager that he will leave most of his men at the bottom of the road. He is just being cautious coming across town. He has never been liked in Chihuahua by others in addition to us. Ray, why don't you go find Carlo and let him know. Make sure he has planned for the larger party, but tell him I expect a smaller one."

"Yes, Jefe."

Ray was glad to be out of the room. He stepped across the large main hall to the security room, more to reconnoiter than to actually look for Carlo, for he knew Carlo hardly ever went there. There were two of Carlo's men standing post in the hall, both outside the study. This would likely be the case tomorrow. He wondered what they would do when the diversion at the gate was launched. Would they stay here or go assist those down the hill? Here, the situation would be dangerous for him, especially if there was shooting involved. They just nodded at his passing, acknowledging their complete subservience to his greater position in the hierarchy. He opened the door and walked right into the security room, knowing that no one would question his right to do so. Geraldo was standing looking over Lorenzo's shoulder as he was typing information into one of the terminals; the other two men were monitoring one panel or another and just glanced at Ray before returning their attention to whatever it was they did. Ray wished he did know, but there was no asking without looking overly curious. Geraldo smiled at Ray, something he rarely did, and asked, "Is there something, El Cuchillo?"

"Barega is on his way. Do you know where Carlo is?"

"He was checking on everyone's positioning, last I heard. Try the front."

Four men, Ray thought as he turned and left the room. *There were almost always four of them in the room.* How could he control them and keep his identity concealed without killing anyone? He wasn't even sure if they were armed—it had not appeared so—but appearances could be deceiving. *More goddamn questions without answers,* he thought.

Ray went out the front doors and started down the drive. He saw Carlo plodding his way up the hill with several others, so he stopped and waited for him.

"Aw, El Cuchillo, what brings you outside with the real men," he said, breaking into a hearty laugh.

Ray smiled; it was almost genuine. "Barega is on his way. Three vehicles, eleven men. Jefe thinks he will arrive here with only himself and several others but wants you to know more are possible."

"Either way, all will be fine, my friend. Come; I'll show you what we have set up." Carlo led them through the front doors; through the kitchen, where the cook and several helpers were very busy; and out onto the patio, where a buffet table was being prepared. At the south end of the patio, several tables had been set up with white tablecloths and fine place settings and cutlery for the guards to have lunch.

"Once we get everyone that shows up comfortable and enjoying their lunch, we will surprise them. I'll have a dozen men in hiding with assault rifles, and they will show themselves on my signal. Barega's guards will not put up a fight when they see how many we are and how few they are. Once we have them, you will call Raul, who will be with Jefe and Eduardo in the study, on your private communication network. I will have Miguel go in, and then Raul and Eduardo will have them. You will see; all will be fine."

Much to Ray's surprise and relief, all went as planned. Barega showed up with just one vehicle, his unfortunate second, and two guards. Carlo took the guards to the patio for lunch, and a very happy and relaxed-looking Barega, with his second following, joined Alvarez, Eduardo, and Raul in the Condor's study. When the two nervous guards saw the spread that had been laid out for them and in such an idyllic setting, one could see the tension in them start to ebb. When they both had a plate of great-looking food in their hands and a glass of their favorite drink in the other and were returning to the table, Carlo was suddenly holding his gun on them and, in an almost comical fashion, had his finger to his lips and shushed them softly, intoning them to remain silent.

"You may yet live to see another day, my friends, but you must be quiet," he said. "Sit. Have your lunch." After Carlo's men removed the weapons they were indeed carrying, the surprised and terrified guards did just that.

Ray was in the kitchen, part of a group that had been out of sight when Carlo and his guests had walked through on their way to the patio. Carlo looked over toward Ray and nodded. Ray touched his lapel transmitter of the inner-circle net and simply said, "We have them." There was a click in his earpiece, an acknowledgement from Raul he had received the update.

Ray told the others to go to Carlo, and he went to the hall just as Miguel entered the study. A moment later, it was all over. A stunned Barega and his most-trusted aide came out looking around for help or salvation that they knew in their hearts would not be found. Both recognized Ray standing in the hall, and Ray could not help but feel that both gave him a look that seemed to say, *If not for you!*

Carlo and Eduardo, with a number of others, took Barega and his second away. Ray knew they would be separated and questioned hard about their involvement in the assassination attempt of the Condor. Eduardo would want to know the names of all their contacts in the other organizations who had put them up to the failed attempt. Good information was the only thing that would save them. Eduardo would lie. In an hour or two, they would both be dead. A grim-looking but determined Alvarez came to the hall and said to the few gathered, "Well, it is over, my friends. The worst is behind us."

He turned and walked slowly toward his suite, but his posture and stride did not suggest joy at having successfully defeated another enemy but rather regret or sadness, Ray thought—another disturbing observation to add to the others that were already bothering him.

Ray had not seen but had heard several of the men talking about the unlucky bastards who had drawn grave-digging chores. In the back center of the estate, right against the outside wall, Ray learned there was a cemetery of sorts located there, just as there had been in Monterey. To call it a cemetery was far too civilized. Even to refer to it as a burial ground was not fitting. It was more like a trash dump, Ray thought, or an evidence dump to dispose of those who got in Alvarez's way. There would be no markers for these graves, and soon the native vegetation would take over the freshly turned soil, and there would be no sign of Gerardo Barega's resting place or any of the others' who were buried there whose fatal mistake had been to cross Alvarez somehow.

Ray joined Miguel and the others on the patio, where everyone but Ray enjoyed a great lunch and a lot of spirited humor at the expense of Gerardo Barega. Ray could not enjoy the lunch knowing that two men were to be executed. As was the way of the Condor, the two lucky guards were sent away alive and told they were to tell all of Barega's men that today's business had been retribution for Barega's part in the attempted assassination of the Condor. No further acts of violence would take place if those loyal to Barega accepted this and also accepted that all future trafficking was now to be done by the Condor. Everyone violating either of these two conditions would see themselves and their families killed. Carlo's men down at the mason's business, who were keeping a careful eye on the two remaining SUVs of Barega's entourage, reported that the men looked relieved when their compatriots returned with the news and could not leave the area fast enough. Eduardo still had at least one man in the Barega camp, just as the Condor had others in all the other cartel camps, to advise him of any future mischief.

Alvarez's victory over all the other significant cartels was complete, yet while he did not seem to outwardly celebrate this, everyone else did. As late afternoon turned to early evening, Alvarez's chef put on a great spread on the patio. All but six of the guards were pulled from their posts and joined Alvarez, the inner circle, Carlo, and Eduardo in what was nothing less than a great feast. Ray asked Raul about Jefe's mood—why he did not seem to be celebrating like the others. Raul explained that he was happy that the first great step, striking at the other cartels, was all over, but he was already thinking about all that was to be required to follow up on their victories.

"He understands far greater than you or me how the last several weeks was nothing more than a first step. He knows how much there is left to accomplish, and this is a heavy burden for just one man, but he has chosen to shoulder it. We will help where we can, Ray, but it is his work. Now, enough of that—tonight we enjoy ourselves, and tomorrow we will begin to face the challenges, so drink up!"

Ray forced a smile and drank down the tumbler of tequila that Raul handed him. *In twelve hours or so, we will all face a challenge, all right—just not one you're expecting, my friend. Jesus, I hope I'm doing the right thing. Whatever happens, I have to make sure Raul survives this somehow.*

Alvarez said his good nights at nine and retired to his suite, followed shortly thereafter by Miguel, a heavy drinker whom no one had ever seen drunk. He would reach his limit, usually in silence, and then just disappear. The dinner was still going strong at ten, but Ray excused himself, telling Raul that he'd had enough and needed some sleep. Raul said he was also tired, and they left together. He told Ray as they slowly walked the quiet hall that the times had been hard on him also, but they were nearing the end of Pablo's journey. Even with so much accomplished, the constant worrying about Rodriguez was taking its toll. He and Eduardo were in complete agreement: Rodriguez would have to be dealt with and soon. But it would wait until the returned to the city, he said. There were the two usual guards standing post outside the great hall that led to the north-wing suites. Raul and Ray simply nodded at the men as they passed and went to their respective rooms.

Ray locked the door behind him and went to the bathroom, closed the lid on the toilet, sat, and sent out a short message letting Bennie and the colonel know that all had gone well today. He also told them about the celebration. With any luck, the guards would be less than 100 percent in the morning and give some additional advantage to Alberto's men. He told them of his intention to try to separate himself from the others and get to the security room just before nine. There, he would take care of securing Baca and hopefully keep them both out of the line of fire. Finished, he went back to his room, undressed, and slipped into bed, knowing full well that there would be no sleep this night, perhaps his last night in this assignment. As he lay there, staring up at the ceiling, a completely meaningless thought came to him. It occurred to him that every sleeping room he had had in Mexico had a ceiling fan. He hadn't really thought about it until now, but they had. He realized how much he welcomed the slow, steady, rhythmic sounds it gave off. The sounds actually made sleep possible on the many nights on this assignment he had thought there would be none. A shame it could not help him tonight.

He had to be sharp tomorrow, especially if things went bad and Alberto's men failed. He needed to get out. He had a bad feeling, and knew he was at his emotional limits and that his luck was about to run out. A very small part of him was excited at the possibility that in hours, this assignment would be over. That small part was overruled by the larger part that was scared shitless about the coming attack. So much could go wrong; there were so many possible unintended consequences. What was it Carlo had said? *I always have a few tricks up my sleeve.* What could Carlo have in place that he did not know about? It dawned on Ray that somehow he had to stay in cover until it was clear that Alberto's men had won and that Alvarez and the others were either captured or dead. If he broke cover to help Alberto's men, and somehow Alvarez escaped, his life wouldn't be worth shit.

Ray thought about all the times recently that Alvarez had spoken to him about pursuing more education, perhaps even following in his footsteps and eventually studying philosophy at the university, and how they would be great friends. Ray was deeply torn, but a realization slowly came over him as he stared up at the slow-moving fan; if push came to shove tomorrow, if it came to it, he'd start shooting people: that was all there was to it. He wanted to live, and if that meant others had to die—others he had come to respect, even like—then so be it. What was it Alvarez had said to him a week ago, that to kill others so that you may live was in fact a philosophy? Well, if so, it was not a philosophy lesson that Pablo Alvarez was expecting Ray to teach him.

35

A s easy as Ray's Monday had been as it related to the killing of Barega, so too had Bennie and Alberto's Monday been as it related to the catching of traitors. Bennie and Alberto, along with Roberto and the squad from Los Pueblos Fantasmas, returned by helicopter to General Lozano's base south of the capital about one o'clock. Roberto and his men left in unmarked SUVs for a safe house that the ghosts kept in the city. There they would have showers; new uniforms, those of the Federal Police; plus their new identities and orders. There would also be hot meals and rooms to rest. They would remain in the capital to do the dirty work required to detain the traitors when the time came. Lozano was there to meet them and to take custody of the two pilots. They were most likely innocent of anything, but neither did Alberto want them talking to anyone about anything until after tomorrow's attack. Lozano would explain things to them and how they were under house arrest for security reasons only, and would be free in the morning. The moment they landed, Alberto's government cell phone let him know that he had several messages from the president. He contacted him immediately and told him he had just returned to the city and was headed to his office. When Alvarez asked him how Bennie had enjoyed his sister's place, Alberto was prepared. He explained that they had gone to Zihuatanejo instead, just the two of them. Alvarez remarked what a good choice that had been and then got on to discussing some other business. Alberto knew that Alvarez had had people watching them, and they had seen nothing. Let him ponder that mystery a bit. He'd either question the ability of the watchers or think that Alberto had lied. Both possibilities would bother him. So be it, he thought.

Alberto spent the day in his office reviewing all the follow-up from Saturday's raid. In the course of his routine responsibilities, it was necessary that he meet with both Ramirez and Quito-Perez at times during the day. Each appeared to be working diligently at his new responsibilities, and there had been nothing out of the ordinary during the meetings. During what little small talk they had, Quito-Perez asked him if he had enjoyed his Sunday out of town, but that had been the nearest thing to intelligence gathering by Alvarez that there had been, if it was even that. The media was everywhere outside his building, and he was told the lower-level press room was jammed. He had what seemed liked hundreds of media requests. All wanted just five minutes; they promised to ask him about the government victory, his victory, over the cartels and just what that meant for the future. He declined all requests through his press officer, citing the call of duty to follow up on the investigation. The one question all were asking was, where were the most notorious criminals in the country's history being held? No one in the building knew but Roberto and he, and they weren't telling.

Arellano and the other leaders, plus the five senior lieutenants whom Alberto knew were identified, were at Alberto's secret Las Pueblos Fantasmas headquarters near Tampico on Mexico's gulf coast. Located in what looked like just another international business office and warehousing facility among many, the secret headquarters was hidden in plain view. Like most of the large facilities in the sprawling business park, there were security fencing and security gates, all quite normal. Several, including Alberto's, even had helipads. In one of the typical-looking warehouse buildings of the compound, which was anything but, they had a dozen empty solitary-confinement cells, and that was where the country's most-sought-after criminals were now being held. Each had arrived blindfolded, been stripped, changed into the most minimal of prison attire, and placed in a cell without further word. There was food and water available to them in the cells. Once in each twenty-four-hour cycle, two silent guards would open the steel door that kept them from seeing more than a few feet and order them to stand with their noses against the far wall, and then let themselves in. None of their questions would be answered as one of the guards delivered more food and removed the remnants of the earlier meal, while the other would hold a Taser pointed at their backs. Done with the small housekeeping chores, the guards would leave. Except for ordering the inmates to face the wall, not another word would be spoken by either guard. For any of the prisoners who were defiant, they were simply stunned and then placed on their beds to regain their senses an hour later and wonder.

They would know nothing but this solitary routine for a week and then would be removed individually, always individually, and allowed a shower and a change of overalls before the first interrogation session. Any resistance would be met with quiet, unnerving calm and a return to their cells, where they would again undergo the mind-altering week of pure isolation they had just experienced. Then the process would repeat itself. For those who didn't try to kill themselves, they soon would be quite cooperative.

Alberto wanted to be there when the principal five each had his first session. He felt that Emilio's death had earned him that right. The remaining prisoners captured during the raid were nothing more than cartel soldiers and had been flown out of Cuidad Obregon and arrived at General Lozano's base south of the city late Saturday night. All had been tagged, so to speak, as if they were cattle in an Omaha slaughterhouse. They carried on cords around their necks yellow plastic-coated cards that had all known essential information on the prisoners. All had been taken to the new maximum-security facility there and shown their cells. The wounded were also being flown out when their injuries allowed. The base hospital already had twenty in its care, kept isolated on their own ward floor under heavy guard. Some in the press suspected that a military base was the logical location to jail the criminals, and some outlets had staked out bases known to have significant jail facilities. But there had been no activity at any of the other bases. No one outside a very few in the government knew that a new prison facility had been constructed on General Lozano's headquarters base, so the media had not looked there.

After arriving from Zihuatanejo with Alberto, Bennie was driven from the base to Alberto's home and made the best use of his afternoon, but he had far too much time and little to do. He contacted Charley on his secure phone and gave him a complete update on events. Alberto told Bennie he would be at the house at six, and they would have dinner and then wait for the arrival of the traitors, who had been asked to be there at eight. They had discussed the timing and decided that having the three go missing tonight would not be a bad thing. Roberto and his people would deliver the traitors to General Lozano, who was expecting them.

Bennie was grateful when Alberto showed up almost an hour early. The down time was driving him nuts with all he knew was about to take place. They sat on the patio instead of in the dining room and updated each other on what they knew. Alejandro offered them several fine choices for dinner, but neither was particularly hungry, accepting instead a simple meal of what looked like to Bennie like the Mexican version of a fajita. Bennie had not eaten on the patio since his first day in town. It would be a week tomorrow since he had arrived in the capital city, but it seemed like so much longer. They avoided the wine this night but did share a drink, Bennie his old single malt, Alberto his single-barrel bourbon.

Roberto and his men arrived at seven and Colonel Cordova of the presidential guard a few minutes after that. Cordova had been sitting in his office at Los Pinos late in the day and had been surprised to receive a personal call from the secretary and the invitation to his home. The presidential guard, like all other Federal Police organizations, was under the umbrella of the secretary's office, but typically all communications from the secretary went to the commanding general.

It took all the professional control Colonel Cordova could muster not to break into a huge grin as Alberto explained General Ramos's treachery at being a pawn of a cartel leader. Alberto told him he would be appointed general of the guard tomorrow afternoon. In the meantime, it was important that he bear witness to this evening's arrests. With Roberto outlining his ideas, they went over the simple plan. Alberto would meet with his three guests in the formal living room. There were two ways in and out: the main entry off the foyer and the servant's entry through the butler's pantry. Roberto's ten-man squad would be split into two groups of five armed with their Belgian assault rifles and would enter at the same time when Alberto mentioned a particular phrase. The captain who commanded the national police assigned to protect Alberto knew Roberto as a senior captain in the police but knew nothing about the men he had brought with him or their purpose here this night.

Of the Federal Police assigned to protect Alberto, only the captain was allowed access to the house for the purpose of speaking with the secretary. A few minutes before eight, he came out to the patio and announced that the secretary's guests were just coming through the front gate. The ten men whom Captain Rodriguez had brought with him were nowhere to be seen. Alberto thanked the captain and ordered him to go to the kitchen and seek out Roberto's sergeant major, who had been briefed on how to bring the captain up to speed. The traitors were to be taken out the front to the Los Pueblos Fantasmas vehicles and delivered to General Lozano. Roberto did not want a bunch of curious guards to get excited when this occurred.

Bennie and Alberto were standing in the foyer, drinks in their hands, when Ramirez and Quito-Perez, in business suits as usual, came through the door. General Ramos, in full uniform, the new, shiny gold piping and large gold stripe on his sleeve indicating his new generalship, more strutted into the room as opposed to walking. As was the custom, their protective details remained outside and pulled round to the garage area to await their departure. There were always refreshments served from the secretary's kitchen for the men on duty, another small detail that made the men like the powerful secretary. Alberto greeted the high government officials cordially and directed them to the living room, offering them a drink, which all accepted. He pointed to three overstuffed chairs and asked the men to sit down, their backs to the foyer they had just come through.

"Gentlemen," he said, "there has been a change in plans. We shall not be meeting here this evening." That was the agreed-upon code phrase. As the traitors looked quizzically at Alberto, waiting for his explanation, behind them, very quietly entering the room in their soft-soled boots, were Roberto, Glock 40 at the ready, and five of his men brandishing their assault rifles. They were within just a few feet before the traitors were aware they were in the room.

"Please be still, gentlemen," Alberto said quietly, "and you shall live to see a trial."

The remaining five ghosts came in the server's door, and the astonished Ramirez, Quito-Perez, and Ramos just stared as if in deep shock.

"You are under arrest for aiding and abetting the criminal known as the Condor de Muerte in his unlawful activities against our country." Amid a sudden outburst of desperate overlapping pleas of, "No, Mr. Secretary, there must be some kind of a mistake; we are innocent. I have done no such thing—" Alberto just waved his hand until they became silent and went on.

"We have the evidence of your treachery in hand—the financial records and much more. We have direct witnesses against you. You have been betrayed, gentlemen, by the very criminals you work for. Take them away, Roberto."

The three ashen-faced men were handcuffed and led away through the front door, where the just-briefed captain of Alberto's guard watched in stunned silence as three of the higher-ranking officials in the government were loaded up and driven off. Alberto called for the captain, and he and Roberto went over what the captain could tell his people. It was possible that in his group of guards, there were others who reported to Alvarez. They would be restricted to the estate, their cellphones confiscated, until after the attack was launched at nine. The excitement over with, Alberto and Bennie were once again alone.

"You know, Alberto, except for what Ray has told us, I'm not sure you have any evidence against these guys," Bennie said.

Alberto, a grim look on his face responded, "We will get it, Bennie. Once we have Baca, we will get everything we need. But even without him, once we can start digging into their personal files, there will be evidence. I will also get confessions if it's the last thing I do."

They went upstairs, and Alberto asked Bennie to join him for a nightcap in the living room of his suite. They talked into the night, at first about the raid that was now only hours away but also of the future for Mexico. Alberto shared his sadness at feeling compelled to take on the presidency. Bennie told him that he thought he'd make a good one, but he also knew that nothing he could say would change the way Alberto was feeling. Alberto checked in one last time with Colonel Portillo, who reported that all was ready. All his troops had been thoroughly briefed and were quietly confident and excited about the mission. A recon team had been reconnoitering the estate since just after dark and reporting in. They had watched the dinner party on the patio, which Ray had sent a message about, with amusement. From their perch in the woods up the hill from the rear of the estate, they had a very good view of the rear of the main house and could clearly identify all the major rooms of the central area.

The colonel and the main force would set out at midnight and make the estate by one and make their breach by three. The recon team had identified several heavily wooded areas within the walls where the team could dig in and make themselves invisible until time to launch the attack. All was on schedule. Bennie finally said good night and went down the hall to his room. With the raid only hours away, neither he nor Alberto would get much sleep again tonight, but it was also futile to just stay up; the waiting was just too hard. At least in their own beds, they might get some rest. With what Alberto must have on his mind, Bennie simply could not relate. All he had on his was getting Ray out alive.

36

Estate of El Condor de Muerte
Chihuahua, Mexico
Tuesday Morning

I t had been a day and a week since the 787 carrying President Fernandez had unexpectedly, as planned, crashed on landing at the Hermosillo airport, killing the president and others in his party. The sudden and tragic death of the president had sent the largely Roman Catholic country spiraling into a deep sadness for the week and attracted the attention of people all over the world as a news story. The state funeral brought emotional closure to some, and the country's introduction of their new young president had given them reason to hope by week's end. With the surprising and fantastic victory by government forces over the cartels on Saturday, as Alvarez had predicted, the people had celebrated with a vengeance in plazas and squares in a hundred towns and cities all over the country through the weekend. Hundreds of churches and a dozen cathedrals celebrated Sunday Mass with glowing sermons and biblical tales of good overcoming evil. Many a priest stood in his pulpit and retold the story of Saul and the Israelites and their victory over the Philistines in the Valley of Elah as told through 1 Samuel 17, with the young David's victory over Goliath. The irony of the metaphor of a country as the young David and groups of drug traffickers as the Goliath was lost on all, but it perhaps most accurately described just how bad things had truly become in Mexico.

In less than a week, the country had seen historical highs and lows and had reason to be optimistic about the future. The greatest unknown irony was that the source of their optimism and hope had been orchestrated by a single man, who, despite his considerable contributions to the good defeating the evil that was at the heart of the people's hope, was in fact the people's greatest criminal.

In his heart, Pablo Alvarez did not see himself as a criminal. Accepting the life his father had left to him and using the means that he felt had been delivered him by the God he deeply believed in, he had done for the people what a half dozen presidents before had failed to do: gain the upper hand in the war with the criminal insurgency that had been threatening to take over his country for years. His accomplishments would forever be obscured however by his tragic personal failure years before: when presented a choice between right and wrong, because the choice had been a hard one, maybe even an impossible one for any son. It was fantasy to believe that a grateful people would come to forgive him and even embrace him when came the day he told them the truth about his life, as he wished one day to do. To his closest friends, there could have been no greater clue or evidence of the depth of his departure from reality, had they realized he harbored such a notion. But as he had not shared this personal dream with anyone, there was no protecting Pablo Alvarez from himself, no matter how the day's events played out.

This task, the impossible task, of protecting Pablo Alvarez from himself fell to Raul Ortega, who had enlisted Eduardo and Ray to help. But with Alberto's ghosts already hidden within the estate walls awaiting the start of their attack, Alvarez's great and true friend likely would not be granted the time he required to save his friend. As Raul awoke this Tuesday morning, his mind was on the plan he had devised in the night to assassinate Alberto Rodriguez. He would enlist the fool Quito-Perez in his scheme. Raul was thinking of a small explosive device to be placed by one of the paramilitary assassins covered as a bodyguard to Quito-Perez. At some time in the future, Perez would undoubtedly have the opportunity to visit the Rodriguez home. With the assassin now on the grounds, there would be opportunity to place the bomb on Rodriguez's official vehicle. Once this was done, it was only a matter of triggering it as he drove to the office some morning.

As he made his way to the dining room for breakfast, Raul was feeling better for the first time in days. He would set his scheme in motion when they returned to the city. Quito-Perez would be the weak link, of course, for however powerful he looked and acted, Raul knew the man inside the shell who had allowed himself to become the traitor he was. Life being life, Raul had no idea that his key link in his new brilliant scheme was already a totally defeated man, lying on a jail-cell bed, sobbing at the injustices of life that had brought him to such a small, cold gray space.

For Colonel Portillo and the men of Los Pueblos Fantasmas, to a man, they felt this clear, calm Tuesday would be a good day. None of the ghosts had any idea that the president of their country was inside the grand house they were watching. They were attacking with the intent of capturing the last of the known cartel leaders, the Condor de Muerte. None of the troops had heard the name before. Portillo and Major Garcia had, only because they had conducted other raids against the man, so they knew whose organization it was they were eroding. Before last night neither of the sharp courageous offices had had any idea the Condor was Alvarez, although Ray's messages of the day before had started to enlighten Colonel Portillo. The references to an Alvarez had not aroused his curiosity, as the name was too common; however, when coupled with the mention of a Baca, he had started to think the impossible. Alberto told his two senior commanders in his last stunning communication with them who their targets were. Shock hadn't been able to begin to describe their emotions at first. After midnight, as they prepared for the advance to the estate, the two officers had talked in hush tones, and shock had turned to anger and then determination to put an end to the abomination that was the Alvarez presidency.

The ghosts, forty-two in all with the addition of the squad that accompanied the Major and Colonel Portillo from Zihuatanejo, had silently and flawlessly executed their penetration of the outer walls of the Condor estate by three in the morning, right on schedule. The march to the top of the hills and then back down to the rear of the estate through the scrub forests was nothing more than a pleasant walk under the quartering moon and clear, cool, star-filled night for the superbly conditioned warriors that were the people's ghosts. The forecast called for a few clouds, and these were welcomed, as the light from the iridescent moon was no friend of a night fighter. The pathfinder teams had laid out the approach to the estate and had pinpointed their points of entry based on the aerial photos. The lasers of the perimeter warning systems, sophisticated and dangerous to the inexperienced, were as bright as the sun through the troops' special night vision equipment and were easily avoided as the men scaled the walls and dropped silently on the other side.

The diversion team, numbering six now with the added men, was in their position in the woods across the road from the main gate. All were armed with the HK G36 assault rifle with the AG36 single-shot 40mm grenade-launcher assembly. They were a lethal force for so few. When given the order, they would start hitting the front gate with multiple grenade shots. The devastation and noise would be terrible for those on the receiving end. From the aerial intelligence provided by the colonel, the lieutenant in charge of the diversion had spent the early-morning hours reconnoitering north of his position opposite the front gate to find a suitable place to control the road coming up from the valley floor. The colonel had advised him that there could be reinforcements called that would arrive by the road from the valley below.

His secondary task to the diversion at the gate was to make sure no one got up the road. Any reinforcements that should try would have little chance of success. Several hundred feet down the valley from the estate, the road made one of the three or four switchback curves as it snaked its way up into the hills. The crest of a promontory the last curve in the road carved around before straightening up and passing the Condor's estate on its climb provided the perfect point from which the road could be controlled. The long uphill curve could be seen in its entirety from the high promontory fifty feet above the road. By only having to shift positions by twenty or thirty feet, the two-man team at the promontory could control some four hundred feet of road. It was the perfect ambush site, and one of the two-man teams the lieutenant had to work with at the gate could be in position there within minutes of being warned of reinforcements. And they would be warned.

Unknown to the troops but nevertheless flying overhead were two Predator drones of the US Army. The first drone was at a distance of five thousand feet vertically and horizontally from the center of the estate in its nearly silent and invisible circular path. For a week now, this bird and several others had been keeping watch on the Condor's estate and reporting back through digital telemetry all they saw. The second drone was a new addition to the watch and was making lazy figure eights at seventy-five hundred feet above the valley floor, focusing on a construction business below with an enclosed yard of a dozen trucks of all sizes.

Manny was fully aware of Colonel Portillo's plan to deal with any possible reinforcements from the construction business and thought it satisfactory. But Manny being Manny, he decided to improve the overall response posture of the attackers with a little reinforcement of his own. This drone had only arrived on station this morning, and unlike its mechanical twin, which could circle for hours with the added fuel in the auxiliary tanks, this second drone had just six hours of total fuel aboard, as its auxiliary tanks had been replaced by the two Hellfire II air-to-ground missiles it carried—another gift to Alberto from his American cousin. The sixty-four-inch long, seven-inch-diameter missiles packed twenty pounds of ultrahigh explosives, delivered on target by the onboard laser-sighting system at an incredible Mach 1.3, or 950 miles per hour. Manny contacted Alberto first thing in the morning on their see-tee system to let him know what he had done. Alberto was of course grateful and contacted Colonel Portillo, now on the grounds of the estate and perfectly hidden, and told him what he had available until ten this morning. At that time, with just enough fuel to make it back, the Predator would have to begin its flight back to Fort Bliss. Colonel Portillo acknowledged receipt of the message with a double click of his transmitter. The only drawback to the air support arranged by Manny was the communication lash-up. The colonel would have to contact Alberto, who then would contact Manny, and the instructions could be executed, whatever they may be. While it would of course never be ordered, the devastating punch of the two Hellfires would, if electronically told to do so, level the Alvarez mansion.

In addition to his diversion team of six ghosts, Colonel Portillo had already divided his force within the walls into three groups. His main striking force of fifteen men, who would be with him and taking the main house from the rear, was dug in near the center of the rear area of the estate in a tangle of underbrush and twisted pinion pines. They would first silently take out the sleeping guards who came off the night shift and returned to the casitas. They would then regroup and reposition to approach the house under cover.

His second force of sixteen men under Major Garcia was dug in toward the front of the house near the south wall, in a position to quickly redeploy to two lines that the major had picked out straddling the private drive as it came up from the gate below. With his two eight-man lines, the Major would be able not only to keep the guards at the gate from coming to the aid of those in the house when it became obvious that was where the heart of the attack was, but he also would be in a position to attack downhill and force the guards there to give up or die. The guards at the gate thought of their defensive position as a fortress, with its twelve-foot-high walls and heavy steel gate, but that assumed an attack from the road. Trapped as they were about to be between the diversion force opposite the front gate and the major's force, their position was more accurately described as a crossfire.

The colonel's last and smallest group was his two two-man sniper teams. They had dug in downhill from the major and had the six guards at the front gate, four of whom were actually on the wall, and the two on the south wall in their sights. What the shooters discovered that previous intel had not mentioned was that on the inside of the tall perimeter wall, hanging from it, was a continuous narrow steel scaffold accessed here and there by steep ships ladders. Not unlike the wall walks of ancient castles, the scaffolding allowed the men to run along the entire length of the walls that overlooked the road protected by the wall. From there, they could easily shoot over it. The only thing differentiating the castle defenses of old to what was constructed for the defense of the Condor was the lack of a crenulated top in the wall. The architecturally ornate entry gate, as viewed from the road, was really a portal beneath the continuous scaffolding. On the colonel's command to the diversion team to initiate the attack, the snipers would start taking down the men on the south wall. With the guards who would already have been killed or captured at the casitas, of the known twenty-four guards at the estate, roughly half would already be eliminated. A one-sided fight would ensue with what few guards survived the grenade assault at the front gate.

Of the remaining known guards, they would be in or near the main house, and the plan counted on most of them trying to reinforce the gate. As they rushed down the drive to help, they would be cut down by Major Garcia's lines. If all went according to plan, the Condor and his inner circle of guards, one of which the troops now knew was a good guy and their intel source, the Condor's two chief lieutenants, Carlo and Eduardo Vargas, plus a communications team of four men in the security room, would be largely on their own. Once Major Garcia and his team had all the onsite guards accounted for, with the diversion and sniper teams under cover still and in reserve where they were, the major's team from the front would augment the attack on the house, which would hopefully be over with by then, if all went well.

The only question the colonel had in the back of his mind was one that he had raised initially and the secretary put in his head again just before he had flown out of Zihuatanejo on Saturday night: an unknown second way out. It did not seem logical for one as intelligent as Alvarez clearly was to not have an alternative means of escape. What was really bothering the colonel was the secretary reminding him of the grotto at the seminary, an underground exit of some kind. The simplest exit would be some sort of door through the wall from one of the casitas. That would mean those in the main house would have to get to the outer wall. That was not going to be possible for anyone in the house if he attempted to do it in the open. That left making such a move unseen, and the possibilities were endless. A tunnel, of course, was the only logical speculation. Maybe Intel One would be of some help, but up till now, there had been no mention of any second way out, so he would concentrate on what he knew.

For Command Sergeant Major Jeff Green, the opportunity to get back into a potential combat environment had his juices flowing. He and the young captain assigned by Colonel Romero as the team leader had gone over the overheads provided by a drone and had decided on a parking area for a scenic overview of the reservoir Alberto had suggested as a possible staging area. Free of overhead powerlines or other obstructions, its flat paved area made a simple and ideal site to stage. Tourists or others driving the north lakeshore road would come to a larger main parking area and boat launch ramp long before they wound up at this spot. The aerials showed a lot of traffic at the boat dock but little at the overlook.

They had flown down at first light at a quick 180 miles per hour at no more than four hundred feet altitude, hugging the western hills of the Rio Sacramento Valley. If there had been radars looking for them, they would have been very hard to see in the cluttered reflection from the foothills. They had flown over few inhabited areas, mostly farms and fields, and arrived unnoticed. At six in the morning, the parking area had been empty. The squad of twelve counterterrorist troops that Jeff had with him had been split equally between the two choppers. After landing, they had quickly set up a defensive perimeter that would keep all civilians away from the birds. Had any of the hungover guards at the Condor estate been really listening in the cool, still morning, they would have heard the distant echoing up the valley of the *whacka whacka whacka* the two US Army–marked choppers made as they approached their staging area.

From the higher lot, Jeff and the captain had a great view across the valley to the slopes beyond. They could not actually see the Condor's estate, as it was further up the narrow, smaller valley that climbed the opposite hills. They thought they had the construction company site from which possible reinforcements could be sent spotted, however. They certainly could see the road intersection through their high-powered scopes. Jeff had lobbied the general for a more active role in the fight but had been told no. They had two jobs; their primary mission was to fly in and extract an American covert operative when called upon to do so. Secondly, and it was thought to be a remote possibility, if the action somehow went unexpectedly bad, the colonel in charge on the ground knew he had additional air assets he could call in. The two US Army Sikorsky UH-60A helicopters were each carrying two door-mounted M60D machine guns in addition to the fourteen soldiers they could deliver. So as the morning slowly unveiled itself, CSM Green and his troops would just have to be patient and let the action evolve.

37

Departamento de Seguridad Pública y Justicia
Situation Center
Mexico City
Tuesday Morning

For Alberto Rodriguez and Bennie Santiago in the capital city 650 miles to the south, they were both up early and had a light breakfast at six. At six thirty, Alberto started making his calls: first to Castillo and then to the chief justice and the two leaders of the Assembly and the Senate. He explained that a matter of grave consequences had arisen and their presence at a meeting at his office this morning was of the highest national priority. When asked, and all did, just what the emergency was, he declined to answer, saying that what information he had and could pass on could only be disseminated in the utmost secrecy. Several asked if the president had been informed, and he lied and said the president was and would be heard from at nine. He advised the leaders, most of whom were much older men, that he had members of his national police outside their residences to augment their personal protection details and get them to the Zocalo safely. Most of the leaders assumed there must have been some cartel retribution planned or discovered that had Alberto all worked up. Even the few who did not know him well could tell by his tone that something serious indeed was taking place. It was just the tone that he had wanted to set and confer. He then called his department heads and ordered them to the office and then, with Bennie at his side, left for his office at the Zocalo, arriving just before seven thirty.

They were met there by Roberto and his troops, all decked out in their version of the army combat uniform. The light cotton-polyester fatigues differed from the American counterpart in that the shirt tucked in and the pants had a black fabric belt to complement the black-and-gray camouflage pattern of the uniform. With their black berets and compact Belgian assault rifles they all carried, they were an intimidating presence on the fifth floor of the old government building.

Alberto implemented the same security precautions that had been used for Saturday's raid. Bennie assured him he was not being totally paranoid, and taking the precautions was warranted by just whom they were pursuing. Everyone getting off the elevator had to clear a metal detector and give up their cell phones, to be returned at noon, they were told. His department heads and their chief deputies assembled once again in the main conference room. The dozen very curious men were surprised to see the secretary of defense, General Lozano, and Colonel Cordova of the presidential guard, as they entered Alberto's conference room. Also unlike Saturday, the attorney general was in attendance, and then the four old, very recognizable senior members of the government. It was not lost on anybody that except for the president himself, the political and governmental power of Mexico was gathered in this room.

For the ones who had been at the Center on Saturday, they had woken up this morning with a feeling of euphoria at the success of the raid on Saturday and also had been feeling a bit full of themselves that they had been at the Center and a witness to history. All had risen this morning thinking that the republic was in the best shape it had been in a long time, only to receive the call from the secretary informing them to be at his office by eight. For most of the bureaucrats, that was an hour earlier than they typically arrived. *What now?* most thought. This thought was reinforced when they walked off the elevators and were faced with the same tight security they had faced on Saturday. Now their curiosity, almost fear, was really intensified. They had just found their seats when Alberto and Bennie walked in from his office.

"Good morning. If you will, please join me in the Center; I will fully brief you on the serious circumstances that have required this extraordinary meeting."

With that, Alberto took control of wheeling former president Castillo down the hall, his aide having been told he could not be admitted, and with Bennie leading the others, he took them down the hall and into the bunker-like room, where all but Alberto, Castillo, Lozano, and Bennie once more had to clear a security screen with armed police standing and scowling at them. Once they were all seated, with Alberto at the head of the table, Bennie at his right hand, and Castillo at his left, Alberto spoke. All those present had known Alberto for a long time and many were thinking they had never seen him looking so grim and determined.

"Gentlemen, Saturday was an important and historical day for our country, but I'm afraid the terrible business we started is not yet complete. Many of you have been wondering, I'm sure, at the presence of Special Agent Santiago of the American DEA in my company for the last week. It is now time you know what I have known for some time. As you are aware, we felt for many years we had identified the six principal cartels in our northern states. What we only learned recently, with the help of Mr. Santiago here and his associates in America, is that perhaps the most powerful cartel of all is one called El Condor de Muerte. Where we believed that the Mendoza brothers of Chihuahua and the Vasso-Barega group of Hermosillo and Monterey were major players in the trafficking, they were in fact fronts, the puppets of others more powerful. What we learned is that a family by the name of Vargas, two brothers and a cousin from Chihuahua, has for many years run the other two groups. The brothers are Eduardo and Carlo, and the cousin is Pablo, who also goes by the nom de guerre "the Condor" and is the leader. He has several other aliases as well. To stay unknown as they have for these many years and not attract our attention, I think you would agree, is quite an accomplishment. Furthermore, we now believe that most of the confidential information we have been receiving that has allowed us to deal with the cartels and other gangs effectively has all been provided by this Condor.

You looked surprised, my friends; why, you are asking, would he do such a thing? Well, the answer is obvious. The Condor is attempting to take over all significant trafficking in Mexico. He alone has been responsible for many of the deaths that have occurred in the intercartel fighting. We have hard intelligence that he recently killed or ordered killed the Mendoza brothers and both Vasso and Barega. Within the week we will be able to further document this, as we know where several of these notorious men are buried. We have learned from an intelligence source provided by the American DEA that the Condor has been among us for at least twelve years with the sole goal of consolidating his control over all trafficking. Because of information provided us by our friends in America, we are in a position this morning to strike at this Condor and put an end to his attempt."

Those around the table nodded, the earlier tensions they were feeling now leaving them as they thought they understood why Alberto was being so melodramatic with all the security and secrecy. Some even smiled, but not for long.

"You will have noticed that we are missing the presence of AFI Director Ramirez and Commander Quito-Perez of the national police, my most re-cent replacement. I regret to have to inform you that they were arrested last night and are now in custody for being informers and conspirators for this Condor and for aiding and abetting his trafficking."

There were audible gasps from all around the table.

"I also must inform you that we also have evidence that General Ramos of the presidential guard is also complicit in this illicit business, and he is also under arrest. Colonel Cordova here will be promoted to general later this afternoon but from this moment is my choice as the commander of the guard."

Former president Castillo spoke up first in his slow and sometimes halting way but nevertheless his voice was clear and strong. "These are grave accusations indeed, Alberto. I presume you have the evidence to prosecute these men on these charges? I have known all three for a very long time."

"Yes, Mr. President, I do have proof and will share it in good time." Castillo nodded.

"I also believe, Alberto"—Castillo looked over to Colonel Cordova—"that the prerogative of appointing General Ramos's successor is President Alvarez's and not yours."

Alberto accepted the subtle rebuke but responded politely. "President Castillo, it is my appointment, as the guard is under my responsibility; the president can either accept my recommendation or ask that I consider another. I am confident, knowing how our president feels about Colonel Cordova, that he will agree."

Castillo nodded and smiled. The look on his wise old face that only Alberto could read said, *OK, Alberto, what are you up to and why?*

The chief justice asked, "Secretary Rodriguez, you have the necessary proof in hand? These are senior members of the government. The case will need to be clear and convincing."

"When the attorney general makes his case, Chief Justice, he will have complete records and irrefutable documentation as to the guilt of these three men, but gentlemen, in most cases, he will also have confessions. Quito-Perez opened up like a flower in spring last night as he was being placed in his cell, and he was not even being formally questioned. We will have no trouble getting convictions. But that's not why we are here this morning. We are here because of this morning's raid and its importance to our country. If we are successful, all will become clear."

The president of the Senate, Alonso Alarcon, was a short, stout man always known for having a far greater sense of his importance than others had of him and one of those who saw himself as a future president even if Castillo and the party had overlooked him when selecting Fernandez. He piped up now. "Secretary Rodriguez, with all due respect, we are all busy men here with our own responsibilities. Police action against criminals is yours, but not mine. I see no reason I have to be here wasting time watching you do your job." He stood up moved his chair back. "So if you will excuse me, I have a schedule to maintain."

"Senator, we will be communicating with the president at nine; you are required to be here. Please sit," Alberto said evenly.

"If the president wants me here," the defiant little pissant of a senator said, "have him call me personally."

Alberto was ready to simply not allow anyone to leave the room. It was, after all, his armed men standing in front of the only door, but to his immense relief, it was the wise and good old Castillo who diffused the situation before it got ugly. "Alonso, old friend, please, sit down."

The pompous senator looked at Castillo and slowly sat down. If he ever was to be made president, it would be because of the old man, as long as he was alive.

"It is clear that there is more going on here than Alberto feels he can tell us at this time. I presume, Alberto, that at nine, you will tell us what has happened and why you are so concerned?"

"Yes, Mr. President, and thank you. I apologize for being so cautious, gentlemen. I assure you, for security reasons that will be self-evident to you all, it is necessary. And if you would just give me an hour, all will become clear."

Those in the room who had known the senator for years all felt they knew what the pompous ass was thinking, given the pained expression on his face: *Why could you not have just died, Castillo, as a result of your stroke. If so, I'd be the power in the party, and you'd be rotting away in some grave.*

In fact, what the pompous, secretly scared-shitless old senator was thinking was, *My God! If they get the Condor and his cousins, how soon will it be before they find the evidence to get me? I should not have helped him, but what choice did I have? He would have killed my family otherwise. Please, God, take the Condor to you!*

All but two or three of the others admired and respected Alberto Rodriguez as much as they despised the Senate leader. They would gladly support their friend and wait. It was after 8:30 a.m., and Alberto was kind enough to have provided pastries and coffee, so what were thirty or even sixty minutes? Most were curious as hell and looked forward to whatever show Alberto was putting on, in spite of the tensions that dealing with cartels brought out in all of them. Most of the men were still reeling from the knowledge that in addition to the cartel leaders taken down on Saturday, the notorious Mendoza brothers and Vasso and Barega were also dead. This was not yet known in the country.

The six-man technical staff that would be monitoring the communications and computer equipment of the Center sat at their terminals facing their equipment but could not help but be tense. Just the distinguished and powerful personages in the room were enough to make most of them nervous, but the secretary's information had not made them curious; it simply made them more nervous and apprehensive about what was going on. Between the secretary and General Lozano, they had the necessary frequencies to monitor whatever was going to be transmitted.

For Ray, hundreds of miles to the north, this day was one he had looked forward to for weeks. It was day ninety-eight inside the cartel; he could hardly believe it had been that long, and it felt even longer to him. He had lain on his bed and stared at the ceiling all night thinking about many things, but most of all, he had thought about how desperately he wanted to survive the coming day. This had been a new and troubling experience for him. In all the police actions he had been involved with in Sacramento, he'd never imagined himself hurt or worse. On this day, he had doubts. There was so much out of his control, so much he did not know.

He knew he had been extraordinarily lucky the past fourteen weeks—even longer when he considered his time as Carlo's cellmate. Any slipups he had made were so close in character to his role they had gone undetected, and as a result, he had lived. Since four, he had been going over possible ways to get himself out of the study and into the hall before the attack, but ironically, it was his body that gave him his way. The incredibly high levels of nervous anxiety he had been feeling had finally manifested itself into the granddaddy of all gut aches. Ray was physically ill. He got up and showered and then dressed, being extra careful to check his knife and his Glock. He made sure he had the second clip, which normally he just carried around in his luggage. He had never carried it on him, but to-day was different. Twenty-four total shots; he might need them all. It was only six, but he was anxious to get out of his room. But first, for mostly personal reasons, he simply wanted contact with the outside world. He also had an idea on how he could let the good guys know what he looked like. He texted:

Ray to world, com check.
Have thought of way to bag
baca. Will do best i can.
For portillo, am headed to
patio with coffee. Will
give you chance to identify
if in position.

Colonel Portillo was quick to respond:

intel one portillo, am near all
well. Will check you out.
can initiate any time after 8
on your signal stay strong
will meet you soon.

Bennie's message came in as he was reading Colonel Portillo's. It was also simple, and he was grateful for the contact:

Hang tough kid all parts of
plan set. Have chopper standing
by to take you to el paso
fort bliss. you'll be there by
noon. Stay low, you go and
get shot and I'll chew you
a new asshole. Bennie.

A chopper for me! Ray suddenly felt a lot better. Bennie wouldn't have to worry about chewing him out; the cop in him started taking over. He'd been on the inside more than once when the cavalry started kicking doors in. Admittedly these perps had just a few more brains and guns, but he'd been there. He left his room at six thirty and nodded to the two guards in the hall who had just come on duty. He decided it was time to start gathering information.

"Just come on?" he asked the first man, whose name he realized he didn't know.

"Yes El Cuchillo, thirty minutes ago."

"A good party last night, how is everyone feeling?" he asked with a small smile. Both young guards relaxed a bit. They were actually about Ray's real age, mid-twenties, and his demeanor made the dangerous El Cuchillo seem less intimidating. "A good party, but we all drank too much. The two we just replaced will sleep till noon. But we are fine."

"Good," Ray said. He smiled and walked off toward the kitchen. There was always an urn of coffee warming in the kitchen, and he walked in and helped himself. The cook manning the kitchen was a middle-aged woman who almost curtsied to Ray and then asked him if he wanted any breakfast. He thanked her, said no, and went out on to the patio.

Damn, Ray thought, *how many on staff here really and how many women? Probably six to eight, like I told them, but I wish I knew. There's nothing I can do, but hope they all hit the deck when the shooting begins. Shit!*

He walked out onto the terrace and stood in the expanding light of the new day and sipped his coffee. He looked carefully across the clear part of the rear yard, if that's what it could be called. It was just native grasses and wildflowers in the large clearing between the house and the scrub forest. *Why did they never have it cleared?* Ray wondered. *How could they not think of it as potential cover?*

He tried to look bored, just staring out into space, but Ray was looking very hard for any sign of the troops. There was none. He could see the roofs of six of the eight casitas near the rear walls through the woods and wondered if Alberto's men had started their attack yet. If so, eight or ten of the men he had had dinner and drank toasts with last night might already be dead. He shivered at the thought—or maybe the cool morning air. He wasn't sure which.

Every time he turned around on this assignment, people died. He was still adjusting to the two fresh graves from yesterday, and already there were perhaps more. He heard steps coming out the door from the kitchen and turned to see a smiling Raul walking up.

"Ray, you're up early."

Ray pretty much always looked serious to the others, but this morning looked more so given all he knew was about to take place and his need to create an opportunity to get out of the dining room or the study at nine.

"Morning."

"You don't look yourself; too much fun last night?"

"No, not that. I drank little last night, like you. No, it's my guts; I'm not well. Maybe something I ate."

Raul now took on the concerned look of an older brother. "Look, Ray, we have nothing planned today of any importance. Take it easy, OK? If I need you for anything, I can find you."

"Well, I thought I would start with you and the others, at least at breakfast. I'm not hungry, but I like being around."

"Sure, fine. But like I said, we have plenty to do figuring out how we will absorb the transshipment routes of the others we killed or caught Saturday with our own. Mostly that's Pablo and Eduardo who figure that out, but it will take all of us to get things organized in the weeks ahead. In the meantime, Pablo also has a country to run. I do not know how he does it, frankly."

"He is a good leader, a good man," Ray said, even believing it a little.

"Let's go in. Swing by Geraldo's office and see if there are any overnight messages."

"OK," Ray said as he nodded his acceptance of the order and went to the security room.

Lorenzo was there with one operator only. "Any traffic for Jefe, Lorenzo?"

"Some, El Cuchillo. All routine."

"When do Geraldo and the other man come on duty, and have you been here all night?"

Lorenzo smiled at what he thought was an attempt by the frightening young killer to be nice. They had really never talked much at all, he and El Cuchillo.

"Only Felix here had the all-night; I came on at six." Lorenzo looked at the other technician. "Felix, you can go now; get some rest."

The operator nodded and silently left the room.

"Geraldo will be checking in anytime. He and Rafael, our other signals tech. I pretty much do six hours on, six hours off, both me and Geraldo. Except for midnight till six, there are usually three of us here most of the time. You would not believe the traffic we have now."

"I'm sure you're busy. Thank you for this; I need to get it to Jefe. See you later."

Ray left, not realizing that he had made Lorenzo's day, what was left of it. Ray was completely unaware just how frightening he appeared to most of the others. His quiet, almost aloof behavior and his killing of Guzman, and then Luis—with his knife no less—had put a version of Ray into their minds that was completely beyond anything Ray could have done overtly. Lorenzo was pleased that someone as important and dangerous as El Cuchillo had taken the time to talk to him. He wondered if they might become friends.

Ray joined Raul in the dining and handed him the folder of messages. It was barely seven. After going over the messages, Raul put them aside and looked at Ray.

"I had some thoughts on our private project. Let me run them by you, and tell me what you think."

He went through the assassination scheme he had come up with involving Quito-Perez. Ray listened, tightly controlling his emotions and the look on his face. When Raul was done, Ray suggested that he might want to send a team of two assassins as guards, each with a bomb. One could distract the real guards somehow, just by talking with them or maybe an argument, which would allow the other one to place the device.

Raul smiled at Ray and then said, "that's good thinking. That is exactly what we will do." He slapped him gently on the back and smiled. Eduardo wandered in, looking grim as usual, and then Carlo, and finally about eight, Alvarez. Eduardo took the time before Alvarez came in to update Raul on what was happening in the north. There could be no doubts now: his man Corro was still missing, and there was nothing to follow up on. No rumors, no news reports on murders or accidents with victims who matched Corro's description. His contacts in the DEA and the El Paso police had finally called in and also knew nothing. Eduardo grew silent when Alvarez came in, looking better than he had yesterday. Maids had been in and out, bringing coffee and juice and breakfast for those who had ordered it. Alvarez noticed that Ray had nothing but toast and asked him about it. Raul answered for him, telling Alvarez that Ray was having stomach troubles and would be taking it easy today. Alvarez turned to Ray and told him to not to worry about anything today and just rest. Ray thanked him and said he wanted to start off the morning as usual, if that was OK, and see how it went. Alvarez smiled and said it would be fine. He'd come to expect no less from his new young friend.

It was about eight thirty when Alvarez got up and headed for the study. Raul, Eduardo, and Miguel followed, while Carlo said he was going to check around outside and would be back later. Ray got up and followed the others and was as tense as he had ever been. He had not looked directly at his watch once during breakfast but hardly ever took his eyes off it now as the second hand crawled around the face. He stepped up beside Raul as he was entering the study and said, "Raul, can you excuse me for a moment? I must go to my room."

Raul looked at Ray and was concerned. "Of course," he said quietly, thinking he understood why Ray had to go. One look at Ray told him instinctively that he was not himself.

"Do not come back until you feel better. Really, you are important, young friend, but we can manage without you," he said warmly.

Ray thanked him and headed to the north wing. The guards who watched the north hall at night were now in the main hall, and there were only two. Geraldo stopped by the dining room on his way to his security room, so Ray felt good about how things were shaping up. Everything was going pretty much on routine. When he and Raul had come through the kitchen an hour earlier, there had been several men grabbing something to eat, but by now they'd be on duty. There was no one in the north wing but him as far as Ray could tell. He went into his room and closed and locked the door. He went into the bathroom and turned the fan on and also the shower. He realize that he was being completely paranoid and his actions were likely stupid, creating background-noise clutter, but he wasn't sure if he was listened to or not, and he wanted to hear Bennie's voice. He pulled out his phone and did what he had wanted to do for weeks. He punched speed dial number one. Bennie answered on the first ring.

"Ray, that you?"

"Me, Bennie. God, is it great to hear your voice. Can you hear me over the background noise?"

"Sure, fine. Talk to me. What's going on?"

"I need to know if Portillo is on the line; how can I be sure?"

"Just dial two and then hit conference; we will both be on."

"OK sure, I see—conference."

Ray did as he was told, and he had them both. "Colonel, you read?"

"Affirm, One."

"Did you see me?"

"Yes, One. Troops know."

"Alvarez and the others are in the study. A total of four. I say again, four: Alvarez, Eduardo, Raul, and a bodyguard, three armed with Glocks. Two guards in the main hall outside the study. Baca, Lorenzo, and one other are in the security room. That's where I will be. I'll wait for the attack to begin and then order the two guards in the hall to go to the gate. Carlo Vargas is out looking around."

"One, we have Carlo Vargas sighted. Can we initiate in five minutes. I say again, five minutes."

"Yes, Colonel. I'll be ready."

"OK, five minutes on my mark…mark. Portillo out." Ray looked at his watch, noted the time, and then looked at his screen. It showed Bennie still on and the colonel off. "Bennie?"

"Yeah, Ray?"

"Got to go, boss. Stand by."

"No hero shit, Ray, you hear me?"

"Got it."

In the study, Alvarez sat at his desk, his back to the expansive windows that looked out to the west, and started glancing at the papers that were placed there for his review. Raul and Eduardo sat facing him in the large comfortable side chairs. Miguel sat on the couch. Raul was taking Alvarez through the overnight reports, while Eduardo placed some calls.

Eduardo was more worried than Raul about the business with Rodriguez and his American DEA friend. There were too many unanswered questions for there not to be some connections. Valentine Corro going missing weighed heavily on him. His people reported that there was no one at the farm and no sign of violence. So where was Corro? Why didn't he answer his phone? He had checked the local papers on the Internet, and there had been no mention of any arrest of any kind that seemed connected to Corro. He had called his wife and identified himself as a friend and wanted to know if she had heard from him. She hadn't, and Eduardo knew that he had scared her, but it couldn't be avoided. He had to find him. He had been wondering what else he could be doing when it had occurred to him to check his message drops. *Shit*, he muttered to himself, *why didn't I think of that before?*

He hadn't because Corro was one of the few of his subordinates who had direct access to him. The message drops were for those he wanted no direct contact with. But he simply forgot that whenever he dumped a phone, if in the few minutes he was switching the programming, over he got a call, it was diverted to the message drop. The chances were remote that Corro had tried to call him at the exact moment, but it was worth a check. He dialed the number and entered the proper code, and to his amazement, there was a message from Corro. He was stunned at what he heard and silently repeated the message several times.

The escape staged? Most likely by American law enforcement? My God, why? To follow Carlo—is that it? Did they trace him to here? This is where he came the first day with Ray…with Ray. Jesus Christ, it can't be that. Can it?

Eduardo looked up from his thinking, his face stricken at what he believed was a possible explanation. Alvarez was looking at him quizzically, as was Raul. Both had known Eduardo a very long time and had not seen such a look on his face since the assassination of Alvarez's father, Armando, an event Eduardo had always blamed on himself.

"What is it, Eduardo?" Alvarez asked.

As Eduardo stared at his cousin, a cold, terrible realization coming over him, he opened his mouth to speak, and then the entire wall behind his cousin just seemed to explode, and he knew in that terrible instant he had failed his cousin, just as he had failed his father.

38

For Colonel Portillo and his troops, the fight had begun, quietly and deadly, several hours earlier. From their concealed cover, the men of Portillo's team had watched as just after six, the rested guards, still yawning and moving slowly, had left the outlying casitas and sauntered slowly to the main house, to be followed some time later by the guards from the overnight shift heading to bed. A total of nine guards had made their way back to the casitas by six forty. To Portillo's displeasure, they had gone to six different casitas. Things would have been so much easier had they gone to just a couple, but what the hell he had thought—when did a plan ever go like you wanted it to?

Portillo employed the same basic tactic that he used at the seminary very early Saturday morning, only this time he would use four teams of two men, two teams to a casita. The team leader had gone in with a silenced FN F2000 assault rifle with laser sight. His teammate had carried the same weapon but also carried a hip pouch with a Taser. If the sleeping guards could be taken alive, they would be. Any sign at all of resistance or the possibility of alerting the estate would be met with instant death. Every deadly call was up to the team leader, and no decision he made would be questioned. Each casita had a small living/dining area and two sleeping rooms. Portillo had no idea how the casitas were wired for emergencies. They could not take the chance that there were panic alarms or other such devices, and his teams had been briefed if in doubt, kill.

Two two-man teams had entered each casita, and two casitas had been hit at a time. In all it had taken the stalkers twenty minutes to clean out the six casitas. Of the nine guards, they had taken five alive, stunned them, and then bound them wrist and ankle and gagged them. The force medic had followed the stalkers and judged each man's weight and then also injected each with a strong sedative to keep the prisoners immobilized for several hours. Three guards had been awake in their living rooms, and there had been no choice but to come in shooting; another had come walking out of a darkened bathroom and again given the stalkers no choice. By just after seven, the stalkers had been back under cover and focused once again on the rear of the main house.

All members of the assault team were on one of two radio nets and had combination earpieces and mics, making it possible to hear and to talk quietly. All team leaders were on the command net and all others on their team nets. Portillo had alerted his team that their intel source was going to show himself, and all were to note his appearance and not mistake him for any of the others. All had done so and had been surprised at how young he was to be doing what he evidently was doing. After Ray had given Portillo his last heads-up and the report on where the principals were in the house, Portillo had passed the word down his command—go in five minutes—and timepieces had been synced up. When it was time, he had simply said, "Team three, *go*," and all hell had broken loose.

The six men of team three each triggered off a 40mm grenade at the front gate. At a distance of only eighty feet opposite the gate, high on the hillside and concealed by the cover the undergrowth and scrub pines provided, they had a clear line of sight. When the team leader got the go signal from the colonel, he had said quietly to his team over his net, "On one, men: three, two, fire." The entire area of the gate seemed to explode. Parts of the heavy but decorative steel gate flew skyward as chunks of stone and masonry from the surrounding pilasters rained shrapnel in a fifty-foot radius. The guards on the catwalks above and to the side of the gate went flying; those on the ground simply ceased to exist, their bodies blown apart due to their close proximity to the blasts.

The second six-shot volley followed the first three seconds later, some shots again at the gate area, others toward sections of the wall where guards had been seen before the attack. The diversion team leader sent his alpha team of two off to the promontory and told them to be prepared to report any attempts at reinforcement. He had been assured of a heads-up but saw no reason to wait. The gate was blasted to hell, and he and his three other troops could have just walked in. Instead, as planned, from cover, they started to fire their assault rifles through the gaping opening, seeing no targets of value to actually aim at. That didn't matter, however; their job was to distract and entice a response. Of the six guards at the gate, two were certainly dead, having taken the brunt of the explosive force. The four on the wall had certainly been blown off of it, and their condition was unknown except it was clear they were not firing. The two guards at the extreme north end of the front wall were firing wildly, and any success on their part would have been pure luck.

The sniper teams were lying in their shallow depressions molded to their bodies, their personal ghillie suits draped over and around them in a way that blended into the native ground. If not for the protruding silencers at the end of the barrels of the sniper rifles, one could have walked within a few feet of the two sniper teams and never realized that the patch of wildflowers and grasses were men, and lethal ones at that. They had received the five-minute word and had sighted in on their targets. The four guards who had reported to the south wall overlooking that portion of road were essentially in loose pairs—the easternmost pair at the corner where the front and the south wall met, the other two further up the south wall to the west. At the first devastating explosions at the gate, one each in the pair of guards had simply collapsed as the 7.62 mm projectiles passed through their chests dead center. The second pair of guards did what anyone probably would have done when conditioned and trained to defend a fixed point as they had been. They simply ducked down below the top of the wall, assuming the shots that amazingly had taken out their partners had to have come from outside the wall. In their crouched positions, they made more difficult targets for a single-shot kill, but not much. Both were felled by single middle-mass shots and lay unmoving on the scaffolding. Neither shooter felt the desire to shoot them further, and one, the youngest, secretly hoped for their survival.

Team two commander, Major Garcia, was alternating between glances at his watch and following the one senior cartel leader he recognized from the police mugshots that had been part of their preraid planning package, as the leader trudged up the steep driveway from the direction of the gate. Garcia knew his name was Carlo and that he was one of the Vargas brothers and a high-value target. Getting him alive was preferred, but getting him period was more important, in the major's mind. From what he had been told, the wide, round-shouldered Carlo was the thug part of the cartel and not the brains. Garcia would risk no one in his command in order to take him alive.

As he watched Carlo huffing and puffing his way up the driveway, he heard one of his men on the team circuit. "Major, from the house, two more, and they seem to have a purpose."

Garcia looked, and indeed, two young guards were running down the drive. He glanced again at his watch. *Anytime now*, he thought. The two excited guards were obviously aware that something was about to occur. *How?* Garcia wondered. The now very alert Carlo stopped them and wanted to know where they were going and why. Before they could answer, the diversion team initiated the attack. With the first thundering of explosions, the thick Carlo spun and sprinted down the drive for the gate. Major Garcia quickly said over his mic, "Charley team, take them."

From a point between Garcia and the three running men on the road, there were the rapid miniature explosions of automatic weapons fire, and Carlo and the two young guards seem to pirouette through the air then tumble and roll off the driveway on the other side. The major barked the practiced commands that would have his force of sixteen men split into two squads of eight straddling the drive. "Alpha squad, three men down across the road. I don't want them circling back to the house if they are able. Establish your line, and then work downhill and find them."

"Confirm, Major," the sergeant major leading his alpha team responded.

The action was not a full minute old, and not counting those guards who had been taken in the casitas, there were six known or suspected dead and six wounded, status unknown, plus one of the leaders, Carlo.

Three minutes before the explosions at the front gate, Colonel Portillo and his men made their move. The eighteen men of team one would split into three groups as they reached the house. Portillo took eight men and swung wide to the north around the clearing, always staying in cover, and slowly came down the north wing of the sprawling house. His group would hit the tall windows of the Alvarez study with their flashbang grenades and then follow up with gas, then the assault. A captain led the other two squads of five in a wide arc around the rear clearing to the south. A kitchen staff of three was clearly visible through the doors and windows that opened to the patio. The team moved through the underbrush in their flanking move to the south end of the house and started working their way up the back side against the wall. There were sleeping quarters here for the Vargas brothers, Baca, his technical staff of three, and a few guards. They had deduced this largely by knowing where everyone else was quartered. By eight o'clock, most if not all of the rooms had looked empty through the spotting scope as people had gotten up and headed out, which made sense. There would be no prying eyes here. The captain and his ten men would flashbang the kitchen and then move in clearing the kitchen and then the south wing. Four men would defend the team from any support from the front hall as the others busied themselves securing staff and anyone else they found. The staff would be bound initially and placed someplace safe. At their final staging points with a minute to spare, they waited for the recognizable sounds of the forty millimeters; that would be their signal to attack.

While Colonel Portillo and his team were edging up the rear wall of the house, the other teams were waiting for the initiation of the attack by team three down the hill. In the house, Ray was just getting ready to leave his suite. The members of the inner circle had their own communication system, and he had his earpiece on, but there was nothing on his net, nor would there be with Raul and Miguel in the same room, Baca, who hardly ever initiated communications in the security room, and Carlo not yet on their net. He turned everything off in the bathroom, which immediately struck him as silly, and went to his door and watched the seconds tick by. He needed to time this just right. With forty-five seconds remaining, he headed out. He walked up to the two guards in the main hall, holding his hand to his ear as if he was receiving some communication. All of the estate guards of course knew of the private communication system those in the inner circle used. Many a time they had been ordered to do this or that by one of Jefe's circle; it was routine. Ray said, "Yes, immediately," and then looked at the two curious guards and said quietly, "Go to the front gate now. There may be trouble there."

They both nodded and went right for the front door and then bolted from under the porte-cochere down the driveway. Ray glanced at his watch: fifteen seconds. He went to close the front door and saw Carlo's head in the distance as he was chugging up the driveway. He closed it and watched out one of the narrow side windows that framed the beautifully carved doors. The two guards would get to him in a matter of seconds, and he would of course stop them and ask them where they were going in such a hurry. *Shit!* Ray thought. *This is going to be close.* They would tell him they were told by El Cuchillo there was trouble at the gate, and while Carlo's first thought might be to ask what kind of trouble, surely his second would be, *How in the hell does Ray know?*

He looked at his watch; any second now. Carlo had the guards and was just starting to talk to them when, thank god, there were multiple explosions down at the gate. Carlo's head jerked around at the sudden sounds, and he and the guards took off at a dead run in that direction, and he lost sight of them beyond the horizon caused by the hill. Ray immediately went to the security room and entered without knocking. The security room had no windows but was on the front of the house, and Geraldo for sure had heard something; he was unsure of just what. Ray entered and drew his Glock to the wide-eyed surprise of the three men in the room.

"It looks as if some of Barega's men may be up to something at the gate. If you can, focus on your work; I will stand guard," Ray said coolly and reasonably. This seemed to make them all relax a bit. All three men knew of the number of men and guns that lay between them and the front gate, and while concerned, they were not overly so. Once one had been on the winning side for years, as all three of these technicians had, a certain feeling of invincibility manifested itself, and Ray could see it. *These people really think they are bulletproof,* he thought.

Carlo and Eduardo always carried around small two-way radio communicators, like small walkie-talkies, that allowed them to communicate with the guard forces at the estates. Lorenzo and the others were not on the inner circle net or that one. In the security room, only he and Baca were on the circle net, so only they heard Raul start to scream—there was no other way to describe it—what sounded like "Pablo" as the distant sounds were suddenly drowned out by very loud vibrating explosions close by. Unlike the muffled explosions Baca thought he might have heard, the concussion grenades that had just gone off in the study were deafening, even through two solid doors.

"Get on the floor," Ray shouted to the others. Ray cracked the door and looked into the hallway, which was already starting to fill with smoke and gas. From what seemed like all points on the compass, Ray could hear crashing glass, more flashbang explosions, and rapid small-arms fire. The study door burst open, and a very badly disheveled Raul and Eduardo, bleeding from a bad head wound, states of shock and terror on their faces, were half carrying, half dragging a limp Alvarez, holding him under the arms. Raul and Ray's eyes locked, and Raul shouted, "Ray, get Baca and Lorenzo, and follow me, quickly!"

Ray shouted back, "What's happening, Raul?"

"No time! Get to Jefe's rooms. There is a passage there from his closet; we need to get him out."

Ray, who was glancing to his left and right the entire time, suddenly turned and started firing his Glock high toward the south end of the hall. "Assassins, Raul! *Go, go!* I will cover you!"

As Raul and Eduardo, their backs already to Ray, lunged up the hallway toward Alvarez's suite, Raul screamed over his shoulder. "Quickly, Ray, the others—follow us!"

Ray had taken five shots. He had seven more plus the clip in his pocket. He aimed and could drop Eduardo and Raul easily, but he simply could not bring himself to shoot them in the back. He might have thought differently had he known that Eduardo had figured it all out and he was now exposed.

His phone was buzzing and had been. He ducked back in the security room, where the others were still on the floor, almost under their tables. Ray yelled at them to keep their heads down. He reached for his phone and hit "1," conference, and "2" and spoke rapidly.

"In security room, with three. Top three headed to Condor suite. From a closet there's a secret passageway. Hall is clear."

What had to be the colonel's voice came over the phone. "We're in at two points. Stay where you are. We are facing light resistance but will prevail shortly and then will pursue."

Ray was watching the other three the entire time, never taking his eyes off them. This was when it was going to get hairy, he knew, because they'd have to be morons not to realize that Ray had been talking to others, and these others were attacking the Condor. Lorenzo and the tech were not morons; they simply were too afraid to have paid attention. The sound of gunfire was everywhere, including in the house, and getting closer. To even the trained, the cacophony of sounds was horribly frightening. Lorenzo had his hands over his ears he was so terrified. There apparently had been at least one guard in the south end of the house who got it into gear and had managed to make a bit of a fight of it, and of course the devoted Miguel was defending in the study. Geraldo Baca, however, had a very puzzled look on his face that was slowly giving way to understanding. "You?" he asked. Ray's cop instincts were in full force now.

"Baca, crawl over here, on your face, now," he yelled, pointing his Glock. "Lorenzo, Baca and I must help Jefe. You stay where you are. Do not move, and you will be safe. Do you understand?"

Lorenzo had not even looked up, preferring to keep his face pressed on the floor. "Lorenzo, answer me! Do you understand?" Ray yelled.

Lorenzo shakily looked up from the floor, his face ashen with fear. "Yes, El Cuchillo, I understand."

"Baca, on your feet now, quickly!"

Even Baca was afraid now, looking at Ray with wide eyes filled with terror as Ray kept his Glock pointed at him. The sound of firing was beginning to diminish to sporadic bursts in lieu of the constant clattering of small-arms fire that had been going on for the last minute. Ray grabbed Baca by the collar and opened the door to the hall and looked out. It was clear of people but full of smoke and gas. Holding Baca firmly by his collar, he said, "Let's go now and fast to Jefe's rooms. Fight me or say anything to the others, and you will be the first one shot—do you understand?"

Baca's response was a whimpered yes. Ray knew his impulsive decision to follow Alvarez and Raul was probably a bad idea, but he simply could not take the chance that they would somehow elude Colonel Portillo's men. Ray had learned never to underestimate Alvarez's or Raul's intelligence. He had no idea where or what the secret passageway was or where it led to, but he had to follow. Raul was too close to the truth about him, and if he escaped and figured out that Ray was a traitor, Ray knew his life wouldn't be worth shit. He knew the next move was perhaps the most dangerous. If some of Portillo's men should happen into the hall as he and Baca were running, they might just shoot first and yell stop second, but Ray had to chance it. He and Baca moved quickly up through the main hall past Ray's room and entered the open doors of the Condor's suite. They had made it past the first critical moment alive. Ray had never been in the suite before and glanced around quickly to locate the closet Raul had screamed at him to find. There was nothing immediately visible in the living room they first entered, so Ray pushed Baca toward a door that was likely the bedroom. Once in the bedroom, here he saw another door open to a large walk-in closet and dressing room.

"There!" Ray said intensely. "In there!"

As they entered the large, finely detailed closet, they could see a small dark opening in the back wall. From the dark space beyond, there was a dim glow of light. The open panel would have looked just like all the others in the detailed cabinetry of the closet had Raul not left the panel open. "Baca, any move on your part to warn the others if we catch them, and I shoot. Got it?"

"Yes, yes, El Cuchillo," the completely terrified little man said.

They ducked through the opening and found themselves on a heavy steel grate landing in a narrow passage between unfinished walls, with a steep metal stair leading down. With Ray holding on to Baca from behind, they descended into the cool, dark space below. The narrow stair ended in a five-foot-wide concrete tunnel that headed back to the south. The tunnel's concrete ceiling was a good seven feet tall, so they could shuffle down it without having to bend over. There were exposed metal conduits on the ceiling, and every ten feet there was a bare bulb in a light fixture creating pools of light. Ray knew they were heading back down the entire length of the great house but beneath it. So thick were the concrete walls that nothing could be heard of the battle going on above them, if indeed there was a fight still going on. Ray was certain that the only logical destination for the escape tunnel, given the direction they were headed, was one of the two casitas along the south wall. Ray had not been in either one, knowing one was where some of the domestic staff lived, and the other he had thought was a storage building. Obviously there was more to the storage building than met the eye, but what could it be?

After what seemed like a very long minute to pass down the long tunnel, Ray could see more light from what looked to be a small room at the end. Ray moved up beside Baca and grabbed him under the arm as if helping him. "Remember, you little shit," he hissed quietly, "one sound out of you, and I start shooting and explain myself later. If you warn Raul, and there is a fight, and I somehow survive, I swear by all you find holy I will gut you like a fish with my knife."

All Baca did was shake his head yes. Ray hoped that his threat, as grisly as he hoped it sounded, was enough to keep Baca silent until he could get control of whatever situation he was about to enter. They stepped into the small, cool, barren, ten-foot-square room. There was a steel ladder fixed to the far concrete wall leading up to a hatch. So far it looked to Ray like no attempt had been made to go up. Alvarez was lying on his side, to all appearances unconscious or dead. Eduardo was sitting on the floor, his back against the wall, with Raul on one knee bent over him, trying to stop the bleeding from Eduardo's head wound. Raul heard motion in the tunnel entrance and snapped around, his Glock in hand, when he saw Ray and Baca enter the room, and then he just as quickly relaxed.

"Thank God you made it, Ray. I cannot get Pablo up the ladder by myself. Eduardo is hurt worse than I feared and cannot stand. We have a few minutes before the attackers realize we have disappeared and even more time before they will locate the closet door panel. You did close it behind you Ray?"

"Yes," Ray lied. "We have time, but time to do what?"

"There's a Land Rover in the storage building, and a section of the outer wall is actually a door painted to look like the wall. We need to get Jefe and Eduardo into the SUV and go up the road. A mile from here where the road ends, near the top is another small villa we own. We have some accountants who work and live there. To the rear is a clearing from which we will be met by a helicopter that I have already called in, so we must hurry."

Raul stood up and stepped away from Eduardo and started climbing the ladder. As he started up, Eduardo seemed to regain his senses momentarily, raised his head from his chest, spotted Ray, and, his eyes widening, screamed, "You, you traitor!"

With more quickness and strength than one might have expected from looking at him, Eduardo raised the Glock that was sitting in his lap. Ray was still standing beside Baca, his gun in his right hand, his left still holding on to the terrified IT expert, watching Raul and contemplating his next move when Eduardo screamed. Before Ray could do anything, Eduardo squeezed off several wild shots, the first two ricocheting loudly down the tunnel, but the third nicked Ray in the side, the jacketed slug cracking a rib as it passed mostly harmlessly through him in a shallow flesh wound that still nonetheless spun him around a ducking and cringing Baca.

Eduardo's scream also startled Raul as he was fidgeting with the latch release on the hatch above his head, and when he quickly looked down, he could not believe his old friend was shooting at Ray. Raul jumped off the ladder toward Eduardo and kicked at him to stop the attack, thinking that his friend must be delusional from his loss of blood or the head trauma that he had suffered. Unknown to Raul, his old friend was dying a slow death from the concussion and fragments he had taken in the initial grenade attack in the study. The bleeding in his brain was severe and only getting worse. The mild kick, which had knocked Eduardo onto his side, was inconsequential to the fatal wound his lifelong friend had already suffered. He would be dead in minutes.

Ray was in pain. The impact of the shot and his natural reaction to spin away and get Baca between him and Eduardo had caused him to lose his balance and his grip on Baca. Baca also attempted to dive out of the line of fire in a completely understandable reaction and sprawled on the floor out of Ray's reach. Ray's Glock had also gone flying during the spin and had bounced off the adjacent wall a few feet from where Ray bounced off the floor, just out of his reach as he lay there slightly stunned from the sharp pain he was beginning to feel from the wound. Raul first quickly bent over his old friend Eduardo and saw that he was again unconscious, and then just as quickly he came over to Ray.

"Good God, Ray, you are wounded. Forgive Eduardo; he is out of his mind. His head wound, I fear, is very serious. Let me look at yours."

"It's not serious, Raul. You go. I will stop the bleeding; you must get the hatch open."

Baca, who had raised himself to a sitting position, seeing Ray's Glock on the floor beyond Ray, saw an opportunity and mustered the courage to yell.

"Raul, Eduardo is right—Ray's a traitor. I heard him speaking with the attackers, I swear. Kill him—kill him now!"

Raul, now more confused than ever, looked at the terrified Baca and then at Ray and back to Baca. In that short several seconds, all the variables he had been mulling over and over in his head since he had become aware of the American DEA's search for Carlo suddenly coalesced in a bright light of understanding at the one possibility that had been there in the back of his mind—but that he had not quite been able to grasp. Suddenly the answer was there in his mind's eye, right in front of him. *The mystery about the escape is that it was no accident—it must have been planned! But why? So Carlo would bring Ray back to the cartel with him?*

"My God Ray," Raul said with a husky voice filled with great emotion as he started to pull his handgun from his belt, "what have you done to us?"

Ray sensed immediately from the look in Raul's eyes as he looked at Baca and then back to him that the truth was there; it was simply a matter of a few seconds before Raul's sharp mind would get around the idea, and it would all make sense to him. Ray's HK was still safely in its scabbard up his left sleeve. With a little flex from his forearm and his wrist, the small spring-loaded device that held the deadly switchblade quickly and quietly propelled the knife into Ray's palm, and he hit the actuator button that unsheathed the shiny, deadly serrated four-inch blade. Given how Raul was kneeling over him, he was actually concealing Ray's left hand from himself.

As Raul started to pull his Glock from his waistband, Ray, his emotions deeply conflicted at what was likely to take place but in real fear for his life for the very first time in his young career, pleaded, "Raul, no, stop, please. Just stop. It's over, its over."

Raul slowly pulled the Glock free, but before he could level it at him, Ray, a terrible, deep sinking feeling coming over him, did the only thing he could do. He struck straight up with his left hand from the floor, his knife deeply penetrating Raul's chest just beneath his rib cage. As much as it hurt physically to do so, Ray very quickly reached up with his right hand and was able to push Raul's hand with enough force to keep the gun it held aimed away from him as Raul managed to squeeze the trigger once before collapsing on Ray, the bullet ricocheting harmlessly down the tunnel. With visions of Zandro Guzman flashing through his mind, Ray heard Raul gasp a breath before becoming still.

Ray felt instant and terrible hurt and remorse. "God, I am sorry. I'm so sorry—forgive me," he said out loud, thinking it was a thought and not spoken words until he heard himself.

My friend, my friend—I've killed my friend, Ray thought as he slowly laid back down on the cold, hard floor. He was crushed at the turn of events and sinking physically and emotionally, both from the wound and what had just happened.

Ironically, it was Baca who brought Ray to his senses and gave him the shot of adrenaline that he needed to survive the moment. Baca was stunned at first by the quick and deadly scuffle between Ray and the now-dead Raul lying mostly on top of him. Seeing Eduardo's gun in the unconscious and nearly dead man's hand, he had scurried on hands and knees across the floor toward it and what he saw as his only chance at safety. Ray heard Baca's sudden rush and painfully pushed Raul off of him and lunged for his Glock lying a few feet from him, the searing pain in his side focusing his mind. Ray won the deadly race and reached his before Baca could get to Eduardo's. Ray did not really think, more just reacted, letting his training take over. As Baca reached out from his knees for Eduardo's gun, Ray got off several quick shots at his right foot, knowing that any wounds would be horrifically painful but not life threatening. He needed Baca alive for Bennie and Alberto. There were no arteries to accidentally hit but lots and lots of little bones, any combination of which, when shattered, would produce intense pain as the nine-millimeter Parabellum slug blasted its way easily through both bone and soft tissue. Ray had no idea which of his two shots shattered Baca's ankle, but it had the effect Ray knew it would. Baca's scream reverberated down the tunnel as he instantly stopped reaching for Eduardo's Glock and instead reached for his ankle.

"Roll away from Eduardo Baca, now!" Ray ordered as he started to rise to his knees. He realized that his telephone was buzzing; how long this had been going on, he had no idea. As he stood up he reached for it and saw both one and two illuminated on the small screen. He pushed the button and spoke. "Colonel, can you hear me?"

"Barely, Ray. I am in the tunnel at the ladder. My men are in the casita above you. We found the SUV and the escape door. I heard shooting; are you OK?"

"Yes, but I need help now. I have them—come quickly."

Ray never took his eyes off Baca the entire time, but he needn't have worried. Baca was in so much pain that he was reduced to a crying, broken man, curled up on the floor clutching his wounded leg. Ray could hear running footsteps echoing down the tunnel and getting closer. A man about his size, maybe fifty years old, in fatigues and a black beret, holding his own version of a Glock, walked in, surveyed the scene, and then yelled over his shoulder, "Three men in here now. And get the medic down here."

The soldiers quickly entered and dispersed, each going to one of the other bodies in the room. Ray finally took a painful deep breath and looked at the colonel and extended his hand. "Thank you, Colonel. I'm Ray Cruz, American DEA."

"Lieutenant Colonel Vicente Portillo of the secretary's Los Pueblos Fantasmas. It is my great pleasure to meet you, Senor Cruz. You're hurt," he said, a concerned look coming to his face as he saw the blood on Ray's shirt, "you must sit".

"I'm fine Colonel, and please, its Ray. Alvarez is there; he's been unconscious the entire time. I have no idea if he's even alive. Eduardo Vargas is also down but was alive when I got here. That's Baca; he knows about me. We have to get him to the secretary alive, and we have to keep him from talking to anyone whom the secretary does not control and trust."

"And this one?" Colonel Portillo asked as he stared down at the lifeless body at his feet.

"That's…that's Raul Ortega. I had to kill him with…with my knife. He gave me no choice."

The colonel could see that Ray was deeply affected by the stabbing and said gently, "Do not dwell on it, Ray. My men and I had many such happenings this morning."

Colonel Portillo reached up and touched the small mic he was wearing. "Doc, the end of the tunnel, now."

It was only a minute later, and a young medic reported to the colonel.

"The wounded one there—sedate him, but make sure you don't kill him."

"Yes, sir," the medic said as he kneeled down, rummaged through a rucksack, pulled out a hypodermic, and, after sizing up Baca's relative weight, administered a shot. "Eight hours or so, Colonel."

"Thank you." Portillo turned to Ray. "As I understand it, there is a helo less than five minutes from here that will take you out as soon as we make sure there are no cartel eyes to see you leave."

Ray was looking down at Raul and was having difficulty seeing due to the moisture in his eyes. He looked up at the colonel and then forced a small smile at the reminder of the helicopter nearby to take him away, away to the United States.

"Colonel, you can't imagine how that makes me feel knowing that helo is close by. Thanks."

"Now," Portillo said, "let's get you moved back to the suite we came through and get the doc here to patch you up. What did that to you?"

"Eduardo Vargas gained consciousness, saw me, and opened up when I wasn't looking. A lucky shot got a rib, I think. I heard a snap, and breathing is a bitch. I was worried that Vargas and Raul were close to figuring me out. I got lucky. Eduardo apparently did but was too hurt to do anything effective about it. Raul didn't figure it out until he was trying to help me and that miserable shit Baca told him. He heard me talking with you during the fight. I had no choice but to use my knife; it was all I had."

Portillo nodded his understanding. He had seen a lot of death this morning from a distance. He could only imagine what Ray had had to do and cringed at the thought of having to stab a man at so close a range. More of the colonel's men entered the small space, and they picked everyone but Ray up and moved back down the tunnel and up the steps with some difficulty given the narrow space, and finally they had everyone in Alvarez's suite. Portillo's medic told Ray and the colonel that Raul and Eduardo were dead but that Alvarez was alive and had probably been concussed, either from the grenade attack itself or from close proximity to the flashbangs. He had some burns from the flashes and superficial cuts from flying glass but should live.

Ray was lying on Alvarez's bed as the medic finished dressing Ray's wound. Colonel Portillo, who had been watching but obviously listening to the chatter and taking calls on his net, said to Ray, "We are getting the estate totally under control. We will keep you out of sight until we get the staff and the prisoners away from the main house."

He paused and touched his ear. He then spoke. "Major Garcia, send a reinforced squad to team three. They have stopped two truckloads of cartel reinforcements, but there are survivors, and they are fighting back. Remain here for a bit, Senor Cruz, while we get the situation under control."

Portillo smiled and headed out, listening to incoming calls and issuing orders. Ray called Bennie, in part to give a situation report and tell him he was OK but mostly just to hear his voice. Their short conversation was very emotional for the two of them. Bennie said he had to go, as there was a lot going on in the Situation Room as the second phase of the operation was being mounted.

"Listen, Ray, I've got to run. I need to be with Alberto as he explains all this to the government and the people. Because you're wounded, I will refrain from tearing you a new asshole for disobeying my orders and not hiding in a closet. I have enough to explain to your dad without you having a goddamn hole in your side. You get your ass to Fort Bliss and lay low there. Charley Willis will meet you there and start the debrief. I will join up just as soon as I can shag my raggedy ass out of here. See you in a couple of days, and Ray, great job, son."

"Thanks, boss," was all Ray trusted himself to say.

Bennie's words meant everything to Ray, and he was surprised at the emotion in him. Ray did as he was told and just stayed in Alvarez's suite as the ghosts went about their business. He could make out the distant clatter of automatic-weapons fire, but it gradually grew silent. Portillo came walking down the hall with a smile on his face as he saw Ray, who was standing in the doorway.

"We have everyone, Ray. Here's the situation. We have the president and Baca unconscious. The president is still in his disguise at the instructions of the secretary. We have two men who have been broadcasting our actions back to the Center in the capital, but they have not yet shown Alvarez. I am awaiting further instructions from the secretary as part of what he calls the second phase."

"The second phase, Colonel?"

Colonel Portillo raised his eyebrows in question. "Your guess is as good as mine. As for Baca and his two associates that you bagged in the security room, they will be isolated from all others. I have alerted the secretary, and he has discussed this with Senior Santiago."

"I heard quite a bit of small-arms fire, Colonel."

"No longer a concern, not that it ever was. About twenty of Alvarez's men from town tried to make it up the hill. One of my teams hit them as they came around the last curve, and I'm afraid few of them survived. My lieutenant in command of the diversion chose his defensive position brilliantly. After we hit their vehicles, four or five tried to move on foot to the estate. They were obviously well paid, for their determination to come to Alvarez's aid was commendable, if not suicidal. My men have them; all are wounded to one degree or another. Most are dead."

"Goddamn it, Colonel, I am so sick of all the killing. How about your men—OK?"

"Three wounded, none seriously. It was a very one-sided fight, just like at the seminary. The fact is, for as powerful as the cartels have been and the number of murders they have committed—and we are talking tens of thousands over the last decade—their fights have always been against innocents or weak opposition, and they have always dictated the parameters of the engagement. They have been like the bully on the playground, only fighting those who that are weaker. They have rudimentary weapons skills at best and have used sheer terror and numbers to dominate their victories. We had the intelligence on them, we picked the killing ground, and we have the skills. Both engagements the last several days were nothing more than organized slaughters I'm afraid, but necessary."

"I hate all the killing, Colonel, but I'm glad you did what you did. I suppose I'll be sorting this one out in my mind for years to come."

Colonel Portillo put his hand on Ray's shoulder, a fatherly look in his eye, and responded, "As I said earlier, do not dwell on it, my friend. It was necessary. They gave us no choice, none of them. There is simply too much money and power in play for them to have done anything else."

In the background, Ray could hear the sound of arriving helicopters. "Colonel, Jesus, I forgot. Raul said something about ordering up a helo for a rescue of Alvarez from a villa up the mountain."

"Not a worry, Ray. We observed an unidentified chopper coming up the valley, and I had one of my gunships do a flyover at the villa you mentioned when it was clear that was where it was headed. Alvarez's helicopter is burning up on the ground as we speak. A squad of my men is headed up there now to reconnoiter the area. There is no escape up the mountain; the road dead-ends. Whoever Alvarez had up there will be ours shortly. What you hear now are my evac choppers. We must get Alvarez and Baca and the others to my staging base and then the few surviving guards and staff. We have a field hospital set up there to treat the wounded beyond what my medics have been able to do here. National police units from our Chihuahua barracks are on their way. I must go meet with them and give them their orders. Major Garcia knows everything I do, Ray, but no other. He will be here shortly and stay with you."

Colonel Portillo's choppers started to arrive. With Major Garcia's blessing, Ray moved down the hall to the shattered study to watch from within; he was alone. Miguel was still lying in a twisted shape on the floor, an agonized look frozen on his face, multiple gunshot wounds very evident. Ray hadn't expected to come across more bodies of men he knew, and it affected him. A short time later, Portillo walked into the study, saw Ray and his interest in the devastation, and explained.

"Alvarez was able to survive the initial assault because his study windows were three-millimeter-thick bulletproof glass. No one knew. My initial burst of flashbang grenades shattered some of the glass but did not penetrate fully. I had my two launchers quickly reload, and we hit the wall with grenades and blew the end of the room to shit. The slight delay evidently gave Ortega and Vargas enough time to protect Alvarez and get him out of the room. His guard there stayed behind to provide cover fire and was killed in the assault."

Ray felt strange. It wasn't really sadness knowing that Miguel was dead. He had never been close to the quiet older man over the last three months.

But he did feel something, and it was confusing. As one of the colonel's choppers departed, another landed, taking Alvarez and the others with them.

"Colonel, what about Carlo Vargas—big guy, Alvarez's cousin."

"He was near the front of the house, he and two others who came running out. I'm guessing you had something to do with that?"

"Yeah, they were the two in the hall. I told them there was trouble at the gate just before you hit it. I don't even know their names. Both were young, fairly new, I'm guessing. Just me talking to them scared the hell out of them. Did you get them alive?"

"Afraid not, Ray. I'm sorry. Garcia's men took them out as they were headed down the drive. That was their job. The big one, Carlo, he lived for a while. He was the one responsible for two of my wounded. Tough bastard was playing dead and came up firing as my men were checking on them. Had several very bad wounds, I'm told, and then put up a fight. My men had to defend themselves, so I'm afraid he didn't survive. One tough bastard, though. I'll give him that."

Ray was looking at his shoes, shaking his head.

"What is it, Ray?"

Ray looked up, grim determination on his face to control his emotions. "It's hard to explain. Carlo was completely corrupt, a murderer. I know of at least four murders, executions really, that he committed just since I joined the cartel. All cartel members, really bad men, but they supposedly had rights. But I liked Carlo. It's not Carlo that's really bugging me; it's Alvarez and Raul Ortega, the way they treated me, befriended me. This could well be the goddamndest thing I have ever said, Colonel, but there was a connection there. I liked them, even admired them—a part of me, anyway. Alvarez is the most morally complicated man I have ever met. So much of the defeat of the cartels is his doing, and for all the right and good reasons. It was his father, you know, who turned him into a trafficker. He was a lawyer, a good man, until his father gave him the choice: arrest me, or follow me. What's been bothering me for a very long time is this question: Am I any better? Would I have made a different choice? I simply don't know. I love my dad, like I think Alvarez loved his father. What I am very glad of is that I have never been forced to make such a choice. I feel that if he could, he would end all trafficking. I know that's how Raul felt. I cannot believe I'm saying this out loud, but Raul had become a friend. I really liked him, his loyalty, his character, his intelligence, and his compassion. Shit, Bennie will probably throw my ass in the loony bin for talking like this. I'll never be able to forget the look on his face as he realized I'd betrayed him. He looked so… sad, hurt, I guess. And I feel as if I did betray a friend; that's what's so crazy. God forgive me. I feel so bad."

Portillo smiled, the fatherly like smile he had already shown Ray. He grabbed Ray gently by the shoulder and said softly, "Give it some time. You will sort it all out—you will, OK? You did what you had to and for all the right reasons. Your humanity is intact, my young friend. Your conscience is the price you pay for being human."

Ray, who had been looking down so that the colonel could not see his eyes and the tears there, looked up. "I suppose, Colonel. In time."

A videographer came in and filmed the study, and then others removed Miguel's body and placed him in black rubberized zip-up body bag. Another officer stuck a yellow tag on the bag, giving the body a number in lieu of a name. The national police from Chihuahua began to arrive and were set to work on the grounds documenting the site as a crime scene and removing the bodies to the local morgue, where Portillo ordered they be placed under guard. It took a couple of trips each for his choppers to do their work and remove all the wounded, the prisoners, and the staff to the staging area.

As the ghosts' choppers left and headed south over the hills, Ray could hear another approaching. The colonel came back to the study and told Ray his ride was approaching. They stepped through the gaping hole that had once been the beautiful glass-and-stone west end of Alvarez's office and watched as the US Army–marked helicopter slowly descended. A typical young but sharp-looking captain and a very large fierce-looking senior sergeant stepped out of the chopper and walked toward Ray and the colonel. They saluted the colonel, warriors to warrior, and then the big dark sergeant said to Ray as he extended a big meaty hand, "Mr. Cruz? Sergeant Major

Green. This here is Captain Johnson. General Rodriguez from Fort Bliss asked us to come on down and give you a ride back to the world."

Ray wanted to cry again. It was maybe the third time in the new day that the emotion to do so had come over him. He held everything back behind tight lips, determined to get out of there without breaking down. He took a quick, deep breath, took the sergeant's hand, and said, "I don't know what else to say, Sergeant, but thanks—thanks a lot."

Jeff Green looked at his captain and then at the colonel. "With your permission, Colonel, we'll get this man out of here. He's fucking well earned it, sir."

"Of course, Sargento Mayor. I agree. Captain." Portillo turned to Ray. "Ray, I hope this will not be the last time we meet. I am very interested in your story and would look forward to talking with you again at a better time. You are a most courageous young man and a credit to your DEA."

Ray took the colonel's extended hand in both of his and shook it. "Colonel, thanks. I'd look forward to it."

With that, Jeff led Ray to the chopper, helped him in, and showed him where to sit and how to fasten the restraints. The pilot increased power and took the bird straight up fifty or sixty feet and then, rotating until the nose was pointed north, pushed the collective in his hand forward. The nose of the powerful helo dropped down, and they accelerated quickly, leaving the estate far behind and below them. The big sergeant leaned over to Ray and said loudly above the engine and rotor noise, "Two hundred and forty miles and we got plenty of gas. About ninety minutes, Mr. Cruz, to a cold beer."

Ray said back, equally loudly, "It's Ray, Sergeant Major. Call me Ray. Any way I can buy the first round? I got some back pay coming, about five months' worth."

Jeff Green, known to thousands of US soldiers at the sprawling base northeast of El Paso as the scariest, most dead-serious hard-as-nails motherfucker at Fort Bliss, smiled broadly at the young man like a kid in a candy store, slapped him on the knee, and said, "Hoo-ah. I can arrange that, Ray. That's an affirm."

39

I n Mexico City, about the time Ray was excusing himself from Raul and heading to his room at the estate, in the fifth-floor Center, as the assembled group of leaders of the Mexican government watched the second hand tick off the time until the attack, there was little to do but nervously wait and have the coffee and pastries Alberto had provided. Despite Alberto's explanations of what was to come, the old president's comment about Alberto clearly having more to say had each one of them guessing in nervous anticipation. Bennie joined Alberto in the glass walled office with Colonel Cordova and watched as Alberto organized the second phase of this morning's raid. Using the terminal and video hookup the technicians had set up for him, he contacted the national police commander in Baja and also the colonel of the presidential guard, both living in temporary housing in the compound constructed across the paved road from the Alvarez estate. It took several minutes to get the two commanders together in a private location in front of a camera, and then he informed them of the arrests the night before and the pending raid in the north. The news surprised both men, but they maintained a veneer of professionalism until he told them what he was ordering them to prepare to do.

In a word, both men were flabbergasted. After regaining their composures, they were told to very discreetly pick twenty good men from each of their commands. There would be two teams, each composed of ten men from each service. They also were to select two television media camera crews of their choice, one to accompany each team. Both camera crews could take one reporter who would serve as pool reporters for all the media. The crews were to use the special camera equipment flown to Baja the night before and broadcast on the frequency provided. The only people viewing the broadcast would be those in the Center, for now.

Alberto told the two colonels who was in the Center with him, which of course impressed them. He then told them that on his orders, they were to force their way into the Alvarez estate and the Pena estate next door. Everyone in the Pena estate was to be arrested, taken to the detention trailer, and kept away from everyone, especially the press. Alberto also wanted the press confined to the press tent until he ordered otherwise. A third media crew was to be picked and placed with the national police who were watching the estates from the beach. All Alberto would say in response to the reservations both colonels had to the orders was that the safety of the presidency depended on their obedience. Both colonels were ordered to be part of the group that entered the Alvarez estate.

"Now, gentlemen, listen to me carefully," Alberto said slowly and deliberately into the camera lens, his face reflecting the tension he felt and the seriousness of the events. "What you will find when you enter the president's home is his mother and her domestic staff. There may be some security personnel—two brothers, to be specific—Guillermo and Alejandro Sanchez. Photographs are being faxed to you as we speak. If you find them, they are to be arrested. They will either be with Senora Alvarez or next door at the Pena estate. What you will not find is our president or his personal entourage."

Both men stared into the small camera broadcasting their image to the Center, as if Alberto had just told them they each had two heads. They simply did not believe what they heard. Colonel Pacheco, Alberto's handpicked man to head up the units that supported the presidential guard, spoke up first. He owed his entire career to Alberto Rodriguez, who had mentored him and advanced him over others. There was no one in the police or government he trusted or respected more, but he was still stunned by what his superior was asking him and Colonel Torres of the guard to do. And now to be told that their president was not even there was simply too much.

"Mr. Secretary, with great respect, all this is astounding. Are you telling us that someone has kidnapped the president from under our noses—is that it?"

Colonel Torres was nodding as if that was also the conclusion he had drawn from Alberto's statements. General Ramos had picked Torres for the plum assignment of being the day-to-day commander of the presidential guard. Alberto did not know him well and would not have been the least bit surprised if a check of the Baca computer files showed Torres to be a traitor. Alberto felt that anyone General Ramos would handpick for commander was likely wanting in some way.

"In a manner of speaking, Alonso, a manner of speaking. I cannot tell you everything at this time, just that the president is not in his home. Secure the estates, and have all your actions captured on video. Senora Alvarez is to be treated with respect and care; she is not well. If she asks, just say we are there to protect her son. Wait for my order, but get ready to move in and attract as little attention as possible."

While Alberto was giving his subordinates their instructions, Bennie's phone to Ray signaled an incoming call. He slipped out of the glass box and quietly took the call from Ray. When he was finished, he went back into the office. Several groups of officials in the Center had eyed Bennie with curiosity, but none had approached. Alberto was finishing up his communication with the colonels in Baja when Bennie looked over and said, "Five minutes and all hell breaks loose."

"Right, thank you, Bennie."

The three of them returned to the large polished conference table and sat down. Old President Castillo was sitting quietly watching everything around him. As nervous and curious as all the others were and despite the debilitating effects of his stroke, the old president was as cool as the morning sand on the beach at Zihuatanejo. On the many flat-screen monitors in front of the technicians, images began to appear. From the images, it was obvious there were two cameras transmitting. As if from an African safari documentary, those shooting were clearly in tall underbrush or twist-ed, gnarly trees, one focusing on a beautiful, sprawling hacienda, the other looking through some trees at what looked like a fancy estate gate. Only this one, as the lens slowly zoomed in, was being manned by a number of heavily armed men. The two images were being shown on multiple screens. Everyone at the table had a very good view. There was no narration, but there was sound. As the cameramen moved, the mic picked up the rustling sounds a man makes when moving through dry native underbrush. Also the steady breathing of the cameramen could be heard. There was static in the background and then a whispered voice: "One minute, all units stand by."

Alberto said evenly but softly to those assembled around the table, "You are seeing the Chihuahua home of El Condor de Muerte. A reinforced pla-toon of our best antiterrorist police are about to take it. The significance of this will be clear, gentlemen, if all goes well."

Without warning, the screens showing the gate and the armed men talk-ing and smoking there suddenly erupted in what looked like a massive single explosion, which was, in fact, six 40mm grenades hitting within the same area within fractions of a second. This was followed several seconds later by the second volley. The stunned men in the Center had all jumped, everyone but Alberto, Bennie, and old Castillo. Alberto and Bennie knew what was coming; Castillo must have sensed it. The transmission showing the large house began to tighten focus on a large room near the center of the hacienda that protruded out from the main rear wall. Clearly, it was an important room, with tall windows framed by the beautiful stone walls, limestone sills, and the dark-tiled peaked roof. There were suddenly explosions here as well, but different ones, not as devastating. Then suddenly, a few seconds later, came more fierce explosions. Soldiers could be seen now, real-looking sol-diers in their black camouflage fatigues, firing weapons into the broken and smoldering ruins that had been a room.

For the next twenty minutes, those assembled watched the twisting, turning, dizzying images as the cameramen ran here and there, sometimes standing, other times ducking low, all the while broadcasting. The high-tech sound system in the room flooded it with a cacophony of weapons fire, a symphony of high-pitched shouts, desperate and angry screams, and the occasional rational documentary-like narration by the cameramen of what was going on. All during the melee being broadcast, from time to time, those in the room could hear the radio communications being sent to the attackers: precise, clipped orders that none in the Center really understood. "Alpha two across the drive; charley three to the point."

Some of the images had been hard to watch for those who had never served in the military or the police, as images of broken and twisted bodies filled the screens. For many in the Center who had randomly picked the scene of the gate to be watching at the instant of the attack, the image of shattered human beings flying through the air and landing in motionless heaps would be seared into their consciousness. The heretofore abstract notion of "fighting" the cartels that they had arrogantly and with little emotion discussed at cabinet meetings or their privileged cocktail parties, as if they really knew what this meant, become suddenly transformed with the images on the screens. Fighting meant death: sudden, stark, horrific death.

As suddenly as it had started, the battle the men had been watching stopped. There was occasional distant and sporadic weapons fire, but even that didn't last long. A tough-looking soldier who had an air of command about him was walking up to one of the cameramen, who was standing and focused on his approach. The soldier stopped and spoke into the lens. "Mr. Secretary, we have Intel One. He is wounded—not seriously—and safe. We have the two principal targets alive. The others, I'm afraid, died in the fighting. I have three wounded, none serious. We are getting the situation under control and will be sending out the high-value prisoners within the next few minutes. The Chihuahua barracks is on the way. They will seal and document the site. There's a hell of a mess on the state road, as there was an attempt to reinforce the cartel from the valley below. I will report back when we reach the staging area so that you may begin your next phase."

Alberto picked up his special cell phone and spoke. "Colonel, can you hear me?"

The man standing in front of the camera tilted his head, his hand to his ear, and then said, "Yes, Secretary, go ahead."

"Cartel casualties—can you be more specific?"

"No, Mr. Secretary, not yet, but I'm afraid we did not take many alive, maybe half. Of the eight domestic staff, we have all eight, mostly unharmed but several badly concussed. All will be transported shortly to the staging area as planned."

"Thank you, Colonel. I need you to get to the staging area and prepare for the next step as soon as possible."

"Thirty minutes, Mr. Secretary. Out."

The assembled government leaders listened to the conversation without really understanding it much. Alberto looked around the table. He began to speak, softly but confidently, each word clipped and strong.

"We have achieved a great victory over the criminal insurgency that has plagued us for so many years, my friends. The significance of today is even greater than our success on Saturday. I must tell you now the hard truth, a truth so monstrous that your first reactions will be denial, astonishment, and disbelief, but it is the truth nonetheless. Three months ago, Mr. Santiago here successfully infiltrated a covert operative of his into a cartel in the north. At great personal risk, this operative confirmed for us the existence of El Condor de Muerte, for it was his cartel that Mr. Santiago's man infiltrated. The details of this, we will set aside for now. We had suspicions of such a cartel but no proof. Mr. Santiago got us the proof. I mentioned earlier that this Condor's given birth name was Pablo Vargas. He also had two very well-known aliases. Vargas is also known as Nicolas Pena."

There were the expected startled gasps as Alberto mentioned one of the richest and most well-known philanthropists in the country. Several had actually met the recluse. And now Alberto was telling them he was a cartel leader. Impossible, they thought!

"A hard truth, gentlemen, but a truth. The harder truth is that for many years now, Vargas has moved among us here in the capital. He has socialized with each and every one of you, done business with you. For some, he is a friend. For me, he was a friend for most of my life."

There were more gaping mouths and head shaking. "For the last twelve years, Vargas has moved among us as Jacques Pablo Alvarez, my childhood friend, and as of this past Monday, the president of our republic."

As Alberto had feared and expected, the room exploded in excited and animated outbursts and denials. *It can't be! Impossible! A slanderous accusation! What proof!*

Alberto raised his hands like a performer trying to get an appreciative audience to stop their applause. Castillo was looking intently at Alberto but seemed totally in control of his emotions. If he was shocked, it didn't show. There was a reason he had achieved the highest office in the land. It was Castillo who got everyone's attention as he shakily stood up from his wheelchair. "Shush, shush, gentlemen, please. Alberto, go on. Answer the question. What is the proof?"

"My proof is simple, gentlemen. You all believe our president is at his mother's estate in Baja Sur, yes? You saw his brief press conference from there on Sunday, I'm sure, and watched as I did as he entered the estate. The media and all our protection agencies have been watching from outside the gates since then. You agree?"

There was acknowledgement of this fact all around the large table.

Colonel Portillo, who you all just saw make his report, has told you all we have just captured him alive outside Chihuahua. President Alvarez was the high-value target, along with his cousin Eduardo Vargas and several others, including Geraldo Baca."

There were more murmurs of astonishment at the mention of Baca. Alberto nodded to the chief of communications, who, along with the other stunned technicians, were awaiting Alberto's order. "Bring up the colonels in Baja, please."

The senior tech turned and typed a few commands into a computer, and an image appeared on the central screen. Most everyone in the room recognized Colonel Pacheco of the national police and Colonel Torres of the presidential guard.

"My colonels, can you hear and see me?"

"Yes, sir," they said in unison. "Is all prepared?", Alberto asked.

"Yes, Mr. Secretary."

"Then please, execute your orders."

The gathered group watched as the two men, who had been standing outside in the shade of one of the temporary trailers across the road from the Alvarez estate, climbed into an American-manufactured Humvee with the top off, a curious field reporter and a cameraman broadcasting the events. They and their troops, in Humvees of their own, drove the very short distance to the front gate of the Alvarez estate. An SUV parked in front of the impressive gate started to back away, and they could see that there was a cable from the truck to the gates. Slowly, as the truck backed away, one leaf was forced open, and the colonels' Humvee led the large group of men in. After arriving at the front of the mansion, the colonels, with the camera crew broadcasting their every move, walked directly in through the unlocked front doors. A maid was the first person they saw, and Colonel Pacheco said, "Do not be alarmed; we are here for the president's protection. Where are he and his mother?"

The obviously very shaken maid led them out to the patio, where the thin and frail-looking Senora Alvarez was sitting at a glass patio table having her breakfast. She turned and watched the approaching men without any visible sign of fear. She appeared only to be curious. She looked up, one hand reaching for and caressing the simple wooden cross she wore hanging from the delicate gold chain around her neck, and said, "Yes?"

"Forgive us, please, Senora Alvarez. We are the commanders of the president's security. We need to urgently see the president."

The small, pious woman gave everyone in the room all the proof they would ever need. Her face turned from curious to sad, and she said, "My son is not here, Colonel. He has been gone since Sunday, visiting his cousins in the north. How is it you do not know this?"

The camera crew documented everything as the men of the security forces searched the estate. A second monitor was showing what was going on at the Pena estate. Senor Pena was not there, of course, but the security forces were able to detain everyone, including the two Sanchez brothers, without firing a shot. In all there were eight total people taken at the Pena estate. The security team removed them to the detention area of the compound across the road and put them under a tight guard.

Senora Alvarez, her nurse, three maids, and a cook, all the inhabitants who could be found, were allowed to remain in the Alvarez home. A desperate-looking Colonel Pacheco came on the screen. "Mr. Secretary, we have checked every inch of both estates. The president, his personal bodyguards, and the two communication people we saw enter on Sunday are nowhere to be found."

"Thank you, Colonel; you did well. Each of you take a couple of men and the camera crew and go back to the guesthouse. I am told that in the lower level, if you look along the north wall, you will find a hidden door panel leading to a tunnel that connects the Alvarez guesthouse with that of Senor Pena. Do what you can to confirm this. Then report back."

The colonel's looks turned from pained to curious at the order and the mentioning of a tunnel. *How could he know of such things?* was going through his mind as Pacheco acknowledged the order and took off.

With his mother's statement and no other explanation possible on the whereabouts of the president, the gathered group turned and looked at Alberto and, without a word, accepted the evidence Alberto had presented. There was one last piece of evidence, and Colonel Portillo's image came over the central monitor.

"We are ready here, Mr. Secretary." He was standing outside a walled military tent. In the background the men could see the clearing being used as a staging area and the scrub forests beyond. The colonel entered the tent with the cameraman following him. The camera lens adjusted to the difference in light, and as it did, the image became very clear from the translucent light penetrating the canopy. Lying on sleeping bags or blankets were four men, all who appeared to be sleeping. The deputy who was now the temporary head of the AFI, having assumed the post on the revelation that Ramirez had been arrested, said first what most men in the room started to realize: "That's Geraldo Baca, for Christ's sake, the one on the left. The other there, on the right, there can be no doubt—that is Ortega, the president's senior aide."

A young medic, the red cross on his sleeve easily identifiable, was kneeling next to one of the two men on the ground whom they did not recognize. The one in the center had long, disheveled white hair and a beard. Very gently, the medic took the man's head in his hands and slowly turned it until it was looking straight up at the ridge of the tent, and with great care, as the camera zoomed in closer, he slowly removed the wig and the beard. Even though the men in the room now knew the truth, knew what they were going to see, there was a collective sucking in of their breath as the man, his eyes closed but looking peacefully up at the camera, was clearly their president.

"Thank you, Colonel, and thank you to your brave men. Please get Alvarez out of there as soon as possible."

The camera lens had pulled back to find the colonel, who was standing with hands on hips, looking grimly down at the four men. He turned and looked in the camera and said, "Three hours, Mr. Secretary. I will report from base."

The transmission stopped, and all in the room turned to face Alberto, who said, "The man whom none of you recognized was Eduardo Vargas, cousin to Alvarez. He's dead, along with Raul Ortega, the president's aide."

A weak and trembling voice said very quietly, almost in a whisper, "I knew who it was." All heads turned to Senator Alarcon, now looking completely broken.

"I have known Eduardo Vargas for twenty years, since my days as the chief magistrate in Hermosillo. I have had a death sentence on my head since the day I met him. From time to time, he has asked me for information, and I have provided it. I have never accepted money. I did what I had to do to keep my family alive. Those of you who have known me for years—you, Mr. President, and you, Mr. Secretary—remember when my oldest daughter was kidnapped, and we got her back, safe. That was Eduardo Vargas sending me a message after I refused a service. Please forgive me; I had no choice."

The senator broke down, weeping uncontrollably. No one wanted to condemn the man. Some even felt compassion. Alberto motioned to Roberto and whispered a few words and Roberto went to the senator and gently escorted him from the Center. While the sad faces around him watched, Alberto consulted a notebook he had produced and contacted the next senior-most senator, who acted as secretary of the senate and deputy to Alarcon. He told him there was a crisis of national importance and that

Senator Alarcon and he required his presence immediately at the Situation Center at Justice. The senator was only ten minutes away and said he was on his way. Alberto was sure he was a decent and reliable man, a Castillo man.

Alberto knew that the entry of the presidential estate would not escape the media and all others present across the road from the Alvarez home. "Gentlemen, we have much to do and not much time to do it. Certainly within the hour, if it has not started already, there will be rumors about what I just had to do to show you the proof. Everyone will want to know where the president is and how he is. Without answers, the country will fear the worst. But the truth will be so much harder than they expect. The moment we entered the grounds, people will have noticed and will want a statement. We must take decisive action, and we must prepare a statement for the people."

All the men in the room knew that what Alberto was saying was the truth, and they were now prepared to help with the answers. For the next hour, they planned for a news conference and a temporary transfer of power. Castillo had been the one to bring focus to the discussions early on. His speech and ability to walk had been altered by his stroke, but the mind was still there, intact and reasoning its way through the issues.

The old president stood slowly, early in the conversation, and the whole room noticed and quieted, giving him their full attention. "Am I not correct, Attorney General Farias, that the provisions of Article 84 of the Constitution are in play?"

"Yes, Mr. President. I would defer to the chief justice for confirmation; however, I would say that the arrest and detention of President Alvarez constitutes a case of absolute absence of a president. As such, the Permanent Commission should be called on to elect a provisional president until the legislature can be called into a full extraordinary session."

The old chief justice nodded his agreement. "Mr. Farias is quite correct, Mr. President. We are now in an Article 84 succession. As you are the chairman of the Permanent Committee, might I suggest that your first duty is to nominate the provisional president."

Castillo nodded. "Thank you, gentlemen. I agree. Alberto, do you have the numbers of the others on the commission in that little book you keep?"

Alberto nodded.

"Then I ask you to call them, please, so that we may convene a session. My friends, under these terrible circumstances, I will first ask that the commission join us here, where Alberto can explain to them what we all now know. We will then meet privately, and there we will select our provisional president. I am sure it will come as no surprise to any of you that I will use all my powers of persuasion to have Alberto named to that post. I believe I will prevail."

Castillo turned and looked at Alberto, who was staring down at the table. In his halting but clear voice he said, "Alberto, I know how you feel about this, but I must ask you to rise up and accept this appointment. I do not think I am overstating the situation when I say you have saved the country. I know you would prefer not to be president, but I ask you, on behalf of the people, will you please serve?"

Alberto looked up. Bennie had never seen the man look sadder in the short time he had known him—perhaps even sadder than when they had spoken of his brother, Emilio, and his death. "I will reluctantly accept, Mr. President, if the commission so votes."

It took an hour to get a quorum of the Permanent Commission assembled in the Center. The others who had been there all morning gave up their seats at the table so that Alberto could take the commission through a summary of the events of the morning. They were shown videos of the action in Baja and of the revelations in the clearing in the mountains south of Chihuahua. When he was done, Castillo once more rose from his chair and addressed the shaken commission members.

"My friends, I will be nominating Alberto Rodriguez for the presidency. We may go into private session and discuss it among ourselves, but I see no need. Unless anyone of you disagrees, I am calling for a vote of acclamation on the point at this time."

As the wise old man knew, the shocking truth they had just learned was still overwhelming their senses, and to a man, they were unable to do anything more than agree with the old president and nodded their acceptance around the table.

"All those voting for Alberto Rodriguez as the provisional president of the country will please raise their hand." All did. Castillo turned to Alberto, who was still sitting in his chair at the end of the table. Castillo put his trembling hand on Alberto's shoulder. "Congratulations, Mr. President. What would you have us do next?"

Alberto looked up and nodded at his old mentor; then he slowly stood. "It is with a heavy heart that I accept this appointment. And I only do so out of a deep concern and love for our country. I must address the people as soon as we can set it up. They must know the truth and that their government goes on."

It was decided that the government would take over the airways again under the provisions of the National Emergency Act. Alberto called in his press secretary, who had not been in the meetings. He was clearly already agitated when he arrived and, when asked, told those assembled that there were thousands of rumors out of Baja, but the one with traction was that the cartels had hit back somehow, and the president was missing. Other rumors speculated he was already dead. Several of the major stations had broken in and aired stories about the presidential guard forcing their way into the president's house. Since that time, neither of the men in charge of security for the president had been seen. The entire situation had been exacerbated when the press outside the Alvarez estate had been forced to return to the large media tent and literally told they could not leave. All power from the large emergency generator that powered the camp was cut off to the press tent. All the broadcast vehicles had been placed under guard, but this was the age of cell phones, laptops, and instant communications, and reporters still called their editors and filed stories. Everyone was thinking and believing cartel retribution. Alberto gave his secretary a brief summation of the situation, and, after swearing him to secrecy and sending one of the armed ghosts along to make sure he did what he was told, Alberto sent him to arrange with the networks for an address and a press conference for the world to see. Alberto asked, and all in the room agreed that they would be at the press conference, which was to be held in the much larger briefing theater at the presidential palace across the Zocalo. It was nearly time to adjourn. Most of the men in the center felt weak in the knees at the day's events. There was one last task to be performed, and Alberto had been dreading it. The old chief justice approached Alberto.

"It is time you take the presidential oath, Mr. Secretary."

With one of the techs videoing the entire scene, a very reluctant Alberto Rodriguez stood, raised his right hand, and repeated the fifty-nine words of the oath. The chief justice smiled a wan smile and said simply, "Mr. President," and shook Alberto's hand. The senior men of the government, their emotions from the day stretched to the limits of sadness and despair at the terrible events they had witnessed, took solace from the fact that they were still a democracy, and the powers of the executive once again had changed hands quietly and peacefully, as it had since the revolution. One by one they filed by Alberto and bid him good wishes and congratulations. Out of the Center and free to return to their offices, they too were sworn to secrecy until the press conference and national address set for three o'clock. Alberto once more took control of Castillo's wheel chair. Castillo looked at Alberto and signaled he wanted a private word, so they watched in silence as the others left the room. Bennie had discreetly moved to the glass office a few minutes earlier and called Manny with an update. With no one else within earshot, Castillo asked, "Where are you taking him, Alberto?"

"With all the respect I can muster, Mr. President, and for all the reasons that must be obvious to you, I must keep that information to myself. Let me just say that we have the proper facilities, very highly secured and known to just a few. Until I have a chance to get out of Baca all that he knows, I must keep silent. Please understand and forgive me."

Castillo smiled and nodded. "I always knew you would be a good choice for president someday; Emilio would be very proud." With Alberto behind him pushing his chair, the old president could not see the tears on Alberto's cheeks.

40

I t had been quite a Tuesday, as far as Tuesdays go, for all those involved in the events of the day. When viewed through the prism of time and history, this Tuesday had been more significant than most but less significant than others. It had been a Tuesday in January of 1610 when Galileo Galilei had looked into the heavens through the device he had invented that brought the heavens closer and was the first man on earth to see the small dots of light ringing the great Jupiter and, with his observations, confirmed the then-heretical views of Copernicus and toppled the Roman Catholic Church's myth of geocentricism. It was a Tuesday in July of 1776 when a band of revolutionaries in Philadelphia mutually pledged to one another their lives, fortunes, and sacred honor and adopted a resolution severing ties with England in the hope that a just new country might be born, founded on the principal of those governing having derived their power from the consent of the governed. It was a Tuesday in February 1836 when General Santa Anna set siege to a small Texas stronghold, and the battle of the Alamo began, and with it, the continuing fight for what was to become Texas. It was a Tuesday in February 1848 when, with the signing of the Treaty of Guadalupe Hidalgo, a border war was finally put to an end, and Mexico ceded a half-million square miles to the aggressors from the north, and the states of California, Arizona, and New Mexico would be born there and a new border between the two countries would be established. And it had been a Tuesday in October of 2016 when the American legislature would finally agree to the wording on a bill whose language as the law of the land would send millions of illegal immigrants back south across that border, many to the chaotic and poor cartel-ruled towns or cities that they had fled years before, and contribute further to a chaos that allowed a good man, turned by unexpected events to a life of crime, an opportunity to try to usurp a country.

And so too it happened to be a Tuesday in late July of 2017 that—because the usurper was revealed to be a criminal and charlatan, exposed and condemned to spend the rest of his life in a small cell by the good and decent policeman who had planned and executed the actions so that a republic would be righted—a man who for years had called the charlatan friend and who would have preferred the anonymity of his chosen field found himself instead the newly sworn leader of a dazed and confused country. There would be chapters in future books and footnotes in history documenting the significance of this Tuesday; historians would judge the history created and conclude it indeed had been more significant than some and less significant than others.

For Alberto Rodriguez, composed, resolute, and compassionate, he stood before the cameras and the press of not only his country but the world and took them clearly and calmly piece by piece through the events of not only the day but the days leading up to this Tuesday. The young and old men of the leadership who had known the truth for hours and had seen it unfold stood behind their new president and looked on. The rumors of a missing president had shot like wildfire around the globe, and for several hours before the press conference, confusion and doubt had gripped Mexico, and curiosity had captured the attention of the world.

He took a full sixty minutes going through the process and evidentiary trail that had brought them to this day. He stood and answered every question the excitable and oftentimes inane press had to ask, for that was the price as their leader he had to pay to calm a nation and reassure a people. And when it was over, the new president returned to his Mexico City estate with just his one new and greatly trusted friend from the north, and as they had done on many occasions in the last week, they sat together for hours in the beautiful dining room of the old mansion, the soft light from the crystal chandelier creating a warm and pleasant atmosphere, eating, talking, and drinking, with only the occasional presence of the faithful and trusted manservant to distract them.

For Bennie Santiago, a witness to the history of this day and one of its principal architects, as significant as the day had been for the Mexican people and their country, his thoughts were with his young operative and the knowledge that he was safe and dining with an American general in his simple but warm home, safe for the first time in months from a mistake or a casual whim that would have violently ended his young life. Even when he knew that his man was airborne and headed for home, his anxiety had not diminished until he received the call that he was there and as such finally truly safe. With the information that would be pulled from him in his debriefing and the data recovered that had been carefully created and stored by Baca, the fight against the traffickers would go on, but for the first time ever in the history of this particular war, the good guys had the advantage. And it was exploitable.

He had endured much over the last five months—nothing, he admitted to himself, like what his operative had endured or the friend he was dining with, who had finally temporarily lost the stoic composure he always maintained when Bennie had proposed a toast to the fallen brother who could not be with them. For Bennie, while he could say he knew and liked many people, he could count his true friends on one hand—not for something lacking in himself or in others; it was just his way, his belief. True friendships were hard to come by and usually took years to develop. In his dinner companion, in just over a week, he knew he had made such a true friend for life. He had remarked earlier in the week, on the occasion of his first dinner with a head of state, that he would have preferred to pass, knowing the true nature of the man. As the two new friends sat for dinner this Tuesday night, Bennie, knowing the true nature of this man, remarked on what a great honor and pleasure the occasion held for him. It was a memory he would keep with him always. He would be a house guest just one more night and then return to America to begin his work once again.

For Ray Cruz, the ninety minutes on the helicopter flight from the hills south and west of Chihuahua to the sprawling American base northeast of El Paso felt so much longer. It had been 98 days since he and Carlo had escaped jail and almost 160 days since he and Bennie had last seen each other and shaken hands, excited and confident in their mission. To finally be going home was the most emotional experience of Ray's life. He tried to understand his feelings and thoughts, but there was just too much, and he was overwhelmed. He had been told months before that there would be a period of decompression and perhaps great emotionalism after the tensions associated with being undercover for so long. Ray had dismissed the discussions then, believing he could handle anything, but now, it took all the strength and fortitude he had to not just curl up in a ball and cry like a baby.

They landed about noon, the temperature so hot that he could see the shimmering heat rising from the concrete tarmac where they landed. He was greeted by an American army general whom he had never met and knew little about but knew enough to know the man had been a principal contributor to his rescue. Also there was Charley Willis, down from Washington, whom Ray had only met the one time during his mission briefings but understood would begin the process of extracting all the intelligence he had absorbed in the last three months. After running Ray by the base hospital to better treat his wound, the small party had driven to the headquarters building. The cold beer and large cheeseburger, taken in the cool of the air-conditioned privacy of the general's mess, were necessary, tangible first confirmations of home. This Tuesday, there would be no further work. He was shown to his simple quarters, where only Charley accompanied him to show him the video of the new president being sworn in at the Center, and later, they joined the world and watched the press conference and relived what they already knew through the careful explanations of their new friend and, for a 110 million people, their new president.

For Ray, this Tuesday had ended as differently as was possible from the dawning as he had dinner in the warm and comfortable dining room of the general's quarters with his lovely wife hosting. They were joined by the now first lady of Mexico and her widowed sister-in-law, their personal stories being illustrative of the great pain and suffering the unrealized dreams of a wanting philosopher king had created.

And for Jacques Pablo Alvarez, appointed president of the Mexican Republic, successful lawyer and businessman, philosopher, devoted son, and reluctant drug trafficker, his Tuesday had ended when he slowly regained consciousness and, after a struggle, sat up on the edge of the firm, uncomfortable bed he was lying on, looked around, and realized where he was. A dim light in the dark, hard ceiling beyond the bars leading to the harsh-looking steel door shed just enough light to make the observation and reach the terrible conclusion. The dream was over, he realized, but how? His last recollections were of muted explosions and Raul's shouts, and then his world had caved in, just as the wall of his study had from the great explosion that had knocked him senseless. He thought he remembered hearing, through a fog and din of terrible sounds, his young friend, his savior, scream *go* and something about cover fire, followed by many shots. His next thoughts were of his friends Raul, Ray, and his cousins, and he prayed they had all survived, even if the God he had deeply believed in for so long had abandoned him.

The earth continued to spin on its axis, giving the appearance that the growing quartering moon had raced across the night sky, and Tuesday became Wednesday, and a new day was born. As the day dawned both literally and metaphorically, Alberto Rodriguez, the reluctant new president of Mexico, personally took his good friend to the airport and put him on what was now one of his government's executive jets for his flight north to El Paso. The unannounced trip and early-morning departure assured that there would be no press around to record the affectionate hug of friendship between the two men, a friendship that had been forged through the most difficult of times, before Bennie said a last good-bye, turned, and climbed up the few steps of the luxurious private jet.

It was two hours to Fort Bliss, and after landing and the short taxi, Bennie could see the general, Colonel Romero, Charley Willis, Sergeant Major Green, and Ray standing in the wide opening of the hangar. Bennie descended the steps and enthusiastically shook everyone's hands. Ray was the last in the line, and the handshake quickly turned into an embrace, with Ray thanking Bennie for all he had done to get him safely out and an emotional Bennie Santiago asking Ray to forgive him for what he had put him through.

Ray and Bennie spent two weeks at Fort Bliss. Ray wanted to be in Mexico City to personally witness the public swearing-in ceremony of Alberto Rodriguez as the new president of Mexico, but that had been out of the question. He would not be going back south anytime soon, at least looking like he did. From morning to evening, Bennie and Charley took him through his fourteen weeks undercover a day at a time until they were certain they had squeezed every bit of information they could out of his memory and recorded every word. Except for the occasional appearance by the general, Colonel Romero, and the big sergeant major, no one else was allowed into the room.

When finally the sessions were finished, Ray and Bennie, in the company of the general and his faithful sergeant, walked toward the agency Citation business jet that Charley had arranged for, and after handshakes and smiles, they boarded for the three-hour flight to Sacramento. Ray had talked with his folks almost every night since he had been back, but there was more to be said, and it needed to be said face to face with his dad. He only hoped his dad would understand, for there were parts of his saga that he could not yet understand himself.

Ray had slept poorly when he was in the cartel, and he was finding sleep difficult now that he was back, but for entirely different reasons. On his and Bennie's second night back together, with Charley away on other business, Ray had finally broken down. He had quietly told Bennie of his confusing feelings for Alvarez and Raul Ortega as he had stood in the shattered ruins of Pablo Alvarez's study, staring down at the broken body of Miguel. He was having bad dreams, most reliving the final fateful seconds of his friend Raul Ortega's death. Bennie had looked on questioningly but compassionately, not really understanding Ray's emotions, but he had accepted Ray's admission—if that was what it was—that Raul had indeed become a friend.

The complex feelings Ray had were heightened when word had come from Alberto that he had had his first face-to-face conversation with Alvarez, who had asked him who of his friends had been killed and who had survived. Alberto had told Bennie and Ray that he had lied and added Ray to the list of those who had been killed. He wanted no one looking for Ray in the highly unlikely event Alvarez discovered Ray's true identity and could arrange for something like that to get out. Alberto told them that learning of Ray's death had hurt Alvarez the deepest, and he had expressed to Alberto the greatest sorrow for the loss of his young savior, promising student of philosophy, and friend and had not been able to talk further, as his emotions had so overcome him. Alberto had meant well when he spoke of this, a tribute to the effectiveness of Ray's professionalism as a covert operative, but the knowledge of Alvarez's feelings had hit Ray hard.

Bennie had told Ray afterward he thought he knew how he felt and why, when in fact he admitted to himself that he had no fucking clue. Bennie had promised Ray that he would have whatever help he needed, be it from him or professionals, but he would listen for as long as Ray wanted to talk, and they would get through this together. Bennie's most reassuring words to Ray had been that he had done nothing wrong on the assignment and that Bennie said he hoped he would have conducted himself just as Ray had and with the same courage. Maybe it was finally having broken down and confronting his mixed feelings, perhaps it was their subsequent talks, maybe it was just time, but Ray began to feel a little better, more sure of himself, and he started sleeping some the final few days they were in Texas.

Once airborne, as the flight smoothed out, Bennie got up out of his seat and went to a small refrigerator opposite the main cabin door and removed two cold Coors from the six-pack he knew Sergeant Major Green had stashed for him. He walked back, handed Ray the cold beer, and sat down in the open seat facing him. He looked at Ray for several seconds, trying to find the words that needed to be said, knowing full well they were not there.

"You know, Ray, I have imagined this scene for months, thinking about what I would say to you when we finally could leave Mexico and Texas behind us, but I'm at a total loss to find the words to thank you. There is nothing that I can say that would mean enough or express how I really feel. To say you did a wonderful job just seems so inadequate. It's not every covert operative who places himself in a position that helps bring down a corrupt president of a sovereign country, but that's exactly what you've done, son, so just let me say here's to you."

They touched beers and took a couple of drinks. For Ray, Bennie's simple beer toast was all he needed to hear, and he was touched. He looked at Bennie, smiled, and said, "I'm just glad I could help and that it all worked out. I had my doubts about that and a lot of other things for a very long time. It was a helluva first assignment, though; I will have to admit that."

There was a pause as Ray took another swig of the cold beer and then, with a normal, interested look on his face, asked his boss, "I know you have had your hands full lately, Bennie, what with all of the time you spent in El Paso and down south, and I don't want to put you on the spot or anything, but have you given any thought to my next assignment?"

Bennie stopped drinking and just stared in disbelief and surprise at Ray's sincere look and question and could only shake his head and marvel at the resiliency of youth. From deep inside him, a feeling came over him that he had not felt in months, and he threw back his head and laughed, thinking, *What a fucking hotshot.*

About the Author

Chris Thomas graduated from the University of Colorado in 1977 and embarked on a long career in architecture. At age fifty-five, after seeing his three children graduate from college, he scaled back work at his architecture firm to pursue writing. He has since written three books, two of which are in the *Until Philosophers Become Kings* series, and he is at work on his fourth novel. Chris currently lives in Denver.